$2

THE EXPEDITION

CHRIS BABU

PERMUTED
PRESS

A PERMUTED PRESS BOOK

The Expedition
© 2018 by Chris Babu
All Rights Reserved

ISBN: 978-1-68261-835-6
ISBN (eBook): 978-1-68261-836-3

Cover art by Cody Corcoran
Interior design and composition, Greg Johnson, Textbook Perfect

PERMUTED
PRESS

Permuted Press, LLC
New York • Nashville
permutedpress.com

Published in the United States of America

For Michelle

*I'm eternally grateful for your unshakable belief in my writing,
and for enduring the sacrifices that came along with it,
including my sudden constant presence in the living room.*

Also by Chris Babu

The Initiation

CHAPTER 1

They say you don't shoot to kill; you shoot to stay alive.

Drayden peered through the sight of the M16A4 rifle and tried to control his breathing. He pulled the trigger at the top of his exhale.

The gun fired with a loud, metallic bang, recoiling hard into his shoulder.

"Hold your fire!" Sergeant Holcomb yelled. "Bring 'em in!"

Unfortunately for Drayden, the safest spot in the practice range was *on* his target, still pristine after twenty minutes of shooting. He removed his earmuffs.

I'm a flunk.

Catrice remained on her stomach to his left, propped up on her elbows, her skinny legs splayed out behind. She glimpsed through the rifle's sight, her golden hair in a ponytail.

Charlie and Sidney stood to Drayden's right. They clutched their weapons, beaming with pride. When the white paper targets arrived, theirs showed only bullseyes.

Drayden thought Charlie looked like Rambo from the old movie—a soldier capable of single-handedly defeating an entire nation. They all wore their gray camouflage Guardian uniforms, but Drayden didn't get why. It was just target practice. And did Charlie really need the war paint under his eyes?

"Private Arnold," Sergeant Holcomb said to Charlie. "You were born to be a Guardian, son. You're a natural."

Charlie stood at attention. "Sir, yes sir!" he barked.

Oh, for crying out loud.

They weren't training to become Guardians. Since Guardians would escort them on the expedition, the probability of needing a gun was almost zero.

"I'd say you were the best young shooter I've seen if Private Fowler weren't here," the sergeant said, hooking his thumb at Sidney. "She's destined to be a sniper. Where'd you learn to shoot a gun like that, young lady?"

"I've never shot one before this week, sir." Sidney blushed. "Am I actually good?"

"Remarkable."

Sergeant Holcomb stared at Drayden's target, his expression like he was reading something written in Swahili. The sergeant spent so much time yelling you rarely got a clear picture of his face. He removed his drill sergeant hat, which resembled a cowboy hat, and scratched his head. Though a grizzled old man, he still seemed like he could whoop your butt in a fight. As always, he chewed on the end of an unlit cigar.

"Private Coulson, if you need to use your weapon, you might be better off throwing a rock."

Drayden lumbered to his feet. "We're not privates, sir, and this isn't Guardian school."

Catrice got up and joined him.

"You're privates-in-training when you're with me. Your target's cleaner than when we started, son. How can you explain this? Where in God's name are your bullets going?"

Drayden shook his rifle. "I don't know, sir, I think there might be something wrong with my gun."

"There's nothing wrong with your gun!" He threw his hands in the air. "It's your trigger mechanics. Private Zevery here hit the target twice. Nicely done, Private," the sergeant said to Catrice, giving her a thumbs-up.

She fumbled with a button on her shirt, displaying her usual discomfort with compliments. "Thanks, Sergeant."

Drayden patted her on the arm. "Well done, Catrice."

She rubbed the spot on her shoulder where the gun recoiled, grimacing.

"Private Coulson, it's a good thing you're skilled at hand-to-hand combat with that jiu-jitsu of yours. You're crafty with a knife too. You'll have to hope the enemy is right in front of you. If you have your gun drawn, maybe just hit him with it."

Drayden internally rolled his eyes. "Sergeant, I don't anticipate many enemies."

"Son, you hope for the best but prepare for the worst. Let's switch to pistols. I want you standing." Sergeant Holcomb leaned his head back to the group of young Guardians behind them. "Let's get some fresh targets in here! Except for Private Coulson, that is, his can't get any fresher. Move it!"

Drayden scowled at the sergeant. He had a point, though. Drayden sucked at shooting, plain and simple. They'd worked on it every day for most of the week as part of their training. They would spend time with the scientists in the morning, and the Guardians in the afternoon. He switched his rifle into safe mode and laid it on the grass.

The May afternoon was gorgeous, sunny and warm, with a cool breeze coming off the Hudson River. The firing range was in Battery Park, at the southern tip of New America, where the Palace Guardians maintained several training facilities. In the past week, Drayden and the others had also used the explosives depot, the fighting gym, and the fitness center.

He drew his pistol, a Glock 22, and inserted the magazine loaded with ten rounds. After handling the heavy rifle, the Glock felt like a toy gun. "Hey, nice shooting, you guys," he said to Charlie and Sidney.

"Don't look at me." Charlie waved his Glock around a little too casually. "Sid's cocked, locked, and ready to rock."

"Thanks," Sidney said. "Your form is solid, Dray; stick with it. You'll get it."

Charlie holstered his pistol. "Dray, given how crummy your aim is, I'm glad we don't share a bathroom." He howled. "I'm just teasing, bro. I'd trade my accuracy for your brain in a heartbeat."

"Thanks, I guess," Drayden said.

"Okay, boys and girls," Sergeant Holcomb said. "Gimme rapid fire this time, all ten rounds in less than six seconds. And Private Coulson, if you don't shoot any people, that's good enough." He sneered.

Drayden pressed his lips together to keep from saying something he'd regret. He snapped his earmuffs on and cocked his gun. With his feet shoulder-width apart and knees slightly bent, he raised his pistol with his right hand, cupping it underneath with his left. He lined up the rear sight and the front sight with the target and placed the top pad of his index finger on the trigger. After concluding his routine, he waited for the sergeant.

"Fire!" Sergeant Holcomb yelled.

The firing range erupted with violence.

Drayden squeezed the trigger over and over, the gun popping with each round. He battled to stabilize the gun against its powerful recoil.

Seven seconds later, the range fell silent.

Please, one hit.

"Bring 'em in!" the sergeant shouted.

Drayden holstered his gun and pulled his earmuffs down so they hung around his neck. His pulse quickened as the targets zipped down wires toward them. Despite his argument for not needing a gun on the impending journey, he'd feel a heck of a lot better if he could shoot one.

The targets arrived. Zero hits.

Drayden released an exasperated sigh. He had a bad feeling about the expedition.

Drayden sat at the round table in his kitchen, still in his gray fatigues, debating whether to eat a banana or a pear. They'd been in the Palace only a week, and already he'd become accustomed to the superior food. He couldn't help but feel guilty, though, thinking of the crummy and limited food his father and brother were eating back in the Dorms. In fairness, he needed the better food to recover from all his injuries sustained in the Initiation.

He opted for one of the sugar cookies Catrice had baked for him. It was chewy, sweet, and scrumptious. The two of them had been taking advantage of the incredible food variety by trading baked goods. Hopefully she liked the apple pie he'd made for her.

As usual when Drayden found himself alone, his thoughts returned to his mother. Investigating her exile had proved challenging, to say the least. The few people he could find to ask about it had no clue what happened. She was probably an unlucky victim of the Bureau, which was exiling random people in the Dorms to shrink the population. They couldn't produce enough food to feed everyone because the special batteries that stored power from the windmills and solar panels were failing.

Drayden needed to know for sure she wasn't singled out, which was another possibility. Her exile was wrong either way. Nevertheless, for him it made a huge difference whether she was one of many banished to cull the population, or if a specific person targeted her. Had it been the latter, he would find a way to avenge her. Nobody knew what became of exiles, since none were ever seen again. It was highly probable they died, so getting her back wasn't an option. His only recourse now was revenge.

He'd exhausted every avenue except one. Nathan Locke. The head of the Food Distribution Centers, and Mom's boss, he'd carried on an affair with her. If she'd broken it off, he could have ordered her exile as retribution as a jilted lover might.

As much as Drayden ached to burst into Locke's office and attack him, he needed to be cautious. It was merely a theory and visiting Locke in person would be aggressive. Locke would feel threatened. However, with the expedition a week away, he was nearly out of time and might need to confront the philanderer. Assuming Drayden's father and brother moved to the Palace on the day he departed, as the Bureau had promised, he had to possess some information to pass along to Wesley. Otherwise, he could die on the expedition and his mother's murderer would get away with it. As non-Bureau members, Dad and Wes wouldn't have the same access to people he did. There was a nuclear option too: Get the expedition delayed to buy more time to figure it out.

A knock at the door snapped him from his thoughts.

Drayden limped through the kitchen and opened it.

"How's my favorite patient today?" Shahnee asked, beaming in a white lab coat over pink scrubs.

"Come on in. I'm all right." He closed the door after she entered and followed her into the living room.

Afternoon light flooded the space. Immediately after the Initiation, the Bureau had placed Drayden in an apartment on a high floor at Seventy-Five Wall Street, adjacent to the other pledges. Two floors up, on seventeen, was the rooftop deck.

Shahnee plopped her black duffel bag on the coffee table and removed various objects: a thermometer, massage oil, a blue stretchy band, and an ultrasound machine. Drayden joined her on the couch.

Shahnee was cute. She was African American, late twenties, and always upbeat. Her mother worked as a surgeon at the hospital that treated the pledges after the Initiation.

"So, tell me how you're feeling," she said.

Before he could answer, she jammed the thermometer in his mouth, under his tongue.

He gave her a look.

She made a silly face.

During the Initiation, the pledges were savagely wounded. While most of their injuries resulted from the bomb that killed his best friend Tim, the riskiest ones were from rat and cockroach bites. Drayden would never shed the mental scars of crawling through millions of the little monsters. On top of that, a bite from a diseased critter was like an injection of infection straight into an open wound. Aeru was the specific super bacteria that had wiped out most of the world's population, either through direct infection or by destroying the food supply. But all bacteria became antibiotic-resistant, rendering any cut a potential death sentence.

The thermometer beeped and she pulled it out. "Perfect, no fever. I think you're in the clear on any infection, my friend. Were you saying something?"

"Ha ha. I'm feeling fine, thank you very much. Everything's basically healed except my ankle." He hoisted his leg up and plopped his left ankle between them. "It's only gotten a little better."

"You know the deal; there's a lot of soft-tissue damage in there." She poked and prodded it. "Ligaments stretched or torn. You can't expect to fall off a rock wall and snap your fingers and be cured. We're talking a minimum of eight weeks to heal, if not sixteen."

Drayden cocked his head. "Shahnee, I leave New America in a week. We're going to have to speed this up a tad."

"You're not ready. You won't be ready. You should see if they can push it back." She pulled a syringe and a vial of opaque white liquid out of her bag. "Speaking of being ready, you need your Aeru booster."

Drayden's heart rate accelerated every time he received the Aeru vaccine. The Bureau was injecting him with the very bacteria that had killed most life on Earth. It seemed insane. "You sure that bacteria's dead?"

Shahnee pretended to be deep in thought. "We'll find out, won't we? If you develop a nasty cough, and then a fever, we'll know it backfired." She pulled his sleeve up to his shoulder and rubbed alcohol on the back of his arm.

Drayden turned away, focusing on the wall.

The needle pinched his arm and the familiar burning sensation spread through his triceps. Shahnee wiped his arm with a tissue.

"Now lie on your stomach," she said. "Let's start by massaging your ankle, and then do the ultrasonic treatment."

Drayden flipped onto his belly and rested his cheek on the brown sofa cushion.

Shahnee touched his foot to roll up his pant leg.

He erupted in laughter.

"Sorry!" She snatched her hands away. "Sorry. I forgot."

He was ridiculously ticklish, and not proud of it.

Shahnee shook her head. "First kid to pass the Initiation in eight years. If the Bureau only knew. All they had to do was tickle your feet and you'd be vanquished." She paused, tilting her head. "How are you *really* doing?"

Drayden hesitated and released a long, slow breath. "I'm a flunk."

"Say what? You're a hero! It's all anyone can talk about in the Palace. You're famous."

"I can't shoot a gun for shkat. Can someone be allergic to guns? Everyone else can do it. Even Catrice can hit the target. Charlie and Sidney are both sharpshooters after four days."

"Who cares? Tons of people can shoot guns. You don't have to. There're very few people that can do what you can. Let them have their little guns."

Drayden stared into the interwoven fibers of the couch, wishing he could curl up on it forever and forget about this expedition stuff. The Initiation high had worn off. Right after it, he'd been cautiously optimistic about the adventure of exploring the world outside the walls. Now that it was imminent, he was more anxious than anything. His ankle hadn't healed. They were a week into the two weeks the Premier had given them to recuperate. It wasn't enough time. Of course, the others had made full recoveries. The problem wasn't exactly that he couldn't shoot. Between the Guardians, Charlie, and Sidney, the team was flush with assassins. The issue was broader than that. He was the weak link.

The Initiation had been a mix of brainteasers and bravery challenges. Though he ultimately found it within himself to conquer his fear of the bravery ones, they remained his weakness. Not fearing them didn't make him *good* at them, as Sidney and Charlie were. Yes, he'd summoned the courage to swim through the frigid underwater maze in the Initiation, but he almost drowned. The intelligence challenges were his thing. However, the expedition would effectively be all bravery challenges, or one prolonged bravery challenge. Even healthy he'd struggle. With a bum ankle it could be a serious problem. As with probing his mother's exile, he needed more time.

He'd love to blame his jitters on the ankle. If he was being honest, it was more than that. Whether it was witnessing how strong and skilled Charlie was or being around so many Guardians the past week, this much was clear: Drayden wasn't as strong as they were. All the bravery in the world would be worthless if he lacked the physical strength and skill to overcome the expedition's challenges. Like someone with the knowledge and courage to scale a mountain, but no legs.

While surviving should be his primary concern, he was also worried about Catrice, who seemed to be his girlfriend at the moment. Her interest might fade as the expedition wore on and he was the Achilles' heel of the group.

"Shahnee, you're not married, right?"

She straightened. "I do. I accept. I'm so excited! We're getting married!"

"Very funny. I'm just wondering, what kind of guys do you like?"

"I go crazy for math whizzes."

Drayden groaned. "I'm serious. What are you looking for in a guy?"

"Are you concerned about Catrice? You think she won't like you because you can't shoot a gun?"

"Not exactly. I don't know…I guess I'm a little afraid she only dug me because of the Initiation and everything. Here, in real life, who cares if I can solve a brainteaser? I'll never have to solve one again. Doesn't seem like they pop up much in the Palace. If you had to crack a riddle to get your meals, I might be the cat's meow. But here, or out there on the expedition, I'm just some gimpy kid who might shoot himself in the foot." Drayden craned his neck around to see her. "I feel like I need to show her I'm not some weakling."

Shahnee whacked him with the blue stretchy band. "Boy, you don't know anything, do you? It's not a competition to see who has the most skills. It's not a job. You guys have a *spark*. That's all you need. That spark. There's something between you two, you both feel it, yet you can't define what it is or why it exists. That's what I'm looking for, that spark. I don't care if you're a rocket scientist or a janitor—if you're an expert marksman or a guy with two left hands. You shouldn't worry so much."

Hmmm. Perhaps she was right. Or not. "Yeah, that's not *totally* true. Why do the girls flock to the star of the basketball team then?"

"Do you know him? Can you introduce me?" She smirked.

"You joke because you know I speak the truth."

She leaned closer to his face and spoke firmly. "Drayden, be confident, and be yourself. She adores you. Who *you* are. Don't try and be something you're not. Don't worr—"

A knock on the door interrupted them.

"It's open!" Drayden shouted.

Charlie strolled into the kitchen. "Nice." He eyed them up and down as he approached. "I know how this goes. You massage his feet, and he offers to massage your back, but your shirt is getting in the way, and he suggests you take it off, and then—"

"Charlie, what do you want?" Drayden asked.

"Hey, Shahnee," Charlie said, a stupid grin on his face. "Man, how did you snag Shahnee? My nurse is Jeff. Oh no, did she give you the booster yet? Turns out I'm terrified of shots."

Drayden sighed and buried his face in the sofa cushion. "I know there's a reason you're here, chotch."

"Right. We have to be at Bureau headquarters in thirty minutes. Some big meeting with a senior Bureau member."

Drayden needed the expedition delayed. Even a week would help. Since he couldn't tell anyone about his clandestine investigation into his mother's exile, his ankle provided a perfectly legitimate excuse. This meeting could be his only chance.

CHAPTER 2

Drayden was overcome by *déjà vu.*

He and the others sat facing a desk in a palatial office at Bureau headquarters, in the former Federal Reserve Bank of New York. The setting was eerily reminiscent of their meeting with Premier Holst after the Initiation. Even the late afternoon sun draping the room in gold mirrored the recent memory. They were alone besides a Guardian posted at the door.

"It's quieter than a mouse at the library," Charlie whispered to Drayden. "What do you think this is about?"

"I don't know. I hope they're delaying the expedition. My ankle's still a mess. I need more time. Anyone else have *déjà vu,* by the way?"

"Totally," Sidney said.

Charlie snickered. "You know that old saying? 'It's like *déjà vu* all over again.'"

A tall man with an elongated face, a sizeable nose, and a patch over one eye entered the room and sat at the desk. A red Bureau pin adorned his tailored gray suit. He neither smiled nor spoke. After adjusting the black eye patch and placing both hands together on the desk, he surveyed them, pausing on each face. "My name is Harris von Brooks, and I'm Premier Holst's chief of staff," he said, his tone stern. "I'm responsible for the expedition. I've summoned you here today to go through the specifics of your mission. I must apologize. We should have met sooner, but I've been working out the details with the scientists."

So much for postponing it.

"Even though you only became involved in this project a week ago, it's been in the works for quite some time." He rose from the chair and walked in front of the desk, leaning against it.

"We've decided you will head to Boston. Early in the Confluence, when Aeru first appeared in the United States, many cities were discussing quarantines. Ultimately, as you know, cyberterrorists wiped out communication systems, satellites, and the internet. We have no idea what became of other cities after contact was cut off, or if their quarantines were successful. We were very fortunate that Manhattan was an island, easy to seal off. Boston would have been much tougher to quarantine, but it's our best bet. It's the closest large city that we know was discussing a quarantine. We believe there's a possibility that people remain there today. Logic suggests they would have constructed a wall, though it would have taken years to build, as it did here."

Von Brooks raised his index finger in the air. "Now, in three days, you'll meet the four Guardians escorting you on your journey. They are the very best. The elite of the elite. You'll be in good hands. They understand the goal of the mission and the leadership hierarchy. You are in charge. Premier Holst selected you to lead this mission because of your intelligence, problem solving skills, teamwork, and ability to overcome adversity."

Charlie raised his hand, as if they were in class.

"Yes, Mr. Arnold?"

"Are you sure about that? I mean, we've been training with the Guardians. They call the four of us 'privates,' which is what they call the new kids. I can't see how a lieutenant or a captain will be taking orders from us."

Von Brooks nodded. "I understand your concern, I do, but trust me when I say they have signed off and accept it. Premier Holst spoke to the most senior of them, Captain Lindrick, personally."

Sidney raised her hand.

"Yes, Ms. Fowler?"

"Boston is pretty far. How are we getting there?"

"Please, allow me to finish, and I believe all your questions will be answered." He plopped down at his desk. "You will travel by boat. It is specially designed, built by our scientists, with a top speed of twenty-five miles per hour. You should reach Boston in approximately ten hours. Being on water rather than land will limit your exposure to Aeru as well. The scientists will teach you everything you need to know about the boat, navigation, and your route. The Guardians will receive the same training."

Drayden glanced at Catrice, who was squeezed between Sidney and Charlie. Why hadn't she sat next to him?

She picked at her fingernails.

"You will depart next Monday, a week from today," von Brooks said.

Sweat beaded on Drayden's forehead. He wasn't ready for this mission. "Mr. von Brooks, I'd like to request we delay the expedition…a few weeks, so my ankle has a chance to heal. I'm told it's an eight-week recovery, and we've only had a week."

"Mr. Coulson, there will be no delay. You're already aware power storage in New America is failing. Deep-cycle batteries and solar cells die after about twenty-five years. What you don't know is it's getting worse by the day. We lost another wind turbine yesterday, the seventh. That leaves us with thirty-seven active. For all we know, the rest could shut down simultaneously. Without power, we cannot produce food or water. It's critical you leave a week from today. You travel to Boston, make contact, ask to see their leader, and gather information. Establish communication, let them know New America exists and needs assistance. Then you return home. Once we test you for the Aeru infection and you're cleared, you will reenter the city and your mission will be complete."

The teens shifted nervously in their seats.

Drayden asked what he knew the others were thinking. "What happens if we've contracted Aeru?"

"In that case, you will not enter the city," von Brooks said matter-of-factly. He paused. "As a courtesy, we would honor your request to be executed if you prefer not to die a slow death outside."

Drayden swallowed hard. *Now* it was quieter than a mouse in a library. Something else gnawed at him. "How can the person who tests us stay protected?"

The corners of Harris von Brooks's mouth turned up in a faint smile. "They will be wearing a protective suit."

Drayden's jaw dropped. "Why don't you just give us those suits to wear when we're outside?"

Von Brooks's cold eyes bored a hole through Drayden. "Part of your mission is to test the success of our vaccine." His faint smile returned. "Would you have preferred I lie? No? I didn't think so. We have every reason to believe it is one-hundred percent effective."

In his mind, Drayden was punching the guy in the mouth.

"That is it," von Brooks said with a casual air of finality, as if closing a meeting about ordering new office supplies. "That's the whole mission. You should be back here in two days, safe and sound. We will not see each other again until the day you depart. Oh, I almost forgot." He walked in front of the desk and reached into his jacket pocket. "Your Bureau pins."

He handed a pin to each of them. "Welcome to the Bureau."

Drayden plunged the butcher knife into a red bell pepper, which he tossed into a frying pan with broccoli, onions, carrots, and garlic.

It sizzled, a steamy cloud of deliciousness billowing out.

He checked the pot of boiling noodles. "Hungry?"

Catrice forced a smile. "Honestly, no. I can't stop thinking about that word. Executed."

Drayden shrugged. "All right, fine, more for me."

After pouring the noodles into a colander, he opened a drawer to fetch tongs. A white paper rested atop the kitchen utensils, so he picked it up and flipped it over.

It was a superb drawing of a giant, glossy heart balanced on the spire of the Empire State Building, in astounding detail.

A lump formed in Drayden's throat. He'd told Catrice about his eighth birthday, when his mother took him for a climb to the top of the iconic structure. Catrice was a gifted artist and had made a habit of leaving brilliant drawings hidden around his apartment. He clutched the picture to his chest.

She raised her eyebrows. "You like it?"

He sniffled. "I love it. Thank you."

Drayden portioned the noodles onto two dark green plates and spooned the sizzling vegetables over them. His stomach growling, he set the plates on the white table and sat across from Catrice. "*Bon appétit.*"

"Thanks, this looks delicious. Where'd you learn how to cook anyway?"

"From my mom. Stir-fry is my specialty. I can't make much else." Drayden shoveled the food into his mouth, savoring the sweet onions and crunchy broccoli.

"Are you even chewing?" Catrice asked, barely picking at her food.

He swallowed. "Chewing's overrated."

"What are we going to do about this? The expedition, I mean."

Drayden wiped his mouth with a napkin, staring into space. They'd had a few hours to digest the details of the expedition, so at least some of the shock had worn off. "I was hoping to delay it because of my ankle. After that chat with Harris von Brooks, I wouldn't mind getting out of it completely. I know it has to be done. Still, I have a bad feeling about it."

"Me too. I'm scared."

"I am too. It's not just my ankle either. What if the Aeru vaccine doesn't work?" He felt embarrassed after admitting his fear. "Does that make me a wimp?"

Catrice cocked her head. "No, Drayden. It makes you realistic, and smart."

"There's something else. I don't trust the Bureau. It's as if they're not telling us everything. Feels like there's an inside joke and we're the only ones who don't know the punchline."

She pushed her food around the plate. "I don't think I'll be much help on the expedition either. It's not like the Initiation where there were brainteasers and riddles."

"You can totally help. You're a lot stronger than you think."

"I've been thinking about a way out for days. So far, I've come up with nothing."

Drayden tugged on his ear. "Makes more sense for a team of scientists to lead the expedition. A group of sixteen-year-olds is hardly qualified."

"They don't want to sacrifice the scientists. They're too valuable."

"Exactly."

"We're going to have to do this. And we're going to die." She chewed a nail.

"We have a week. While we continue with our training, we'll keep brainstorming. Tomorrow afternoon we meet with the scientists. Let's see if anything they're doing could be an alternative to the expedition." He reached for her hand across the table.

"Catrice, if we have to go, I'll handle it. We can do it. I'll make sure you're okay."

She set her fork down. "Drayden, I just wanna say...thank you for watching out for me. Like, in the Initiation." She gazed into his eyes. "Nobody's ever treated me like that before, or cared. My parents sure as heck didn't. It makes me feel special. You're the first person I've ever trusted."

Drayden blushed. "Wow. Thank you. Um...you're welcome." He cleared his throat. "Listen, we're gonna be fine. We survived the Initiation, and that was a lot tougher than going on a boat ride with armed guards."

She tucked a strand of blonde hair behind her ear. "Even though extra protection sounds nice, I almost wish it could be the four of us alone, you know? We kinda got into rhythm during the Initiation."

"Yeah." Drayden flashed a mischievous look. "You know what would be better than that? The two of us."

It was Catrice's turn to blush. She stood, took Drayden by the hand, and led him to the couch in the living room. After pushing him down to sitting, she climbed onto his lap and lowered her face to his, her lips grazing his ear. Her silky hair draped over his shoulders. "And what we do out there on that boat?" she whispered.

Drayden's heart raced. "Um..." He swallowed. "I guess if it was only the two of us, one of us would have to drive."

She laughed and nodded. "True."

Drayden brushed his hand on her soft cheek. He pulled her closer until their lips touched, and electricity zoomed through his body.

The spark.

As long as he had Catrice, everything would be okay.

CHAPTER 3

The following afternoon, Drayden and the others found themselves in a monstrous room resembling an airplane hangar. Wide open inside with a soaring roof, it occupied part of the science lab at the former Pace University. Although they'd met with the Palace scientists every day, they hadn't seen this part. Black-topped wooden tables contained all sorts of experiments. Row after row of those tables created grid-like walkways throughout the space.

Drayden absorbed everything, contemplating how much he'd love to work here. While it was difficult to identify most objects, one was clear: the boat. The wooden craft had been polished with some type of shiny sealant, glistening in the center of the room.

Drayden had never seen a boat before in person. It was smaller than he'd expected, around thirty-five feet by his estimation. An undersized, enclosed cockpit in the center housed the controls. There was a deck with bench seating and a table in the rear, with another deck in front of the cockpit. Two huge propellers hung off the back. The scientists had constructed the boat on rolling trolleys, presumably to wheel it the few blocks to Pier Fifteen.

It was ironic that they lived on an island, yet building a boat was a huge project. Obviously, there were walls around the city and nobody had ever been outside because of Aeru. No one in New America had ever needed a boat before.

Today marked the final session with the scientists, in which the goal was to learn how to drive the boat to Boston.

But that wasn't Drayden's goal. His was to find a way to delay the expedition so he could buy himself more time in the Palace. Some scientific reason they couldn't go, or an alternative solution. If he needed to wander around the warehouse, he'd find a way.

Doctor Samantha Miller, the scientist tasked with their training, paced before them. She was a lovely, warm woman who insisted they call her Sam. She fished her horn-rimmed glasses from her white lab coat and put them on. "I want you to know it's been a pleasure getting to know the four of you. I wish you the best of luck on your journey, and I'm confident you'll be fine. You're well prepared. Before I show you how to operate the boat, let's spend a few minutes reviewing the essential highlights from our last few meetings."

Drayden noticed Catrice again didn't sit next to him. Since her face showed concern, he winked at her.

Sam held up a box of matches. "Remember, should something go wrong and you find yourself on land, you've learned several ways to start a fire. If your matches get wet, you'll each have a magnifying glass, plus a battery and a paperclip. The boat will be well stocked with water. If on land, collect rainwater or dew. Do not drink any natural water you find, but if you must, be sure to boil it first. I would not recommend eating any animals, should you encounter any. You will have a few fishing rods aboard the boat, and eating fish should be fine. We don't know which species of animals have survived Aeru, so beware of predators. We've gone over what to do if you encounter any. You each will have a compass and maps in your pack."

Sam picked up a neat stack of folded papers. "We've reproduced maps with detailed layouts of many of the cities between here and

Boston so you can find your way. That includes a map of Boston and its surroundings. In addition, we've gone over how to find the North Star to get your bearings. Any questions?"

Charlie raised his hand.

"Yes, Charlie, only if it's a real question and not a joke."

He dropped his hand. "Never mind then."

Sam couldn't help but laugh. "Good. As for the Aeru superbug, while we've researched it in labs, we really don't know its status outside the walls. Clearly, nobody goes outside. That it can exist without a host is one of the unfortunate characteristics of *Pseudomonas Aeruginosa*. In other words, it can just be out there, in nature. Bacteria such as *E. coli* live in the rectums of cows and die outside a host. When—"

"Rectum?" Charlie shouted. "Damn near killed 'em!"

Sam put her hands on her hips. "Are you finished?"

"Yeah, nah. I have a question."

"We don't have time for your colorful sense of humor."

"No, it's a real question. I was wondering if you'd heard about the sick chemist."

Sam closed her eyes and pulled off her glasses. "No, Charlie, I haven't."

"If you can't helium, and you can't curium, you may have to barium." He cracked up.

Drayden's patience with Charlie was wearing thin. He was such a flunk sometimes. "C'mon, Charlie."

"Guys, we might be dead in a week," Charlie said. "Let's have some fun; let's take that boat out for a spin."

Sam grumbled under her breath, placing her glasses back on. "Can we continue, please? We're not taking the boat out for a spin."

Drayden raised his hand. "Sam, Charlie raises a valid concern. How can you be sure this boat, you know, floats? Has no leaks?"

"Excellent question, Drayden."

"Yeah, sure, excellent question when *he* asks it," Charlie mumbled.

"We've tested it," Sam said. "We built a trailer for it, towed it behind a vehicle, and sailed it in the reservoir in the Meadow, in Central Park. It worked quite nicely."

Sam wheeled over a giant map of New England with Manhattan in the lower left. A bright green line snaked from the east side of Manhattan to their final destination in Boston. It ran up the East River, through Long Island Sound, then through a tiny canal in Massachusetts, which cut off Cape Cod. It concluded by running alongside the eastern Massachusetts coast and hitting Boston.

With a pen, Sam tapped the green line. "Here is your path. It's pretty straightforward. You're going to hug the Connecticut and Rhode Island shoreline, which will be your guide. The only tricky parts will come after darkness falls, and here." She circled the tiny canal. "You need to enter Buzzard's Bay and weave through this narrow canal in Bourne, Massachusetts. If you miss Buzzard's Bay, you'll have to go all the way around Cape Cod, making the trip much lengthier and more dangerous. Essentially, you need to go left of Martha's Vineyard and Cuttyhunk Island, which is tiny. The inside of Buzzard's Bay is also confusing because lots of peninsulas jut out into the water."

She pulled a miniature digital clock from her coat pocket. "Now, this part is critical."

Catrice was paying attention, Drayden noted, while Charlie was whispering something to Sidney, who shoved his head away.

"You need to find landmarks and note the boat's speed. This is how you will determine your location, which will be crucial at night. You've each received a digital watch. Depending on your speed, and how long you've been traveling, you can determine where you are on the map. Most likely it will be dark by the time you reach Buzzard's Bay. That means you'll have to know precisely what *time* you should bear left. Once you traverse the canal, you'll be in Cape Cod Bay, and it's a straight shot to Boston from there. Simply hug the Massachusetts coast on your left. Any questions?"

"Yeah," Charlie said. "Do you know what happened when the red boat crashed into the blue boat?"

Sam feigned interest. "What, Charlie?"

"The crew was marooned," he said, laughing before he could deliver the whole punchline. "C'mon, that was good."

"Charlie," Sam said, scratching her head, "have you heard the one about the boy who didn't pay attention in navigation class and got lost at sea?"

"Is that the one where he finds a genie lamp and wishes for the ocean to be made out of beer, but then realizes he has nowhere to pee?"

Sam threw her hands in the air. "I give up."

Drayden exhaled audibly. "Charlie, quit being such a nerf."

"Um, like I can understand any of this. This is why we have you. You're smart, I'm not. You say stuff like 'kerfuffle.' I don't even know what that means."

Drayden wrinkled his forehead. "What the...I've never used the word 'kerfuffle' in my life."

"Whatever, man. It's the kinda thing smart people say."

Sam tucked her pen into the chest pocket of her lab coat. "Okay. We're done. Let's run through the boat operation. Follow me."

The group trailed her through a long corridor flanked by tables. A jumble of wires and circuit boards covered one. Another held several tanks of water in all different colors. Various types of toilets furnished one section.

Drayden scanned the room as they walked, searching for anything related to exploration or communication. "Sam, after the boat, can you tell us about some of the other experiments? Especially ones related to your attempts to contact other civilizations?"

She glanced back. "Sure, if we have time."

Toward the rear of the boat, a ladder extended up to the uncovered deck. With everyone following, Sam climbed the ladder and strode into the enclosed cockpit section in the middle. It was a tiny room; the five of them barely fit. A wooden seat faced the boat's controls on the right. Straight ahead a narrow staircase led down below the front deck.

"What's downstairs?" Sidney asked.

"It's a basic bathroom. We didn't develop anything else below deck and sealed the area off. This boat is primitive, built with the sole purpose of getting you to Boston and back."

Sam ran them through the controls: a steel steering wheel, roughly a foot in diameter; a throttle to control speed, which also worked in reverse; an odometer that displayed their speed; a compass; and a switch to turn on the boat's headlights. After, she showed them the manual anchor, which was operated with a crank, on the front deck.

"This is a motorboat. What about gas?" Drayden asked Sam. "Will we have enough? And where did it come from?"

"Years ago, the Bureau hoarded as much gasoline as they could find. They drained it from all the cars in New America before dumping them in the East River. They preserved it in pressurized, sealed containers, in case it was ever needed. We'll stock the boat with reserve fuel. You will have plenty."

Sam climbed down the ladder. When everyone else reached the concrete floor, she clapped her hands together. "That's basically it. The boat is simple to operate. Sure, it'll take you some time to get the feel of it. Anyone could drive this, though."

This was Drayden's chance. "Sam, you've told us about some past failed attempts to contact anyone outside New America. A battery-powered airplane with a message but no control over it. A glorified message in a bottle. Attempted radio communications. Are there any others? Are any ongoing right now?"

Clearly losing interest, Charlie wandered off.

"Well, there is one, the most promising attempt to date."

That got Drayden's attention. Catrice perked up as well.

Sam pointed. "It's another airplane, solar powered. It's very cool. Here, I'll show you." She walked deeper into the warehouse, with Drayden, Catrice, and Sidney in tow.

His excitement built as they reached the sleek aircraft.

It was white and similar to a glider, with solar panels covering the wings and a propeller jutting out from the nose. Its eight-foot length was dwarfed by the nearly twenty-foot wingspan.

"Hey, you guys!" Charlie hollered from back the other way. He was sitting on one of the toilets, his pants around his ankles.

"Oh God." Sidney shielded her eyes.

"I hope he knows those toilets don't work," Sam said.

"Idiot." Drayden rubbed his temples. "Sam, please, tell us about this plane."

"The problem with radio control is range. We're limited to around five miles. But one of our scientists devised a way to bounce the radio waves off the ionosphere, which is a layer of gas about sixty miles up the Earth's atmosphere. Radio stations Pre-Confluence used to broadcast signals across large distances that way. Using that technique, in theory, we could maintain radio contact over great distances. That's the simplified explanation anyway. In practice, it's quite difficult. Plus, it'd be a bit like old space exploration. We would have to know the exact time of flight, speed, and direction to determine its location. Hypothetically, we could fly it straight to Boston."

Drayden could barely speak he was so euphoric. "With this plane we wouldn't need to go on the expedition. Our lives wouldn't be at risk. Why wouldn't the Bureau try this first?"

Sam readjusted her glasses. "I don't disagree. But I don't make those decisions."

"Is it ready to go?" Catrice asked.

"Almost."

Drayden practically choked on his spit. "How soon?"

"Very. Probably a few weeks."

His heart sank. That was way too long.

The group rode their bicycles south on William Street toward their apartment building. The bikes were yet another abundant luxury enjoyed in the Palace versus the Dorms. Their former school, Norman Thomas High School, owned four bicycles governed by a signup sheet with a two-month waiting list. Only a few lucky families owned bikes. Despite their scarcity, pretty much everybody in the Dorms had learned to ride a bike, even Catrice. Charlie, though gifted at all other athletic endeavors, couldn't ride a bike with gears. He rode a "dirt bike" since it didn't require any shifting, while everyone else rode ten-speeds.

The overcast sky and blustery wind portended rain. The deserted streets here, about five blocks north of Bureau headquarters, were narrow, lined with rundown shops, restaurants, and former banks.

"I got a lousy feeling about this, guys," Charlie said after they had ridden in silence for a few minutes. "When Charlie gets a lousy feeling, well, watch out."

"Forget delaying it," Sidney said. "I don't want to go at all."

Drayden groaned, his ankle flaring up from the pedaling. "I think that solar airplane is the key. Sam said it would be ready in a few weeks. Maybe they can speed it up. If they have that, why would they send us and four Guardians out to possibly die?"

"Because they don't care if we die," Catrice said.

As usual, she was right, and cut straight to the heart of the problem. Even if the plane were ready now, the Bureau might move forward with the expedition anyway.

"You nailed it," Drayden said. "We either need to show that an alternative is superior to the expedition or that we're incapable of going right now."

Charlie held up his fist. "Want me to break everyone's legs?"

"No, Charlie," Drayden said, "but that's kind of the idea. If we literally couldn't go, they couldn't force us, right? If we stalled long enough for the scientists to complete the solar plane *and* it was successful, the expedition might be scrapped."

A smartly-dressed middle-aged couple headed toward them, arm in arm. After slowing and whispering to the woman, the man waved.

Drayden and the other pledges stopped when they reached them.

The man appeared to be fighting back a grin. "Excuse me, aren't you the kids who passed the Initiation?"

"Yeah, that's us." Drayden said.

The woman's face lit up. "Congratulations. Which one of you is Drayden?"

Charlie nodded at him. "He is." He stood tall. "I'm Charlie."

Sidney pinched him on the arm. He pretended it didn't hurt and smacked her hand away.

"You guys are legends in the Palace already," the man said. "It's an honor to meet you. I hope you enjoy life here. Take care." The duo strolled off.

The pledges had become semi-famous in the Palace, with episodes like that growing more common. They walked their bikes south as the streets became too crowded. When they reached Maiden Lane, the golden Bureau headquarters came into view.

"Listen," Drayden said, "we're all on the same page, right? I say we show up at Harris von Brooks's office and convince him to postpone the expedition. Suggest they try the solar airplane first."

Catrice looked pained. "He seemed pretty firm about *not* delaying it."

"We're right here," Charlie said. "Let's just do it now."

"No," Drayden said. "We need to think about this, to construct a persuasive argument. Catrice is right. Von Brooks doesn't seem like the type of guy who's going to suddenly agree and call it off. We'll go tomorrow morning."

"Von Brooks is a one-eyed cockroach," Charlie said. "What if we say we're sick or something?"

"They can check with the nurses," Catrice said.

"Yeah, they'll know it's shkat," Drayden added.

As they passed Bureau headquarters, more people packed the streets. Some stared at them closely, whispering, pointing, and even offering congratulations. Charlie puffed his chest out, held his chin high, and strutted with swagger, relishing the attention.

After crossing Pine Street, a strikingly handsome man in a tight-fitting suit approached, waving as he neared.

"Who is *that*?" Sidney muttered.

The comely man stopped in front of them, clapping his hands together. "Hello, *pledges*." He winked. "I'm Dennis Robinson, the new Bureau rep for the Dorms. I'll be spending a lot of time there, working closely with Lily Haddad, your 'mayor,' and taking Dorm concerns to the Bureau."

He pursed his lips for a moment. "I'm taking over for Mr. Cox."

Thomas Cox had been the liaison between the Palace and the Dorms, the zone the teens had lived in until completing the Initiation. Cox had been arrested, charged with plotting to overthrow the Bureau, and executed.

Thomas Cox's execution had bothered Drayden ever since Holst told them about it. Drayden personally knew about the plot; he'd heard it with his own ears. Before the Initiation, he'd hidden under Lily Haddad's desk in her office after sneaking in to question her about his mother's exile, and accidentally overheard the conversation between her and Cox. It was clear they were indeed plotting to overthrow Holst. What bugged Drayden was, how did the Bureau find out?

"I've only been on the job a few days," Robinson went on, "but I'm quite familiar with you four. Unlike previous years, the Bureau is spreading the news of your success in the Initiation. Finally, someone lived through it." He stroked his fancy chin beard, smiling.

Drayden felt the urge to slap him.

"They want people to be aware of kids passing, in hopes others will enter next year. On that note, congratulations. What an amazing feat. I'm honored to meet you guys."

He extended his hand to Catrice. "Are you Sidney or Catrice?"

His petty jealousy flaring up, Drayden couldn't help watching her greet this ridiculously dapper guy.

Catrice, who appeared frozen, was saved when Sidney thrust her hand out for a shake, a sly grin stretched across her face. "That's Catrice. I'm Sidney. So nice to meet you."

Gross, Drayden thought. Was she flirting with this guy? He had to be thirty years old.

"That would make you Charlie," he said, shaking his hand. "And last but not least, Drayden."

"Pleasure to meet you, Mr. Robinson," he said with a firm handshake.

"Please, call me Dennis. My dad is Mr. Robinson. Anyway, even though my work will mostly be in the Dorms, I'm here for you guys too. If you need anything, at all, feel free. My office is around the corner at Sixty Wall Street, in the old Deutsche Bank building."

Sidney touched him on the arm. "I'm sure we'll be stopping by...Dennis."

Dennis checked his watch. "Hey, Drayden, can I grab you alone for a minute?"

"Uh, sure, yeah. I'll catch up with you guys later," he said to the group.

"See ya, Dray," Sidney said.

When the others turned left on Wall Street, Catrice glanced back, her face a question mark.

After they walked away with their bikes, Dennis's smile faded. "Drayden, from what I hear, you're the reason everyone passed the Initiation. That's amazing. Between you and me, I don't think there are many people in the Palace who could pass it."

"Thanks," Drayden said. "But is that really what you wanted to tell me in private?"

He reached inside his suit jacket pocket and pulled out a white envelope. "No, there's something else. I'm working closely with Lily Haddad now, helping her deal with issues in the Dorms. She went on and on about how she'd been mentoring you over the years, and how close you two were."

What in hell is he talking about? Drayden had met Lily once. "Okay."

"She asked me to give you a letter." Dennis scanned the area before continuing in a lowered voice. "Now, this is unusual. Borderline inappropriate. Since it's not by the book, I shouldn't do it. I need Lily to trust me, though, and I'm the new guy. Nobody trusts the new guy. While I agreed, I *did* have to read it first. Can't say I understand it, but there's nothing improper." He handed Drayden the open envelope.

"Thanks, Dennis. Yeah, Lily was like an aunt to me. She and my mom were close."

"Drayden, I meant what I said. If you need anything, stop by my office. Cool?"

"Yeah, uh, cool, thanks a lot."

Dennis stuck his hand out in a fist, apparently hoping for a fist-bump.

He bumped it.

Dennis headed down William Street in the other direction, toward Bureau headquarters.

Drayden waited till he was out of sight before ensuring he was alone. He took a deep breath and pulled out Lily's note. Totally perplexed, he shoved his face right up to it.

"Memory is a fragile thing;
A bee's honey, and its sting."

CHAPTER 4

It had rained overnight, giving the Palace a wonderful fresh smell, as if the water had washed the city's dirtiness away. A thick, misty layer of clouds still lingered overhead, the air cool and humid.

Drayden and crew huddled on Liberty Street in front of an enormous glass and steel skyscraper towering behind them. Across the way stood the arched doorway to the Bureau headquarters' main entrance.

The usual cast of Guardians, all heavily armed, milled around the structure. Several eyed the four teens suspiciously. On previous visits to the building, someone had escorted them.

"Follow my lead," Drayden whispered. "Look confident, like we're supposed to be here." He marched across the street, the others in tow.

An older, husky Guardian stopped them. "Can we help you?"

"Yes, sir, we're here to see Harris von Brooks," Drayden said. "We're the kids who passed the Initiation."

"No kidding. Hey, Jack!" he yelled to another Guardian. "These are the kids."

Jack, another stocky, middle-aged Guardian with glasses and a mustache, walked over. "We heard about you guys, the Initiation and everything. Was it crazy hard?"

Drayden nodded. "Yeah, it was pretty bad."

"I always wondered how I'd do, you know?" the first Guardian said to Jack.

"Pffft. Nobody knows the details, but word is there's some math in there. You'd spend the whole time on the first problem and then get it wrong anyway." He couldn't stop laughing.

"Like you'd do any better, Einstein. You can't even count to eight." They both cracked up.

Drayden laughed along. "Can you take us to Mr. von Brooks?"

"Is he expecting you?" the first Guardian asked, instantly all business again.

"We're working with him on a project," Drayden said. "He said to stop by anytime."

"I'll take them in," Jack said. He patted them down, checking for weapons. "Follow me."

Drayden raised his eyebrows at the others and tilted his head in the direction of the doors.

They trailed Jack, who led them to the security desk and spoke to Guardians seated there. After a few minutes of discussion, Jack offered to escort them up to von Brooks's office. Once in the elevator, he said, "Mr. von Brooks is a terrific guy, isn't he?"

Nobody answered. The teens shifted uncomfortably.

Jack belly-laughed. "Don't worry, no surveillance in here."

A lengthy, carpeted hallway gave way to the foyer outside von Brooks's office, a spacious room with a magnificent red Oriental rug. Von Brooks's assistant, a nerdy middle-aged man with glasses and a turtleneck, sat at a desk. Two burly Guardians guarded the door to the office.

"Here you are. Good luck," Jack said, walking away.

"May I help you?" the assistant asked coldly.

Drayden tried to sound authoritative. "We're here to see Mr. von Brooks. It's very important."

"I'm sure it is." He offered a fake smile. "Unfortunately, Mr. von Brooks is quite busy. Leave your names and we'll contact you when he's available."

Drayden's face flushed hot. He wasn't about to be denied by this snooty man. This was life or death. He couldn't embark on this journey and die. He needed to find out what had happened to his mother. "Sir, we need to see him right now. It can't wait."

"Young man," he said, raising his voice, "you are not the only one with important business needing his attention."

To hell with you, Melvin von Turtleneck.

Drayden jutted his jaw and stormed toward von Brooks's office. "Drayden!" Catrice shouted.

The Guardians didn't hesitate. Both rushed him with their weapons drawn. "Freeze," one said.

Drayden stopped in his tracks. "Mr. von Brooks!" he yelled. "It's Drayden Coulson. I need to speak to you. It's urgent!"

One of the Guardians lowered his rifle. With his right hand, he seized Drayden by the shirt near his left shoulder, shoving him backward.

A flash of searing pain tore through his left ankle. Without thinking, he used his left hand to peel the Guardian's hand off and twisted it outward, applying a brutal jiu-jitsu wristlock called *Kotegaeshi*. He pressed with his right hand to twist it further. If he kept going, he would break the wrist.

The Guardian let out a scream and crumpled to the floor.

Drayden pinned the Guardian there, maintaining the pressure on his wrist just short of breaking it. That was the beauty of jiu-jitsu; he was causing intense pain but not injury, and the guy would be fine in ten minutes.

The Guardian moaned in pain.

Starting a fight with two huge guys brandishing guns may have been a mistake.

The other Guardian charged him with his rifle drawn. He held the muzzle inches from Drayden's head. "Let him go! Now!"

The doors to von Brooks's office burst open. He stutter-stepped back, his mouth wide, processing the scene before him. "What the hell is going on out here? Lower your weapon!" he yelled at the Guardian. "And let that man go," he said to Drayden.

Drayden released his hold.

The Guardian scrambled to his feet. He clasped his wrist, scowling at Drayden. "You're a dead man, punk," he snarled.

Drayden's heart thumped in his chest. He swallowed hard, trying not to look scared.

Charlie, Sidney, and Catrice stood frozen in shock.

"Mr. von Brooks," Drayden said, clearing his throat, "may we have a word with you please?"

Von Brooks pursed his lips and narrowed his good eye. He stepped to the side and extended his arm toward his office.

Drayden entered, and the others followed him inside, taking seats before von Brooks's desk.

The Guardian hobbled into the room and hovered by the door, clutching his wrist. Von Brooks plunked into his chair. "Now, what was so urgent that it couldn't wait and led you to attack my guards?"

"Sir, to be fair," Drayden said, "we calmly requested to see you. When your assistant declined, I yelled to get your attention. Then your guards assaulted me. I had to defend myself."

Von Brooks did not appear amused by the details of the encounter. "I will not ask this a third time. Why are you here?"

Drayden leaned forward in his chair, having rehearsed his speech. "Sir, I think we're all in agreement that New America needs to contact Boston. We have a problem here. An imminent one. We need to pursue the best solution. We've analyzed our proposed expedition, and it's fraught with potential complications. The boat may not work. We could contract Aeru and die before we arrive. We could be denied entry into Boston."

Drayden placed his hand on his chest. "I believe Premier Holst intended for me personally to lead this, but I have a severely injured ankle. I may be a liability out there. And there is an alternate solution that simplifies this. The scientists have constructed a solar plane which they can fly to Boston using brand-new technology. It's virtually ready to go. It can carry the same message we would deliver. We feel it's in the best interest of New America to send that plane first. If it's unsuccessful, then we go forward with the mission."

He should have stopped there. He didn't.

"I mean, you're basically asking us to go on a suicide mission when there's a superior alternative available."

"Hmm, very interesting," von Brooks said, filling out some paperwork on his desk.

Drayden studied him. Was that sarcasm or honesty?

Von Brooks set down his pen and walked in front of his desk, cupping his hands together. "It's a good thing you decided to come to me with this...*problem*. If you had gone to the Premier, for example, I don't think it would go too smoothly. I can be more reasonable than the Premier sometimes. I believe he would force you to go. I'm not going to do that. I can understand your apprehension. You are, after all, still children. However, if you'll recall, the only reason the Premier granted you entry into the Palace was to undertake this mission. Therefore, if you are refusing the mission, you are no longer welcome in the Bureau."

Von Brooks returned to his seat behind the desk. "Your families are lucky; they will merely be exiled. You, on the other hand, are Bureau members. Bureau members are never exiled. They are executed. If that is the option you would prefer, I can get started on the arrangements immediately."

Holy shkat.

The others looked exactly like he felt.

"Which will it be?" von Brooks asked, an evil smile growing across his face.

Drayden didn't need to confer with anyone. "We'll be going on the expedition," he said quietly, defeated.

"Ah, excellent choice." Von Brooks's smile faded. "We've made further changes to the plan. Instead of leaving Monday, we're pushing your departure day up to Friday, just two days from now."

Oh no.

That only gave Drayden two days to solve his mother's exile.

Von Brooks crossed his arms. "Tomorrow you'll meet your Guardian escorts, and I think you will feel much better about your mission once you do, but let me be crystal clear this time. If we have this conversation again, I will be deciding your fate. Understood?"

"Yes, sir." Drayden stood and shot his friends a look.

They rose from their seats and headed for the door. When the Guardian opened it, he zeroed in on Drayden.

"Watch your back, kid," he whispered.

The four teens walked up William Street toward their apartments.

"Soooo," Charlie said, "that went well."

Drayden shook his head. "What a flunk that guy is."

"I've heard of exiles that have gone smoother," Charlie said. "Hey, do you guys remember Julia Singer? She was in our class. I asked her once if she wanted to come over, have some alone time with Charlie. She kicked me in the shin. Didn't say a word. Just hauled off on my shin. That went better than this."

"We get it, Charlie," Sidney said. "Drayden, what are we going to do?"

He waved a hand through the air. "Apparently, we're going on the expedition. In two days. What a bunch of shkat." He cursed under his breath, thinking of his mother. "It's...my damn ankle."

"Dray," Charlie said, "that was sick the way you tossed that Guardian on the floor. He was, like, three times your size. Can you teach me that move?"

"That was stupid. I don't know what I was thinking. If von Brooks hadn't bailed me out those guys would have pounded me into dust." After years of suppressing his jiu-jitsu skills, Drayden finally had the confidence to let them shine, thanks to the Initiation. Still, he even surprised himself a little by reflexively securing the wristlock.

"What you did worked," Sidney said, draping her hand on his shoulder. "You got us in there. That was really brave."

Catrice held her stomach as if she were going to get sick.

"You all right?" Drayden asked.

"I guess. Just trying to wrap my head around doing this."

"I don't think it'll be that terrible, you guys," Charlie said. "We go for a boat ride and come back. Sounds a heck of a lot easier than the Initiation."

It struck Drayden how weak he must look to Catrice. Here he was, allowing his fear to pervade his life again, like early in the Initiation. It wasn't that he was scared as much as too weak for the expedition and in need of more time.

Sidney gawked at Charlie. "The Initiation didn't have any challenges that involved avoiding the bacteria that killed everyone in the world."

"They're probably saving that for next year's Initiation," Charlie mumbled.

They reached Wall Street and stopped.

Charlie scratched his head. "What do you guys want to do? We've got a free day."

"I—I need to go take care of something," Drayden said, fumbling with the enigmatic note from Lily Haddad in his pocket. It was late Wednesday morning, and the boat departed for the expedition on Friday morning. That gave him the rest of today and tomorrow to untangle the web of his mother's exile. A week of investigation had revealed zippo thus far. He needed to finally make the uncomfortable meeting he'd been avoiding, and he no longer had the time to wait.

"You want some company?" Sidney asked excitedly.

Catrice glowered at her. "What is it, Dray?"

"Nothing, it's just...it's nothing." He kicked around a few pebbles on the sidewalk.

She pulled him by the arm away from Charlie and Sidney. "What's going on?" she whispered.

"I'm investigating my mom's exile."

"I could help you," she said.

While he'd love Catrice's help, digging up dirt on an exile would likely be considered a serious offense if he got busted. He'd be putting her life at risk. Drayden hugged her and kissed her forehead. "Thank you. I'd love your support, and I have you no doubt you could help me figure this out. Unfortunately, I need to do this alone."

She couldn't hide her disappointment. "Okay."

"I'll come find you in a little bit." He touched her arm. "This shouldn't take long."

She walked away with Charlie and Sidney down Wall Street, toward their apartment building.

It shouldn't take long at all. Nathan Locke's office was only five minutes away.

Drayden hurried in the other direction, toward the old New York Stock Exchange. As he passed it, he imagined the tourists that must have flocked here PreCon, snapping photos, documenting their trip. He reached Broadway, with the crumbling Trinity Church across the street, and the crowd of people thinned out. He turned left, heading for Twenty-One Broadway.

It was barren here, a ghost town of deserted office buildings. He stared at his reflection in the floor-to-ceiling windows of the abandoned drug stores and cafés, noticing he hadn't bulked up despite the superior food in the Palace.

Something caught his eye.

A person was walking behind him, around thirty feet back. Not really anything special; there were other people in the Palace after all. But it was how he was dressed, in a long coat with an old-fashioned hat tipped low in the front, obscuring his eyes. It resembled the type of hat the gangsters wore in that mafia movie *The Godfather* the Bureau had played once. He was a rather large man as well.

Drayden pulled out the letter from Lily Haddad, reading the poem:

"Memory is a fragile thing;
A bee's honey and its sting."

He held it up to the sky, thinking it might have contained a hidden code. There was nothing other than the poem. What did it mean anyway? Memory was like a bee's honey, and its sting. Or *memories*. Sweet, or painful? If it was a reference to his recollection of the Dorms, he was thinking more along the lines of 'painful.' He stuffed it back into his pocket and sneaked a peek behind him.

The man was still there. A little closer, in fact.

Hmmm.

Drayden tried to appear casual as he strolled across Broadway to the right side of the street, noting that the man didn't follow. He breathed a sigh of relief.

As he approached the famous Wall Street bull statue, the road forked. Twenty-One Broadway was past it to the right.

Quick glance back.

The shadowy man had crossed and was behind him again.

His body instantly went into panic mode: nervous sweating, rapid heartbeat.

Morris Street, a narrow street, almost like an alley, led to the right. Drayden darted down it about halfway before stopping and facing back toward Broadway. He backed himself against one of the brick walls of the alley, vaguely aware he was holding his breath. His stomach twisted in knots when the man followed him onto Morris Street.

Well, that answered that. He *was* being followed.

He could turn and bolt, certain he could outrun a burly, grown man. But whoever this man was, he wanted something and had found him once already. He'd probably be able to locate him again. More than that, Drayden was done running. He'd been running in fear his whole life before the Initiation. He stood his ground and tried to exude confidence as the man reached him.

Mere feet away, he tipped his cap back, revealing that *he* was a *she*. A towering woman. Not fat, just big, like a Pre-Confluence football player or pro wrestler. Before Drayden had a chance to say anything, the powerful woman gripped him by the shoulders and slammed him backward into the brick wall. It hurt, a sharp edge of brick digging into his shoulder. She leaned in as if to kiss him; an oncoming bus of short red hair, strawberry skin, and freckles.

What in the hell is this?

She brought her lips to his ear and whispered, *"Memory is a fragile thing; a bee's honey and its sting."*

CHAPTER 5

His head spinning, Drayden followed the ginger giant back the way he had come, up Broadway toward Wall Street. He'd tried to say something to her before they left, but she'd covered his mouth with her banana hands and instructed him to follow her, without looking like he was following her. When he attempted to ask her a question again, she'd whispered forcefully, "Shut your piehole."

He tried to act casual, as suggested, despite the woman's brisk pace. It was challenging to seem like he wasn't following her when he had to walk so hastily. But he needed to talk to her. Although she was scary and this whole scenario was dangerous and uncomfortable, she was evidently the key to unlocking the puzzle of Lily Haddad's note.

She disappeared left down an alley. Drayden followed.

It was dark inside, about ten feet wide, and smelled like wet cement. A giant gray stone building towered on the right. On the left, a building constructed of glass and dirty brown brick rested atop huge brown stone pillars. The woman was waiting about halfway down, now wearing pants and a button-down shirt, her coat and hat in a pile on the ground.

When he reached her, Drayden extended his hand. "Hi, I'm Drayden Coulson."

She regarded it as if it were poison. "I know who you are, kiddo. Obviously."

"Okay. Who are you?"

"My name is Kimberly Craig. I run surveillance for all of New America. Right over here, 90 Trinity Place," she said, tilting her head back. "I know you're confused and probably a little scared, and I'm going to do my best to explain what's going on. But I also need to ask you some questions, because I'm a little confused too. Yeah?"

"Um, sure."

She blew out a long breath, puffing her cheeks out. "A decision was made about you. To bring you in. I don't know why yet, but that's what we're going to figure out. You were contacted by Lily Haddad? With that poem I recited?"

Drayden nodded. "Yes. What does it mean?"

Craig made a face. "Hell if I know. I'm no poet. It was a code for this scenario we're in right now, so we could be sure to trust each other. It's not like Lily could call on a phone and tell me what's up. Communicating with her is very difficult, particularly with Thomas Cox gone."

It occurred to Drayden that just because this woman knew the poem didn't mean he could trust her. The new Dorm rep, Dennis Robinson, had read the note. What if he'd shared it? How could he be sure she wasn't an agent of the Bureau digging into Lily Haddad? He decided to play along for now.

"Got it."

"I found you because certain people think you should be in. I'm here to make sure it happens. What I don't understand is why Lily *wants* you in. How do you know her?"

In for what? Drayden wondered.

"I'm one of the kids from the Dorms that passed the Initiation," he said. "I only met Lily once, the day before the test."

"What did you talk about?"

"I asked her if she had any idea why the Bureau exiled my mom. My brother had mentioned she'd been spending a lot of time with Lily, which I found odd because I didn't recall them ever socializing."

"What was your mom's name?"

"Maya. Maya Coulson."

Her eyes widened. "Ah. Maya was your mom. What did Lily tell you?"

"That she had no idea what happened. My mom was accused of conspiring against the Bureau, but Lily said that was shkat."

Kimberly Craig hesitated, scratching her head. "Is there anything else you're not telling me? About you and Lily."

"Uh...I..." Drayden recalled how he'd hid in her office.

She put her hands on her hips. "What is it, kid? I need to know everything."

Now was the moment he'd have to decide if he trusted this woman or not. Any further information could expose him, or Lily, or who knew who else. He recalled that his best friend Tim had often told him to stop thinking so much and trust his gut. Sure, the context was often in regard to a fight or jiu-jitsu, but it applied during the Initiation as well. Maybe her bulk reminded him of Wesley, the most trustworthy person he knew. Plus, she seemed authentic. His gut told him to trust her.

"I didn't think Lily was telling me the full story. I broke into her office to press her. Then I heard her approaching with Thomas Cox. It was too late for me to escape, so I hid under her desk. She and Cox had a conversation, then left. After they were gone, I snuck back out."

A lightbulb appeared to go off. "Did anyone see you leave?"

Oh yeah, he'd forgotten about that. "Yes. Her receptionist. She yelled after me, but I ran."

"In that case, Lily would have found out you'd been in her office." Craig rubbed her temples. "That means she knew you overheard what she discussed with Cox. What were they talking about?"

Drayden hesitated again. "I—I don't want to get Lily in any trouble."

Kimberly Craig smirked. "Do you have any idea why we're talking here? I run surveillance. I know where all the cameras and microphones are in this entire city. We're secure right here. This is one of the only places not monitored besides the Meadow. I'm on Lily's side, sonny boy. You can tell me; it's fine."

Why wasn't the Meadow surveilled?

He hoped his gut instinct was right. "They were talking about getting rid of Premier Holst. Cox said they needed to move swiftly. Lily said they weren't even close to being ready, and expressed fear that Cox was going to get them exiled. Cox told Lily about the power outages and the exiles in the Dorms. The Bureau couldn't produce enough food to feed everyone. He said exiles would skyrocket. He actually said nobody was safe in the Dorms. It's one of the main reasons I entered the Initiation."

"Now we're getting somewhere," Craig said. "Lily knew you were in her office and overheard that conversation. She knows you uncovered the plan, and that you were upset about your mother's exile. That, combined with you being smart enough to pass the Initiation, explains why they had me find you. I get it now." She checked up and down the alley for people.

"I'm lost, lady."

She stepped back a little. "You're clearly a smart kid. We need you in our movement and I'm here to officially recruit you. I was sent to find you. You're an asset, yes, but you're also too big a risk to keep on the outside considering the information you possess. Get it? We can't have you running around out there aware of a plot against the Bureau. I can't tell you many details yet. What I can say is there's a plot, and Thomas Cox's execution did nothing to slow it. There are people in all zones involved, including some Bureau members. I control surveillance. If I'm aware of a sensitive conversation that's taking place, I'll shut those cameras or microphones off. If someone screws up and gets recorded, I'll guarantee that feed never sees the light of day."

"Ms. Craig, how did Thomas Cox get caught then?"

"You *are* sharp, aren't you? Let's just say Cox screwed up. Had a conversation outside, in an unexpected place, where he was overheard yapping before I could do anything about it. Jeez, now that I think about it, it might have even been the day you were hiding under the desk."

Drayden connected the dots. "That would mean the Bureau knows about Lily."

"They can't touch her, Drayden. She's the leader of the Dorms. The Bureau knows her exile would lead to a revolt."

Craig stepped closer to him and puffed up like a balloon. "Now we've got a little dilemma here. You might be questioning why I'm telling you all this since we just met. It's because you don't leave here today without either joining us or dying. It's one or the other. Many people would be executed if this information got out. What you knew before I found you today is enough to blow the whole thing. The safest thing for me to do is kill you. It's possible that's why Lily connected us. I could, by the way. Like that," she said, snapping her fingers in his face. "However, I don't think so. They want you to be a part of this and felt you'd be on board, based on your mother's exile and having suffered through the Initiation. A kid smart and brave enough to pass the Initiation would be quite a tool in our box. What do you say, string bean?"

Drayden imagined this mountain of a woman killing him with her bare hands. But it was more than that. The Bureau had exiled his mother, killed his best friend Tim, and put him through hell in the Initiation. This was a no-brainer.

"I'm no fan of the Bureau, and I'd love to see the walls knocked down. I'm in, on one condition."

"Your choices are join us or die. You don't get to set conditions."

After years of bullying, Drayden wasn't getting bullied anymore. "You can't kill me right now, Ms. Craig. I may have already told other people about this. If you kill me, you won't know who they are."

To be fair, he hadn't told anyone, but he'd thought about confiding in Catrice.

She smiled. "I like you, Drayden Coulson. Call me Kim. What's your condition?"

"Can you help me figure out why my mom was exiled? Who was responsible, who ordered it, if it was random? Anything about it."

She tilted her head back and forth. "That information is highly classified. I can try, though." She checked her watch. "Meet me right here at noon tomorrow. Do not speak a word of this to anyone. I think you know what that would mean for you. And them."

Drayden sported a pair of beat-up red boxing gloves, pounding away at a heavy bag inside the Guardian fitness center. After his fortuitous meeting with Kim Craig, he needed to think, to strategize. He was no longer sure if an uncomfortable confrontation with Nathan Locke made sense. Recounting the events of his mother's exile had also gotten him fired up and he needed to blow off some steam.

One–two: left jab, right cross. Repeat. He'd picked up a few combinations from the Guardians during their training. Huffing and puffing, dripping sweat, Drayden collapsed with his back against the wall, resting the bulky gloves on his knees.

Finally, a solid lead had emerged, and just in the nick of time. Whatever her reasons, Lily Haddad had connected him with Kim Craig, the first person to offer support. Kim's demeanor was a tad surly, but her toughness somehow enhanced her authenticity and appeal. You got the sense she was totally upfront about everything. Nothing was masked behind pleasantries.

Still, Drayden wasn't sure he could trust her. How could he know for sure? She hadn't revealed anything he didn't already know, except mentioning the Meadow wasn't under surveillance, and that seemed to have been an accidental slip. Meanwhile, Drayden had sung to her like a canary, telling her everything he knew.

He had little choice in the matter since he needed her help *and* she had threatened to kill him. He was firmly on the rebels' side in theory, he just wasn't sure he wanted to be directly involved in this overthrow plot. While he'd welcome the Bureau's destruction, there was a broad gap between being an idealistic supporter and an active participant. He imagined many overthrow plots had been concocted over the years, and each one had failed, its rebels executed. Perhaps Lily and Kim and the few other members of each zone had a brilliant scheme. Yet witnessing firsthand how strong the Palace Guardians were, the idea of a rebellion seemed laughable.

He could cooperate until Kim produced the information he needed about his mother, then afterward tell her, "Yeah, nah. Thanks anyway." Drayden snorted out loud at the thought. Kim would snap his neck on the spot.

He should have asked if his mother was involved in this plot. Kim recognized her name, so she could have been, or they sought to recruit her. He couldn't imagine his mother associating herself with anything that would jeopardize her ability to care for her children. If that was true, her exile had nothing to do with this plot. Not to mention, Kim controlled surveillance. If a camera or microphone caught Mom talking about it, Kim would ensure the clip disappeared. That basically ruled out her exile having anything to do with the conspiracy.

As a result, two possibilities remained. She was randomly exiled to match the declining power and food production with the population size, or it was something else altogether. Like, Nathan Locke. The affair between his mother and Locke still ate away at Drayden. Her exile and the fling were simultaneous shocking events. How could they be unrelated? What were the odds?

Drayden's supposed involvement in the plot to overthrow the Bureau overlooked one major problem—he would be leaving New America in two days. Despite the assurances from everyone, he gave himself a fifty-percent chance of returning alive and healthy. He wouldn't be much good to the movement outside the city.

He got up and returned to the heavy bag. Having never seen Nathan Locke's face, he pictured a creepy old guy's mug on the bag. The anger simmering inside him, he pummeled it with all his strength.

Kim Craig could come up empty tomorrow, and he couldn't leave any stone unturned. He'd been avoiding this, not just because it was risky, but because it would be difficult. The decision was clear. He needed to confront Nathan Locke.

CHAPTER 6

Drayden rode the dimly lit elevator up to fourth floor of Twenty-One Broadway. The building smelled old and musty. Since the offices to the left were dark, he headed right, reaching a door that read "Food Distribution Center Main Office" etched into translucent glass.

Nathan Locke ran all the food distribution centers, or FDCs as they called them in the Dorms. Drayden's mother had been the manager of the local one on East Thirtieth Street. Until Wesley told him about her affair with Locke, Drayden barely knew who he was. Even now he didn't know much about the man. Locke supposedly visited the Dorms on Mondays and Fridays. That was the extent of Drayden's knowledge.

Despite his not knowing Locke, Locke might know him, or at least his name. If he wanted to make sure Locke agreed to meet, he'd have to lie about his name. He couldn't imagine Locke would desire a sit-down with the son of a woman with whom he'd had an affair and possibly exiled.

Drayden opened the door and entered.

Immediately to the left was a dark wood desk. A stunning girl, not much older than he was, reclined in a chair with her face buried in a book. She read for another few seconds, twirling her luminous brown hair before looking up. She dropped the book on the desk, scooted her chair in, tucked her hair behind her ears, and smiled.

Butterflies fluttered in his stomach. He felt guilty for finding her attractive, thinking about Catrice. Dammit, she was gorgeous, though. Drayden suddenly wished he'd dressed cooler, instead of wearing imitation jeans and a wrinkled T-shirt. He called to mind his best friend Tim and how he would own this situation. He'd get in to see Locke *and* leave with a date.

Drayden tried his best to channel Tim's gift of gab. "Hi. How are you?" He started to lean on the desk but decided that was stupid and straightened.

Her smile faded a bit. "Can I help you?"

"Oh, yeah. I'm Dr—Charlie. Charlie Arnold. What's your name?"

She furrowed her brow. "Hi, Dr—Charlie. What can I do for you today?" She was becoming increasingly businesslike by the second.

How did Tim make it look so effortless? "I'm here to see Mr. Locke. I have a message for him."

She pulled out a notepad and pen. "Why don't you leave the message with me, and I'll pass it along to Mr. Locke?"

Drayden surveyed the room. Lacking the elegance of the headquarters' offices, it was functional rather than aesthetic. Dented metal filing cabinets, notebooks, and stacks of papers littered the space. Fluorescent white light brightened the room, which featured an ugly turquoise rug. Like the offices at headquarters, however, two rather bulky Guardians flanked Locke's door.

"I was instructed to deliver the message to Mr. Locke myself. It's from Dennis Robinson, the Bureau rep for the Dorms. He's sick and couldn't come. I know Mr. Robinson because I'm from the Dorms. I joined the Bureau last week."

Her blue eyes lit up. "Oh my God, you're one of the kids who passed the Initiation?" She excitedly rubbed her hands together. "I can't believe I'm meeting one of you! Though, no offense, Charlie, I'm dying to meet Drayden."

You've got to be kidding me.

He stood there for a moment, paralyzed by the irony. You couldn't make this up. He might as well have some fun with it.

"Yeah, Drayden is incredible. They say he's one of the smartest kids ever. Strong and brave too. And funny, with unconventional good looks."

She stood and extended her hand. "I'm Katelyn." She gave him a solid shake. "Let me tell Mr. Locke you're here and I'll show you right in." She walked to the door, knocked twice, and poked in her head. After saying something, she opened the door a tad further, and returned to the desk. "Go right in, Charlie," she said with a sultry smile.

"Thank you, Katelyn." Drayden took a deep breath and approached the door.

Now that he was here, he waffled on the proper approach. He could go super aggressive, or play dumb and pretend he didn't know about the affair. Maybe he wouldn't even reveal his identity. After walking through the door and closing it behind him, he faced Locke.

Locke was sixty-something, overweight with a round belly, and had a receding line of flawlessly coifed gray hair. He also carried an air of authority about him. Classic bureaucrat. He'd risen from his desk and approached, a jolly grin on his face. He stopped in his tracks five feet from Drayden and his smile faded, inverting into a frown. "Hello, Drayden."

How did he know? There were no pictures. Drayden racked his brain to recall whether he'd met the guy once while visiting Mom. Or, Locke might have seen her in his features. "Mr. Locke, may I take a seat?"

He tugged at his tie, apparently lost for words.

Perhaps he was debating if he should summon the Guardians outside, Drayden worried.

"Please do," he said, motioning toward the chairs facing the desk. He walked behind his desk and sat. "What can I do for you?"

You know exactly why I'm here, you shkat flunk.

"I'm trying to find out about my mom's exile. Since she worked for you and you're a senior Bureau member, I figured you might have some information."

"I'm sorry, Drayden. She wasn't just one of the best managers in the FDC system, she was also a friend. I was devastated and angry when I found out."

Nervous sweat glued Drayden's T-shirt to his back. "So you didn't know about it?"

"No, absolutely not. Believe me. I made a big deal about it the very next day in the Bureau." He radiated indignance. "They don't announce exiles either before or after. It's not like the Bureau posts them up on a board somewhere. If I had known about it beforehand, I may have been able to stop it. That's what got me so angry. It's a disgrace." He shook his head.

Locke was playing it perfectly. Very convincing. He seemed sincere. Drayden was about to drop the bomb on him, though.

"I know, Mr. Locke."

"Exactly, a real travesty. As upset as I was, I can't imagine how much it must have distressed you and your family."

"No, Mr. Locke. I *know*. About you and my mom."

"I don't know what you mean."

"Yes. You do."

Silence.

Locke's face turned red. "Life...life is...complicated, Drayden. Things happen. Unexpected things. You'll learn that as you get older."

A tiny spark of rage ignited inside Drayden. A little ball of fizzling fire, growing more intense with each passing second. He pictured this fat scum trying to kiss his mother.

"She was married," he said through gritted teeth. "To my father."

Locke remained calm, leaning back in his chair. "I didn't expect my own wife to die, years ago. Like I said, life often has twists and turns we can't foresee."

Drayden felt angry tears welling. "Mr. Locke, it's not like an accident, like she tripped and her lips landed on yours. I don't know why you're talking about it like you had no control over it."

The slightest smirk appeared on Locke's face. "It takes two to tango, doesn't it?"

Drayden almost leapt out of his chair. How dare he? His mother was dead; he shouldn't be sullying her good name. He took a breath. He had to hold it together. He needed information from Locke and any more aggression would lead to him being escorted out.

"Drayden, just so you know, your mother talked about you constantly. She loved you so much and was so proud of you. I knew you were a genius and deserved to live here in the Palace, among the greatest minds in New America. I invited her to move here with you and Wesley."

Drayden's jaw practically hit the floor. How could all of this have gone on under his nose? How could his mother have kept these secrets from him?

"She—"

"She said no," Drayden exclaimed. "Obviously. Is that why you had her exiled?"

Locke's outrage was visible. He jabbed a finger at Drayden. "I'm going to grant you a pass on that very serious accusation because you're just a child. One who lost his mother." He took a few deep breaths, regaining his composure. "You clearly don't know how exiles work. Bureau members can't go around exiling whomever they want," he said. "I'm the last person in the world that would exile her anyway." He leaned forward. "She said yes, Drayden. She was going to leave your father."

No!

Drayden balled his hands into fists. This guy was a liar, plain and simple. A snake.

"Oh please. For you? I don't think so."

It was a mistake to come here. What did he think, that Locke would simply admit what he'd done? Apologize? Of course he would deny it. Now that Drayden knew what a liar he was, his words were irrelevant anyway.

Locke cocked his head. "I can understand that you're angry, but instead of looking to take that anger out on other people, I suggest you examine the source of your anger. I think you're angry at your mother."

Drayden shot to his feet, the ball of fire inside him exploding.

Locke reached for a button on his desk.

Drayden turned to leave before he called in the Guardians.

"Drayden!" Locke shouted.

He stopped.

"One more thing. Be careful asking questions about this. The Palace is a small place, and people talk. They would not look kindly upon you if they find out you're investigating this."

Drayden slouched on the steps of Federal Hall across from the New York Stock Exchange. The late afternoon sun was trying and failing to break through the clouds. People passed by, some of whom waved at him. These people must have been either oblivious or indifferent to the plight of New America.

The meeting with Nathan Locke hadn't cleared anything up. On the contrary, it scrambled things further. While Drayden couldn't believe anything he said, his denials around the exile were forceful. What motivation did he have to lie about it? If Locke was responsible, he knew Drayden couldn't do anything about it. He even seemed like the kind of guy who would admit what he'd done just to anger Drayden.

It could be time to accept that the Bureau spoke the truth. They picked people at random in the Dorms to exile, and his mother was simply unlucky.

The Bureau's policy was barbaric and unfair, but it wasn't illogical. The city didn't have enough resources to support the population anymore. They believed they had a choice between exiling a few people or allowing everyone to die. It was the essence of the philosophy of utilitarianism, which his original mentor Mr. Kale had taught them about in school. It also echoed the words of Spock, from the one *Star Trek* movie played in the Dorms—*The Wrath of Khan*. He said the needs of the many outweighed the needs of the few. The red-and-green-hats challenge in the Initiation was even designed to drive the message home. *All might be done, but for one*, was how they had phrased it. They'd said a group's well-being superseded any individual's.

Lily Haddad had claimed nineteen people were exiled in April alone. It was not as if Drayden's mother was the only one. Maybe he was trying to solve a mystery that didn't exist. If one evil person bore responsibility, it was easier to comprehend and simpler to punish the monster. If it was just the Bureau-at-large executing a strategy, it wasn't as easy to direct his wrath. Holding the entire Bureau accountable wouldn't be so straightforward. Still, it could be done. Mr. Kale had encouraged him to enter the Initiation to fix this broken system of government. In an ideal world, overturn it.

He beheld the giant figure on his left.

The oversized statue of George Washington towered on the steps leading up to Federal Hall. He was, arguably, the greatest revolutionary in United States history. Or one of the most famous anyway. Overthrowing British rule must have sounded insane at one time too.

Drayden removed the green Yankees cap his mother had given him and held it with his eyes closed. On more than one occasion during the Initiation, he was sure she had contacted him when he touched that hat. In the Initiation's final moment, when he'd swiped it to run through the finish line, he was overcome with the feeling that he should save Charlie instead. He'd believed she protected him sometimes. During the red-and-green-hats challenge, he had a fifty percent chance of surviving. It wasn't luck that had saved him.

It sounded crazy, revisiting it now. Back then he was under incredible stress, exhaustion, and the influence of narcotic pain-killers, but something told him he wasn't imagining it. As he felt the hat now, he could sense his mother watching over him. Possibly even contacting him.

In that moment, he felt unsettled. Something was off. Was it something Locke had said? It wasn't that he'd denied exiling Drayden's mother. That was expected. He could've been telling the truth as well. He'd made some valid points. Besides that garbage about blaming his mother for their affair. His *mother,* the saint of the Dorms. What a load of shkat, trying to flip the blame onto her.

Drayden held his head in his hands. He supposed she hadn't exactly been a saint. Not that Locke was right.

But dammit, Mom, why did you do that? Why?

What a mess he was in now. Almost dying in the Initiation, probably about to die on the expedition, and it all led back to this stupid affair with a fat old guy.

No. No no no. I'm sorry, Mom, I didn't mean it.

This was not his mother's fault. She could never have known she'd be exiled. No, it was something else about the confronta-tion with Locke that felt off. It could have been Locke recognizing him, or his veiled threat about investigating the exile as Drayden departed. That was a chess match, and Locke had made an error, except Drayden couldn't see what it was yet. There were still too many pieces on the board.

Premier Holst's explanation of the exiles also bothered him for some reason other than its cruelty.

After the Initiation Holst had said that once the Bureau decided to shrink the population, they wouldn't exile scientists or Guardians. They were too valuable, which was why they focused on the Dorms. That implied they considered someone's value to society when deciding whom to exile. If that were the case, they would have applied the same logic inside the Dorms, where a clear hierarchy of importance also existed. Drayden's mother was one of the most invaluable and senior Dorm members. She managed the FDC, and she was tremendous at it. Obviously, every life was meaningful, which was why the idea of exiles was so repugnant. But by their rationale, why not exile a seamstress instead? There were hundreds of them. Mom's exile was inconsistent with the Bureau's reasoning.

He couldn't give up yet. Hopefully the rendezvous with Kim Craig tomorrow would put the issue to bed; then he could focus on the other pressing issue: not dying on the expedition.

CHAPTER 7

Drayden and the others wore casual clothes to meet their Guardian escorts. Imitation jeans and sweatshirts all around. Although they were meeting in the Guardian facility in Battery Park, it wasn't a training session.

Finally, the skies had cleared, and while the air was cool, the morning sun was warm. Charlie and Sidney walked in front, and Drayden and Catrice followed. The route to the park took them down Broadway, right past Nathan Locke's office.

"Dray, I hope these guys dig you more than Sergeant Holcomb does," Charlie said. "He likes you about as much as Alex did."

Nobody had spoken about Alex, Drayden's former nemesis and Charlie's best friend, since he'd died in the Initiation. Nor had anyone mentioned Tim. It was refreshing to hear Charlie joking about it. Drayden sure as hell wasn't ready to laugh about his deceased friend.

"I guess it doesn't feel normal if someone doesn't hate me." Drayden took Catrice's hand, holding it as they walked. Even recalling Tim's name evoked memories too painful to revisit.

They entered Battery Park, and hearing gunfire, headed toward the shooting range. When it emerged in the distance, one man stood on the range shooting pistols with another watching him.

"Hold your fire!" the watcher yelled. Both men wore their gray camouflage fatigues, and camouflage baseball caps. They turned and faced the teens, remaining expressionless.

"They look like fun guys," Charlie whispered. "Can't wait to go on a twenty-hour boat ride with them."

Sidney whacked him on the arm. "Shut up, Charlie!" she whisper-yelled.

The man on the range holstered his weapon and joined the other guy, who appeared much older and wore a different hat than most Guardians. His was more like an actual baseball cap, while everyone else wore military baseball caps, with flat tops. The shooter seemed to be a teenager.

Drayden stopped a few feet away, awestruck by their obvious strength and toughness.

The two Guardians stood at attention and saluted.

He exchanged an awkward glance with the girls, unsure of whether saluting back was disrespectful. They weren't Guardians themselves and hadn't been shown how to do it.

Charlie, naturally, straightened and gave a hearty salute.

"At ease," the older Guardian, presumably the captain, said to the younger.

Drayden, Catrice, and Sidney hadn't yet decided whether to salute or not.

Good start, Drayden thought ruefully.

The captain had piercing blue eyes, and a brutal face, overtaken by scars. He removed his cap, walked up to Drayden, and extended his hand.

Drayden shook it, the captain squeezing with such force that it hurt. He had what Drayden referred to as "old man muscle." While he didn't seem like a guy who lifted weights, he was rock solid and powerful, despite being in his mid-fifties.

"Captain Jonathan Lindrick. It's an honor to meet you," the captain said, his tone serious. "Completing the Initiation is an incredible feat. Well done." He rubbed his mustache, which was gray like his short hair. "Beside me is Corporal Eugene Austin, our most junior team member. The other two soldiers will be joining us in a moment."

Corporal Austin smiled like a kid at Christmas.

Drayden couldn't help but notice how handsome he was. Tall and muscular, strong jaw, thin nose. He hated him immediately.

Sidney and Catrice both regarded the young corporal. Sidney smiled equally wide back at him.

Drayden sighed. Looks aside, the kid was probably a flunk.

Captain Lindrick stepped back, his hands clasped behind him. "I'm going to refer to you as privates. Please don't take this as a sign of disrespect or rank respective to us. It's just an old habit. Young people in our world are always privates. If I should yell out 'privates,' I'm addressing you all." He glanced at Corporal Austin. "Now, we're well prepared for this mission, as I trust you are. You'll be in safe hands with us. Judging by your performance in the Initiation, we'll be in safe hands with you."

"Thank you, Captain Lindrick," Drayden said. "We look forward to working with you."

Captain Lindrick nodded at Corporal Austin, who approached.

Drayden didn't think it was possible, but Austin's smile grew even wider.

"Hey, you guys, I'm Corporal Austin. Call me Eugene. I'm eighteen, only two years older than you are. I hope you'll forgive me for being so excited. This is insane! I'm meeting the legends who passed the Initiation, and I get to hang out with you for a few days. I don't get to hang out with kids my own age too often either, so this is pretty special for me."

Already, Drayden was having a hard time not liking this kid. He was strapping, tough, and handsome, yet childlike and innocent in his excitement. It was charming.

"Hi, Eugene, I'm Sidney," she said, batting her eyes, fighting him for world's widest smile.

He shook her hand, clasping it with both of his own. "Nice to meet you, Sidney. I hear you're quite the shooter. That happens to be my specialty too."

Drayden thought Sidney might faint.

"You must be Charlie, great to meet you." Eugene gave him a firm shake. "I heard that after the mission they want you to join the Palace Guardian force. How awesome would that be? I'd love for us to be friends."

Charlie was visibly as emotional as he could get. He stood tall, his lips pursed, and saluted Eugene. "Sir, yes sir," he whispered.

Eugene shifted over in front of both Catrice and Drayden. "Catrice, Drayden, I...I'm sorry. I'm in awe of you guys. I know you wouldn't guess this about me, but I love math and science." He touched his hand to his chest. "I mean, I'm nothing compared to you guys. I read math books at night to educate myself. I'm reading about stochastic calculus now, which is probably cake for you two."

Drayden didn't know the first thing about stochastic calculus.

Although he was six feet tall, Eugene was a little taller. He hunched over as he spoke, as if he were trying to seem small in front of him and Catrice. While he addressed them together, he largely focused on her.

"It's nice to meet you, Eugene." Catrice held out her hand.

He shook it with both of his.

"Yeah, Eugene, the pleasure is all ours." Drayden shook his hand, noting how powerful it was. His skin was calloused and rough, in contrast to Drayden's, which was soft like a baby's butt. "The fact that you teach yourself math at night is incredible."

"So, Eugene," Sidney said, touching his arm, "you're as big and strong as Charlie and as smart as Drayden and Catrice."

"You're like the lovechild of me and Drayden," Charlie deadpanned.

Drayden nudged Charlie. "I think I would have preferred if you said you and Catrice. I'd hate to imagine how we'd produce a lovechild."

Eugene held his sides he was laughing so hard. "You guys are hilarious! And Sidney, I'm not anywhere near as smart as they are." He inched a little closer to Catrice. "I'd love to pick your brain, see what I can learn from you." He glanced at Drayden at the last possible second, as if suddenly remembering he was there. "Drayden, do you think you could walk me through the brainteasers from the Initiation on the boat ride? We'll have a lot of time to kill."

All Drayden could do was nod, because he was speechless. Eugene was amazing—tall, brawny, movie-star looks, humble, deferential, eager to learn, and possibly bright. Drayden sensed everyone else agreed. Catrice hovered close to him, and Sidney had already touched him a few times. Catrice also seemed intrigued. In situations where they met new people, she was painfully shy. It was one of her more endearing qualities. Not today, though.

She started firing questions, which was especially odd for her. "Eugene, how did you get picked for this unlucky assignment?"

He pulled his head back. "Unlucky? I'm not sure what you mean. This was like winning the lottery. I volunteered for it. So many Guardians volunteered, the colonel had to select the team. I feel blessed to have been chosen."

Jeez, Drayden thought. *Slightly different view of the expedition.*

"You do realize we could die out there from any number of things, right? I think Aeru is the most likely."

Eugene eyed him like a disappointed parent. "Yeah, I understand the risks, but we have a chance to save New America—to save tens of thousands of lives. I'd happily give my own in exchange. The real kicker was getting to do it alongside you guys. I was on cloud nine the day they told me. I couldn't sleep that night."

Two other Guardians strolled up, joining Captain Lindrick without so much as a glance at the privates. They spoke in hushed tones.

As Eugene droned on about how lucky he was to be selected for the expedition, Drayden considered if he should introduce himself to the other two men.

"Privates," Captain Lindrick called out, cutting off Eugene mid-sentence. "I'd like to introduce you to Lieutenant Juan Duarte and Sergeant Peter Greaney."

Neither Guardian approached. Sergeant Greaney, a totally bald, stocky African American man, almost smiled and offered an informal salute. Lieutenant Duarte didn't even glance at them.

In a most unfortunate association, Duarte reminded Drayden of Alex, his former nemesis. Only Alex was sixteen and this guy was thirty-something. His whopper of a nose, and ears that flared out also stood in stark contrast to the model-esque Corporal Austin.

Doubt crept into Drayden's mind about his authority over the Guardians. It wasn't explicitly discussed, and neither Greaney nor Duarte had given them the time of day. He disliked Lieutenant Duarte straightaway. While it may have been his similarity to Alex, his body language spelled trouble. He didn't respect this group of teenagers.

Catrice flipped her hair. "So, Eugene, what else do you like to do besides study math?"

He chewed on his lower lip. "I love art, especially drawing."

Oh, for crying out loud.

It was like he'd seen a profile of Catrice. Drayden felt the sudden urge to clutch Catrice's hand in front of him. Except she stood just out of reach; in fact, closer to Eugene.

"Corporal Austin!" Captain Lindrick bellowed.

"Coming, sir!" Eugene rolled his eyes. "See you guys soon."

"Privates, thank you for coming," Captain Lindrick said. "We'll see you tomorrow."

As Eugene marched toward the other Guardians, he turned his head back, for a second, and smiled at Catrice.

She smiled back.

CHAPTER 8

Drayden approached the alley alone for his meeting with Kim Craig, having brusquely left the others.

What the hell was that?

It was the most interest Catrice had ever shown in another person. He'd known Catrice practically his whole life before she ever spoke to him or asked him a question. Five seconds after meeting Eugene it was as if she were conducting an interview. Fine, the guy was handsome and cool. So what? Just because someone loves math doesn't prove he's smart. He might suck at it. Though Drayden ultimately discovered his own bravery in the Initiation, he still wasn't strong or physically gifted. Not like Charlie and Sidney were anyway.

She also didn't show any signs they were a couple in front of Eugene. A simple touch, anything. It was like she didn't want him to know.

The only consolation came right after they'd left and Sidney called Catrice out. She'd said, "Hey, math nerd, hands off this time. You already stole one guy. You don't get to have both." Catrice had scoffed at the threat, but Drayden had loved it because it delivered the message without coming from him. If he said anything he would have come across as an insecure weakling, which, fine, perhaps he was. He was probably being stupid and oversensitive about the whole thing.

Drayden arrived at the alley and checked his digital watch. 11:34 AM.

Kim was nowhere in sight, which made sense. He was way too early.

The alley was cool and dark inside, running downhill from Broadway toward Trinity Place. He walked down it and turned right toward Ninety Trinity Place, where Kim had said she ran surveillance. He just wanted to check it out. After a few blocks he stopped across the street from the bland structure.

Fourteen stories of brown stone blocks rose up, with seven square windows on each floor. It was wedged between two ugly, filthy buildings—on one side, the former American Stock Exchange; on the other, a former school.

Surveillance cameras blanketed New America, and most were concealed. To everyone's knowledge, they only existed outside. All the video feeds would lead to this one building, full of people watching the action across the city.

It was weird to imagine that the people inside had observed Drayden before. How many times had he popped up on those cameras? Allegedly, the cameras existed to bust criminals. When the Bureau witnessed a crime, they moved fast. If a Chancellor deemed the crime serious enough, they would enforce an exile. The Bureau set the bar for "serious" much lower than a rational person would. If someone skipped work or school, they risked exile. A whole team of Special Forces Guardians and a Chancellor would raid the home at night. After the raid, they drove the victim in a bus up to the top of the city and pushed them out a gate. As they did with Drayden's mother.

He recalled sitting in Premier Holst's office immediately following the Initiation. Holst had said to Drayden that, contrary to what his father thought, the Initiation wasn't a trap. It had shocked him at the time. There was no way Holst could have known his father had said such a thing. Dad had said it to him in private, inside their apartment. He argued the Initiation was nothing more than a ruse to exile extra people. His father would never have uttered those words outside their home. He was too smart.

Was it possible that, unbeknownst to anyone, the Bureau hid cameras inside people's apartments? While using cameras outside to enforce the law was one thing, the Bureau invading homes would constitute a gargantuan violation of privacy. It could trigger a revolt if people found out about it.

Drayden headed back toward the alley, a chilly breeze smacking into his face. Although it was May, today was cool and the air smelled wintry.

Kim was waiting in the alley this time, pacing. "Hey, kiddo."

"Hi, Kim. Thanks again for doing this."

She gave him a look. "Don't thank me yet; you don't know if I found anything."

Drayden's pulse quickened. "Did you?"

"Yes and no," she said, tilting her head from side to side. "Before that, I need to know you're on board with our effort. Don't worry. Your name won't be on some list of people. Nobody will even know except me. You could be a real asset."

He already knew what his answer had to be. He was on board with taking down the Bureau, but he didn't feel great about it, because he wasn't entirely sure he could trust Kim. Who knew what her motivations were in recruiting him? Still, he needed the information she had about his mother.

"I'm in. Have you heard about the expedition? I don't think the Bureau's told many people about it, besides the ones directly involved. They're forcing me and the other kids from the Initiation to go on an expedition to Boston. We'll have a team of four

Guardians to protect us. Because of the power crisis, Holst needs to reach out for assistance. I'd been trying to delay it, but Holst's chief of staff, this shkat flunk named Harris von Brooks, said either we go or he'll exile our families and execute us. We leave tomorrow."

Kim muttered something to herself then said, "I didn't know about the expedition. The failing power storage, on the other hand, has become the worst-kept secret in the Palace. It's one of the reasons we feel compelled to move quickly with our plans. They're getting desperate if they're sending you outside the walls. They probably consider you kids expendable. I'm sorry."

"Yeah. My point is, I'm not sure how useful I'll be. I'll be gone and most likely will die on this trip."

She blew out a long breath, her cheeks puffing out. "I think you can still help. First of all, try and gauge if your Guardian pals are disgruntled with the Bureau. We have people who could approach them when you return."

A terse laugh escaped Drayden's lips. "Just met them. I wouldn't be surprised if they have the Bureau insignia tattooed on their bodies."

Kim shrugged. "Hey, you never know. Be discreet but gather as much information as you can on the trip itself. Take note of everything in the outside world. Are people alive outside the walls? That would be mind-blowing, since nobody has been seen or heard from in a quarter century. Same goes for the exiled, who everyone believes are dead. Are they actually alive and well in some community because Aeru is history? If there are large groups outside, we might be able to mobilize them to join us. And you have to make it to Boston." She paused and cracked her knuckles. "This is where you're going to have to fire up that oversized brain of yours. It's highly unlikely there are people. How could we not know by now if there are? On the off chance we've been deceived, find someone you can trust, speak to them away from the Guardians. Tell them what's going on here, appeal to their sense of humanitarianism. See if we can persuade them to bolster our effort. We could use weapons, for one thing. Be careful, though, because it could be even worse there in Boston. Who knows?"

Drayden was beginning to feel overwhelmed.

"This'll sound nuts," Kim said, "but I used to have an aunt in the Boston area before the Confluence. She'd be in her sixties now. Her name is Ruth Diamond. She's probably dead, but if you can locate her, she would help you figure out who to talk to. It's worth a shot if you're lost.

"Whatever intel comes out of this mission, I bet the Bureau will fight to prevent it from leaking out. That's how they control things, by controlling the information, brainwashing everyone. Telling everybody the system is equal, while guaranteeing nobody could ever check."

Kim hocked up some phlegm and spat. "Now that I'm saying it, you may want to be careful when you return. It's quite possible the Bureau plans on executing you to contain whatever information you deliver. You might need to have some bargaining chips to prevent that. And not something they can torture out of you. Remember how I threatened to kill you? It was clever of you to say that I didn't know who you've told. Like that cute little blonde girlfriend of yours." She smirked.

"How do you know about Catrice?"

Kim put her hands on her hips and cocked her head.

"Oh, right. You run surveillance." He blushed. "You haven't seen us...like...making out, have you?"

She belly laughed. "No, no cameras in the apartments."

"Kim...I have to know. Are there cameras in the Dorm apartments?"

She pressed her lips together for a few seconds. "No. But there are microphones. They're quite sophisticated, programmed to start recording when voices rise above a specific decibel level. If people are arguing, or if certain words are said, such as Bureau, or overthrow, things like that."

My God.

Drayden's heart stuttered. That was how Holst knew what his father had said. What else had they overheard?

"Focus here, sonny boy. This isn't an interview. I'm just saying, that simple bargaining chip you used on me wouldn't work on the Bureau, because they could torture you to find out what you're hiding. It has to be stronger than that. Like, unless you give a signal, an attack is going to happen. Something they need you alive and well for. I don't have any specific ideas off the top of my head. You're a smart kid, and you have a few days to think of something."

"Kim, thank you. Whether Lily intended it or not, you've been a great mentor. If I don't die, either on the journey or when I come back, I'll come find you."

She raised a finger. "That reminds me. If anything happened to me, you wouldn't have any contacts." She pulled an envelope, sealed with wax, from her pocket, waving it in Drayden's face. "For everyone's protection, including yours, I can't tell you too much about our effort. Only open this envelope if you get back and find me dead. Otherwise, burn it. Just so you know, there's nothing incriminating in it. If someone else got a hold of this, it would be meaningless out of context. But it wouldn't be to you, yeah? Good," she said before he had a chance to answer.

Drayden stuffed the envelope in his pocket. "Got it. Now, Kim... I've got to know about my mom."

"All right, sonny. I had to break some rules to find out what I did, and it's not much. I don't have access to the files that store that information. We're talking computer files here. I can get a smidge outside of it. So I can tell if the exile was directed or non-directed. Directed means a Bureau member ordered it, usually because someone committed a crime. Non-directed signifies a random exile; that would be your population-shrinking exile. Your mother's was directed. It wasn't random."

Drayden clenched his jaw. "I knew it. It wouldn't make any sense to randomly exile my mom. But—"

"I know what your next question is, and I don't have the answer. Who ordered the exile is inside the file."

He threw his hands in the air, his frustration building to tears. "Dammit!" This was his last chance to find out. "Is there any chance this had to do with my mom being caught up in this plot against the Bureau?"

"No, definitely not. Lily was trying to recruit her, but she'd resisted from what I hear. In any case, none of their conversations about it were recorded, I made sure of that."

Drayden wiped his teary eyes with his palms. It was tough to separate his emotions from the logistics of the exile.

Kim rubbed her chin.

"What is it?"

"Why not?" she mumbled. "It's your life after all."

A chill ran through his body. "What? Tell me!"

She waved a hand through the air. "It may be nothing. On directed exiles, the person who ordered the exile is in the file, as I told you. But there is often a username alongside the filename. It's usually the name of the Chancellor who reviewed it. The Chancellor may or may not be the person who ordered it. The username might also be the last person who viewed the file. Understand? It may be meaningless. Some have no name listed."

Drayden's eyes bulged. "Who is it?"

She pursed her lips. "I've been watching you the past two days. Seeing where you've been. I don't want you to do something stupid."

"Kim. Please."

"It says Nathan Locke."

Drayden stormed toward Twenty-One Broadway. He wiped away tears, gathering himself.

As soon as Kim said the name, it clicked. He realized what was wrong with his conversation with Nathan Locke. It wasn't Locke's offensive claim that his mother was to blame, nor his insinuation that Drayden was actually upset with *her*.

Locke had said he'd made a big stink about the exile in the Bureau the very next day. That would have been impossible. He said himself they didn't post the exiles anywhere before or after. The exile occurred on a Wednesday night, and Locke only visited the FDCs in the Dorms on Mondays and Fridays. No phones existed in the Dorms. The Dorm rep at the time, Thomas Cox, came on Mondays, Wednesdays, and Fridays. Locke simply could not have known by then. Knowledge of exiles were limited to the Chancellors and Guardians who executed them.

Plus, Locke had warned him not to investigate this further. He wasn't looking out for Drayden. He was protecting himself *from* Drayden.

It confirmed what Drayden suspected all along: Locke was a liar. That weasel.

He arrived at Twenty-One Broadway, with its massive arched doorways. What exactly was he going to do? He couldn't attack Locke. Two giant Guardians protected him. It might be smarter not to inform Locke he knew. If Drayden accused him and survived the expedition, Locke might orchestrate his execution when he returned. This guy was a slimeball, and a powerful one. He exiled Drayden's mother after she dumped him. If he couldn't have her, nobody could.

On the other hand, if Drayden died on the expedition, Locke would believe he'd gotten away with murder. Fooled everyone, including Drayden.

To hell with it. While he couldn't physically assault the guy, he could apprise him of the recent discovery. He couldn't tell him how, because doing so might expose Kim. Drayden knew nothing about computers, which might log who viewed particular records. Since Kim was a surveillance expert, however, she would have taken precautions to shield her identity. She was obviously smart.

Drayden closed his eyes and touched his hat, channeling his mother's strength. He needed to do something before the Bureau sent him outside the walls to die.

I'm going to make them pay, Mom.

CHAPTER 9

Drayden wondered if Locke would meet him again. This time there would be no fooling anyone about his identity. Locke was clever, in a sleazy way. If Drayden visited him a second time, Locke would probably realize he had figured out the truth.

It was time to see how spineless the guy was. He opened the door to the office.

Katelyn lounged in jeans and a T-shirt, her legs up on the desk, reading a book.

She lifted her head and beamed. "Hey, Charlie."

Drayden reflected on the meeting with the Guardians. Catrice had basically thrown herself at Eugene. He whirled around to Katelyn's side of the desk and eased on top of it, inches away from her.

She reacted with a mixture of shock and intrigue.

He gazed into her eyes. "Katelyn, I have to tell you something. I needed to protect my identity the other day. I lied to you. I'm sorry. I'm not Charlie. I'm Drayden. Part of it is, I don't want people to treat me differently because of the Initiation. I'd rather people like me for who I am."

Katelyn practically swooned, biting down on her lower lip. Intentional or not, her chair inched forward, and her knee brushed Drayden's leg.

Maybe he had learned something from Tim. "I need to speak to Mr. Locke again. Can you help me out?"

She didn't respond at first; she just stared. "Yeah...yes, of course. Gimme one sec, *Drayden*." She sashayed to Locke's door, where she knocked and opened it enough to stick her head inside. After a few seconds of conversation, she glanced back, no longer smiling. When she slid in the room, the door closed behind her.

That wasn't a good sign.

A minute later, she emerged and sulked her way back to the desk. "Mr. Locke says he's too busy to see you now. I'm sorry."

Locke was lying, and she knew it. "Thanks for trying, Katelyn. Can you do me another favor?"

"Sure, anything." She flipped her hair.

"Can you sit back down at your desk? Stay there. I don't want you to get hurt. I'm sorry for the scene I'm about to cause." Drayden marched toward Locke's door. He recounted the pain this weak man had inflicted on his mother, his family, and himself. This self-important sleazebag believed he could sentence someone to death with impunity, simply because he got dumped. He represented everything wrong with the Bureau.

One Guardian trained his rifle on Drayden and the other drew his pistol. Both blocked the door. "Where you think you're going?" the first one asked.

Drayden stopped a few feet away from the guns, balling his hands into fists. "Mr. Locke!" he shouted. "I know you can hear me. It was you! You hear me, you piece of shkat? You were the one who had my mother exiled. You sat in front of me, lying your face off. You thought nobody would find out. Guess what? That's not the end of the story!"

The Guardians exchanged looks, clearly unsure of what to do.

"I've told several other people about this, so don't even think of trying to get rid of me. I'm leaving New America on a little tour.

But I'm coming back. And when I do, I'm coming for you! You hear me?"

The Guardians had had enough. The one with the pistol holstered it and rushed Drayden.

He wasn't stupid enough to fight these guys. Jiu-jitsu or not, he didn't stand a chance. Nobody would be rushing out of Locke's office to bail him out, as Harris von Brooks had done. He raised his hands in the air and backpedaled, revealing a slight limp. "Okay, okay, fellas, I'm leaving."

The Guardian stopped himself before he tackled Drayden to the floor.

Drayden could have easily dodged it, but why engage in a fight he would lose? He stood tall and strutted out of the office, finally sure who his enemy was.

That night, Drayden fumed alone in his apartment on the brown couch. He hadn't calmed down at all. In fact, he was even more fired up than before.

He wasn't quite as sure of himself as he was when he left Locke's office fueled by emotion. Confronting him may have been a tactical mistake. Locke was a senior Bureau member and could pay a visit to Holst or von Brooks and tell them what had happened. He could arrange Drayden's execution before he reentered New America, or ensure he was never allowed back inside. By doing what he did, Drayden guaranteed he could not safely return to the Palace. He couldn't come home and build a pleasant life for himself here, not after threatening Locke. Assuming his family would move to the Palace, he may have put them in danger as well.

He was so frantic and upset after Kim dropped the bombshell, he hadn't stopped to think straight. It was a remote possibility, but she might have lied about Locke. Since she'd been watching him the past two days, she was aware he'd visited Locke once. Kim itched for him to join the insurgency against the Bureau. What better way to seal the deal than to supply the motive needed to sway him? While his gut told him to trust her, he couldn't honestly say he knew the first thing about her.

In their original meeting, Locke had steadfastly denied involvement in his mother's exile. If he was lying, he was a master. If he was innocent, he'd probably refused to meet Drayden again because he didn't feel the need to repeatedly defend himself to some over-zealous sixteen-year-old. Once, sure, but not twice in two days. Yet, Drayden believed Kim. Call it intuition. He was going to trust his gut, heeding Tim's advice. Kim had also appeared authentic and struggled to decide whether to reveal Locke's name or not. Locke had a much greater motivation to lie as well.

Ultimately, it didn't matter whether it was Locke. He merely represented everything wrong with the Bureau. The Bureau had exiled his mother. It was either random, as if she were an expendable piece of trash, or ordered by an evil weakling whose feelings were hurt. Whichever it was, an organization that would wield its power that way, without regard for every human life, needed to be destroyed.

At one time, Premier Holst may have had his heart in the right place, attempting to save as many lives as possible. Somewhere along the way though, his logic became poisoned, twisted into something sinister. Despite the diminishing resources, there had to be a better way than exiles.

Drayden was going on this expedition. With his own mission. He would damn sure reach Boston, but he was returning with an army. Or a plan. He would prove to Catrice, and Eugene, and the rest of the Guardians, that he was no weakling. First and foremost, he did need to ensure he didn't die on the journey. He had to return so he could help take down the Bureau and Nathan Locke. Justice would be served.

A knock at the door interrupted his thoughts.

"Come in!"

Sidney burst through the door, followed by Charlie and Catrice, who both lingered by the kitchen. Sidney charged like a bull, a huge grin on her face, almost as wide as the one she had when she met Eugene.

Charlie wrinkled his nose and sniffed the air. "Man, smells like something swam in here and died."

"I think I dropped a chunk of salmon behind the stove, chotch," Drayden said.

"Guess what?" Sidney plunked down beside him on the edge of the couch.

He raised his hands. "What?"

"The Bureau kept its promise. Our families are coming tomorrow. We get to see them before we leave, and they're staying here in the Palace, for good." She covered her mouth, her eyes moistening. "My little sister is coming here, and I'm going to give her the biggest hug." She wiped her tears.

Drayden embraced her. "That's great news. I bet our families will be pumped to see us too. We suffered through a lot to get them here." He'd tried to block it from his own mind in case it didn't happen, but he'd reunite with his brother and father tomorrow. He choked up a bit.

Catrice was throwing away garbage in the kitchen and putting Drayden's dirty dishes in the sink. She always took care of him that way.

He walked over to her. "Hey."

"Hi," she said, without making eye contact.

"I'm sorry about earlier," Drayden said, recalling how he'd stormed off after their meeting with the Guardians. "I guess looking into my mom's exile has riled me a bit." It was probably best to lie about why he was upset with her; otherwise, he'd seem like a jealous flunk. She was smart, and hopefully she knew the real reason without him saying it. In an ideal world, she would apologize herself for acting all gaga around Eugene, without any consideration for how it made him feel.

"Don't worry about it," she said, her tone impassive.

Or not.

Drayden suspected she was most likely dismayed because she wouldn't have any family coming. That was her choice, but still, everyone else was ecstatic.

"Would you like to meet my father and brother with me tomorrow?" he asked.

"Yeah, sure."

"Hey, you guys," Drayden said, addressing the group, "I've changed my mind about this mission. I'm ready for it. We're gonna go out there and kick the crap outta this thing and come home safe. Let's do this."

CHAPTER 10

Catrice chewed on her nails. Charlie yawned and checked his watch. Sidney tapped her foot, peeking back at the doors to the atrium every few seconds.

They sat in plastic chairs at a round metal table in the sprawling atrium that adjoined Sixty Wall Street.

Drayden wore the green hat he'd refused to take off since his mother's exile. The others had stuffed their military baseball hats in their pants' pockets. All the privates sported their gray camouflage uniforms for the mission, with their Bureau pins over their chests. Catrice, like Sidney, had pulled her hair back in a ponytail.

The mission would commence as soon as they said goodbye to their families. The reunion was supposed to happen hours earlier so the boat could depart at sunrise, giving them as much daylight as possible. But there had been some complications with getting the boat to the pier, and everything had gotten pushed back a few hours. It was past 9:00 AM now.

They were alone in the atrium, a massive space over three stories tall, which stretched the whole block from Wall Street to Pine. Battered white tiles covered both the interior walls and the square pillars that supported the ceiling. The walls facing both streets were made wholly of glass, containing revolving doors.

The space had not been well maintained, with many of the brown floor tiles cracked or missing. It also had no lights, and the gloomy morning made it cool and dark.

Charlie drummed on the table. "I'll bet anyone an egg both my parents are bawling their eyes out when they see me."

Sidney tapped both feet now. "Ugh, I can't take this waiting. Where are they? I can't wait to see my sister."

"Your grandparents are coming, right?" Charlie asked. "You know how slow old folks are. They probably had to use the bathroom like five times before they left. How old's your sister?"

"She's eight. Her name is Nora."

Drayden rubbed Catrice's back.

She forced a smile.

"My dad's name is Adam and my brother is Wesley. I call him Wes," he said.

"I know. You've told me."

Drayden peered over Sidney's shoulder.

A young girl zipped down the Wall Street sidewalk and pushed her way through the revolving doors, struggling to turn them. A gray-haired couple, followed by a Guardian, tried their best to keep up with her.

Sidney drew in a quick breath and squealed. She leapt and sprinted toward the child.

Nora was wearing green overalls and the happiest smile, her brown hair flying behind her as she ran. "Sidney!"

Sidney scooped her up and squeezed her. Nora buried her face in Sidney's neck and wrapped her tiny legs around Sidney's waist. Crying, Sidney spun around and bounced her sister. As her beaming grandparents approached, Sidney plopped Nora down and hugged them both.

"We should go introduce ourselves to them," Drayden said. He scooted his chair back.

Wesley and his father walked through the revolving door. Wesley jogged in Drayden's direction, his arms extended wide.

Drayden froze, his heart fluttering. He couldn't believe his eyes. Wes was the spitting image of Mom. One-hundred percent Korean. "Catrice, c'mon!" He dashed to Wesley, meeting him halfway.

Wesley wrapped his muscular arms around Drayden, hoisting him in the air. "Who's my boy? Who's my boy, huh?" Wesley whooped. "Did I tell you or what? I knew you could do it!" He set Drayden down.

They held each other's arms, grinning like they were little kids again. "It's good to see you, Wes." They hugged once more.

Wesley howled. "Boy, you are the *man*!"

Drayden looked over Wesley's shoulder at his father.

He lingered a few feet away, awkwardly staring at the floor with his hands in his pockets. Drab clothes hung on his tall, slight frame as if they were still on the hanger. When he raised his head, his eyes were filled with tears.

Drayden released Wesley and approached him. Not having seen his father for a few weeks, he was struck by their resemblance. It was like a peek at the future. Tall and skinny, with graying hair, and hazel eyes every bit as bright as his own.

Weeping, his father pulled Drayden into an embrace. "I'm so proud of you, son," he whispered. "I...I love you."

"I love you too, Dad. I did it."

"You did. I'm sorry for doubting you. And for not saying goodbye."

"Don't worry about it. You were trying to protect me."

Catrice hovered a few feet away, ostensibly aloof.

Drayden snagged her hand and ushered her into the reunion. "Dad, Wes, meet Catrice."

"Hello," she said softly.

Drayden cleared his throat. "Catrice is my girlfriend."

Catrice shot him a look that just about stopped his heart. She furrowed her brow and frowned, as if she didn't know what he was talking about or she didn't agree.

"Isn't that nice," Dad said. "Where's your family, Catrice?" He scanned the atrium.

Drayden tried to get his father's attention with his own furrowed brow, shaking his head.

"They're not coming," she said.

His father looked concerned. "That's terrible. Why not?"

"Dad," Drayden said.

"It's okay," Catrice said, her eyes downcast. "I didn't invite them."

He seemed confused. "I see. I'm sorry to hear that, then."

"Dray, check it out." Wesley glowed. "They're giving us an apartment in the same building as you. They're also going to reinstate Dad as a doctor here in the Palace after he does some training. Isn't that awesome? I'm not sure what my job will be yet, but it can't be worse than stacking boxes at the FDC."

"That's great, Wes. It's great." Drayden wiped tears, surprised at how emotional he became. Being with Wes and Dad in the Palace, knowing they were safe and reunited, was overwhelming. That the reunion would be short-lived was heartbreaking.

A woman wailed on the right side of the atrium. Charlie's parents both sobbed, pawed at him, and stroked his cheeks. Charlie made eye contact with Drayden, raised his index finger, and mouthed, "One egg."

Drayden giggled, appreciating how Charlie could manage to bring levity to any situation. "Do you guys know about the expedition?" he asked Dad and Wesley.

"They told us on our way here," Wesley said. "They said we'd only get a few minutes together." He scowled. "That's total shkat. You guys finished the Initiation. They should let you stay here. How are you feeling about this thing?"

Drayden gave him the "so-so" hand gesture. "We're ready. They told us about it as soon as the Initiation was over. They said it was the only reason we were all allowed to join the Bureau. We've been training the past week and receiving the Aeru vaccine they created. I mean, don't get me wrong, it sucks. My ankle's busted, we'd rather not go...but we have to." He quickly scanned the atrium. "Wes, I need to speak to you alone for a minute."

He gripped Wesley by the arm and dragged him to a corner, unsure of how much time they had left. When the Bureau said they'd have a few minutes with their families, they were probably being literal.

Drayden remembered Kim and the surveillance cameras and microphones. He whispered in Wesley's ear. "Wes, listen. I'm going to tell you some things you're not supposed to know, and you need to keep them secret." He proceeded to tell him about the failing power storage and New America's desperation.

Wesley looked horrified. He was speechless.

Drayden peeked behind him to ensure no one was around. "That's not all. They're exiling people at random in the Dorms to shrink the population. There's not enough power, so they can't grow enough food to support everyone. I thought that was the reason for Mom's exile. But I've been digging into it, and I don't believe it was that. I have evidence it was Nathan Locke. He—"

"No way! That g—"

"Wes, Wes." Drayden held up his hands. "Let me finish, I need to get this out before it's too late. He wanted Mom to move to the Palace with me and you. He claimed she said yes, but I doubt it. I'll bet Mom said no and he had her exiled. Even though I'm not one hundred percent sure, I'm ninety percent sure. I don't want you to do anything about it, at least not before I return. I just wanted you to know in case I don't make it back."

Drayden peered back again. "I also did something stupid. I confronted Locke, told him I knew. He denied it, as expected. Then I threatened him, and said I'd told other people about it. I may have put you and Dad in danger because he'll assume I let you know. In reality, I haven't told anyone else. Plus, I doubt he'd do anything, since he doesn't know how many people I've told. Getting rid of you and Dad wouldn't help him if he believes I've told others too. Still, I think it's best to avoid him."

"Holy shkat." Wesley rubbed his chin. "That's a lot of...are you sure about all this? Shouldn't we tell Dad?"

"I don't know." Drayden grimaced. "I don't think so. Like you said a few weeks ago, if Dad didn't know about the affair, why crush him? And if he did, why embarrass him by letting him know we know?"

He debated telling Wes more, about Kim and the plot to overthrow the Bureau, for the same reason he told him everything else: in case he didn't return. Kim had forbidden him from saying anything, however. Wes was a hothead and likely to accidentally expose it, endangering the people involved. Drayden also carried the envelope from Kim in his pocket and briefly considered leaving it with Wes, but figured he should hold onto that as well.

"Privates!" Two Guardians stood on the Wall Street side of the atrium. "Time to go!" one yelled.

Wesley held Drayden by the shoulders. "You're going to make it back, bro. You're special, Drayden. Like the Initiation. Nobody was supposed to pass that, but you did. This is the same thing. You'll find a way. I know you'll be smart, because you always are. I need you to be tough—strong. There's no math problems out there, only stuff that can hurt you." He clenched his jaw. "Be *tough*, you hear me?"

Drayden fist-bumped him. "I will, Wes. I love you. I'm making it back."

They hugged one last time and headed over to their father, who was chatting with Catrice. When Drayden reached them, both Dad and Catrice smirked.

"What?" Drayden eyed both suspiciously.

"Oh, nothing," Catrice said, pursing her lips, stifling a laugh. "Your dad was saying how even though he'd never met me, he'd heard a lot about me. Because you planned on marrying me."

"Dad, no," Drayden said. "What? Just...oh my God." He buried his face in his hands.

Catrice couldn't contain her laughter.

CHAPTER 11

Everyone was shaken by the brief encounters with their families. Drayden almost wished he hadn't seen Wesley and Dad, because leaving them again was so painful. They'd finally begun to adjust to daily life without their families around. It was yet another cruel tactic by the Bureau. Why did they have to do it that way? Their families could have come right after the Initiation.

The two Guardians escorted them to the open gate in the wall at Pier Fifteen, a few blocks away. The sight offered a view they'd never experienced—the East River at eye level, and straight over it into Brooklyn.

Their boat bobbed in the water beside the pier. Right past the gate, the dock consisted of seemingly new, reinforced wood. Further out, a few stumps of ancient wood jutted out of the water, where the original pier must have been. Several unfamiliar Guardians were loading supplies onto the boat.

When Drayden stepped onto the pier, his gaze caught deep, arced grooves in the dock that matched the gate's trajectory. The gate must have dug those grooves, which struck him as odd. Was this gate used often?

The air already reeked this close to the East River. Once he walked further onto the pier, the smell punched him in the face like a fist of raw sewage. New America's human waste was dumped into the East River. Charlie groaned somewhere behind him.

Drayden stopped abruptly, positive he was about to vomit. He hunched over and braced his hands on his knees, unable to stop gagging.

"Sweet mercy," Charlie said. "It smells like a rat died inside of another rat's rectum. And I'm not even going to crack a rectum joke."

Sidney held her nose closed. "How are the Guardians not affected by this?" she said, her voice nasal.

Catrice covered her mouth with both hands, as if physically holding her breakfast down. She grew paler than usual, something that didn't seem possible.

Drayden started moving again. "Breathe through your mouth for a while, until we get used to it," he said, although he struggled to follow his own advice.

The four brawny Guardians were crammed inside the boat's tiny cockpit, huddling over their unfolded map. Captain Lindrick craned his neck and saw the teens. He said a few words to the other Guardians, exited the cockpit, and approached them. "The smell is arresting, isn't it?"

"It's like taking a bath inside a dirty toilet, sir," Charlie said.

"Indeed, Private Arnold. Everyone come aboard. Your packs and weapons are already loaded in the stern of the boat. We'll be off soon. Harris von Brooks will join us shortly to say a few words. Otherwise, make yourselves comfortable. We've got a long journey ahead." He returned to the cockpit.

"I think it's time to accept that we're the privates," Sidney said. "First we were the pledges; now we're the privates. When do the four of us not need a group title?"

The day was overcast and windy, generating little white ripples of foam on the waves in the river. Though tethered, the boat rocked and bounced, periodically slamming into the dock.

They hadn't discussed who would be driving the boat. Technically, the privates were in charge, so, in theory, they should be driving. But operating the boat safely could be construed as a method of protection, or service. It didn't necessarily represent a breach of hierarchy if the Guardians drove. Still, Drayden thought they should discuss it. Captain Lindrick was already sitting in the driver's seat.

"This is our first challenge," Sidney said. "How do we get in the boat?"

"Charlie," Catrice said, "can you snag that nearest rope and hold the boat close to the dock?"

He knelt by the rope. "Yeah, lemme see."

Eugene burst out of the cockpit. "Hey, guys! Boy, am I glad to see you. Here, let me give you a hand with that, Charlie." He grasped the rope from inside the boat and pulled until it slammed into the dock. "I'll steady it. You guys jump in."

Eugene to the rescue.

Drayden pondered how many times this would happen on the expedition. Given how strong the young man appeared, probably often. Thankfully, Eugene seemed thrilled to see everyone, not just Catrice.

Charlie and Sidney jumped into the rocking boat and Eugene stabilized them when they landed. Catrice stepped to the edge of the dock.

Drayden stood close, extending his arms to guide her across.

"I got it." She leapt the two-foot gap to the boat.

Eugene caught her when she landed. "One sec, Drayden," he said, "let me pull us close again." He secured the rope and pulled, the tendons in his neck bulging from the exertion.

With the boat a foot away, Drayden jumped onto the side, and then in, where Eugene steadied him. "Thanks, Eugene."

Captain Lindrick popped his head out of the cockpit. "Corporal! Untie all but one rope. Let's get ready to depart. Lieutenant, give Corporal Austin a hand."

"Sir, yes sir!" they both said.

Drayden didn't like this one bit. The Premier had put him in charge. "Captain Lindrick," he said with as much authority as he could muster.

Lindrick raised his eyebrows.

Drayden fiddled with the button on his shirt. "Um, should I drive the boat?"

Lindrick shared a slight chuckle with the other Guardians. "No, no, I think I've got it. Why don't you kids relax in the back and enjoy the ride. We'll do the heavy lifting. The Bureau piled up some life vests back there if you want to wear them. They make you float if you fall overboard." He proceeded to make himself comfortable in the driver's seat.

The privates settled in the rear around the table. After Eugene finished untying the boat, he headed their way.

"Corporal!" Captain Lindrick hollered.

Eugene spun around and joined the Guardians.

A familiar feeling washed over Drayden. It was the same one that bubbled up as a child when he got in trouble, which wasn't often. It was a nervous combination of his face overheating and his neck stiffening. While he obviously wasn't in trouble, something wasn't right about this whole situation, and his body was trying to let him know.

Charlie, Sidney, and Catrice were watching him, their faces question marks.

"No, I'm not happy about this," Drayden said. He picked up a life vest and examined it before putting it on.

It was a navy cloth vest, all puffed out in numerous places, appearing to contain empty plastic water bottles inside. He tied it on tight, and the other privates followed suit.

None of the Guardians wore theirs.

The hint of a power struggle seemed to be budding between the privates and the Guardians. Or between Drayden and Captain Lindrick. If so, the Guardians and the captain had won before it started.

Captain Lindrick had asserted his dominance over Drayden with ease. In school, they learned it happened much the same way in nature. A group of male lions would fight each other to lead the pride as alpha male. In schools of fish, one established himself as the leader and the rest fell in line behind him.

Except, Drayden didn't even fight. Captain Lindrick was stronger, and he made a show of it. He embarrassed Drayden in front of his friends and the girl he thought was his girlfriend until thirty minutes ago. He didn't care to imagine what Catrice was thinking. Probably that he was a weakling. He should have addressed hierarchy right off the bat with Lindrick. If Drayden had the sponsorship of the Premier, he was in the right here. But the captain was a battle-tested military leader. Apparently, it never crossed his mind to confer with Drayden about who would drive.

"Looks like everybody is ready to go," said a man's voice from the dock, sounding like he had a cold. Harris von Brooks stood beside the boat, wearing a clip that held his nostrils closed.

The four Guardians exited the cockpit and approached. None of them acknowledged the privates. Greaney and Duarte hadn't even said hello yet.

"Mr. von Brooks," Captain Lindrick said.

"Captain Lindrick," von Brooks replied. "I think it's best if you move along as soon as possible. The weather is unstable. You should complete as much of the journey as possible in daylight." He pointed to a large secure bin in the stern. "Inside that box, each of you has a backpack that was carefully assembled by the Bureau. It contains food, water, bandages, painkillers, loads of extra ammunition, batteries, rope, flashlights, maps, and other useful items. The maps are very detailed. We added one thing in each pack that may confuse you: a Bureau flag. This is for your return to New America. It is to guarantee you will not be shot by the Guardians, particularly if you dock somewhere other than this pier. As you are all aware, this mission is a secret. The Bureau flag will identify you as friendly. There's also a white flag for your arrival in Boston. They should recognize it as a sign you are peaceful."

Von Brooks regarded the privates with a disapproving sneer. "Now, one final thing. In case any of you are struggling for motivation on this trip, the Premier has come up with the perfect solution. We *need* you to reach Boston. If you do, your families will be handsomely rewarded. Luxurious apartments normally reserved for Bureau members, and double food allocations for life. That applies to every one of you, including the Guardians."

This expedition was suddenly looking up. What was the catch?

"You must prove you reached Boston. If it is full of people, this will be easy. Bring back the help we seek. If it's deserted, bring back a relic that could only be found there. Either way, you must prove you made it. Do not test us on this matter." His nose in the air, he looked directly at Drayden. "For our four young members, we felt you needed additional motivation based on our little conversation the other day." He paused. "If you fail to reach Boston, your families will return to the Dorms."

No!

Drayden wished he could grab von Brooks by the throat. How could they be so evil?

The other privates' faces showed a mix of anguish, fear, and anger.

"That is all," von Brooks said smugly. "Good luck."

As expected, Captain Lindrick drove erratically at the start, as any of them would have. He needed to motor far away from the coast of New America, over to the east side of the East River, near Brooklyn. The west side of the river was a graveyard of cars from the aftermath of the Confluence. Since the Bureau had deposited all of the city's cars in the water—a task which employed many people and took years to complete—they were piled up on the west side of the river.

Eventually Lindrick figured out how to drive, and they headed north. They crossed the ruins of the Brooklyn Bridge, the Manhattan Bridge, and the Williamsburg Bridge. The Bureau had blown up those bridges during the Confluence, when the quarantine went into effect. After it became clear the quarantine was permanent, the Bureau destroyed most other bridges too. Some remained, such as the Henry Hudson Bridge at the top of the city where the Bureau dumped the exiled.

As they approached the intact Fifty-Ninth Street Bridge, the sewage smell all but vanished. Nobody lived this far north in New America. Drayden located his pack and removed the big map to track their location. Fine, Captain Lindrick could do the driving. He wasn't about to leave the navigation up to the Guardians.

Despite his mood about von Brooks's new "motivation," being out on the water on a boat was the coolest thing Drayden had ever experienced. He was out in the real world.

Gliding through the water, the wind blowing in his eyes, felt like flying. Between the roar of the engines and the frothy wake they generated, riding in the boat was loud. East River water periodically sprayed them, which was totally gross considering the water quality. Regardless, it was a new experience.

Drayden tracked their progress by correlating observed landmarks with the map, using an actual ink pen the Bureau had included in his pack.

They passed to the east of Roosevelt Island, a narrow enclave in the East River, which once housed a small community of New Yorkers. A giant hospital crumbled on its northern border to the boat's left, while the borough of Queens ran along the right side.

It reminded Drayden of his mother, who grew up in Flushing, Queens. She was Maya Song back then, not yet Maya Coulson. At the tender age of thirteen, she'd taken a rowboat on these very waters with her big brother Dan to enter Manhattan under the cover of darkness. They'd sneaked in after the quarantine went into effect during the Confluence. It was assumed all life outside the wall succumbed to Aeru afterward. Now they would find out for sure.

When they sailed east of Randall's Island, they officially left New America behind. It disappeared from view as they passed beneath the barely standing RFK Bridge. Both towers of the suspension bridge stood, but one leaned precariously forward, and a primary suspension cable had broken off.

So far, the Guardians were following the correct path. According to the map, the islet on the right was Rikers Island, an ancient prison notorious for its violence. The barbed wire fencing surrounding it was missing or rusted away in many places.

"Whoa, look at that!" Sidney jumped to her feet.

Drayden couldn't believe his eyes. "Holy shkat."

In the distance, the entire tail section of a passenger airplane, a jumbo jet, jutted out of the water. Though green algae or mold covered it, you could tell it was originally white. Past that, the ruins of other large planes lay scattered on a runway, some appearing to have crashed into each other.

He checked off LaGuardia Airport on his map.

After breezing past the Whitestone Bridge, the boat slowed as they approached the Throgs Neck Bridge, which formerly connected the Bronx to northeast Queens. While the two towers remained, the roadway had plunged into the water. Captain Lindrick eased off the motor, and they floated over the barnacle-covered asphalt, which was mere feet beneath the surface.

They took a sharp left. Shortly thereafter, they passed City Island in the Bronx, and then Hart Island.

Drayden noted them on the map.

The Guardians had successfully negotiated most of the tricky initial navigation. Now that they'd entered Long Island Sound, the next several hours of travel would be in a straight line. They would cruise between the north shore of Long Island and south shore of Connecticut. Eventually, Connecticut would give way to Rhode Island, and then Massachusetts. It seemed simple enough. Once darkness fell, however, navigation would become infinitely more complex.

Although they motored in Long Island Sound, protected from the open Atlantic Ocean by Long Island, the waves surged. Their tiny boat rocked further and further, bouncing off each swell.

Drayden felt the first tinge of nausea. It lasted only a second, but for that moment he was sure he was going to lose his breakfast.

Catrice and Charlie both turned green. They remained still, as if not to amplify the already dramatic motion of the boat.

According to the map, the distance between the Connecticut and Long Island shores varied between five and ten miles. Captain Lindrick drove much closer to the Connecticut shore, albeit nearly a half mile off.

Drayden remembered his true mission. He hadn't the slightest idea how to assist with the overthrow of the Bureau, how to gather an army, or even more simply, to determine if anyone was alive outside New America's walls. But one thing was certain—he couldn't do anything at such a distance. They needed to hug the Connecticut coast much closer.

It was time for him to start directing this mission. He'd deferred to Lindrick too much already. He stood, taking a full minute to get his balance, and shuffled to the cockpit.

"Captain!" Drayden yelled so Lindrick could hear him over the wind, waves, and engine. "We need to sail closer to the Connecticut coast on our left. We need to watch for signs of life."

The captain didn't respond.

"Captain!" Drayden shouted again, louder.

Lieutenant Duarte chuckled a bit, shaking his head. He drew his glistening hunting knife, smooth on one side and serrated on the other. He polished it with a rag while glowering at Drayden.

What the hell?

Drayden glanced back.

The other privates were scrutinizing him with concerned faces.

"Captain Lindrick!" he screamed.

Lindrick turned his head back, visibly annoyed. "Go have a seat in the back, son."

CHAPTER 12

The silence around the table in the back of the boat was deafening. Captain Lindrick had ordered Drayden to sit down, and he did. He didn't take charge. He put his tail between his legs and got owned by the captain all over again.

"What is going on?" Sidney asked. "This isn't what we signed up for."

"I don't know," Drayden said. "I gave Captain Lindrick a direct order and he laughed and told me to sit down. After he ignored me for a while. That freaking Duarte shkat starts polishing his knife in front of me, trying to intimidate me. I mean, what am I supposed to do?"

Catrice touched his knee. "Don't worry, it's not your fault. There's nothing else you could have done. You can't physically wrest control of the boat from four Guardians."

"Do you think they were never told that we would be in charge?" Drayden asked. "Holst and von Brooks could have lied to us."

"Or," Sidney said, "they always planned on taking over once we got out here, where nobody would find out."

Charlie kicked the table leg. "Charlie's pissed. I know these guys are super strong and everything, but people should leave decisions to smart guys like you, Dray. Can you imagine if I was driving? We'd wind up in China."

Sidney reached into her backpack and pulled out a bag of apples. She handed one to each of them. "We're only like an hour and a half into this; we've got a long way to go. Hopefully it won't matter."

"Thanks, Sid," Drayden said. He tore into the apple, which was sweet and crunchy. What if they did need to make an important decision? He never enjoyed hearing Charlie talk about being dumb. Nevertheless, he also loathed the idea of these meathead Guardians making a critical choice if one arose. He hadn't consulted the map in a while; he should figure out where they were. He dug into his pack and fished it out.

Everything on the Connecticut coast looked the same. Lots and lots of trees. Another reason they needed to hug the shore.

Charlie started talking with a mouthful of apple. "How about the bomb they dropped on us about reaching Boston? Shkat flunks."

"I don't care what happens. We have to make it," Sidney said. "I can't have my sister sent away. How could they even do that to an eight-year-old? She's just a child. It's so cruel."

"I'm not sure we can trust the Bureau," Catrice said.

"We can't," Drayden said. "Let's not give them a reason to make good on their threat, though."

Eugene emerged from the cockpit and joined them at their table, beside Charlie. He wore an apologetic expression.

Drayden glared at him. Eugene-the-great sure as heck didn't defend him in there. Then again, he was the lowest-ranking Guardian. Taking orders and keeping his mouth shut came as naturally as shooting for him.

Everyone remained silent, waiting for Eugene to say something.

"Hey, Drayden, don't worry about that back there," he said. "The captain's a grizzled old veteran. It's hard for him to take orders from anyone, let alone a teenage civilian. He doesn't even like taking orders from his commanding officer. He's actually an amazing guy.

He served in live combat with the Marines Pre-Confluence. When push comes to shove, he knows you're in charge. Driving the boat and all that isn't a big deal."

"I guess," Drayden said. "Thanks, Eugene." Yet to him it *was* a big deal. Given the stakes, and his own secret goals, he wasn't about to kowtow to the captain.

"Would you like an apple?" Sidney asked Eugene.

He rubbed his hands together. "Yeah, love one. Thanks, Sid. Is it okay if I call you Sid?"

She tossed his apple high in the air. "You can call me Sam if you want, as long as you're talking to me."

Eugene caught it and took a bite.

"What's going on with your gun there, Euge?" Charlie asked. "Can I call you Euge?"

Eugene cracked up. "Dude, you are hilarious." He drew his pistol, which appeared to extend through his holster. An elongated metal cylinder protruded from the muzzle of his Glock 22, the same gun they used. "This is a silencer. I made it. Check it out."

He raised it with one hand, aiming out over the water. He squeezed off two quick rounds, the sound like a coin dropping into a glass jar.

"What do you need a silencer for?" Catrice asked.

Eugene shrugged as he holstered his weapon. "Who knows? There might be a situation where you need to kill someone without the rest of the world hearing. We prepare for every contingency. Let me ask you a question. How many Guardians are there in the Precinct?"

"Around fifteen thousand," Drayden answered.

"Exactly," Eugene said. "There are only a few hundred Palace Guardians, yet we're prepared to defeat fifteen thousand Guardians if they ever tried to overthrow the Bureau. Every Palace Guardian is Special Forces–trained. We're picked when we're eight to begin training, based on observed strength or athletic ability."

"Are you happy you were picked?" Catrice asked.

He stared out over the water. "I'm happy being a Guardian. No regrets. But if were totally up to me? I might have become a scientist. As I told you when we met, I love math and science. Hey, can you guys share any brainteasers from the Initiation? I'm so curious."

Charlie raised his finger in the air. "I'm probably the guy to walk you through those, Euge."

Eugene leaned toward Charlie, apparently ready to do some thinking.

"Oh, I was joking," Charlie said. "I was as confused as a homeless guy on house arrest."

Eugene held his sides, laughing out of control. "You guys must be constantly cracking up with Charlie around."

"Yeah, he's a gem." Drayden rested his chin on his hand. "You want to tell Eugene about that time in the Initiation when you tried to kill me, chotch?"

Charlie frowned. "Drayden, I thought we agreed we wouldn't talk about that anymore?"

"Whoa, what's that about?" Eugene asked.

"Ah, I'm just busting Charlie's chops," Drayden said. "In the final challenge we had to cross a chasm, like two hundred feet deep, with a raging inferno at the bottom. Charlie's best friend, Alex, tried to throw me in, and I thought Charlie was helping him. He claims he was trying to stop Alex. The jury's still out." He smirked at Charlie.

Charlie flicked Drayden on the arm. "Draaaay...c'mon, you're my boy." Charlie scooted toward Eugene. "After Dray fought him off, I tried to save Alex, who was dangling over the chasm." He shook his head. "I couldn't do it. He fell. Then I almost fell but Dray saved me instead of finishing the Initiation in time. Holst admitted both me and Dray to the Bureau because of what Drayden did. He wanted all of us for this mission."

Eugene's mouth hung open. "Dray...I'm...I'm blown away. Forget Lindrick. You're battle-tested. You're a freaking hero. That should be in the history books or something. I knew you and Catrice solved the brainteasers, but I don't think people know about those heroics. Man, I wanna be just like you."

Although Drayden hated it about himself, he was still a sucker for flattery. He needed that reassurance, for people to like him. He wished he was confident enough not to care what other people thought. Instead he glowed from Eugene's praise.

"I can tell you some of the brainteasers if you want," Catrice said.

Eugene licked his lips. "Yeah, I'd love that."

Drayden was probably being a little selfish, but he was irritated that Catrice had stolen his moment in the sun, the studly young Guardian heaping him with praise.

Catrice tucked a strand of hair behind her ear. "We only had five minutes to solve the brainteasers. There was a tough one with two wicks. What—" she stopped and covered her mouth with her hands.

Drayden looked at his feet and tried to blink away the tears that were coming.

Don't cry, dammit.

"Oh my God, Drayden, I'm sorry," Catrice said. "I'll pick a different one."

Drayden kept his head down. "No, that's all right, it was a cool problem, you can tell him." She had to choose the one where he screwed up and killed his best friend. Real thoughtful.

Catrice reached over and touched his arm. "Drayden."

"I'm...I'm sorry, you guys," Eugene said. "I didn't mean...you don't have rehash this for me. The Initiation was traumatic for you guys and I'm treating it like a game. That was insensitive of me. I was—*am*—blown away that you guys did it. That's all. Please forgive me." He got up and headed for the cockpit.

"Eugene!" Drayden called out. "Come back."

Eugene hesitated for a moment before returning and sitting next to Drayden. "Something awful happened on that challenge. You don't have to talk about it. I wouldn't be able to either."

Jesus, he wanted to rest his head on Eugene's shoulder. He wished Catrice would be that considerate.

Drayden removed his hat and ran his fingers through his hair. "Basically, we had to disarm a bomb. We figured out how to do it right, but I messed up pulling out the detonator and my best friend, Tim, was killed. I was seriously injured and everyone else was hurt too."

"You didn't mess up," Catrice said emphatically. She faced Eugene. "While the rest of us hid behind the steel pillars in the subway station, Drayden and his best friend Tim handled the bomb. Even though Drayden did it right, the detonator didn't come out. I don't think the Bureau intended for it to come out. They *wanted* the bomb to go off. At the last second, Drayden ran for cover. Tim stayed and tried to rip the detonator out. Unfortunately, it exploded."

Wait…was Eugene crying?

Eugene wiped his eyes. "Wow. I'm sorry, Drayden. Catrice is right. You can't blame yourself. Surviving the blast probably was the challenge. You should have run for sure. I'll bet you tried to get Tim to run, and he didn't. He must have been very brave." He wrapped his arms around Drayden and hugged him.

It was insane, but the first person to ever truly comfort him over Tim's death was Eugene. He buried his face in Eugene's chest and cried.

CHAPTER 13

Three hours into their journey, Drayden didn't know where the hell they were.

It was 1:00 PM. He'd spread his map out over the table, his eyes darting from the map to the Connecticut shore and back. The Long Island shore was barely visible. Even the Connecticut coastline didn't offer much in the way of clues. So many insignificant peninsulas jutted out and harbors cut in, like the unfinished border of a jigsaw puzzle. Tiny islands dotted the coast everywhere. He needed a meaningful landmark.

According to the map, a major group of islands clustered off the shore around Norwalk. They lay further out than some of these other rinky-dink islands. He needed to find that.

Although hours of daylight remained, once darkness fell he needed one additional and crucial piece of information to navigate—their speed. He would need to enter the cockpit with the Guardians. He hadn't been back in there since Lindrick shut him down earlier.

Whether intentional or not, Captain Lindrick had steered the boat closer to the shore. It wasn't as close as Drayden wanted, but at least you could distinguish trees, docks, and buildings.

After three hours on the boat, they'd all become restless. While the senior Guardians huddled in the cockpit, the privates and Eugene milled around, searching for any way to occupy themselves.

Drayden sat alone at the table, thankfully. He was eager to move on from the awkward cry that had left an owl-shaped wet spot on Eugene's shirt. Catrice did genuinely seem to feel horrible about having brought up the challenge in which Tim died. Regardless, he was embarrassed for having bawled in front of everyone, particularly Catrice and Eugene. Not only was Eugene strong and confident, he turned out to be sensitive and compassionate too. Drayden, on the other hand, was a worried crybaby. It was a tough comparison. He didn't want to imagine what Catrice was thinking.

He walked around the cockpit onto the deck in the front of the boat so he could check for approaching landmarks. Charlie and Sidney were slouched there, chatting.

Drayden squinted, digesting the distant landscape.

A sizable island lay in their path about a mile ahead, and other islands were visible beyond it. That was Sheffield Island, the first of the Norwalk Islands.

He wanted to check their speed. Why should he be afraid of going into the cockpit? He headed back to the rear of the boat and strolled inside.

Sergeant Greaney and Lieutenant Duarte sized him up without speaking. Captain Lindrick, who sat at the controls, stared straight ahead.

Drayden peered over Captain Lindrick's shoulder and checked the speed on the boat's odometer.

They were traveling at twenty-two knots. Since one knot equaled 1.15 miles per hour, twenty-two knots translated to twenty-five miles per hour, which was the boat's maximum speed.

Before leaving, Drayden noticed the Guardians didn't even have their maps out anymore. Perhaps they intended to wing it. That would be a brilliant strategy after it became dark.

Idiots.

He walked back to the table in the stern and took a seat.

Against the boat's rear wall, several tall plastic cylinders rested beside each other. They were dark green and bound together, with water trickling down their sides. That was the backup water supply. A few other gray metal boxes, secured with chains and locks around them, sat beside the water. The Guardians had loaded those. Drayden found it odd that they were so well protected, wondering what they contained.

Catrice knelt by the water tanks, examining the knots that secured the cylinders together. With extra rope in her hands, she attempted to replicate the knots.

"It's called a bowline knot," Eugene said, approaching her with his own rope. "Want me to teach you?"

She held her tangled rope like an offering. "Yes, please. I should be able to figure this out, but I can't."

He sat cross-legged in front of her, rope in hand. "In Guardian training, we learn to tie all kinds of knots."

Catrice followed suit, sitting the same way, tucking her hair behind her ears.

Like a magician, Eugene whipped his rope into a complex knot that culminated in a loop. "Okay," he said, "hold the ends of your rope in each hand. Yup. Now stick both of those through this loop."

"Okaaaaay..." She pushed both hands through.

He yanked one side of his knot and the loop snapped tight around her wrists. "That's called a handcuff knot. I made that one up." He giggled. "The more you struggle, the tighter it gets."

Catrice couldn't stop laughing. "Nice, funny man. Are you arresting me?"

"Honestly, knot training is so damn pointless I wanted to finally use it for once!" Eugene untied the knot and she pulled her hands out. "Let me show you this knot. The bowline knot is a great one, since it doesn't slip but it won't get any tighter. Up in the Meadow where the sheep live, the farmers could tether them with a bowline knot. It'll never get too tight around the animal's neck and hurt it. It's also easy to untie."

"I can tell you really love this knot," Catrice said. "I want to learn the handcuff knot too."

Drayden couldn't take it anymore, hoping Eugene could tie a noose for him to hang himself. It wasn't just his jealousy and insecurity. They were *cute* together. Eugene wasn't sleazy like Charlie, he was...dammit, he was cute. Innocent. He was childlike and endearing. Why wouldn't Catrice dig him? She'd be crazy not to. Drayden couldn't compete with that guy; not in strength, charm, or physical attractiveness anyway. He was so damn confident, so comfortable in his own skin. Although he was tough, he never worried about *looking* tough. Still, there was one way Drayden could outshine Eugene.

"Hey, Eugene, you want to hear another brainteaser from the Initiation?" Drayden asked. "This one was downright stupefying. I mean, I solved it, but it was crazy tricky." He immediately regretted asking, invoking the Initiation all over again. The test that saw his best friend killed, and he was trying to use it to embarrass the guy.

"Yeah, definitely," Eugene said. "I'm sure I won't get it. Why don't you come join us over here? There's not much I can teach you, but I'm basically a certified knot instructor." He winked at Drayden. "Here, grab some rope, have a seat."

Catrice waved him over. "Come on, Dray. Eugene's holding knot school."

"Nah. I'm going to do some work on navigation. I'm afraid your Guardian buddies will sail us to China. Thanks anyway. You guys have fun."

He stood, his head back and his chest puffed out, and strode toward the front of the boat. Unfortunately, he tripped on the table leg and stumbled. He refused to peek back and witness the giggling. Once up front, he collapsed alongside Charlie and Sidney, burying his face in his hands.

"Sometimes I forget you guys lost your best friends during the Initiation," Sidney said. "Or I'm afraid to bring it up, even to tell you how sorry I am, because I know how upset you'll get. Drayden, I felt terrible for you having to cry on Eugene like that. None of us have been there for you—or for you, Charlie, about Alex. I'm sorry, you guys."

"Thanks, Sid," Drayden said.

Charlie fist-bumped her. "Thanks."

"I'll still never understand why you liked Alex," she said to Charlie.

Charlie touched a finger to his chin. "Alex...was an acquired taste."

"Well," Sidney said to Drayden, "I assume Catrice has been super supportive." She gave a sarcastic nod.

Drayden snickered. "She's too busy entertaining Eugene."

"Awesome, another guy that picks her over me." Sidney play-punched him on the shoulder. "Don't worry, I'll go break that party up." She straightened her uniform and walked toward the rear of the boat.

The sky had darkened further, and the winds had picked up. The ocean swells ballooned, violently rocking the boat. If they grew large enough to capsize their vessel, they should angle themselves so the waves didn't hit them broadside. Drayden bet Captain Lindrick hadn't thought of that.

"You'll get over Catrice pretty fast," Charlie said. "I did."

"What?" Drayden asked.

"Catrice. You had a good run. She picked you over me. I know, I know, I gave it my best shot. Sadly, she's smart, you're smart, and I'm an idiot. There was no way I was winning that battle. Bravo. But, I mean, Eugene? I think your ship has sailed. Sorry, not sorry for the pun, by the way. It's the love. It moves quickly man, like wildflowers."

Drayden held his hands in the air. "Like wildflowers? *Wildflowers?* What the hell does...do you mean *wildfire*?"

"Yeah, like wildfire."

"I haven't lost Catrice. I don't think."

"That boy's game is slicker than snot on a bald guy's head," Charlie said quietly. "All innocent and charming. I wish I was that smooth. Instead I get kicked in the shins."

"You think it's an act?" Drayden asked, scanning the boat to make sure Eugene wasn't around.

"I'm not sure. I don't think so. The guy is just awesome."

The guy *was* awesome. If he'd indeed lost Catrice, then she must prefer Eugene to him. What was it about the kid exactly? Assuming he and Eugene were equally intelligent, that only left Eugene's better looks and superior strength. You could scratch looks from that list. While Drayden wasn't particularly handsome, she was into him before Eugene entered the picture. That meant appearance wasn't that important to her, leaving Eugene's strength, with which he could protect her.

He needed to show Catrice that he was strong, tough, and manly like Eugene. It was probably his jealousy, but given the other Guardians' actions thus far, he wasn't sure they should blindly trust the young corporal.

"Charlie, I'm not sure about him. I agree the guy is cool, nice, charming. Still, he's too perfect. Who's like that? Nobody. Have you ever met anyone like him before? Something bugs me about him, and it's not just that he's stealing my girlfriend."

Charlie pointed at him. "Stole."

"Thank you. All I'm saying is, I think the four of us should stick together, not totally embrace him in our group yet. Let's be a little cautious. Plus, the kid has two first names. Eugene Austin. You can never trust someone with two first names."

Charlie scratched his head. "I have two first names. Charlie Arnold."

"Exactly. And you tried to kill me once." Drayden smirked. "Listen, we have no idea what the Guardians are up to—if they're even on the same mission *we* believe we're on. They're sure not acting like it."

Charlie held out his fist for a bump. "We're sticking together. I got your back; don't worry."

Drayden bumped his fist. "Thanks, Charlie. Now if I could only figure out how to take over control of the boat from Captain Pinprick, I'd feel better. I have to show him I'm not weak. Any sign of weakness, a guy like that eats you for breakfast."

"Listen, bro," Charlie said, "you're a lot smarter than me, so I shouldn't be giving you advice, but there's already a lot of muscle on this boat. Know what there's not a lot of? Brains. Maybe leave the tough stuff to guys like me and Captain Chick-Flick...Captain Bone-to-Pick...Captain Limp—"

"Charlie, I got it."

"You do *you*," Charlie said. "That's all I'm sayin.'"

It was more than being strong for the mission's sake; Drayden was fretting about the Catrice situation. Thinking he should refocus on navigation, he surveyed the coast, searching for landmarks.

A sizable peninsula jutted out ahead of their path. On their current trajectory, they would pass within a few hundred yards of it.

He rose to fetch his maps from the boat's stern when something caught his eye, and he drew in a quick breath.

"Oh my God, Charlie. Do you see that?"

CHAPTER 14

A young boy, around five years old, was frolicking on a beach, wearing only shorts.

"Look!" Drayden pointed. "There's a kid there! A person!" He dashed to the rear of the boat.

Eugene was holding court between Catrice and Sidney, recounting some story. Both girls were engrossed.

"Catrice! Look!" Drayden frantically jumped up and down.

Sidney leapt to her feet. "Holy shkat. There are people out here! Alive."

Catrice waved at the little boy. "Drayden, shouldn't we stop?"

If there was a boy, he had parents. It was possible a whole community of people lived here. Drayden's mind swirled pondering all the implications—survivors, immunity to Aeru, gathering an army.

Mom.

He rushed into the cockpit. "Captain Lindrick! There's a young boy on shore. Over there!"

Sergeant Greaney and Lieutenant Duarte exited the cockpit to check it out. Captain Lindrick squinted, ducking to see out the side window. Then he resumed driving without a word.

"Captain, what are you doing? We have to go investigate that!"

Captain Lindrick ignored him.

Drayden mulled taking hold of the throttle and pulling it back. What would Lindrick do?

They passed the beach, leaving behind the boy who was now waving. Sidney, Catrice, and Eugene waved back.

"Hello!" Eugene called out.

Drayden balled his hands into fists. "Captain Lindrick, I'm *ordering* you to turn the boat around so we can go talk to that boy. People are alive out here. We need to find out what they know. This could be critical for New America."

Lindrick stared straight ahead. "That's not part of our mission, Private."

Drayden's face flushed hot. "Like hell it isn't. We could get to Boston and find the city deserted. They might not let us in. This may be the only live person we see on the whole journey. Captain! I gave you a direct order."

Sergeant Greaney and Lieutenant Duarte pushed by him to reenter the cockpit, both remaining silent.

Drayden could appeal to Sergeant Greaney, who was at least cordial the first time they'd met. "Sergeant, I believe we need to go back and talk to that boy. It's the first proof we have that people are alive outside the walls of New America. If there's a young boy, he has parents. There may be a community of people. They might hold the key to surviving out in the wild."

Sergeant Greaney's eyes flicked to Captain Lindrick.

His voice raised, Lindrick spoke without turning around. "Private, clearly you don't know much about the military chain of command. I'm the senior officer here, and I've decided we continue on our mission. When you have a mission, you must exercise discipline to stick to it. And you complete it, at all costs."

By now the other privates and Eugene had gathered outside the cockpit door.

"Captain!" Drayden shouted. "Am I in charge of this mission or not? Turn the boat around, now! This is the first proof of life outside New America in twenty-five years. We need to find out how those people are alive."

Lieutenant Duarte leaned into Sergeant Greaney. "I don't believe he's too in charge of this mission, what do you think?"

Sergeant Greaney looked at the floor and tried to bite back a laugh, but failed.

"Captain, you need to pull the boat over," Sidney said.

Eugene stood tall. "Captain Lindrick, sir! The corporal requests that we pull the boat over to investigate the issue before continuing on our mission, sir!"

Drayden had to hand it to Eugene and Sidney for having his back this time.

"Stand down, Corporal," Lieutenant Duarte snarled. He scowled at Drayden. "You too, *Private*." He pulled his knife again, polishing it.

Drayden stepped toward him. "I'm not a private. What, I'm supposed to be scared because you have a knife? I have a knife too."

"Yeah?" Duarte flipped his in the air and caught it, waving it at Drayden. "You wanna take yours out and see who's sharper with it?"

Sergeant Greaney pushed Lieutenant Duarte's knife down. "We're too far past the beach to go back now anyway. Why don't you kids go relax? We have hours left to go."

Drayden shoved his way through Eugene and the other privates. He stormed to the rear of the boat, defeated, again.

Drayden fumed at the table in the back. Two hours had passed since his latest failure to wrest control of the mission and investigate the sighting.

No other people had appeared on shore since. That kid may have held the key to surviving in the outside world. Assuming he was part of a larger community, Drayden couldn't believe they'd survived Aeru. The significance of their existence couldn't be overstated.

A walled-in city of people in Boston might not offer information as valuable to survival as a group living in the wilderness. If anything, Boston would be a facsimile of New America, with people living safely within the confines of a protected world. In the wild, people lived amongst the very bacteria that had scourged the whole planet. Those people might have built up a natural resistance to Aeru. Or perhaps the few people with a congenital immunity to Aeru were procreating, rebuilding an entire population impervious to infection.

Drayden also needed to pursue his secret goal. He reminded himself of Kim's instructions to determine if anything out in the real world could assist with their overthrow attempt. A desperate village of people might work. Understanding how to survive outside New America would be transformational. Still, it was a vague, broad goal. He hadn't a clue how to drum up an army.

The other privates wandered around the boat, distressed by their failed confrontation with the Guardians. Two hands behind Drayden massaged his shoulders.

Before checking, he thought it was more likely to be Eugene than Catrice. But the thin, delicate hands were a giveaway. He hated himself for it as he scanned the boat for Eugene.

He wasn't around, unsurprisingly. He was inside the cockpit, speaking with the other Guardians.

Catrice had not yet shown a single sign of affection to Drayden in front of Eugene. Was he being paranoid and way oversensitive? Probably. He needed to push his negativity away. That kind of thinking would make everyone hate him, including Catrice. He reached up and touched her hand. "Thanks."

She sat beside him. "What are we going to do?"

"I don't know. I'm pissed. At those flunk Guardians, at Holst, and at that snake von Brooks. I'm not going to stop trying to seize control of this mission. It's one thing to be going straight in daylight, but it's already late afternoon. Pretty soon it'll be dark, and we're not leaving it to these guys to sail us to Boston after that. They don't even have their map out. All they're doing is hugging the coast."

The wind swirled, blasting ocean-cooled air into their already windblown faces. Fortunately, they were still in Long Island Sound, protected from the open Atlantic Ocean where the swells would be much worse. The boat rocked from side to side, and intermittently jumped and dipped, as if they were sailing off a cliff.

Eugene exited the cockpit, walked over, and sat next to Drayden.

"Thanks for having my back." Drayden patted him on the arm.

"We should've stopped," Eugene said quietly. "That was major, seeing a person out there. I'm sorry about this. Like I said, Captain Lindrick is stubborn; he's used to being in charge. His dedication to a mission is also paramount. One thing is, if we had stopped, we'd be exposing ourselves to Aeru. Those people might be immune, but we might not."

"We got the vaccine," Drayden snapped.

Eugene pulled his head back. "You want to test it out?"

"It doesn't change the fact that the decision should be ours, not his." Drayden gritted his teeth. "That was the deal."

Eugene squeezed his shoulder. "I know. It's not right. Let me try and talk to the captain. He respects me; he chose me for this mission. He'll start to respect you too. Don't worry." Eugene's expression softened. "I remember the first time I met the captain. I was thirteen, well into training. Every time I made eye contact with him, he demanded twenty-five pushups. It was a long day."

He rubbed his chest. "I must have done two hundred pushups. Let me give it a shot, okay? It's probably better than banging your head against the wall."

Drayden wasn't sure how much he could trust Eugene. God only knew what he was saying to the other Guardians in private. But he didn't have much of a choice. "Sure. Thanks, Eugene."

Eugene punched him on the shoulder and walked into the cockpit.

Thunder cracked in the distance. The first drops of rain fell.

The boat violently rocked, shook, and plunged, the hull groaning under the stress of the titanic swells. Rain battered the windows of the cockpit, and waves crashed over the bow. Now that night had fallen, it was impossible to see anything, even with the headlights. The Guardians had finally relented and let Drayden handle navigation.

Captain Lindrick drove, following his instructions. Sidney and Catrice huddled in the cockpit with them. Given the storm, Sergeant Greaney and Lieutenant Duarte had relinquished the safety of the cockpit to them. Nobody else fit. The two senior Guardians stood out back with Charlie and Eugene, the four of them holding on for dear life.

Drayden had stuffed his maps into his pack and was using the Guardians' map instead. His last visual had been Block Island, over two hours ago. Before that he'd noted Fishers Island, which lay right at the border between Connecticut and Rhode Island. It also marked the end of Long Island, their protection from the sea's fury. Now they sailed in open ocean, and with the storm, the waves were enormous.

None of them knew the first thing about boats, and everyone was terrified theirs would capsize at any moment. Was the boat equipped to handle surf this rough?

They needed to execute a slight left turn into Buzzard's Bay, using navigation tools only because they were sailing blind. Drayden had done the calculations by hand after they'd passed Block Island.

Cuttyhunk Island, thirty-six miles past Block Island, marked the entrance to Buzzard's Bay. Their speed had dropped to thirteen knots—fifteen miles per hour—due to the conditions. Heading east-northeast, they needed to bear left of Cuttyhunk Island exactly two hours and twenty-four minutes after Block Island. Hopefully they would see the island before they crashed into it. Unfortunately, between the rain and darkness, they couldn't see anything.

Since they'd passed Block Island just over two hours ago, they would reach the relative safety of the bay in roughly twenty minutes. If they survived that long.

A massive swell rocked the boat's right side, crashing over the deck with a boom. The boat listed dramatically left.

Drayden's heart felt like it stopped. He braced himself against the cockpit walls. They could capsize at any moment. The water was too powerful.

Catrice screamed as they crashed back down.

"Holy shkat," Drayden said, trembling. "Sid, Catrice, we need our packs. Get Charlie and Eugene to grab them."

By now everyone was wearing their life vests, including the Guardians.

Sidney hollered outside the cockpit to Charlie.

He staggered around the deck, bracing himself against anything he could find. A wave knocked him over, flooding the deck, which now resembled a swimming pool. Eugene hauled him back to his feet and flung open the bin holding the packs. After Charlie strapped his on, they held onto each other and stumbled to the cockpit lugging the others. They dropped the privates' packs on the floor inside the cockpit. Both boys were soaked, pale, and shivering.

Drayden had never seen Charlie so scared.

"Everyone put your packs on over the life vests!" Drayden screamed. "And secure your weapons!" He shoved his hat inside his pack.

Sidney and Catrice locked their rifles onto the backs of the packs and strapped them on tight. None of the Guardians wore theirs, though they carried their rifles.

Drayden squinted to see ahead, but with no wiper on the windshield it was impossible. Someone needed to go outside and look. Being a weak swimmer, he was too afraid to do it. If he fell overboard, he was dead. He stuck his head out the cockpit door. "Eugene! Can you see anything in front of the boat? Any land?"

"What?"

"Can you see anything in front of the boat?" Drayden shrieked.

"No! I can't see anything!"

Drayden checked his watch. Fifteen minutes until they reached Cuttyhunk Island.

Another towering wave crashed over the whole boat, even the cockpit. Both decks flooded, thrusting icy water inside the cockpit and down below into the bathroom area, which was under a foot of water now.

Catrice and Sidney held onto each other, shaking.

"Captain Lindrick, we have to pull ashore," Drayden said. "Now. We wait till this storm passes and continue after."

"No, Private, we can make it."

Drayden jutted his jaw. "Captain, that's an order!"

"How much time is left before Buzzard's Bay?"

"Fourteen minutes."

"We can last; we're almost there. Once we're in the bay all this will go away. Don't be a coward, son!"

"Captain, turn left now! Take this boat ashore! It's not worth it!"

Lindrick turned his head back. "Stand down, private! Stand dow—"

An ear-splintering crash rocked the boat.

Either lightning struck or they hit a rock, but Drayden was underwater, in the frigid black sea. The coldness was shocking to the core, blanketing him in pain. His body stiffened instantly, as if zapped by a bolt of electricity. His mind jumped to the pool challenge in the Initiation. This time there was no easing himself in, no well-placed air pockets, and no opportunity to take a deep breath before submerging. This was real, and he had to get above water immediately. His chest ached already. He needed air.

The life vest was buoyant but the pack was heavy, and they were battling for supremacy.

The urge to breathe grew overwhelming. He needed to reach the surface. Without any light, he couldn't even tell which way was up. The disorientation was nauseating.

The life vest gradually pulled him up.

He needed air! He kicked his legs.

Catrice! She can't swim. Oh God.

His head popped up above water, wind and rain pelting it. He sucked in a huge audible breath. "Cat—"

A wave tumbled him underwater all over again. This time he swallowed a giant mouthful of salty seawater.

I could die right here.

He still needed to tell Catrice he loved her. He had to return to New America, to see Wes and his father. He couldn't die yet. He had too much to do. After kicking and kicking, he breached the surface of the water.

Voices. Yelling. Wood scattered everywhere, the boat in pieces.

He latched onto a plank of wood and held on tight. "Catrice! Catrice!" He started hyperventilating.

Another wave toppled him, but he held onto the plank and swiftly resurfaced. "Catrice!"

A hand squeezed his shoulder. It was Charlie, his eyes giant discs.

"Charlie, where's Catrice?"

"I don't know!"

Despite the absolute blackness, frequent lightning illuminated the sky. When it did, it struck pure terror into Drayden's heart. Each flash provided a snapshot of fifteen-foot black swells, splintered wood floating, and heads bobbing in the water.

"I got her!" Eugene yelled from somewhere.

"Drayden!" she shrieked, sounding distant.

"Where are you?" he called out.

"Drayden, I have her!" Eugene yelled.

"Where's Sidney? Sid!" Drayden shouted.

"I'm okay!"

The next flash of lightning illuminated Sergeant Greaney bobbing in front of Drayden and Charlie. "We need to swim that way!" he said, flashing his eyes to the right.

"Eugene!" Drayden yelled. "Help Catrice swim!"

"I got her! Don't worry!"

Drayden clutched his plank of wood like a kickboard and pumped with every frozen muscle he had. His legs felt weighed down with cinderblocks. Up the crests of waves and back down again.

Swells repeatedly crashed over his head, hammering him back underwater.

He was out of breath and freezing. "Charlie! Where are you?"

No reply. The subsequent flash of lightning revealed Charlie fifteen yards ahead.

Based on their former trajectory, they should have been roughly half a mile off the shore of either Rhode Island or Massachusetts, provided they were swimming toward the shore, and not further out into the ocean. By his calculations, they'd capsized near the border between the two states.

A monstrous wave pummeled Drayden, thrusting him underwater again. Another mouthful of seawater plunged down his throat.

When he popped back up this time he vomited. He gagged, swallowed, and struggled for air. His legs were cramping from the strain of kicking and the frigid water chilling his muscles. Hypothermia was setting in. He stopped hyperventilating and his breathing became labored. He'd lost track of time.

Another burst of light illuminated land ahead—close, a hundred yards.

"Catrice! Catrice!"

No answer.

Underwater again. Exhaustion overcame him. Getting back to the surface this time was more arduous. He couldn't catch his breath. So, this was how people drowned.

Push, dammit!

He kicked furiously, and pumped with one arm, gripping his safety plank with the other.

A rapid flutter of light this time. Thirty yards to go, and silhouettes standing on a beach.

His numb legs refused to kick. They shut down.

Hopefully the waves would push him in.

Lightning.

Two people swimming toward him.

Darkness.

Charlie and Eugene grasped him by the arms, and he released his plank. They swam him in the rest of the way.

Quaking, Drayden crawled onto the beach. He collapsed, resting his cheek on the frosty, wet sand.

CHAPTER 15

The disgusting taste of bile and salt water caked Drayden's mouth. After he stopped vomiting seawater, he lumbered to his feet. "Catrice?"

"I'm here!"

Although it was pitch black, he found her with the frequent bursts of lightning. He wobbled over and embraced her. "Thank God you survived," he said. "I was so worried."

"Thank you. If Eugene hadn't grabbed me, I would have died."

That was the harsh reality. He should have been thrilled she was alive, and he was, of course. But if Eugene hadn't saved her, Catrice would indeed be dead. He was the only one strong enough. That wasn't Drayden's opinion, his fear, or his insecurity. It was a fact.

"Eugene," Drayden said, "thank you for rescuing Catrice. You really did save her life."

"Guardians don't leave our people behind. Ever. We've done extensive water training. I would've died myself before I abandoned someone out there."

"Thanks for coming to get me too," Drayden said.

"You're welcome, bud. Even if I die tomorrow, this trip was worth it for me, to get the chance to save you and Catrice."

Goddamn this kid is special.

"What now?" Sidney asked.

The lightning revealed an immense, arched beach.

Drayden felt like walking over to Captain Lindrick and punching him in the mouth. He was taking control of this disaster rather than waiting for Lindrick to assume command. "We need to figure out where we are, and we need shelter. We're obviously on a large beach somewhere."

"Look up there." Sergeant Greaney pointed up the slope of the beach. "There's a building, like an information center or something."

They headed up the beach, which was quite rocky, a blend of pebbles and sand. Rotted wooden stairs led up to a dilapidated structure resembling a cabin. The middle part was open to the air and covered by a high roof. Fully enclosed rooms flanked it on both sides.

"There's an old sign here," Catrice said. "It's too dark to read. Let's wait for lightning." The sky lit up. "Horse...something," she said.

Lightning flashed again.

"Horseneck Beach State Reservation."

"First things first," Drayden said. "We need to make a fire. Charlie and Sidney, see if you can find anything dry to burn. Twigs, wood, old paper, anything. Search this building, or outside if you find areas that are covered. Sergeant Greaney, it's too wet to do it here, we need to build it inside one of these rooms. We need ventilation though. If the windows aren't already broken, can you bust them?"

"Yes, Private. Lieutenant, gimme a hand."

That left Drayden, Catrice, Eugene, and Captain Lindrick standing in the open section of the building.

"Still think we shouldn't have pulled ashore, Captain?" Drayden asked.

"Watch it, Private. You and blondie would both be dead if it weren't for my corporal here."

"Yeah, but we'd be alive *and* have a boat if you'd followed my orders, like you were supposed to," Drayden said. "There's a reason Premier Holst put me in charge of this mission."

"Don't mess with me, son. You don't want to start a fight you can't finish."

Charlie and Sidney returned with armfuls of material.

"We found a trash can with lots of old paper in it," Sidney said. "And the other room had a few wooden chairs. They might burn."

"Well done, guys," Drayden said.

The sound of glass breaking erupted from the other room.

Drayden walked in, followed by the others.

With their rifles, Greaney and Duarte were smashing the crusty windows, which sat high at the tops of the walls.

"How are we going to start a fire?" Charlie asked. "Our matches are ruined."

"Luckily, I was paying attention in science class last week," Drayden said. "Can you break up those chairs and pile up the wood in the center of the room? And crumple up those papers."

"Eugene, can you gimme a hand breaking these chairs apart?" Charlie asked.

"Sure thing."

Drayden and the other privates set their packs down along the near wall. The Guardians collapsed in a fit of shivers with their backs against the far wall. While they retained their weapons, they lacked packs because they hadn't donned them before the boat broke apart.

Drayden rummaged through his pack to find what he was searching for: one AA battery and a paperclip. He also found a flashlight in there, as well as tons of extra ammunition.

Something else gave him pause. The food and maps. The privates had both and the Guardians had neither. Given how the journey had played out, and their current predicament, he realized this could create a situation. Possession of both critical items gave the privates leverage, which he had no intention of forfeiting. They would have to share the food, obviously, but perhaps they could do so without revealing how much they had.

Charlie and Eugene had built a miniature mountain of wood and paper on the cement floor in the center of the room.

Drayden pulled out his knife. "Hey, Charlie, can you shine the flashlight on my hands?"

He took Drayden's and switched it on. "I wish I knew we had flashlights about ten minutes ago."

Drayden leaned in to whisper in Charlie's ear. "Don't say anything about your map or your food. I'm going to tell the Guardians the maps were destroyed in the water. Tell the girls, quietly. If you can do it without the Guardians noticing, burn the maps in the fire."

Charlie nodded.

It was a huge gamble to destroy all the maps except his. But if he had the only map, and the Guardians didn't know about it, he would effectively be in charge of the mission. They would need him to show the way, after he announced that he knew it.

The battery fire trick wouldn't be so easy given Drayden's shivering. With the battery negative side up, he cut away some of the casing around the metal cap. He pried the cap up a smidge, exposing a thin layer of cardboard, then positioned himself close to the crumpled-up paper. After unfolding the paperclip into a straight wire, he stuck one end underneath the cardboard.

Immediately the other end of the paperclip burned his finger.

He yanked his hand away, shaking it for second. He pressed the hot tip of the paperclip into the paper and waited.

It smoked and smoldered for a few seconds, then burst into flame, like magic.

Drayden swiped some of the other papers, lit them, and stuck them under the pieces of wood. Within a few minutes, the fire raged.

"That was impressive, Private," Sergeant Greaney said.

Everyone gathered around, savoring the heat, struggling to dry off and warm up. The smell of seawater saturated the air as their sopping clothes baked in front of the flames. Smoke filled the room, but the broken windows allowed enough ventilation to breathe.

To Drayden, the warmth of the fire was heaven. "We're at Horseneck Beach State Reservation, which is around the border of Rhode Island and Massachusetts," he said to the group. "Unfortunately, our maps were destroyed in the water, but I studied them very carefully before we left. It's about eighty miles to Boston. I know the way." He guessed at the distance, and he roughly knew their location before they sank.

After removing his life vest, he pulled his knife out and hacked at the blue fabric.

"What are you doing?" Sidney asked.

He popped out one of the empty plastic water bottles, which even had caps on them. "Besides the water bottles in our packs, the rest of our water sank with the boat. We're gonna need more."

Drayden glared at the Guardians. "I suggest you guys do the same, since you didn't think to put your packs on before Captain Lindrick drove the boat into a rock."

Each vest contained eight bottles, which was way too many to carry. The opening at the top was also a bit small for collecting rainwater.

Drayden tugged on his left ear. How about using the extra bottles to make funnels? He cut a bottle in half and flipped the top part upside down, taping it to the top of a full bottle. Problem solved. He repeated the process with three other bottles, creating four bottles with funnels on top. When they were ready to go, he set them outside in the rain.

After watching, everyone else copied him, the Guardians borrowing supplies from the privates.

In the ensuing burst of activity, Drayden noticed Charlie depositing a stack of maps wrapped in some old paper into the fire. Charlie winked as he returned to his backpack.

Drayden set his pack down flat to use as a pillow. He discreetly removed his maps and eased them into his pants' pocket, before lying down. Catrice would probably want to cuddle with Eugene the hero, so he might as well get some sleep.

But she dropped her pack right next to Drayden's and laid beside him. She wrapped her arms around him and nestled into his shoulder, her soaked blonde locks smelling like the sea.

Sidney set her pack down a few feet away and collapsed. Charlie plopped his alongside hers.

"Eugene, do you want to share my pack as a pillow?" Sidney asked.

"Yeah, thanks a lot." He crawled off the floor and stretched out adjacent to her.

When Charlie tried to scoot closer to Sidney, she elbowed him in the head.

"Ow, fine, sorry," he said.

"You wanna come snuggle with Sergeant Greaney, sweetheart?" Lieutenant Duarte asked Charlie. He made kissing noises.

"I'd rather go for a swim right now; thanks," Charlie said, mumbling "jerkoff" under his breath.

Catrice kissed Drayden on the cheek.

The spark may be fading, but it was still there.

Drayden awoke cold and disoriented. His chilly, wet clothes clung to his body like they were painted on.

The sun shone into their cabin through the broken windows. Waves crashed on the beach outside, and the smoky smell of ash suffused the room. The Guardians had already left the cabin while the privates were asleep. Catrice was curled up in a ball facing away from Drayden.

He stroked her hair, which remained damp.

She awoke with a startle, her blue eyes sparkling in the sunlight.

"Time to get up," Drayden said.

Charlie had managed to snuggle up to Sidney overnight, spooning her.

Drayden tapped Catrice on the shoulder. "Watch this." He walked over to Sidney and gently shook her arm. "Sid, time to wake up."

"What?" She rubbed her eyes and yawned. "Okay."

Wait for it....

She looked behind her, and elbowed Charlie in the stomach. "Get off me!"

"Ow!" he yelled. "What the...what's going on?"

Drayden cracked up. "Sorry, Charlie."

Charlie scowled at Sidney. "Why do you keep hitting me?"

"You were wrapped around me like a giant baby monkey, you idiot," she said.

"Hmm." He giggled. "Then it was probably worth getting elbowed."

Sidney threw her boot at him. "That's why girls keep kicking you in the shins, because of shkat like that."

Charlie propped up to sitting. "You're right, I should be more like Eugene, so innocent, so nice. 'Hey, let me be your friend! That's all I want!' Yeah, right. At least I'm upfront about it."

Drayden could have kissed Charlie for saying that. He hoped Catrice was listening.

"Hey, what's the deal with the maps?" Sidney asked quietly.

Drayden scanned the area before answering. "The Guardians don't have a map and I'd like to keep it that way. I have the only one, which I need to study since I have no clue where we are. Charlie, can you watch out for the Guardians?"

"Yeah, bro." He strolled to the doorway barefoot and leaned against the rotting frame.

Drayden carefully unfolded his large map and Catrice joined him. A few different options popped up.

After a few minutes, Charlie loudly cleared his throat. He covered his mouth with his hand. "Coming," he coughed.

Drayden hastily refolded the map and stuffed it in his pocket.

Captain Lindrick entered the room, the other soldiers in tow. "Good morning. We've organized your water bottles for you, they're outside. Clearly the rest of this mission will occur on land."

Brilliant observation.

"Captain," Drayden said, "we need to think about food before anything else right now. That water will probably last us until we reach Boston. Since you guys left your packs on the boat, we don't have enough food for the eight of us. We'll certainly share everything we have, but it won't be enough.

"Here's what I think about the rest of the journey. We have no idea what the roads are like. I bet most of them are overgrown, so I suggest we hug the coastline. It'll take a little longer, but we have less risk of getting lost, and we can try fishing along the way. It should take us four days to complete the hike."

"Well done, Private," Captain Lindrick said.

"Let's eat first," Drayden said. He and the other privates pulled a small amount of food out of their packs and shared it. Everyone ate one apple, some nuts, and a carrot. The bread was still soaked with seawater. Hopefully it would dry out and be edible later.

After, Drayden jammed the water bottles into his pack, leaving it too full to zip. He kept the M16A4 rifle locked into it and strapped the pack on his back. If he needed a gun he'd draw his Glock from its holster, but he couldn't hit anything anyway. Sopping wet, and now loaded with water, the pack felt like a refrigerator on his back.

Lugging this thing around would be like giving a friend a piggy back ride for eighty miles.

Lacking backpacks, and with rifles to carry, the Guardians were having a tough time figuring out how to carry their water.

Drayden loved watching them attempt to stuff the bottles into their pockets, only to find these particular bottles too big. Plus, their pockets were loaded with ammunition, among other things.

"What about the life vests?" Drayden asked. "They're cloth. Use them as sacks."

The Guardians stared at him like he'd just invented air.

"Nice!" Eugene said. "Genius. See? This is why we needed you here."

"Yeah. Thanks," Drayden said. "We're going to head north up Highway 88 for roughly ten miles. Then we turn right onto Highway 177 for a mile or two and head east on Route 6 after that for a long stretch."

"Listen up," Lindrick said. "I want a single column formation out there with a scout up front. Lieutenant Duarte is the scout. Privates in the middle single file, flanked by me and Sergeant Greaney. Corporal Austin in the rear."

"Corporal in the rear," Charlie whispered. He couldn't stop giggling.

Sidney flicked his ear. "Shut up, Charlie."

"A refreshing ten-mile hike is cake. We'll reach Route 177 in under three hours, and we don't stop for a break until we do. Move out!"

"Sir, yes sir!" the Guardians and Charlie shouted in unison.

The march commenced. A salty, fishy smell permeated the humid air. The glaring sun and warmth dried their clothes within an hour, and their boots within two, which was more than enough time for wet boots to cause blisters on both feet.

The real world outside New America blew Drayden away. It was exactly as he had imagined when he lay beside his mother in Madison Square Park. They would gaze up at the sky, blocking out the buildings with their hands, pretending the whole world consisted of flora.

Everything was lush, including Highway 88. At one time, it must have been asphalt, like New America's streets. Now weeds, wild grasses, bushes, and even trees had sprouted through it. Though walkable, a bus couldn't make it thirty feet. A crumbling cement barrier, which probably separated the traffic in opposing directions, split the roadway down the middle.

The Guardians described the greenery as bramble, or over-growth. Bushes and weeds sprouted wild and uncontained. The PostCon world was gradually returning to its original state—how it existed before mankind came along and ruined it. Mother Nature was reclaiming what was once hers.

For the first hour, no one said a word, each of them absorbing their unfamiliar surroundings with curiosity and amazement. But the hike quickly grew monotonous and the privates' commitment to the formation and discipline got a little lazy.

The most unlikely of them broke the prolonged silence.

"Eugene, how did your parents feel about you going on this expedition?" Catrice asked quietly, slowing until she walked beside him.

"Uh…they were supportive. They're both teachers in the Palace. The Guardians permitted me to tell them the purpose, and they understood how crucial it was. What did your parents think?"

She hesitated. "I don't know. They still live in the Dorms."

"Oh, I got it. That means you didn't want them in the Palace." He raised his hands. "Say no more."

Damn, he's good, Drayden thought.

"Thank you," she said, staring at the ground as she walked. "Most people don't get that I don't want to talk about it."

"You never learned how to swim, huh?"

Catrice took a swig of water. "No. But that's twice in three weeks I've needed to know how. I guess it's time to learn."

"Wait; if there was a swimming challenge in the Initiation, how did you pass it?"

Charlie raised his finger high in the air ahead of them without turning around.

Catrice chuckled. "Charlie carried me on his back. I just held on."

"You the man, Charlie," Eugene said.

Drayden's neck stiffened. Two could play at this game. "Hey, Sid," he called, "you have any trouble swimming in that water back there? I know you're a great swimmer."

She regarded him as if he were insane. "I'm a good swimmer. I've never even dreamed of water like that. Without the life vest, I would have drowned."

He inched closer to her. "Hey, my brother told me they're placing him and my father in our apartment building. Did they do the same with your sister and grandparents?"

Her face brightened. "Yes! Technically Nora will live with them, but if I want she can stay with me. I'm so thankful to be able to take care of her. She's such an angel. So innocent. I'm praying we reach Boston so we can get them moved to nicer apartments." She cocked her head. "I wonder what jobs we'll have, by the way. If we make it back."

Drayden shrugged. "I think you have a career with the Guardians if you want it. I have no idea if the Bureau will give us options. Nobody's really said."

With it spoken aloud, it was one of the things bugging him about this mission. The Bureau had provided zero guidance on what would happen when they came back. It was as if the Bureau wasn't counting on their return. Originally, Premier Holst had described their apartments as temporary, but nobody had discussed moving them, nor had employment been addressed.

Something caught Drayden's eye. At first, it didn't register as out of place until he looked again. "Captain Lindrick!" he whispered with force.

Everyone stopped. The Guardians raised their rifles. "What is it, Private?" Lindrick asked.

Lieutenant Duarte, who as scout regularly checked on the group, rushed back.

Drayden approached the red object off to the side of the road and knelt beside it.

It was an apple. A half-eaten one. There were no apple trees around, and the eaten part was still white. It hadn't oxidized and turned brown.

"This isn't ours," Drayden said. "It's fresh. Someone just dropped this here."

"Tracks." Sergeant Greaney's eyes followed footsteps in the mud heading into the woods.

"People are alive here," Sidney said. "Should we go search for them?"

Sergeant Greaney lowered his rifle. "We have no idea if they're friendly. They know these woods. We don't. We need to stick to the road."

"The sergeant is right," Lindrick said. "If there was a person here, we're bound to run into others."

Drayden wasn't sure if they should follow or not. He couldn't believe that people were alive out here. How had they survived? What were their lives like?

"Let's keep moving," Captain Lindrick said. "It's can't be much further to Highway 177."

They continued their hike with the lieutenant resuming scout duty. Everyone remained quiet, scanning the woods for people. After half an hour, the excitement had worn off.

The highway ran in a straightaway in this section. Though weeds and tall grasses covered it like an African plain, no trees obstructed it for the next mile or so.

"Guess it was nothing," Charlie muttered.

A man bolted across the street a hundred yards in front of them, from the woods on the left to the woods on the right.

Lieutenant Duarte raised his rifle and fired it in one swift motion. The deafening boom echoed throughout the silent world like an explosion.

"Hold your fire!" Lindrick yelled as the Guardians raised their weapons and everyone got down.

Lieutenant Duarte hustled back.

"What are you doing?" Drayden asked. "How could you fire at him? The poor guy was probably trying to get away from us."

"I'm protecting you and us. And I didn't ask for your opinion."

"Don't shoot these people!" Drayden yelled. "We need to talk to them. Catrice? Do you think we should follow him? There must be a community around here."

Her cheeks were red and sweat beaded on her nose. "We have a four-day hike. I'm guessing we'll see others."

"I think she should be in charge, not you, string bean," Lieutenant Duarte said.

Drayden gritted his teeth. He could foresee a showdown with this Duarte creep at some point in the future.

"Let's move out," Captain Lindrick said. "Guardians, I want your weapons sling-ready, but don't fire on sight."

They continued the slow march. No landmarks stood out before they reached Highway 177. Hopefully it would be marked.

Finally, they reached a part where the roadway widened. A second lane emerged on the right and forked off ahead. That was it. If they considered Highway 88 overgrown, it was just the warmup. Highway 177 was the main event. Barely a trace of roadway remained. It was all bramble.

CHAPTER 16

The group took a much-needed break near the entrance to Highway 177. After peeing in some bushes, Drayden thought about distribution of the food again.

The Bureau had assembled the packs. He was pretty sure the Guardians hadn't taken stock of them before the boat sank, meaning they didn't know exactly how much food each contained, and he preferred they not find out. Not having enough food for everyone could escalate into a dangerous situation. The privates would be easily outmuscled in a physical confrontation with the Guardians.

Rather than aggregating all the remaining food and splitting it eight ways, Drayden collected a few items from each private for the Guardians: a pear, a damp slice of bread, and a boiled potato.

Under the shade of a sprawling tree, Eugene crashed with the privates—or technically with Catrice—while the other Guardians rested off by themselves.

Drayden wanted to show the Guardians he wasn't intimidated, so he personally delivered their food. Only Sergeant Greaney thanked him when he passed it out. On the way back, he watched Catrice, who was sharing other items from her own pack openly with Eugene. Special things, like a cookie.

Although the growing closeness between them was a problem for him, Catrice's misguided generosity was a problem for everyone. It wasn't fair. The food in their packs was effectively community food now, and she shouldn't have been oversharing it with the super cute boy she fancied. Rather than say anything, he grumbled to himself and plopped down beside Sidney.

She took off her boots. "My feet are killing me. Anyone else have blisters?"

Drayden groaned. "Yup. Both feet."

"Mine are numb," Charlie said. "They feel like boiled potatoes."

Drayden chugged water. "These boots aren't made for walking. Sadly, we're nine miles into an eighty-five-mile walk."

Charlie gave him a sarcastic thumbs-up. "Thanks for that reminder."

Drayden couldn't help himself and eavesdropped on Catrice and Eugene.

"Doesn't being out here give you all sorts of ideas for things to draw?" Eugene asked. "I wish I had a sketch pad with me."

"Oh my God, totally. I'd love to draw this tree we're sitting under. We don't have this tree in New America, and the leaves are so beautiful."

Drayden felt sick to his stomach, contemplating whether the two of them could sketch him putting a bullet into his own head.

Charlie poked him. "Told you." He snickered. "Stole."

"Shut up," Drayden snapped. "You also said love moves around like wildflowers. Wildflowers don't move."

"You're wasting your time with that waif," Sidney said quietly. "She has no soul. She's empty inside, Dray. That's so not cool, what she's doing right now. Why would you want to be with someone who treats you like that?"

He wasn't sure. As Shahnee had said, a spark existed between them that he couldn't explain with logic. It wasn't just that they were similar, that they both liked math, and were top students. It was more than that. Wasn't it?

Though she wasn't paying him any attention, and in fact was totally ignoring him, he still liked her. Maybe even loved her. Fine, she wasn't at her best girlfriend form at the moment, but nobody knew her the way he did. They didn't witness how thoughtful and caring she was in private.

Whatever the status of their undefined relationship, she apparently didn't consider it as serious as he did. He'd never forget her expression when he called her his girlfriend. If he acted like a jealous boyfriend now, he might scare her away, or make her think less of him. But if he said nothing, Eugene was free to take his best crack at her, and he was hitting it out of the park. Drayden needed to show Catrice that he was every bit as good, or better, than Eugene.

Charlie rubbed his belly. "I don't know about you guys. I'm stuffed after that half pear and potato sandwich."

Charlie's predictable humor underscored a serious issue. The food situation was a major problem. They needed a lot more, but how? Drayden grew angrier at Catrice for her schoolgirl flirting with the new boy. He needed her to brainstorm with him. This was a life-or-death situation.

They hadn't seen any animals to hunt. Plus, the scientists said not to eat them anyway. If the opportunity arose, they could try fishing, but they lacked gear and wouldn't encounter water for a while. They needed to find a camp of people and ask for food.

"Captain Lindrick," Drayden said, "Charlie raises a valid point. We don't have nearly enough food. The next person we see, we follow. Go where they lead us."

"Fine," Lindrick said. "We go where I say we go. If we find a village, everyone follows my lead. Understood? This is my area."

"Deal," Drayden said. "But no shooting."

Lieutenant Duarte smirked. He tossed his knife in the air and caught it.

Lieutenant Duarte swung the machete with such force and aggression it was clear he relished it. The guy seemed to have anger issues and some inner need to cut things.

Where was he hiding a machete?

Duarte led the trek into the wilderness of Highway 177, hacking and slicing as he walked. The bramble provided some welcome shade from the early afternoon sun. The whole group now walked single file, with Duarte and Lindrick up front, and Greaney bringing up the rear.

Drayden had worked things so Catrice had to walk between Charlie and Sidney, which meant she couldn't discuss drawing with Eugene. Petty, sure, but he had to do something. Unfortunately, they would have seventy-five more miles to marvel at the fascinating leaves. He groaned inwardly, knowing he needed to get out of this negative funk, since he was only making himself uglier.

Eugene quietly whistled with a trill effect, the way Drayden imagined a songbird would sound. Lindrick and Duarte both stopped and turned their heads back.

"Check it out, nine o'clock," Eugene whispered, flashing his rifle that way.

The ruins of a house were hidden to their left, set back a bit from the street amongst the overgrowth. Cement steps gave way to a faded red front door that led nowhere. Everything else besides the chimney was missing. As they carried on, the outlines of additional homes periodically popped up. Some were still standing, though were mostly empty shells.

Nobody lived in these houses. They were long abandoned, which made Drayden curious where that running man lived. He may have been a lone survivor, a nomad, scrounging off the land without the benefit of a larger community. That would make finding food unlikely.

Despite their crawl through the forest, it was only an hour hike to Route 6. After forty-five minutes, the brush thinned, and they entered a wide-open space. What remained of the asphalt of Highway 177 spread out in every direction, with several old buildings around its borders. Duarte stopped, and everyone took stock of the area.

"Captain Lindrick, three o'clock," Sergeant Greaney whispered forcefully.

Captain Lindrick whipped his rifle to the right, panning it back and forth. Everyone saw it at the same time, their eyes heading skyward.

Smoke. A large plume rose to the right, deep into the woods, with the remnants of a road leading toward it.

Captain Lindrick lowered his weapon and faced the group. "Time to go to work. We follow that road until we see who's burning that fire. We go quiet, and we go in heavy. High-ready."

"What does that mean?" Drayden studied the Guardians. "High-ready."

"It means we go in with our weapons up," Eugene said, "ready to act if necessary."

They were talking about people surviving in the wilderness. Drayden did yearn to prove he could be tough and strong like the Guardians, yet there was a difference between toughness and brutality. "Captain, I think that's excessive. We're going to frighten these people."

"I agree with Drayden," Catrice said.

Captain Lindrick turned red, gritting his teeth. "Privates. This part of the mission I'm unequivocally in charge of. If you choose to keep your weapon holstered, I can't stop you, but we intend to make sure everyone is safe until we can .guarantee the situation is secure. We have no idea what kind of threat we're dealing with. Is that understood?"

Drayden hesitated, finally muttering, "Yes, sir."

Lindrick checked his rifle. "No talking. Single file. Everyone as quiet as possible."

Lieutenant Duarte slid his machete into a sleeve in his pants and raised his rifle, leading the way. Though overgrown, the road was passable, bordered by houses that appeared less deserted the further they went.

Duarte dropped to a squat and motioned with his arm for the others to lower down. Everybody crouched.

Drayden's eyes bulged at the sight.

In a clearing ahead, a bonfire raged. Several makeshift wooden stands surrounded it, holding rangy sticks over the fire with objects hanging off their tips.

Food.

People were cooking. A good fifteen survivors, some young children, milled around the fire, and others were coming and going. A mother carried her baby in a maroon sash around her neck. Everyone looked awful—dirty, skinny, swaddled in rags.

Drayden wouldn't have believed it if he hadn't seen it himself. People were *alive.* They'd somehow outlived the Confluence and found a way to endure its aftermath. One glimpse of them revealed survival was a struggle. Either people in this particular region were special in some way, or these survivors had found each other and formed a community. It was astounding. Besides securing food, he needed to ask some questions.

"Everyone follow my lead," Captain Lindrick whispered. "Our goal is to capture food, and clearly they have some. We get in and get out. These people must be immune to Aeru, but we might not be. We can't spend too much time making small talk."

"Whoa, hold on," Drayden said. "They're starving and beyond poor. We can't take their food. We can ask if they'll share some with us. That way we can find out what they know. How they survived. We'll scare them to death if we go in with our weapons out. There are children around."

"We must do it this way for our own protection," Eugene said. "They could be packing weapons for all we know, and might shoot on sight."

Lieutenant Duarte jutted his jaw. "Private, you will follow the captain's orders or I'll cut your throat myself."

"Fine," Drayden ground out.

Captain Lindrick flashed some hand signals Drayden didn't understand, and Eugene joined the captain and lieutenant up front. Only Drayden and Catrice kept their weapons holstered. Sergeant Greaney remained behind the privates while Lindrick, Duarte, and Eugene advanced toward the bonfire with their rifles drawn. Not running, but walking briskly, semi-crouched, Lindrick took the middle spot and the two other Guardians flanked way out to the sides. The privates followed a good distance back, with Greaney close enough to protect them if necessary.

At thirty yards away, everyone around the bonfire froze. Several people raised their hands in the air and one young boy burst into tears.

A man with shaggy brown hair and a flowing scraggly beard, wearing a weathered tunic, stepped forward with his arms up, cutting off the Guardians before they reached the fire.

Captain Lindrick stopped a few feet shy of him, training his weapon on the man's face.

The man neither flinched nor cowered, and even smiled, waving one of his raised hands. "We don't want any trouble," he said calmly. "We are peaceful people."

Enough of this.

Drayden marched up, the blistering air near the bonfire searing his skin. He pushed the barrel of Lindrick's rifle down and offered his hand to the man.

The man shook it, his hand limp.

Lindrick was visibly indignant at Drayden's insubordination.

"Hi, my name's Drayden." He forced a smile. "What's yours?"

"Marty. Pleased to meet you."

He spoke weirdly, sounding far different than they did. When he said "Marty" it sounded like "Mah-ty."

The other Guardians lowered their weapons.

"I'm sorry about that." Drayden shot the captain a scornful look. "We mean you no harm. We're from New Amer...New York. We were sailing to Boston and our boat sank. So now we're hiking there, and we're unfamiliar with the outside world. We're in desperate need of food. Do you have any you could spare?"

Lieutenant Duarte scoffed, his expression saying they didn't need to ask permission; they could take whatever they wished.

"They look like they be eatin' better than us!" someone shouted from the bonfire.

"John!" Marty yelled back without turning around. He cocked his head. "Sure, friend, we'd be happy to share. But we don't have much to spare. As you can see," he tilted his head backward, "we're barely getting by ourselves. Daisy!" he hollered, never breaking eye contact with Drayden. "Get these nice gentlemen a chicken, a head of lettuce, and a loaf of bread, please. How'd that be?"

"That would be amazing. Thank you. We really appreciate it. Can I ask you a few more questions? I'm just wondering...how are you all alive? You weren't killed by Aeru."

Marty shrugged. "No idea. A bunch of us in this area simply didn't die. Some of the others came from farther away and joined our camp. We do some farming to get by."

"Do you know if there are people in Boston?" Drayden asked. "And do you ever see anyone else?"

Marty's gaze started flashing to some of the surrounding houses. "You're the first people we seen in a while. Don't know if there's people in Boston. We used to get harassed by some gangs that would steal our food. There's clusters of people here and there."

A pale woman with hollowed out eyes sidled up to Marty, clutching a cloth sack. He took it and handed it to Drayden. "There you go. Enjoy."

"Thank you for your kindness," Drayden said, the aroma of burnt chicken already making his mouth water. "All of you, thank you. We appreciate your help."

Some of the survivors held each other, cowering in fear. Others stared, expressionless. Nobody responded, leaving only the sound of the crackling bonfire.

Movement inside one of the nearby houses caught Drayden's attention.

"Private, time to go," Captain Lindrick mumbled.

Drayden spun around and sauntered off, joined by the other privates. Sergeant Greaney was already back up the road a bit, anxiously watching the action. Drayden checked behind him.

Lindrick, Duarte, and Eugene were backing away, their fingers on the triggers.

These people shared their food out of fear, not compassion. They clearly could not spare any, and by their own admission, had seen their food stolen before. Who knew how desperate they were to reclaim that chicken?

Once out of sight, Lindrick picked up the pace. "Let's go, now. Run."

Running was easier said than done for the privates, with the heavy packs bouncing on their backs. They sprinted until they reached Highway 177, where they huddled up.

"Why did we run?" Catrice asked through heavy breaths.

Eugene had barely broken a sweat. "I think a few people inside a house were arming themselves to try and get that food back. Captain Lindrick and I both saw it."

Drayden had noticed something as well, though it may have been nothing. "Better safe than sorry," he said. "But I don't think those people were about to start a firefight with all those kids around. They were scared, and relieved we didn't take everything."

"Which we should have done," Duarte said.

"No, we shouldn't have," Sidney snapped. "Those people are starving, and they have children to feed."

Just because their group was stronger didn't mean they should abuse that power. They didn't, and they procured the food they needed without sacrificing the dignity and needs of the survivors. It felt gratifying to be right, and to do the right thing. However, Drayden deflated when he opened the sack. One miniature burned chicken, a moldy loaf of bread, and a tiny head of lettuce were inside. He let the sack flop down by his side.

"We're going to need more food."

One sign read "Fred's Tire Repair." Shuttered businesses lined portions of Route 6, a wider road than Highway 177. A broad section of tall grasses divided two lanes heading east and two heading west. It was badly overgrown as well, with towering bramble and trees sprouting up through the asphalt.

"Eventually, we'll reach a little city called New Bedford," Drayden said to no one in particular. He'd already studied this part of the map, though once in New Bedford, he'd have to sneak a peek at it again. "We should be able to make it there before dark."

Drayden's mind raced as they walked. The discovery of that colony had sweeping implications. One sent a tingle down his spine. *His mother might be alive.* The villagers they'd discovered may have been born with a natural immunity to Aeru, or perhaps some regions were miraculously spared. The other possibility? The Aeru bug no longer existed. With nothing left to kill, the bacteria may have died off.

He was no doctor or scientist, so this was all amateur speculation. He hadn't thought too much about Aeru since they'd been on land. Whatever its status, they might be at risk despite receiving the vaccine. Still, there wasn't anything they could do about it. Worrying about Aeru wouldn't make them any safer, so he vowed to block it from his mind. One less thing to stress over.

They had encountered survivors within the first few hours of their land trek. Sure, it could have been dumb luck, and they'd bumped into the only other people on the planet. That was improbable, though. Marty even said scattered groups existed. Small communities, albeit struggling, were reproducing and growing. Given the vast number of people exiled from New America, they could all live in a village somewhere too. Like in the Bronx, where the exiled were all discarded. But if that were true, why had they never been seen?

Drayden recalled what Kim had said about the Bureau controlling the information. Citizens were always told that no exiled people had been seen again. What if they *had*, and the Bureau lied about it? It was conceivable they'd attempted to reenter New America many times, only to be rejected or shot by the Guardians who manned the walls. If those exiles lived outside the city, they would constitute a considerable assemblage of people eager to take down the Bureau. There was his potential army.

Drayden's excitement grew. He needed to bounce these ideas off someone who could reason through it, although he couldn't reveal his secret objective. He slowed until Catrice and Eugene caught up to him. "Catrice, do you realize what this means? Finding those people."

"Yeah, people are alive. Maybe lots of them. They're immune to Aeru, or it's gone, or something. It's pretty incredible."

"Yup. You know what else it means?" Drayden pressed his hands together, as if in prayer. "My mother may be alive."

"She might be. All the exiles could." Catrice carried on, unfazed.

That was it? His *mom* might be alive. The person whose exile eventually led him to risk his life in the Initiation. Whose exile convinced him to join a team of revolutionaries out to topple the Bureau, though Catrice wasn't aware of that part. That was all she had to say?

"Holy cow," Eugene said. "That's awesome, Dray; you're right. You know what? On our return trip, we should search for her. I can help you."

Drayden was floored. He squeezed Eugene's shoulder. "Would you do that? Thank you, Eugene. Yes, that's exactly what I want to do." He mumbled, "At least someone cares my mom might be alive."

Catrice shot eye daggers at him. "What do you want me to do, a cartwheel? Congratulations, your mother might be alive. I barely ever *had* parents. I haven't a clue what it's like to care if they're alive. Okay?" She folded her arms and sped up, storming ahead of him in a huff.

Drayden and Eugene looked at each other. Eugene made a face.

"You got a real way with the ladies, Private," Lieutenant Duarte said from behind them.

When Catrice was out of earshot, Eugene slung his arm around Drayden's shoulders. "Don't worry about it. Let her cool down. Something real bad must have happened with her parents. I'm sure she's happy for you. But it must bring up some painful memories for her."

Again, leave it to Eugene to be the voice of reason. If he actually *were* angling to steal Drayden's girlfriend, he was an incredible actor. He was also becoming a friend, despite Drayden's own warning to Charlie not to blindly trust the kid.

Drayden gulped warm water from one of his bottles. The Catrice situation aside, a more pressing issue demanded attention. They had enough food for a meager meal tonight, and still had some in their packs, but not enough for three additional days of hiking. Not even close. Add in the exertion of twenty-mile hikes and starvation was on the table.

CHAPTER 17

Drayden's feet were numb from walking. Besides his blisters, which were red-hot.

At any moment he could roll his gimpy ankle. His neck and lower back ached from the heavy pack. His knees throbbed from twenty miles with the extra weight. How could they possibly walk all the way to Boston?

They'd been hiking on Route 6 for a few hours. Lately, their surroundings had become more commercial and industrial. They passed an old pizza restaurant, a furniture warehouse, and a car dealership with an overgrown lot of rusted vehicles.

The car dealership might be worth a shot. Even though the cars outside were scrap metal, the ones inside might be in decent shape. Um, no. On second thought, that was a stupid idea. No chance they would still work.

The group marched up a gentle slope that seemed to go on for miles. Once at the top, the region grew residential. Abandoned homes dotted the area, and side roads branched off from Route 6, which was less overgrown. The following blocks became more commercial again, with stores clustered in long buildings. An intact sign read, "Harve's Shoe Box."

Wooden poles lined the streets every hundred feet or so. Black cables of varying thickness hung from them, coiling on the ground like snakes. Further along, decrepit homes and businesses were bunched ever closer together, as they would be in a city.

"I think we've reached New Bedford," Drayden said. "But we're not in the main section yet."

"When we reach the main part, we'll find shelter and set up camp," Captain Lindrick said. "We'll eat the food we have, then start fresh in the morning."

They reached a major intersection with a wide street called Rockdale Avenue. Past that the road narrowed, with buildings hugging the streets, like in the Palace. Except the structures here, mostly old bars and restaurants, were tiny and in ruins. Vegetation grew over everything, including the buildings.

Drayden recalled one of the lowly Dorm occupations back home—clearing weeds from sidewalks and streets. That task was never complete.

A few blocks past Rockdale Avenue the city returned to residential. Diminutive homes bordered the street, bundled close together. While shoddy, some appeared livable.

Lieutenant Duarte, leading the pack, stopped short and extended both arms. Everyone froze. He touched his index finger to his lips and pointed up to the left. A black plume of smoke rose a few blocks away.

Drayden noted the street sign read Beech Street.

"Listen up," Captain Lindrick whispered. "We don't know when we'll find another camp. We need to go in and get more food. Everyone follows me, the lieutenant, and the corporal, and we go high-ready again. Sergeant Greaney will stay behind the privates."

The other privates looked at Drayden.

No. This was his mission. These people out here weren't the enemy; they were survivors—poor ones. They'd struggled and suffered, with only their human spirit sustaining them day to day. They didn't deserve to be robbed, or even scared. Overpowering the survivors didn't make the Guardians strong. Showing compassion did. Civility might inspire the survivors to aid them in other ways, like giving advice. His chin up and chest out, Drayden stepped up to Lindrick.

"Captain Lindrick, I'm in charge here. We did it your way last time and nearly caused a group heart attack. These people out here are weak and starving. They're harmless. We don't go in heavy or high-ready or whatever. We go in light, I guess, with our weapons lowered. We may come out of this with less food, but we'll leave with our dignity, and they'll keep theirs. They may also help us."

Captain Lindrick spun around and spat, murmuring something before turning back red-faced. "Fine. You want to be in charge? You think this is a game, where things are fair, and there's rainbows and ice cream for people who play nice? Fine. Let's do it your way then."

Lieutenant Duarte glowered at him. "Captain."

"No, no, Private Coulson has been begging to play leader all day. Let's give him what he wants. Then see if he still wants it." Lindrick stretched his arm forward, palm up, inviting Drayden to lead the way up Beech Street.

"Thank you," said Drayden. "And when I say we do it my way, we do it my way. Nobody's weapons raised."

He strode up Beech Street as dusk settled over New Bedford, Massachusetts.

Everyone followed up the short block, and they reached an intersection with an unmarked street, and homes on each corner. The bonfire raged a few blocks ahead, but nobody seemed to be around it.

He crossed the unmarked street and continued. Halfway up the next block they passed a white house on their left and two brown houses on their right.

Something whizzed by Drayden's head. The wind from it kissed his face.

What the...?

"Get down!" Duarte screamed.

Drayden squatted and several more rocketed over him, right where his head had been.

Arrows.

Gunfire erupted behind him. A hand grabbed his shoulder, yanking him back.

Drayden lost his balance and fell backward onto his backpack, twisting his injured ankle. Sharp pain exploded up his leg. He cried out.

"Behind the house!" someone shouted.

His head spinning, Drayden scrambled to his feet and hobbled through the pain toward the white house.

Catrice and Charlie sprinted ahead of him. Arrows zipped all around them.

Deafening gunshots rang out. Duarte and Lindrick stood their ground in the street, firing at the second brown house on the right, pounding it with bullets. They backed up but continued to shoot.

Drayden made it behind the house, his heart pounding, and knelt beside Catrice, Charlie, and Sidney. With a trembling hand, he drew the pistol from his hip.

Arrows flew wildly. Eugene and Sergeant Greaney stood at the edge of the structure, pumping ear-splitting rounds from their rifles.

"Cover!" Lindrick yelled.

Eugene and Greaney slithered back into the street on their stomachs. They blasted steady shots at the same brown home, while Lindrick and Duarte backpedaled faster in the direction of the white house.

Sergeant Greaney rose to his knees and tossed something through the air past the brown house. A massive explosion splintered wood and launched debris everywhere. A mushroom cloud of smoke and fire billowed in the air.

Two emaciated, bearded men hobbled out from the wreckage. Badly injured, they limped across the street.

Eugene dove and rolled into the middle of Beech Street. He unloaded two rounds from his rifle at them. Blood sprayed behind the men. Both crumpled to the ground.

Drayden started hyperventilating. He checked on Catrice, crouching next to him.

Her eyes were crazed, the pupils so dilated they were barely blue. The pistol in her hand was shaking. Beside her, Charlie and Sidney were twitchy, kneeling with rifles in high-ready position.

Captain Lindrick, Sergeant Greaney, and Lieutenant Duarte gathered behind the white house now. Eugene sprinted back and everyone huddled together.

Drayden touched Catrice's arm. "You all right?"

She nodded.

An arrow smashed into the wall and stuck, an inch from her face. She screamed.

The Guardians spun around and pumped rounds behind them, back toward Route 6.

"Get down!" Eugene yelled to the privates, loading another magazine into his rifle.

Drayden and Catrice laid flat on their stomachs. He reached out and clutched her hand.

Charlie and Sidney both knelt, firing their rifles randomly at their invisible enemy.

"Anyone see where they came from?" Greaney yelled, panting.

Eugene pointed. "That red house on the corner, I think."

"We're trapped," Charlie said. "They're in front and behind. How do we get back to Route 6?"

"The same way we came," Captain Lindrick said. "Those little buggers are hiding behind those bushes by the red house. I'm lobbing a grenade there, and the second it detonates, we move. Two-by-two cover formation. On my mark. Me and Corporal Austin up front, the lieutenant and sergeant in the rear. Privates, follow me. Shoot anything that moves."

Lindrick hurled the grenade. Everyone covered their ears.

When it exploded, the ground shook. Branches and dirt flew through the air, and smoke blanketed the area.

Eugene blazed the path, spraying gunfire everywhere.

Arrows flew at them from the right.

The Guardians pummeled the area with bullets.

They reached the unnamed street.

Movement in the yard on the right caught Drayden's eye. A wiry man covered in hair ducked beneath a shrub.

Drayden raised his pistol with his right hand, bracing it beneath with his left. His hands shaking, he fired six rapid shots at the bush.

Pop...pop pop pop...pop pop...

He missed. The man jumped up and charged, aiming his bow and arrow directly at Drayden.

Drayden froze.

I'm about to die.

He raised his pistol.

A bullet pierced the man through the forehead. He toppled backward and landed in an awkward pose.

Drayden looked at his gun before checking behind him.

Sidney stood there, with bulging eyes, her rifle still locked on the man.

"Privates, move out!" Lindrick screamed.

Drayden sprinted his heart out back toward Route 6, fighting through the burning in his lungs and the pain in his left ankle, exploding with each step. Chilly dusk air suffused with smoke blew in his eyes, making them water.

Catrice ran ahead of him, with Charlie and Sidney following.

The Guardians periodically stopped and fired rounds back in the direction of the bonfire. When they reached Route 6, they turned left and kept running.

After a block, cheers erupted behind them from what sounded like a huge crowd of people.

They'd run, block after block, until it became too dark. Lieutenant Duarte stopped and everyone gathered in a circle, doubled over, huffing and puffing.

Between deep breaths, Captain Lindrick said, "We need to camp for the night." He glared at Drayden, as if daring him to try and take charge again.

Drayden lowered his eyes. Any moment now Captain Lindrick would eviscerate him for that disaster back there.

They found themselves in front of a business that resembled a single-story home, with a slanted roof. It contained a narrow parking lot in front, overgrown with weeds. The building itself didn't appear much better, with broken windows, a crumbling facade, and no door. On the street corner, a tall sign advertised the business, reading "E-Z Clean Laundry Center."

"Privates," Lindrick said. "I need a flashlight."

Drayden wasn't about to surrender his flashlight to the Guardians. The privates held a major advantage over the Guardians with the food, maps, and whatever else the packs held.

Sidney pulled one out of her pack and handed it to Lindrick. Switching it on, he shined it inside a window, angling it in different directions.

"This will work," he said, walking back to the others. "It's empty inside, and there's a giant hole in the roof, so we should be able to start a fire." He glowered at Drayden again. "Provided the private here can do his little battery trick."

Lieutenant Duarte spat on Drayden's boot. "You mean, can he do it without getting us all killed."

No one came to Drayden's defense, and he couldn't blame them. He was still trembling from the battle. He'd endangered everyone's lives. That arrow had missed Catrice's face by an inch. How would he ever forgive himself if she were wounded or killed? The image sent chills down his spine. He felt for the survivors who had died too. He saw Eugene kill two men, and Sidney killed the one who nearly shot an arrow through Drayden's head. Many others probably perished from all the bullets and grenades.

He'd only wanted to show compassion toward the impoverished souls in the camps. Just because the result was an attack didn't mean it was the wrong attitude. That would be confusing cause and effect. Treating survivors like animals, and stealing from them on top of it, was wrong. He wasn't sure he'd have too many believers in his faction anymore.

Sidney glanced at Lindrick, apparently expecting him to return her flashlight. Instead he slipped it in his pants pocket without a word.

"Hey, I know there's a lot going on, and everyone's probably hating me right now," Drayden said to her. "But thanks for saving my life, again. I don't even know what else to say, except thank you. You're a hell of a shot."

Sidney hugged him and brushed her hand along his cheek. "It's okay. It's not your fault. Don't worry; we're still with you, always."

He loved her for that. He needed to hear it.

Inside the building, cracks streaked through the tiled floor like miniature bolts of lightning. Random articles of clothing littered the space—a tattered shirt, a pair of jeans. Both front and back doors were missing, generating some breezy cross-ventilation.

Drayden didn't feel inclined to give orders to build the fire. He dug out his battery and paperclip and clutched his flashlight to scour for kindling.

The Guardians rested against a distant wall, flashing Drayden stink-eyes anytime he dared to make eye contact. Eugene was whispering in Captain Lindrick's ear.

"Eugene," Charlie said, "let's find some things to burn."

"Yeah, sure."

Charlie clicked on his flashlight and led the way out the front door.

Drayden approached Catrice, who was sitting alone against a wall, and knelt beside her.

She was shell-shocked, her expression blank.

"Hey, are you okay?" he asked. "I'm sorry about that."

She gazed at him vacantly through puffy red eyes. "I'm fine," she whispered. "That was so scary. I almost got shot in the face with an arrow. What would I have done? What if it didn't kill me? I can't stop thinking about trying to rip it out." She rubbed her cheek as she spoke.

He sighed, staring at the floor, trying and failing not to picture it.

"Drayden, I'm not blaming you." She touched his knee. "There's no way you could have known. You were trying to do the right thing, be a good person. It's not your fault. And I'm fine; I'm not hurt."

He did appreciate her words, though they did little to quell his guilt. "Thanks. Unfortunately, I think everyone else blames me."

Charlie and Eugene returned with a few short tree branches and some yellowed paper, which they piled in the center of the room.

Drayden pulled off his battery trick, and within minutes, the fire was roaring.

Nobody offered compliments this time, but they did crowd around the fire. He and Sidney laid out the chicken, bread, and lettuce. Lieutenant Duarte whipped out his knife and carved everything into pieces, spreading them out on top of the cloth sack.

From each private, Drayden collected a piece of bread, an apple, and a boiled potato for the Guardians. They'd earned it today. He hesitated, not wanting to be the one to deliver it.

Sidney read his mind and picked up the food. "I'll do it."

The privates and Guardians devoured everything in minutes.

Drayden had never eaten chicken before, since it wasn't available in the Dorms, nor in the Palace as far as he knew. Chickens were for producing eggs, not eating. It was the best thing he'd ever tasted, similar to fish but a bit chewier. He wondered whether the Guardians had ever eaten chicken before, having witnessed Duarte expertly slice it up.

Drayden awaited a tongue-lashing from the Guardians, especially Lindrick. The captain had staged a grand display of handing over authority to Drayden, making his failure even more acute.

Besides the dirty looks, nobody said anything. After eating, the Guardians retreated to the far side of the room, kicked off their boots, and collapsed against the wall. Eugene didn't join them, however. He stayed with the privates, who'd lined up their packs against the opposite wall to use as pillows.

Would Catrice still be sleeping with him tonight? Eugene, among others, had saved her yet again. He had demonstrated incredible courage, strength, and skill. It was obvious why they'd selected him for this mission. In battle, he was totally composed, made smart decisions, and executed everything flawlessly. He also appeared to be a perfect shot, taking out two wounded men with only two bullets.

Drayden wasn't worried about his own bravery or intelligence, the traits the Bureau treasured enough to test for them in the Initiation. He could match Eugene in those, but Eugene was simply stronger and tougher, not to mention more skilled. He could protect them, protect Catrice, and he did.

Drayden recalled what Shahnee had said, that life and relationships weren't a contest of skills, that he needed to be himself and stop worrying so much. He also remembered what he'd told her, that the star of the basketball team scored all the girls. Eugene was the star of the basketball team. Drayden was the team statistician. Or the waterboy.

Once again, though, Catrice snuggled up to him. Eugene laid down on her other side, sharing a pack with Sidney, who cuddled up to him. Charlie slid next to her, as close as possible without getting elbowed.

Drayden briefly considered whether they needed a lookout, since New Bedford was obviously home to hostile forces. The Guardians didn't seem concerned, so he figured they must have been far enough away. As he drifted off to sleep, one final thought floated through his mind. Perhaps the Guardians would let this episode slide, eventually realizing it wasn't his fault. Their anger presupposed that the attack could have been prevented by going in heavy. Clearly, they would have been attacked either way. Having weapons raised or not was irrelevant.

He wasn't ceding control of this mission, no matter how pissed they were.

The early morning rays of sunlight through the windows awoke Drayden. The disorientation lasted a moment. Where was he? He had terrible cotton mouth.

The Guardians stirred on their side of the room. They checked their weapons, reloaded ammunition, and strapped on their boots.

Drayden rubbed his eyes. His legs ached, his ankle throbbed, and his back and neck were insanely sore from the heavy backpack.

He debated taking a painkiller before deciding to save them. There was probably more pain to come.

With the fire having died hours ago, the room was chilly. The morning air and ashes smelled of winter, and like New America, was utterly silent.

Drayden's stomach growled, already begging for food.

Catrice had flipped over sometime during the night, and she'd snuggled up to Eugene. In fact, her head rested on his shoulder, her arm draped across his chest.

Drayden wondered if that happened unintentionally while everyone was asleep, or after he fell asleep and they were both awake. His heart sank a little further.

He gently shook her shoulder.

She flinched, waking Eugene. She snatched her arm away, sharing an awkward glance and smile with Eugene. "Sorry," she said.

He yawned and propped up on his elbows. "No worries."

Drayden had to turn away. "Can someone wake up Sid and Charlie?"

Eugene caressed Sidney's cheek. She opened her eyes, looking overjoyed to wake up beside him.

"Charlie. Hey, Charlie!" Eugene called out.

He awoke with a startle. "What? Mom?"

Everyone laughed.

Drayden needed to study the map so he could offer the day's plans, but he wasn't sure how with the Guardians in the room. Based on the prior day's viewing, he knew they continued along Route 6, though he couldn't remember the name of the next major town they should be targeting.

After he gulped some water, he dug into his pack and inventoried his dwindling food: a few apples, a few more slices of bread, some pears, a couple of carrots, and cookies.

"We should probably eat again," Drayden said to the other privates as he got up and stretched. He would have to fake his way through the day's plans for the Guardians until he found an opportunity to consult the map. Being in control of the route afforded him an aura of control and authority over the mission. After yesterday's debacle, he needed every ounce of it. He remained resolute not to surrender an inch to Captain Lindrick.

Captain Lindrick, Sergeant Greaney, and Lieutenant Duarte watched him. Lindrick whispered something to them before storming over. His eyes were narrowed slits, burning with rage. He stopped a foot from Drayden, his red face twitching.

"Let's get one thing straight," Lindrick said, seething. "I am in charge of this mission from now on. Whatever authority you thought you had, I'm relieving you of it. We're lucky to be alive. You're just a kid. You may be a smart one, but you don't have any experience. And you're weak. Are we clear?"

The room was quiet enough to hear a Bureau pin drop. Nobody moved.

Drayden checked behind him.

The other privates and Eugene were scrutinizing him, awaiting his reply.

His fight response kicked in, the adrenaline coursing through his veins.

Stand your ground.

He had the advantage. Although the Guardians might be stronger, they didn't have the maps or the food. Plus, it was more than strength and toughness that would lead them to Boston. He wasn't picked to head this mission due to his physical ability. Maybe he didn't have much of it, but he was strong in his own way.

"No. We're not clear," Drayden said as confidently as he could.

Lindrick cocked his head. "Excuse me, son?"

Drayden stepped closer, right in his face. "You heard me. The Premier put me in charge of this mission, because he knew you couldn't do it without me. You may be strong, but you're not too smart. We would have been attacked yesterday whether we had our weapons drawn or not. The outcome would have been the same too. And the whole reason we're in this mess is because you sank the boat when you *should* have pulled ashore like I said. I'm in charge of this mission. Are *we* clear?"

Drayden tried to hide his trembling hands. Sweat beaded along his brow. Had he crossed the line? If he'd learned one thing, whether someone was smart or not, nobody liked to be called stupid. He imagined a decorated military commander particularly wouldn't appreciate hearing it from a nerdy sixteen-year-old civilian.

Captain Lindrick's piercing eyes bore holes through him.

Drayden stared right back, never dropping his gaze.

Lindrick blinked first. He smirked, and even started to laugh, peering back at Greaney and Duarte. Both looked confused and apprehensive.

As Lindrick refocused on Drayden, he stopped laughing.

Drayden saw the punch coming a mile away.

Lindrick threw a wide, looping haymaker at his head.

He easily ducked it.

Surprised he missed, Lindrick found himself slightly off balance.

Drayden, still crouched down, drove through Lindrick's midsection. He wrapped his arms around the captain's waist to tackle him to the ground, a move he'd practiced a million times.

Skilled himself, Lindrick raised one knee against Drayden's chest as they fell. It prevented Drayden from achieving mount, the most dominant position in ground fighting.

Nevertheless, Drayden landed on top. Realizing this fight wouldn't last long, he threw a punch before they'd even hit the floor. He connected with a forceful blow to Lindrick's left eye as they crashed to the ground, and brought his arm back up to strike again.

Lindrick pulled a knife from somewhere and held it to Drayden's throat.

The icy steel blade dug into his Adam's apple. Lindrick pressed so forcefully it stung, like it had already cut him.

Drayden froze with his arm elevated, his heart thumping in his chest.

Blood dripped from a cut above Lindrick's eye, running down the side of his face. "C'mon, Private. Finish what you started," he said, seemingly almost amused. "Let's see who's in charge." He pressed the knife in harder.

Drayden drew his head away from the blade, though Lindrick maintained the contact. It was Lindrick's move. Either he would pull the blade away, or he would slit Drayden's throat. Otherwise, they were stuck in a stalemate.

Drayden had studied several techniques in jiu-jitsu to escape a situation in which someone held a knife to his throat. But in their simulations, the attacker usually stood behind him. He would never have imagined it this way, on top of someone who held a knife to his throat from below.

A gun cocked behind Drayden. "Drop the knife, Captain Lindrick," Charlie ordered.

Lindrick's eyes flashed to Charlie, somewhere behind Drayden.

Lieutenant Duarte stepped forward, raised his rifle, and aimed it at Charlie. "Drop your gun. Private."

Lindrick reduced the pressure on the knife, and Drayden could turn his head enough to see behind him.

Sidney aimed her Glock at Lieutenant Duarte. "You drop *yours.*"

Sergeant Greaney stepped forward and pointed his rifle at Sidney. "I don't think so, sweetheart."

Sweat dripped down Drayden's cheeks.

Catrice stepped forward, drawing her pistol from her holster. The gun shook in her hands. Her eyes fiery, she pointed it at Sergeant Greaney without a word.

They still had a stalemate.

One person remained to break it.

"What are you waiting for, Corporal?" Captain Lindrick asked Eugene.

Drayden was the only person who couldn't train a weapon on someone. They were outnumbered because of it. The privates had lost.

Eugene remained expressionless, his pistol hanging down by his side.

"Corporal Austin!" Lindrick screamed.

Eugene released a deep breath. He stepped forward with authority and raised his Glock.

"Drop the knife, Captain."

CHAPTER 18

Captain Lindrick stood with his shoulders back and straightened his uniform, as if he were alone in front of a mirror getting ready for his day. He pulled a handkerchief from his pocket and wiped the blood from his face.

Drayden lingered around the privates and Eugene.

Everyone else's weapons remained live, locked on one another.

"I'm sure we'll be seeing each other soon." Captain Lindrick walked backward to the rear door, spun, and strode through it.

Sergeant Greaney and Lieutenant Duarte backpedaled with their weapons raised. Greaney slipped out.

"You're a dead man, Corporal," Lieutenant Duarte hissed to Eugene, disgust written all over his face. "You too, punk," he said to Drayden before leaving.

The whole room exhaled.

Drayden touched his neck, noting the blood on his fingertips. The cut was superficial, but his immediate concern was infection.

Probably for the first time ever, Eugene looked unsure of himself, chewing his lower lip while taking stock of the room. The reality of what he'd done appeared to be sinking in.

Drayden thought what he'd done was remarkable, the stuff of legend.

The privates stared at him, their respect for this young man growing by the second.

Before Drayden could thank him, Catrice rushed Eugene and clung to him, burying her face in his chest. Sidney and Charlie glanced at Drayden.

He lowered his eyes. Despite the situation, and the seriousness of everything going on, seeing her do that still hurt.

Catrice whimpered. "Thank you. Oh my God, thank you so much for staying with us."

"You're welcome," Eugene said emotionlessly, hugging her with one arm.

Drayden needed to focus on the job at hand and worry about Catrice later. Eugene's courageous act was huge for them. Just when they needed him, he delivered. He also saved Drayden's butt, once again.

"Eugene, she's right," he said. "Thank you. That was incredibly brave. We could use your help, especially now."

He remained solemn. "Okay."

"Charlie," Drayden said, "thank you for having my back. Everybody. Thank you." He knelt by his pack and found the antiseptic wipes, gauze, and tape to dress the wound on his throat.

Charlie holstered his weapon. "Now can you stop telling everyone about how I tried to kill you? I told you I got your back, bro. You're my boy."

For someone who had been the best buddy of Drayden's nemesis Alex, Charlie had become such a loyal friend.

Sidney tapped her foot. "What do we do now?"

Drayden taped the gauze on his throat. "For starters, we need to get out of this building without the Guardians ambushing us. And we need to find more food. Then we need to make it to Boston without them following us. They don't have any maps. Eugene, what's their next move?"

Eugene scratched his chin. "I doubt they'll try to kill us when we walk out of here because it would be an emotional, impetuous move, and they're smarter than that. They'll evaluate the situation first. Since I don't think they know the way to Boston, they'll likely allow us to leave, and trail us. I could be wrong about that though. Captain Lindrick studied the map before we left New America. He may know the way, or another way. He's been letting you lead the way, but he may just not have shown his hand. He hasn't said anything about it to us. If they do know the route, they may attempt to beat us to Boston." He faced Drayden, his lips pressed together. "He's actually real smart."

"I know. He called me weak, so I called him dumb. I didn't mean it."

Sidney held a hand in the air. "Should we just walk out of here?"

"We still need to be careful," Eugene said. "Lieutenant Duarte is a hothead, as you can tell. Despite what I said, there's always a chance he goes rogue, waiting to pick us off with a rifle when we walk out the door. Dray, are there any other ways out of here besides Route 6?"

Drayden snatched his maps from his pocket. Thankfully the scientists had included zoomed-in maps of various cities, including New Bedford.

Eugene almost fell over. "You have a map?"

"Yup."

"Ah, you were hiding it. Very smart, kid. Living up to your reputation."

"Let's not count our chips yet. According to the map, for the next five blocks or so, we can walk on a side street that runs parallel to Route 6. Unfortunately, we have to cross a river after that, and the only other way across other than Route 6 is far out of the way. Our goal for the day will be to reach the city of Bourne, about twenty miles away. That's where the narrow canal is that we should have sailed through."

"Roger that," Eugene said. "This is what we're going to do. They'll be expecting us to leave through the front door, since they went out the back. We'll go out the back too. I'll go out first, with Charlie covering me. Then I'll cover him, and we'll both cover Sid, and Drayden and Catrice will come out. Dray, you lead us to a side street and we run."

"We see if they're following us when we reach the bridge," Drayden took over. "I think we should sprint across. It's almost a mile. After that we'll find somewhere to hide, and we'll eat. Plan?"

"Let's do it." Eugene swung his rifle over his back. He pulled out his pistol and screwed on the silencer.

The privates strapped on their backpacks and drew their weapons.

Drayden decided to go with the pistol again. Not that it mattered for him. Normally he would have checked on Catrice, but at the moment, he couldn't even look at her.

They lined up at the back door while Eugene inspected the lot, assessing the situation.

"I'm going to that tree right there," he said, pointing. "When I make it and I give the signal, you each follow." He darted out the door.

Eugene, Charlie, and Sidney crouched beside a tree. The tall grasses of the rear parking lot provided outstanding cover to escape the building. So far, no sniper shots had rung out.

The Guardians weren't waiting outside the door to shoot them. If they intended to kill the privates, they would squeeze some value out of them first and follow them to Boston.

Drayden and Catrice stood side by side. He still hadn't processed her very public display of emotion toward Eugene. Drayden couldn't exactly blame her. He wanted to hug Eugene too.

Yet if Eugene were a pretty girl instead of a handsome boy, Drayden wouldn't have, because it would upset Catrice. That was the difference. Either she wasn't aware it would upset him, which implied she didn't think they had any relationship, or she didn't care if it did. Or even worse, she did it *to* upset him. To push him further away. He must have freaked her out when he'd referred to her as his girlfriend, although he didn't get why. She acted like his girlfriend when nobody else was around. Then once they were in public, he was invisible. She'd never had any qualms about holding his hand during the Initiation. What had changed? Ah, right. Eugene came along.

Eugene furiously waved at them to exit the building.

"You go. I'll cover you," Drayden said, without a hint of tenderness.

"I'm scared."

He found it hard to be mean to her. "You'll be fine. Three people are covering you out there, and me from inside. Get to that car, beside Charlie. Run; don't stop."

She ducked low, ran, and made it.

Drayden didn't wait. The Guardians obviously weren't going to strike. He bolted until he reached Eugene.

"Your move, chief," Eugene said to Drayden. "Where to?"

Drayden viewed the road in both directions. "We go backward on Route 6, west, to the intersection. Throw the Guardians a curveball if they're watching. We'll go left on Summer Street, two blocks, and left on Elm. Elm runs parallel to Route 6. We run five blocks and rejoin Route 6 where it turns into a bridge. We pause there, and make sure nobody's following us. Once we're on the bridge, there's nowhere to escape."

"Listen up," Eugene said to the privates. "We follow Dray. We got about seven blocks of running. Then we rest. Keep your weapons drawn. Yell out if you have a problem or see something. Drayden goes first; I'll be in the rear."

Charlie giggled. "The corporal in the rear again. He's having a tough trip."

"Charlie, focus," Drayden said. Staying low, he scurried to the street. Moving stealthily was not easy with a weighty pack. His pulse beating in his ears, he peered left down Route 6, which ran in a lengthy straightaway to the bridge.

The street was deserted. No sign of the Guardians.

Drayden ensured everyone was behind him and darted into the street, heading right. He turned left down Summer Street, setting a brisk pace. Pain shot through his ankle and up his leg every time his foot touched the asphalt. After finding it clear, he turned left on Elm Street.

One block later he stopped at County Street, a major intersection. While most of the buildings here were in total ruins, a red-brick church in superb condition towered on the near corner. A dilapidated restaurant sat kitty corner from it. A tall post rose above the remnants, displaying a sign with a rectangular base, supporting two yellow arches, forming an "M."

No Guardians in sight. They continued running until they found the on-ramp for the Route 6 bridge over the Acushnet River. The group huddled around a cluster of bushes.

"Okay," Drayden said, between heavy breaths. "It's a mile across the river. There's an island in the middle, Pope's Island. It's the one place we could be ambushed. Keep your guard up. Once we're on the bridge, there's no escape if we get trapped by the Guardians. We'll have to fight."

He checked once again for any sign of them, but they remained mysteriously absent. "You guys ready?"

"Booyah," Charlie said.

They ran for it. The bridge was more like a highway overpass until they hit the section before Pope's Island. A steel suspension structure rose above the roadway, which morphed from asphalt to a metal grating. Despite the rust, it seemed sturdy enough, and they passed over it with no problem.

Drayden's legs and lungs burned, much sooner than normal with the uncomfortable bouncing pack on his back. He checked behind him.

No Guardians following. The river below was choppy and moved with a moderate current, likely exacerbated by the recent rain. Decrepit stores and businesses housed in short, wide buildings lined Pope's Island.

When they approached the end of the bridge after the island, Drayden stopped.

"Oh no," Sidney said.

The roadway had collapsed, and the river now flowed through it, having carved a new path. Forced to travel in a narrow channel, the water rocketed through.

"If we go back, we can go about a mile north, and there's another bridge," Drayden said. "But we could get there and find that one's out too. I think we should go for it. It doesn't look deep."

Catrice inspected the waterway with obvious trepidation.

It might be too dangerous for her. If she slipped and the river swept her away, she would die since she couldn't swim. This was like a challenge. What was the best way to ensure they crossed safely?

"I could carry Catrice," Charlie said, anticipating the same problem.

"Swimming's not the problem," Sidney said, visibly annoyed at Catrice. "You could slip. *Then* you'd have to worry about swimming."

Charlie's raised his arms. "You guys, I have an idea. An actual idea. We all go together, with our arms interlocked. Keep everyone safe. Hopefully it's not too deep. What do you think?"

"Great idea, Charlie." Drayden holstered his pistol. "Very smart."

"I'm sorry I can't swim, you guys," Catrice said. "How about in addition to locking our arms, we line up parallel with the flow? We have the strongest—Eugene or Charlie—at the top. The water will hit him first and break a bit. If one of you guys is willing, I mean. It'll be rough for you, but much easier for everyone else."

"Wow, that's brilliant, Catrice," Eugene said. "Go, team. I'll be the guy."

Catrice must be terrified. Normally Drayden would comfort her, yet if she chose to hitch her trailer to Eugene, she should seek that reassurance from him.

"Here's the order," Drayden said, taking charge. "Eugene first, then Charlie, Catrice, me, and Sidney." Someone strong needed to hold Catrice, and from his perspective, better Charlie than Eugene. "If anyone gets swept away, we go after them. Eugene, Charlie, and Sidney, you guys are good swimmers. We would need you to step up."

They lined up, arms hooked, and tiptoed into the water. As expected, it was frigid.

Pain engulfed Drayden's feet and ankles within seconds.

"Holy shkatnuts!" Charlie yelled.

"How many times are we going to be in freezing water?" Sidney asked. "It's like every few days now."

The rushing water reached knee level. The river floor proved treacherous, with broken asphalt jutting out at different angles. Everything, including rocks and sand, was slick with river slime. Eugene absorbed the brunt of the river's force, the brown water splashing all around him.

"How you holding up, Eugene?" Drayden shouted over the roar of the flow.

"I'm good."

At the halfway mark, the water reached to waist level on the boys, and lower-chest level on the girls.

"Jumpin' Jesus!" Charlie yelled. "We've hit ground zero. That's the big one. I never wanted kids anyway."

Eugene cracked up. "Charlie, stop. You're killing me."

"That's not the only reason you're not having kids," Sidney said. "You'd have to find someone who'd buy your cheesy lines."

"Eugene buys them," Charlie grunted.

"I hope you two are happy together," Drayden said, through chattering teeth.

Ten feet to go. The water returned to knee level. They were almost out.

Charlie whooped. "This water's colder than penguin du—"

He slipped. He splashed down onto his butt, dragging Catrice with him. She screamed. Eugene stayed on his feet, locking up Charlie's arm before he could slip away. Charlie could barely hold Catrice, struggling for his own balance now that he sat in the water.

Although Drayden remained on his feet, he'd lost his grasp of Catrice's arm.

She was sliding toward him on her back. "Help!" she shrieked.

Drayden panicked, unsure what to do. He dropped to his knees, stomaching the cold water, and the jagged roadway that tore into his flesh. He needed to catch Catrice before the river swept her away.

She slid a foot downstream, nearly breaking away from Charlie's weakening grip.

Drayden wrapped his arms around her legs and squeezed. "I got you!"

Water splashed onto Catrice's back and over her shoulders, spraying Drayden in the face. But she'd stopped.

Sidney wrapped her arms around Drayden's waist to stabilize him.

Charlie regained his footing with Eugene's assistance. "Catrice, I'm going to grab you under the arms and pull you up to standing!" Charlie yelled.

"Okay!"

Charlie scooped her up with ease, and Drayden released her legs. Sidney supported Drayden as he got to his feet, and everyone locked arms again.

Throughout the excitement, Eugene had to remain still, enduring the force of the water. "Everybody all right?" he asked, looking fatigued.

"Sorry, you guys," Charlie said. "Charlie's bad."

They inched their way another ten feet and climbed up onto the roadway. Everyone collapsed to the ground, shivering.

"Who's hungry...for some...wet...food?" Sidney asked through chattering teeth.

Charlie had removed a boot and wrung out his sock. "Remember when we used to think swimming in the Dorms was fun?"

Drayden regarded the continuation of Route 6, his hands on his hips.

"What is it, Drayden?" Catrice asked.

He pointed.

Muddy footprints led down the road.

CHAPTER 19

Drayden studied the cracked asphalt.

The crew followed him down the road, their weapons out. The wet footprints faded with each step. Eventually, the vague hint of a shoe was all that remained before the footprints vanished, as if the Guardians had simply floated away.

He stopped at the end of the trail, squinting down Route 6.

"That's good, the Guardians are in front of us," Sidney said. "Right?"

Everyone appealed to Eugene.

He hesitated, clutching his rifle tight. "I'm not sure."

The Guardians could be monitoring them right now, hunting them, watching from out of sight. They needed to get out of the middle of the street.

"Let's eat and come up with a plan," Drayden said. "Off the road."

Three deer trotted across Route 6, a hundred feet ahead, including one with magnificent antlers.

"Whoa!" Charlie yelled.

Eugene raised his rifle and aimed.

Drayden shoved the barrel down. "What are you doing?"

Eugene flashed him an annoyed look. "There's our food. Or a little target practice."

"What? No, man." The deer disappeared into the forest. "See how delicate they are, how graceful? There are so few living things left in the world, we can't be killing stuff. Plus, the scientists said not to eat any animals."

Eugene switched his rifle into safe mode, his expression more amused than irritated now. "Whatever you say, chief; you're in charge. If you get hungry enough, I think you might change your mind." He patted Drayden on the shoulder before heading off the road.

Following Eugene into the woods, Drayden made a mental note of the deer so he could report back to Kim on the state of the world outside the walls. He wondered how the insurrection plot was going. Surely the way most similar plots in history went—horribly.

The group sat in a circle, in a narrow clearing beneath some trees. The privates dug soggy food out of their backpacks, though Eugene didn't have any.

Drayden felt a tinge of anxiety again at the sparse contents of his pack. About seventy miles to Boston.

"We need to ration," he said. "Let's each have an apple." He finally made eye contact with Catrice. "You'll probably share with Eugene, right?"

Before she could answer, Charlie and Sidney snickered.

Catrice glanced at them, and back at Drayden, a confused expression on her face. "Yeah, sure."

Drayden tore into his apple, the sweet juice running down his chin. It was so delicious he ate everything except the stem.

Charlie burped. "I don't know about you guys, but I'm stuffed. I haven't been this full since I ate that potato yesterday."

"We clearly need more food," Drayden said. "We'll come pretty close to the coast in the next few miles. We could try fishing."

"With what?" Sidney asked.

"We'll have to wing it."

They had little food, and the Guardians had none. Sure, the Guardians had superior survival training, and they were tougher guys, but they didn't have what the privates did: the ability to improvise. While he couldn't out-tough them, he could undeniably outsmart them. Particularly with their new secret weapon—a Guardian of their own.

"Eugene, we may have to stop to fish," Drayden said. "Do we have time? You're one of these guys, or used to be. We all need to reach Boston. Are they aiming to beat us there? Or will they follow us and kill us later? Or was Duarte only trying to scare us?"

Eugene contemplated it before answering, reloading his rifle's magazine. "Just because I know these guys doesn't mean I can predict what they would do in any given scenario. The fact that they crossed the bridge before us is irrelevant. They could be racing ahead of us. Or they could have cut way into the woods, they're watching us right now, and intend on trailing us."

Nobody could resist surveying the woods after that.

Eugene set his rifle down and checked the ammo in his Glock. "If you want my opinion, I think it would be impossible to find Boston without a map. I bet they'll shadow us but stay out of sight. These guys are crafty."

"How will they eat?" Catrice asked.

He waved his Glock at her. "Probably hunt. I'm just saying, after things calm down I think Captain Lindrick will make sure they can follow us. Heck, they might even protect us if necessary, to ensure we show them the way to Boston. Once we reach Boston...it's a different story."

"What if we head back to New America?" Sidney tossed her apple core behind her. "The whole mission is kind of blown now anyway. The Bureau wouldn't really blame us considering what happened, would they?"

Eugene shook his head. "We've got to be close to two hundred miles away. Impossible to hike it without supplies. If the Guardians are watching us, I'm sure they'd kill us if we were heading home anyway. Given how this mission went down, they'd never be allowed back into New America if we got there first. And I hate to break it to you, but if you think the Bureau would give us a pass because the mission didn't go as planned, then you don't know the Bureau very well. Everyone on this expedition needs to reach Boston—period. Especially you guys."

"Yeah," Drayden said. "No discussion there. Our families are back to the Dorms if we don't reach Boston."

Eugene licked his lips. "Even though us Guardians don't have to worry about that contingency, everyone wants the reward for reaching Boston. We talked about it. Boston or bust."

Catrice asked the logical question. "What if they reach Boston first?"

"Depends," Eugene said. "First of all, we don't know if there is a Boston. If there's nothing there, then it won't matter. If there is... them beating us is a serious problem. If they're trailing us, we need to lose them. If they're ahead of us, we need to catch them."

"Thanks, Eugene," Drayden said. "Here's the plan. We hike on Route 6, off the actual road. Let's stick to the woods. Since it's thicker with brush it'll be slower, but it will make it harder to follow us, or attack us. Everyone keep an eye out for the Guardians. We search for the ocean to our south, so we can fish the first chance we get. We hike till sundown so we give ourselves the best chance of beating them to Boston. We should hit Bourne today."

They threw on their gear, and Drayden scanned the thick woods. He touched his baseball hat, overcome with the sense that they were indeed being watched.

The air was pleasantly warm, but the sun was scorching.

After five hours of hiking, Drayden's feet became numb again. All he wanted was his brown couch and a nap. Food and water would be nice too.

Most of the hike crossed flat, rural terrain. In some places, Route 6 was so overgrown it was impossible to distinguish from the woods. For the past hour, buildings popped up with increasing regularity. At first mostly houses appeared, giving way to rundown businesses and crumbling shopping centers.

"I think we're almost in Wareham." Drayden consulted his map as he walked. "More than halfway to Bourne. We've gone about thirteen miles."

"Wareham, huh?" Charlie muttered to himself. "You bet I wear 'em. To the harem. Yeah, I dare 'em. Every time he goes to the harem in Wareham."

"I think Charlie's gone delirious from hunger," Sidney said.

Charlie bellowed, "If they have any fish in Wareham, Charlie'll snare 'em!" He returned to mumbling. "...he'll snare 'em... snare 'em..."

Drayden wiped sweat off his forehead. "We have to cross a bridge in Wareham. We can try fishing off it." His stomach rumbled with hunger pains.

"Guardian check," Eugene said.

Everyone stopped. Hands on weapons, they rotated around in silence. They searched in every direction for any sign of the Guardians, including sounds, like snapping branches. This had become part of their routine, roughly every half hour. So far, not a trace. If the Guardians were covertly following, they were exceptional at it.

Sidney lowered her rifle. "The more time that goes by without seeing them, the more nervous I get."

Drayden holstered his pistol. Why had he bothered taking it out? He couldn't hit Eugene three feet away. "It might be a good sign. If they were going to attack, they probably would have done it already."

"Guys, quiet," Eugene said. "You hear that?"

Running water.

It was faint, like a stream or small river.

"Where's it coming from?" Drayden asked.

"There." Catrice spun toward the woods.

They negotiated the thick bramble, rich with thorns. After about fifty feet, they reached a narrow stream, glistening with gentle, crystal-clear water.

"Nobody drink that," Drayden ordered. They would need to boil it first.

"I just wanna splash my face." Sidney tiptoed down the steep bank and knelt by the water's edge. "Whoa, look! Fish!"

The stream was loaded with fish—big fish, around a foot long. Tiny white spots covered their brown skin. Some glided around while others remained motionless, hovering in the water. The privates watched in amazement. It was the first time they'd seen real live fish.

The way they moved in the water was so elegant, so dazzling, like they were flying. Drayden abhorred the idea of killing these graceful creatures. They'd done nothing other than survive the Confluence to deserve such a fate. Unfortunately, the privates needed to eat.

Sidney washed her face in the stream. "How do we catch them?"

Drayden tugged on his earlobe. They were carrying rope in their backpacks, but it was thick, not fishing wire. They had no hooks. Tie a knife to a stick to fashion a spear? Securing it with such thick rope would be impossible.

"How about this?" Eugene touched a massive rock on the river bank, one of many such rocks lying around. He squatted down, and with visible straining, hoisted the rock to waist level. His lips tightened into a pucker, his cheeks turned red, and tendons bulged in his neck. He stumbled to the edge of the river, and in a shocking display of strength, pressed the massive stone above his head. He paused, scanning the water. With a screech, he launched the boulder into the stream, resulting in an epic splash.

The privates waited till the disturbed sand and silt from the stream settled. When the water cleared, it revealed the fish were quite nimble. Eugene had missed.

"C'mon, Charlie," Eugene said, wearing a stupid grin. "It's kinda fun." He giggled like a little kid.

Charlie picked up a rock. He and Eugene howled as they tried and failed over and over to smash the fish.

Observing them tossing stones he could never lift, Drayden considered his own strengths. They weren't physical ones, and might never be, but he had something else. It was time to start being himself. He caught Catrice staring at him.

Her expression said what he was thinking. *We can do better than this.*

He examined the stream up and down.

It was ten or fifteen feet across. Downstream a bit it narrowed significantly, to a few feet, and the water rushed through that section.

Drayden had an idea. "Does anyone still have the fabric from their life vest?"

"I do," Catrice said, digging it out of her backpack.

"Perfect. Sid, can you and Catrice poke holes in the vest with your knives? Lots of mini holes, enough for water to pass through, like a sieve."

Sidney chewed on a nail. "Sure. Why?"

"You'll see. Eugene, Charlie! Stop. You're wasting your energy; the fish are too fast. And we need those rocks."

Both glowed red and glistened with sweat. "Okay," Charlie said. "What should we do?"

"You see that spot where the stream narrows?" Drayden flung a pebble at it. "Start piling the rocks up there. Make it even more narrow. Leave only a foot of space to pass through."

Eugene put his hands on his hips. "Damn, kid. You *are* smart. This is like being in the Initiation with you guys. I love it!"

Catrice's eyes widened. "So, we narrow the stream to a foot wide there, turn this vest into a net, and hold it in place. If we can force the fish that way, they'll get trapped. Great idea, Drayden."

"Thanks." He turned away. "We'll scare them in that direction with rocks, right into our trap."

Sidney and Catrice savaged the vest, which looked like they'd used it for target practice. Charlie and Eugene piled up the rocks, making the water rocket through the narrow canal they'd built.

Drayden clapped his hands together. "Eugene, Charlie, you guys have to toss the stones, none of the rest of us are strong enough. Keep advancing toward the trap. Sid, Catrice, you guys hold the net. Everybody good?"

"The water's racing through our canal," Catrice said, fumbling with her side of the vest. "I'm not sure if I can hold onto the net."

Sidney glared at her. "We need to eat, girl. C'mon."

"You can do it." Drayden nodded.

She and Sidney struggled but anchored the net in place, the force of the water's flow bubbling it out. Catrice dropped her side and it deflated.

Sidney cursed under her breath, mumbling something about her sister. "Stick your fingers through the holes we cut. And use some damn muscle."

Catrice flushed. She wiped her eyes with the back of her hand before securing the net per Sidney's instruction. "Got it."

Drayden gave Charlie and Eugene a thumbs-up and they hurled the rocks, one after another. The stream clouded up with sand, making it difficult to tell whether their scheme was working.

"How we doing?" Eugene grunted.

"I can't tell; it's too cloudy. Keep going. We'll know soon enough."

Charlie and Eugene were now ten feet from the trap.

"We got one!" Sidney yelled. "And another!"

Catrice turned her face away from the approaching splashes. "And another one!"

They caught five fish in total. Everyone crowded around to see when Sidney and Catrice held the net in the air.

Drayden couldn't bear to watch the fish wiggling around, gasping for air. They were suffering, and he loathed watching any living thing suffer. In this case, the privates were the source of their pain, which made it even worse.

Eugene whooped. "Lunch is served!"

"We can't let them suffocate." Catrice averted her eyes. "It's cruel."

"Fine, gimme the bag 'o fish." Eugene carried the wriggling net up to flat ground, laid it down, and snatched up a rock. "You softies might want to look the other way."

"Dear God," Catrice said, walking off.

Drayden tried to think about his father and brother as a distraction, his stomach turning anyway.

Eugene guffawed as he smashed the fish's heads with the rock, one by one.

Drayden sneered at Catrice, who crouched by the stream. *This is the guy you're ditching me for?*

"Uh, I suggest you guys stay away for a bit," Eugene said. "I'm going to slice the fish open—remove the guts and the bones. Can someone start a fire?"

"If we start a fire, we'll give away our location from the smoke," Sidney said.

Drayden hadn't thought of that. "Great point, Sid."

Charlie hovered over Eugene's shoulder, watching him gut the fish. "We gotta eat. We can't eat that raw. Can we?"

Drayden pondered it for a moment. "No idea. I'm pretty sure we need to cook it. We also need to figure out how. We don't have a pan or anything. I think we have to accept the risk of giving away our location to the Guardians. We need food. We'll go on high alert. Someone will stand guard while the others cook."

"I can start the fire," Catrice said, taking out her magnifying glass and collecting some dry leaves and wood. She knelt and focused the sun's rays into a laser beam of light. A burn hole appeared on the leaf, unleashing a tiny plume of smoke. It burst into flame.

Drayden picked up a long stick, thinking it might work for cooking. "Charlie, help me gather some sticks to skewer the fish. We'll soak them in the stream for a few minutes so they don't burn."

Eugene left the fish intact minus the guts, skewering them through the tail and out the mouth. Each person supported the skewered fish from below with two additional sticks to prevent the fish from breaking off the skewer as it cooked.

The rich, savory smell of the roasting fish made Drayden's mouth water. Eugene worked two skewers, allowing Sidney to scan the area with her rifle raised. In ten minutes, the fish were done.

Drayden ate like a wild animal. He devoured the tender white meat and even the crispy skin.

Charlie burped. "I want another one."

It was the most satisfying meal Drayden had ever eaten. He thought of Wesley, who loved fish and would have gone crazy for this new type of fish that didn't exist in New America.

"We gotta keep moving," he said. "Let's put this fire out, in case the Guardians haven't seen the smoke yet."

Sidney carried one of her empty water bottles toward the stream to retrieve water to douse the fire.

A gunshot rang out in the distance.

CHAPTER 20

Crouched in the bushes, in panic mode, Drayden examined the highway in both directions.

"Did anyone hear where the shot came from?" Catrice whispered.

Everyone answered at the same time. "Behind—ahead—behind us—over there."

"Glad we got that settled," Charlie muttered.

Drayden squinted, looking west. "I think it was behind us."

"I'm pretty sure it was in front of us," Eugene countered.

With no sign of the Guardians anywhere, they resumed their trek east, off the road. Drayden repeatedly peered behind, half expecting to see them charging.

"Cut it out, man," Charlie said from the back of the group. "You're making me nervous. There's nothing back there. I think they're ahead of us."

Sidney held a hand in the air. "If they're ahead of us we should go slow so we don't bump into them, but if they're behind us we should go fast. Great."

Drayden walked beside Catrice up front, with Eugene behind them. Despite her warm embrace of Eugene earlier, Catrice actually seemed to notice Drayden again during the fishing challenge. Even though it wasn't girlfriendy attention, at least she'd acknowledged his presence. That was something.

Eugene hurried past them. "I swear they're in front of us. Let me be up front in case I'm right."

Right after he passed, Catrice locked her arm inside Drayden's.

Drayden internally rolled his eyes. Of course, she'd do that *now*—Eugene wasn't watching anymore. He kept his arm sort of limp. While her touch usually made his heart flutter, he didn't feel much of anything this time. He stared straight ahead and didn't say a word.

Catrice pulled her arm away. "What's wrong?"

Drayden released an exasperated breath and whispered, "What's going on with you?"

Eugene turned his head back for a second.

Catrice glanced at him before returning her attention to Drayden. She crossed her arms. "What are you talking about?"

She spoke a tad louder than he wished, making him regret opening this box. "I don't know, something feels weird, different." He whispered, softer this time, hoping she would take the hint that he desired this conversation to remain private. "You're not exactly talking to me. But you're talking to...other people."

"Are you kidding me?" she whisper-yelled. "What do you expect me to do? Oh, Dray, you're so amazing, let me shower you with kisses. We're in the middle of this horrible journey that's turned into a disaster!" She groaned. "Grow up." She reached into her holster and pulled out her Glock.

For a microsecond Drayden thought Catrice was going to shoot him.

She stormed ahead, past Eugene, and walked alone up front, accelerating away.

"That went well," Drayden mumbled to himself. Was it all in his head?

Eugene slowed until Drayden ambled beside him. He slung his rifle over his back and wrapped his arm around Drayden's shoulders. "Girls." He shook his head. "Listen, I don't have much experience because there's only like five girls my age in the Palace. But I wouldn't go try to fix that yet. Let her cool down."

Incredulous, he studied Eugene. The guy stealing his girlfriend was giving him advice on how to retain her, *again*. Was Eugene messing with his head? He didn't think so. The kid sounded sincere.

Eugene eyeballed Catrice in the distance. "Lemme guess, Catrice was a loner back in school? Not too many pals and no boyfriends?"

Drayden regarded him for a few seconds before answering. "Correct. Go on."

"She didn't invite her parents to join her in the Palace when you guys moved. Obviously, she had a terrible relationship with them. She was unloved, or something. It's clear she likes you." He cocked his head, his index finger in the air. "Maybe it scares her. She's afraid of getting too close and being hurt. By you, like, if you dump her or something. If she couldn't trust her parents, who can she trust? She's keeping her distance a bit, pulling away. She may not even realize it."

Wow. Eugene might be on to something. Perhaps Drayden and Charlie were wrong to be suspicious of him, and he wasn't luring Catrice away. He could just be an incredible dude.

Eugene pulled his arm back and retrieved his rifle. "I would tell her how much you care about her, and, I don't know, probably apologize later."

"Yeah. Hey, thanks, Eugene."

He waved a hand dismissively. "Eh, anytime. I enjoy reading about psychology a lot too."

Drayden allowed Sidney to catch up to him.

"Hey," he said.

She pursed her lips, apparently fighting off a smile. "Hi. Nice fight."

"Yeah, um, thanks?"

"Listen, Dray, it's none of my business. But she got all angry with you and played dumb, like she had no idea what you were talking about. That's shkat. Trust me. I'm a girl; I know. She knows exactly what she's doing."

He arched his brows. "Seriously?"

"Yes. If it was in your head, would me and Charlie have noticed? It's so obvious. It's possible Eugene is, in fact, innocent since you boys are such clueless idiots. She's not, though. She's also totally useless out here, but whatever. You do what you want. I'm just saying you don't deserve to be treated like that. You deserve better."

Drayden surveyed the roadway behind them again, past Charlie. Having been engrossed in the Catrice drama, he'd stopped paying attention to their surroundings. He heard it before he saw it.

Catrice had stopped up ahead, and Eugene had reached her.

As Drayden, Sidney, and Charlie joined them, everyone stood in awe. Drayden rested both hands behind his head.

"*Now* we have a problem," said Charlie.

"This is not on the map," Drayden said.

The river before them raged, whipping right through Route 6 with blazing speed and violence. The white frothy water swirled, splashed, and sprayed, making the air misty and cool. The late afternoon sun blared, draping the world in gold. The map of the Massachusetts coast did indicate lots of water. Still, they'd had enough of it.

"I don't mean to beat a dead horse here," Charlie said, "but Catrice, you *really* need to learn how to swim."

A chill ran down Drayden's spine. Catrice wasn't the only one too weak to swim through that. It was no picturesque stream or piddling ten feet of shallow water to wade through. This river was something out of a movie.

"We definitely can't swim that," Eugene said. "Even I'd drown in there."

Drayden squatted and removed his Yankees hat. Feeling around the emblem evoked memories of his mother, and usually some inspiration. It didn't this time, which was odd, so he shared the first thought that came to his mind. "Since this river shouldn't exist, there won't be any bridges across it, no matter how far upstream we hike."

Catrice refused to look at him. "Further north the water might be calmer."

"We can try that," Drayden said.

"It might be worse," Sidney said.

Eugene turned his back to the river, the sun brightening his blue eyes, and faced Drayden. "What if..." His expression went blank, his gaze suddenly past Drayden's head. He whipped his rifle out. "Get down!"

Drayden dropped to the ground on his stomach. He drew his pistol and rolled onto his back.

The others darted behind trees for cover. Eugene took a few powerful steps back down Route 6 with his weapon raised. He scanned the area through the rifle's sight, panning left and right.

"What do you see, Euge?" Charlie shouted from behind a tree.

He didn't answer.

Charlie dashed out beside Eugene, his rifle raised as well. "What is it?"

Eugene lowered his gun. "Nothing, I guess. Sorry, guys. False alarm. I thought I saw something. Movement, a person."

The Guardians.

Drayden beheld the river, scratching the back of his neck. "Eugene, are the other Guardians strong enough to swim across that?"

"No way."

"Then they must be behind us."

Catrice finally locked eyes with Drayden. "Or they walked upstream, trying to find a safer place to cross."

She was kind of hung up on this upstream thing, but she could be right.

"If so, we shouldn't walk upstream, or we might run into them," Drayden said. "Or if they're behind us, we need to hurry up and find a way across."

"How much rope do we have?" Eugene asked.

Sidney dug through her pack. "We each have a bunch coiled up." She tossed hers to Eugene, who unrolled it. It was marked with lines by foot and stretched roughly fifteen feet.

Eugene wound it back up. "How about we tie them all together, secure it to the other side of the river somehow, and hold onto it as we walk across?" He stood in front of Drayden, squinting with the sun in his eyes again.

"Seems super dangerous," Sidney said, wringing her hands. "It would be real easy to lose the grip and be swept away."

Eugene shifted a few feet to Drayden's left and ducked down into his shadow to block the sun. "That's better."

The shadow.

Drayden strolled to the riverbank and checked both ways before looking up. Most of the trees were evergreens, and they were towering. The others caught up, noting his line of sight.

"The trees?" Eugene asked.

Drayden tugged on his left earlobe. "How wide do you think the river is?"

"Thirty feet? Forty? Hard to say."

"We need to find out. Can you tie those ropes together? And do you think you could toss it across the river so we can measure? Attach a rock to the end or something."

"Wait," Eugene said, "why not just cut down a tree and see if it reaches?"

"Because we don't have anything to cut down a tree with. We have knives. That would take all night. Let's try to find a tree right on the bank with exposed roots that's already leaning across the river. We might be able to tip it across if we dug out around the roots. Even that'll be a lot of work. We need to be certain it's tall enough before we start."

Charlie tapped a nearby tree. "I'm not getting it. So we figure out the distance across the river. How can we tell how tall the tree is? Kinda tall to climb."

Drayden locked eyes with Catrice, positive she would know where he was going with this.

She thought about it for a second. "Its shadow," she said.

The river crossed Route 6 at a diagonal angle. The sun was high enough in the sky that it cast the trees' shadows on the ground, not over the river. Being late afternoon, the shadows were lengthy, but thankfully over land, meaning they could measure them.

Eugene clapped. "Man, you guys have not disappointed. Can't wait to tell my dad about how solid you two were out here."

Drayden wondered why his father would care.

"I'm feeling dumber than a backpack full of soggy food," Charlie said. "Still not getting it."

Catrice stood beside Drayden and rested her hand on top of his head. "We measure, say, Drayden's shadow. He's six feet tall. Pretend his shadow is three feet. Then we measure the tree's shadow. The tree will be twice as tall as its shadow's length."

Charlie's face showed that the lightbulb had finally turned on. "Ahhh."

Drayden gathered all the rope. "Eugene, you're the knot guy. Join these together and find a rock to secure to the end. When you're done with the rope, we'll do the shadow measurements."

After Eugene formed the elongated rope, with a block-like rock anchored on one end, he stepped up to the riverbank. "Okay, you guys, uh, stand back." He held the rope a foot shy of the rock, and twirled it in a circular motion, like a cowboy preparing to lasso a steer. Once it was whipping around, he released it with a final thrust and a scream. It reached three-quarters of the way across and splashed into the water.

"Dude, you gotta get it to the other side," Charlie said.

Eugene put his hands on his hips and gave Charlie a look.

"Sorry."

Eugene reeled it back in and picked up the rock. "I'll try throwing it like a baseball." With a running start and a bellow, he hurled it. It sailed, easily making it across, and the rope dropped into the water. "Gotta do this pronto before the rope gets pushed down the river." He tugged until the rock rested at the top of the far bank and grabbed the rope exactly above their own, marking the length. As the center of the rope started to drift down the river, he retracted it.

Sidney counted out the feet, and Eugene adjusted for the knots he'd tied. "Forty-six feet, roughly," he said.

"Now bring the rope here and measure my shadow." Drayden stood tall.

His shadow measured twelve feet two inches.

"Let's call it twelve feet," Drayden said. "So, I'm half as tall as my shadow. Now the harder part, we need to find a tree candidate."

They explored the riverbank, hunting for a tall tree along the edge that appeared on the verge of falling. Only a handful of trees were close enough.

"How about this one?" Sidney hollered, a bit upstream.

The nominee seemed plenty tall enough. It was one of those skinny, narrow pine trees with almost no branches until the very top. The exposed roots jutted out on the river side, and the tree leaned precariously. Since it lay somewhat alone, they could isolate its shadow from the other trees in the area.

"That one's perfect," Drayden said. "Let's get the rope and measure."

Eugene straightened out their conjoined rope, which extended sixty feet. The shadow was far longer. Sidney marked the end, and Eugene moved the rope. Still, it didn't reach the shadow's top, coming up a few feet short. "Let's call the shadow 124 feet," Eugene said.

"That means the tree is sixty-two feet tall," Catrice said. "It'll clear—no problem."

The group gathered at the base of the tree.

Eugene scraped some dirt with his fingers. "Is this gonna work? Digging out all the dirt around the roots?"

Drayden shrugged. "I don't know. If it was a healthy tree standing perfectly upright, I don't even think a bus could pull it down. But this tree looks like it's about to fall anyway. Does anybody have any other ideas?"

Not a peep from anyone.

"All right then." Eugene gave a double thumbs-up. "Let's get to work."

Sidney kicked the roots. "What do we dig with?"

"Rocks," Catrice said. "I think flat-ish ones, kind of like little shovels?"

Everyone spent some time finding rocks suited to the task. Charlie and Eugene attacked the dirt on the river side, around the exposed roots.

"Drayden," Catrice said, staring at her feet. "We need to dig a wide circle around the tree on the back side to loosen up the root system behind it. So it can tip."

"Yeah. Yeah, you're right. Can you and Sid work on that?"

"Sure."

Sidney frowned at him before joining Catrice behind the tree.

Drayden observed Eugene and Charlie, frantically digging out the dirt, both dripping with sweat. Their jacked arms almost tore the sleeves of their gray fatigues.

He squeezed between them, jabbing his rock into the firm soil around the roots, scraping it away. Digging from the river side required some balance since it was on a steep slope.

After a few minutes, the other two boys had made admirable progress. Drayden, not so much. His feet kept sliding down the embankment, and he hadn't cleared much dirt. He probably needed to hit it harder. Employing every ounce of muscle, he slammed the rock into the unyielding soil. There was no reason he couldn't match Eugene and Charlie.

"Careful, bud," Charlie said.

He swung again with all his force.

His feet slipped. He banged his face into the rock-hard bank and tumbled backward down the hill.

"Dray!" someone yelled.

In an instant, he was in the frigid water, his cheek throbbing. He was coherent enough to realize he was going to be swept away.

Hands seized him, around his collar and on his arm. Strong hands. Charlie and Eugene dragged him out.

Drayden lay on the shore, quaking. He pawed at his busted face.

Sidney squatted by his side, holding his hand, and pressed a piece of cloth against his cheek.

"Dray," Catrice said, "are you okay? Can you say something?"

I'm a flunk? How about that? His weakness was so damn humiliating.

"I'm fine, guys. I'm sorry. I just slipped. Thanks for saving me."

To make it more embarrassing, Eugene scooped him up like a baby and carried him back up to safe ground. Sidney and Catrice stayed with him while the boys returned to digging.

Sidney dabbed his cheek with the cloth. "It's only a small cut, Dray."

He hung his head low.

"Hey," Eugene said, winded. "I think this thing is about to go. It's sagged a few more feet, and the roots in the back where the girls dug are popping out of the ground. Charlie, let's push."

They set down their rocks and doubled over.

Drayden thought about how the two of them had saved his life a moment ago, catching him before the current dragged him away. Then, as if it had been nothing, they resumed digging.

"Sid," Charlie said, "we could use your help here."

They wanted Sidney's hand, not his. Sidney was strong and not likely to injure herself. Once again, though, Drayden remembered what he brought to the table.

"Eugene, don't push. You'll be standing on the roots, which we need to lift off the ground. Wrap your rope around the tree, stand down on the riverbank, and pull. Just make sure to get out of the way once she starts falling."

"Right. Good call."

Eugene tossed the rock at the end of the rope over one of the few low branches. After yanking a bunch of rope over the branch to give him some slack, he threw it over another branch on the other side. He pulled the rock back to where he began, and it was looped around the trunk fifteen feet up. He, Charlie, and Sidney held both ends and pulled. Pull, relax, pull, relax. The ring of dirt and roots behind the tree lifted off the ground.

"Pull!" Charlie yelled.

They groaned and grunted. The tree tilted further.

Charlie screamed and dropped the rope before grabbing his lower back. "Holy shkat! Oh man, my back. Ohh."

Eugene and Sid rested their hands on their knees, watching him with concern. "You all right, bud?" Eugene asked.

Charlie bent over with one hand on his knee and the other on the crook of his back. "Yeah, I'm great," he squeaked. "Feels like my spine burst out of my butt and curled up and stabbed me in the back. Other than that..."

"I think Sid and I can wrap this up. Why don't you go rest?"

"No," Charlie said. "One more humongous pull—I think we got it. I've only got one more tug in the tank. Let's do it."

They gripped the rope, Charlie's face twisted in anguish.

"On the count of three," Eugene said. "One, two, three!"

They pulled with everything they had. With snapping sounds, the tree started falling.

"Go!" Sidney shouted as they scattered.

The tree fell slowly at first, then rocketed down, slamming down onto the distant shore with a crackling boom. It bounced a few times before settling. The roots formed a disc of soil around the bottom of the tree, like the base of a tipped-over wine glass.

"Woohoo!" Eugene clapped. He pumped his fist at Drayden. "That's all you, Dray!"

Drayden returned a thumbs-up. Despite the sun and warm air, he was still chilled from the river, which was odd. The cut on his cheek had stopped bleeding, but the wound was open and the cheek bruised. It hurt. Now, in addition to the cut on his throat from Lindrick, he had another potential infection to worry about.

Some of the tree's branches dipped into the river, straining and bending under the force of the rushing water. Otherwise, their bridge looked pretty solid.

"We gotta move." Eugene yanked off the rope and wound it up. "I'll go last. Don't get all fancy and walk. Too many branches, too easy to slip. Scoot across on your butt."

"I'll start." Sidney mounted the tree as if it were a horse and scooted out over the water.

Drayden draped his hand on Charlie's shoulder. "You okay?"

He stood hunched over, grimacing. "Yeah, I'll be all right." He carefully climbed on after Sidney.

Catrice regarded Drayden with sorrowful eyes and followed Charlie.

"You're up, chief," Eugene said.

The others moved at a snail's pace, with Sidney in front, dictating their speed. Scooting inches at a time, they were deliberate around branches, which demanded some gymnastics to negotiate.

"Aww shkatnuts!" Charlie shook his hand in the air. "Watch out for the sap!"

Drayden mounted the tree at the base—the bark angular, rough, and choppy. It scraped the insides of his legs each time he advanced. After a few feet, he was above water and he paused to watch it race by, so powerful and violent. He resumed and a moment later his hand landed in a patch of slimy, sticky sap.

The sweet smell of pine wafted through the air.

He recalled the wilderness training from the scientists, in which Sam had mentioned some of the extraordinary properties of sap, also called resin or pitch. One of them was to treat wounds. It had antiseptic, antibacterial, and astringent properties. It could stop bleeding and could even treat skin rashes.

Drayden scooped some on his finger and slopped it onto the cut on his cheek, which burned as he rubbed it in. He slipped some more beneath the bandage covering his throat wound.

Mature sap would cake into an amber glob, which had myriad other uses, from medicinal to starting a fire. After several more feet, he saw some. It was as close as Mother Nature came to supplying you with a tool kit in the wild. The pieces were gummy, and Drayden picked off as much as he could, dropping it into his pocket.

He was more than halfway there. While scurrying across wasn't difficult, passing each branch was a tad unnerving, particularly for someone clumsy. In some cases, he could swing his leg over, but others required him to stand up. If he slipped and fell into the water now, there would be no saving him. He'd be dead. More than anything he was exhausted and freezing. Ever since he'd fallen in the water.

Sidney and Charlie had successfully crossed, and Catrice was close. Eugene was right behind him.

As Drayden reached the end, Sidney snagged his arm and guided him off the tree top.

Eugene hopped off moments later. "Let's not waste any time. We gotta move out."

"Wait!" Drayden blurted. "Any chance you can toss that tree into the river? You know, so the Guardians can't follow us."

"Hmm." Eugene appeared to consider it. "It's probably way too heavy."

"I realize I'm not much help," Drayden said, "and Charlie is out of commission, but can you give it a shot, Eugene?" He nudged Sidney. "Can you help him?"

The two stood on opposite sides of the treetop. "On three, Sid. If we can lift it, go toward me. One, two, three." He grunted and pursed his lips.

The tree didn't budge.

Eugene straightened and arched his back. "Nope. Not even close. C'mon guys, let's go." He jerked his rifle out and led the way down Route 6. The others followed, except Drayden.

Sidney turned back, cocking her head. "You coming?"

"Yeah." He was pondering something. Whenever Eugene strained himself, he glowed red and his neck tendons bulged out. That didn't happen this time.

He didn't really try to move the tree.

He was faking it.

CHAPTER 21

It was dusk, the blue hour, in Bourne, Massachusetts.

The group hiked beside the narrow canal they should have sailed through before their final stretch in the Atlantic Ocean. Route 6, which ran alongside it, neared its conclusion, where they would turn north on Route 3.

"This is Sagamore," Drayden said, referencing his map. "It's part of Bourne. We're finally done with Route 6. Roughly fifty miles to Boston. We should set up camp."

Charlie flung a pebble into the canal. "I'm gonna sleep like a baby who's milk-drunk."

"Let's head off the road," Eugene said, "just in case we're being followed."

You made sure that was possible, didn't you, Eugene?

Drayden wished he knew what the Guardians were up to.

It was all forest here, with no buildings in sight. They walked fifty feet or so into the bramble until they found a modest clearing. Everyone collapsed to the ground.

The only other time Drayden had been this tired was during the Initiation. His throat was sore, exacerbated by his coughing. "I don't think anyone has energy to try and find food," he said. "Let's eat what we have. How about a slice of bread and a pear? Leaves us with some food for tomorrow."

"What about Eugene?" Catrice asked.

He hung his head low. "Don't worry about it. I'm fine."

"You've done most of the heavy lifting," Sidney said. "Everyone tear off a piece of their bread for him. Here, you can have my last apple." She handed it to him.

"Thanks, everybody."

Drayden ripped off a piece of the crust for Eugene. He wasn't giving the money part to the guy possibly stealing his girlfriend *and* secretly assisting the Guardians.

Catrice tore off half her slice, handed it to Eugene, and plunked down beside him.

After eating, Drayden coughed again—a barking cough. His chest felt like it did when he swallowed too much water in the school's pool. They called it being "waterlogged." He continued to feel chilled, and the temperature was plummeting.

Charlie poked him. "You okay, bud?"

"Yeah. I think I may have caught a cold falling in that river."

"I'll swap your cold for my back pain," Charlie said.

Drayden pulled out his paperclip and battery. "I guess we're all a little banged up. I'm freezing too; I want a fire."

Sidney piled up some sticks and leaves, the brush dry and cracked from the scorcher of a day.

Drayden performed his sorcery and the kindling ignited. He dropped the paperclip and battery into his pocket, too exhausted to put them back in his pack.

Sidney gathered whatever leaves she could find, scattering them over the forest floor. "Even though it's not a bed, it'll be more comfortable than lying on the hard ground."

"Thanks, Sid," Charlie said. "My back thanks you as well."

After peeing in the bushes, Drayden positioned his backpack to use as a pillow and laid down. He couldn't help but wonder where Catrice would sleep; if she'd finally make the big leap and stay with Eugene.

Nevertheless, she stretched out next to him, her head on her backpack. She wrapped her arms through his without saying a word and closed her eyes.

Sidney craned her neck and made eye contact with Drayden, shaking her head.

What the hell was Catrice's deal? Maybe it was what Eugene had said, that she indeed liked him, but was scared she would be hurt. Or she was having trouble deciding between him and Eugene, who had revealed himself to be a bit more brutal—more "Guardian"—in the past day.

Plus, nobody else had caught Eugene's deceit, and Drayden hadn't told anyone. It was possible he'd misconstrued the whole episode about Eugene pretending to lift the tree. Because otherwise, the guy had displayed an insane amount of loyalty to the privates. He'd risked his life multiple times to save them. Still, that was all part of Drayden's problem with him. He was too damn perfect, as if it were an act, playing a part. He was *always* strong, generous, sensitive, compassionate, and smart.

Regardless of whether they could fully trust Eugene, they couldn't complete the journey without him. Tomorrow he would let Charlie in on his little secret, and they would keep a close eye on him.

Drayden's sinuses had become hot and stuffy, adding to his list of unfortunate symptoms. He wished his mother were here to take care of him. She'd religiously tended to him when he fell ill, like the time he became deathly sick from an infected cut. Even as he grew older and independent, he found nothing more comforting than his mother caring for him when he was under the weather. She'd dutifully put her children first, especially Drayden, her neediest kid.

That was, *until she didn't.* If she were here, he could also ask her what the hell she'd been thinking, having that affair. Suddenly putting her own needs ahead of her children's, getting herself exiled in the process. She would never be there again to take care of him when he got sick, because she'd been too busy thinking about herself.

Drayden groaned. His post-nasal drip irritated his throat, making it difficult to breathe. He turned on his side, facing Catrice. Why did she have to make things so difficult? They'd been on cloud nine together after the Initiation. As angry, disappointed, and embarrassed as he was now, he still liked her...which pissed him off.

Being close to her face, every contour perfectly structured, reminded him how lucky he was to have landed her in the first place. She was exquisite. On that basis alone, she was way out of his league. She was *not* out of Eugene's league on looks, however. Drayden felt he needed to continue proving why he was worth her time.

He kissed her forehead. Still a tiny spark.

Phlegm.

That was Drayden's first thought when he awoke and hacked up a thick green glob of the stuff. He felt awful. Sore throat, dull headache, congested chest, and he was freezing. He gulped water from his bottle, cringing when he swallowed.

The others roused. The morning air was cool, with a slight breeze.

Charlie moaned as he sat up. "Did anyone accidentally stab me in the back overnight?"

"I'm so hungry," Sidney mumbled.

Eugene yawned. "We should try fishing again this morning. We're pretty close to the ocean."

Drayden pulled his maps from his pants' pocket. "This Scusset Beach is about a mile away. We could get lucky and—"

Gunshots rang out.

"Get down!" Eugene screamed.

Bullets whizzed by, splintering trees.

Everyone lay flat on their stomachs. Eugene arched up and pumped deafening rounds from his rifle, each discharge booming.

Catrice curled into a ball, covering her ears.

"Where are they?" Charlie lay on his back, Glock in hand.

Eugene craned his neck and squinted. A flurry of bullets flew over his head and he flattened. "Somebody's straight ahead."

Charlie rose to his knees and squeezed out a dozen rapid-fire shots in that direction, a staccato series of pops.

"Get down, Charlie!" Drayden shouted.

He noticed movement, then a camouflaged man darted from one tree to another on their right.

"Over there!" Drayden shoved the maps into his pocket. With a quivering hand, he aimed his pistol and fired five shots.

Something sailed through the air and landed in the middle of their group.

A grenade.

"Eugene!" Catrice shrieked.

In one motion, he snatched it up and backhand tossed it into the woods, curling into a ball. "Cover!"

An earth-shattering explosion showered them in dirt.

Sidney, her face flushed crimson and filthy, propped up on her elbows. She aimed her rifle in the direction of the grenade-thrower. "I can see your foot, you flunk," she mumbled before firing one shot.

The Guardian screamed and unleashed a flurry of bullets at them.

Everyone lay as flat as they could, arms over heads, feeling the blazing wind from the bullets.

Catrice's eyes were crazed. "Eugene, what do we do?"

"Grab your weapons. Get ready to run that way, six-o-clock!" He glanced south. "I'm gonna cover you with heavy fire. I think they're at twelve and three-o-clock. On my mark."

Drayden holstered his pistol and readied his rifle. He stuffed his pockets full of ammunition and took his flashlight, which was at the top of his pack.

"Someone hand me a loaded pistol," Eugene demanded.

Drayden drew his, jammed in a fresh magazine, and passed it to Eugene. It was no use to him anyway.

Eugene slung his rifle over his shoulder, kneeling up a bit with pistols in each hand.

A hail of bullets from multiple directions pummeled them.

Eugene dropped to the ground again on his stomach. "Dammit. We gotta get out of here. It could be a trap. One of them could be waiting to the south, hoping to pick us off if we run that way."

Charlie stuck his arm in the air and fired off a few rounds in the Guardians' direction.

"Run, and I mean run," Eugene said. "Don't worry about me. I'll get out."

Drayden questioned how they could escape without being shot. It seemed impossible.

Catrice was as pale as a ghost.

"I'll go in front," Drayden said. "I'll fire my rifle in the direction we're running in case someone is back there." What he lacked in skill he did not lack in bravery. He would not let his fear get the best of him.

"On three." Eugene cocked both guns. "One...two...three!" He jumped up, firing steady rounds simultaneously right and straight ahead.

Drayden leapt to his feet and bolted south. He pointed his M16A4 rifle straight ahead and pumped round after round.

Bullets whizzed past and ripped into the trees around them.

He expected the searing pain of a bullet in his back or legs at any moment. Sprinting through the throbbing in his ankle, he powered straight into thorn bushes and low-hanging branches, getting scratched and whacked. A little farther and they might be safe. "You guys behind me?" he shouted without checking.

A chorus of "yeah"s replied.

They reached Route 3 and turned left, heading north.

Drayden peered back. "Where's Eugene?"

"Go, go, go!" he yelled from out of sight behind them.

Drayden didn't slow until he was about to vomit. They must have run a half mile. He was wheezing, his breathing a strained whistle and his lungs on fire. He doubled over, on the verge of fainting.

Eugene caught up, red-faced and sweating. "Let's go, into the woods!" He darted ahead and took a sharp right off Route 3 into the thick forest.

The privates followed. After a hundred yards or so, Eugene squatted. "Everyone get down."

Coated in sweat and panting, they went belly down on the leafy forest floor. The heavy brush kept them out of sight.

"Quiet," Eugene whispered.

Charlie scowled. "Those pieces of shkat."

"Quiet, Charlie!" Eugene whisper-yelled. "We have to hide for a bit."

Drayden's heart was racing. The Guardians had tried to kill them. He always knew it was a possibility. Even so, he couldn't believe it.

The group remained that way, frozen in silence, for a solid ten minutes. They waited for voices, or for the Guardians to run past. Nothing happened.

"Is everybody all right?" Eugene handed Drayden's pistol back.

"We're fine," Drayden said, holstering it. "How about the Guardians?"

"I think I hit one of them in the foot," Sidney said. "I hope it was that Duarte guy."

"What about you?" Drayden asked Eugene. "You get any of them?"

"No."

CHAPTER 22

Sidney was in tears. "We lost everything."

"Almost," Drayden said. "I still have my maps, and I was too tired to put my battery and paperclip away last night. Got my flashlight too."

He tried to put a positive spin on it, but an already desperate situation had become dire. They had *no* food or water. Drayden viewed the map, struggling to navigate the crew through the woods to Route 3a. It ran parallel to Route 3, closer to the coast. It rejoined Route 3 a little further north, and lengthened their journey a tad.

"We have our weapons," Eugene said.

Charlie made a gagging sound. "Is it just me, or now that we have no water is everyone else insanely thirsty?"

Drayden walked alone up front, focusing on the immediate task of locating Route 3a to distract himself from the sudden thirst Charlie highlighted. He stopped when the brush thinned a bit. It was noticeably clearer for fifteen yards before thickening again.

He studied the landscape. "I think this is it. Route 3a."

"This?" Sidney said, raising her palm.

Although the asphalt formerly covering the road was gone, the foliage was thinner and the trees shorter in both directions as far as the eye could see.

It used to be a road. Drayden imagined in another twenty-five years no traces of Route 3a would remain at all. "Yup. At least we'll be safe from the Guardians for a while." He coughed, his throat aching. "They'll stick to Route 3 for sure."

They turned left, heading north. Catrice walked up front alongside Eugene. "Eugene, are you surprised the Guardians attacked us?"

"A little, yeah." He dropped his rifle to low-ready. "I thought they might once we reached Boston if they were following. I didn't think they would do it fifty miles away. I'm not convinced they were trying to kill us, though."

"Could'a fooled me, Euge," Charlie said, walking beside Sidney in the back. "You know, that whole thing where they shot like a billion bullets at us and flung a grenade at your head."

"That's just it," Eugene said. "If they discovered where we were, why not sneak up on us while we slept and execute us, point blank? Even the grenade. You're supposed to pull the pin and wait a second before you throw it, so you can't do what I did. They knew I would toss it out. Consider how many bullets they shot, yet none hit us, and they're superb shots."

"Why'd they do it then?" Sidney asked.

"Our gear, I think. The food and water. They were probably starving. The flashlights, rope, all that stuff."

Drayden tugged on his left earlobe. "Let's think. Stealing our food and water was logical. But why exactly did they leave us alive?"

"Because they're secretly good guys and didn't want to kill five teenagers?" Catrice said with a hopeful tone.

Eugene shook his head. "Nope. They're ruthless. No feelings. If they intentionally left us alive, it was for a definite reason. The only reasonable explanation is they don't know the way to Boston. They need to follow us."

It confirmed Drayden's suspicions about the Guardians. They were bad dudes. While most Guardians were decent people, these three were not. "Hopefully we threw them a mini curveball sneaking over to Route 3a."

"I guess," Eugene said, sounding unconvinced. "But eventually Captain Lindrick may know where they are. Sure, they left us alive this time because they need us right now. Next time we'll be disposable. Their attack confirms it. We need to beat them to Boston without a doubt. They won't let us reach Boston alive; I'm sure of it. If they reach it first, they'll be waiting for us. They sure as hell won't let us return to New America."

The group fell silent, digesting the implications of Eugene's words.

It was barely 10:00 AM, but the bright sun was raising the temperature by the minute. The salty, moist air meant they must have been near the ocean.

"One of them has a shot foot," Sidney said. "Hopefully that'll slow them down a bit."

Drayden coughed again, this time hacking up more phlegm. He spat it out. "Yuck. Okay, so we have imminent needs. Let's lay out what they are and prioritize. We have no food or water. Of those, water is way more critical. The sky is totally clear and it hasn't rained in a few days, meaning no puddles and no water on the way."

"We'll have to find a stream," Catrice said.

Drayden nodded. "Yup. But we'll have to boil that water."

"Soooo, we also need a pot," she said.

"Exactly. Our first order of business is finding a pot of some sort. We need another town. Plymouth is coming up, according to the map. We can try rummaging through abandoned houses or an old store. Let's keep a lookout for streams too."

"We need to get ahead of the Guardians, though," Charlie said.

"If only we could find a way to go faster," Sidney said.

"Yes, all those things," Drayden said. "Of those, water is the most important. Then we'll worry about getting ahead of the Guardians."

He remembered he planned to loop Charlie in about Eugene's possible duplicity. He slowed until Charlie and Sidney caught up, then grabbed him by the arm and let her walk ahead.

Charlie glanced down at Drayden's hand on his arm. "Is this about how Catrice loves Eugene now? She loves him like a fat kid loves cake."

Drayden glared at him. "She doesn't lov—never mind. No, something else." He told Charlie about Eugene pretending to lift the tree, and noted he failed to shoot any Guardians even though the kid never missed.

"So?" Charlie asked.

"So? *So?* He might be working with the Guardians."

Charlie cringed. "Dray, I think you're letting your jealousy get the better of you. He's a smooth-talking, movie-star-looking, strong, tough, smart guy who stole your girlfriend. Without even trying. But listen, that tree weighed like eighty kajillion pounds. He probably went through the motions, knowing it was impossible, because you asked him to give it a shot. When we got attacked he was like Rambo. You remember when the Bureau played the movie *Rambo* in Madison Square Park? Rambo defeated all of Russia and Vietnam by himself. Eugene was like that, except it was real. Kid fired two guns in different directions while totally exposed, standing up. His balls are bigger than—"

"I got it. I got it."

"All I'm saying is the Guardians were dug in, behind trees, that's why he didn't hit them. Those guys aren't rookies. And don't forget: Eugene has saved your life like fifty times."

Charlie was probably right. "I know he has. Just remember what I said, and keep your eyes on him. We stick together."

"We'll stick together like fat, sweaty thighs, bro." Charlie fist-bumped him.

Drayden lingered behind as Charlie walked ahead. He observed Catrice and Eugene chatting up front.

Something unexpected had happened during the attack. In her time of need, it was Eugene she'd called out for. Recalling the Initiation, when she'd almost fallen off the rock wall at the Times Square Station, Catrice had cried out for Drayden. It was one of the first signs she was into him. Although she *had* slept next to Drayden last night, that may have been out of routine. Inertia. Or, so she wouldn't humiliate him. He hated how she made him feel inferior, like a flunk. Tears formed along with a lump in his throat. Why wasn't he good enough anymore? What had he done wrong? Maybe she was trying to hurt him before he had a chance to hurt her. That was stupid, though, since he would never do that.

Eugene's strength and toughness did draw quite a contrast with his own. Drayden had been fighting to show Catrice that he could be strong and tough too. Why were those such valuable traits? The Guardians, and to a lesser extent Eugene, had warped their toughness into something ugly. They dialed the volume on it to the max until it morphed into brutality. It was in the way they treated survivors out here in the wild, and regarded other living creatures for that matter. That wasn't toughness, it was barbarity.

Drayden swallowed, wincing from his sore throat. He remembered the gummy sap in his pocket. You could treat a sore throat by chewing it, as the Native Americans used to do, according to Sam. He pulled out a chunk and tossed it in his mouth. It was utterly horrendous, both crumbly and tasting like chemicals. He continued to chew it anyway. If it cured his cold, it was worth it.

Thinking about Sam triggered a stream of consciousness that meandered from Sam to Kim and her plot, to Nathan Locke, and naturally to Wes and Dad. Drayden loathed the expedition and longed to go home. He wished he had never even entered the

Initiation and still lived in the Dorms, oblivious to the problems in New America. He wanted someone else to deal with it.

"Whoa, check this out!" Eugene called out.

Old train tracks running alongside Route 3a appeared in the brush. Eugene veered over to walk on them and everyone followed. Besides some rotting and missing railroad ties, they were in surprisingly decent shape.

"I'm not sure I like this," Sidney said.

Charlie chuckled. "Having serious Initiation flashbacks right now."

Drayden was as well. After that nightmare, he was sure he never needed to see train tracks again. At least they broke up the monotony of a four-day hike.

When Route 3a became less overgrown and more commercial, with rundown businesses bordering it, the group switched over to the road. They'd arrived in Plymouth, passing Marylou's Coffee, Luke's Liquors, and a tiny white house called Kush-Kone.

"How about we try in there for a pot?" Eugene was eyeing a wide brown building that resembled a barn.

It was set back from the street at the far end of an expansive, overgrown parking lot. The busted sign read "Stop & Shop."

A cool breeze made the tall grass dance.

Drayden liked the feel of the wispy grasses against him. He stretched his hand out, running it through the soft blades as he walked. The same greenery undulated on the roof of the Stop & Shop, as if it had sprouted a head of hair. He wondered when buildings would disappear, swallowed up by vegetation, reduced to dust, and blown away by the wind.

They passed a trio of rusted out cars, brown shells on flat tires, the interiors covered in mold.

"Think any cars out here still run?" Sidney asked.

Charlie kicked one and a chunk fell off. "We'd be golden if we had a car."

Drayden made a mental note: find a car dealership. He'd considered it earlier and dismissed it, but it was worth a check now that their speed of travel was an issue. He eyeballed the Stop & Shop ahead, already debating how they would enter. What if it was loc—

Something leapt in front of him. A large brown blur.

Catrice screamed.

Drayden jumped back and ducked.

A deer bounded away, hopping with impressive speed through the dense lot.

"Holy shkat." His heart racing, he braced his hands on his knees for a moment.

Charlie chortled. "Jeez. It's like we're in the Serengeti! That was awesome."

"Let's keep moving," Eugene said.

With thirty yards to the store, Drayden resumed walking. The building's glass doors were shattered, but intact. And closed. They were probably that automatic type containing motion sensors, which wouldn't work anymore. He could try smashing through it. The separate metal door, adjacent to the glass doors, might be worth a shot too.

Drayden turned his head back to the others. "What do you think, break our way in? Use our rifles?"

"Let's try that steel door first," Catrice said.

As Drayden contemplated the best way inside, his peripheral vision caught rapid movement to his right.

Something furry and stinky slammed into him, knocking him to the ground.

He cried out as he crashed down, holding his ribs from the surging internal pain. It felt like he got punched hard in the stomach.

The silvery beast blew by him and spun around.

Drayden scrambled back to his feet, nauseated from the stomach pain. He froze.

A wolf. Or some sort of wolf-dog hybrid.

Guns cocked behind Drayden.

The wolf locked its icy, menacing eyes on him. Its bristly fur was patchy, its back hunched, and its ribcage bulging. The wolf emitted a low growl, curling its lips and baring its teeth. It was only feet away.

There was virtually no defense against a wolf, save for a weapon, according to the scientists. You couldn't outrun it, and it would consider you prey if you ran anyway. You couldn't turn your back on it, or look it in the eyes. If a wolf pounced, it would likely eat you while you were alive, disemboweling you first. As a last resort, you could try to appear hulking and it might not attack.

Rather than reach for his gun, Drayden raised his arms and widened his stance. He fixed his gaze on the ground. "Don't shoot it unless it charges me," he said in an authoritative voice. "I'm going to back away, slowly." He inched backward.

The snarl grew louder, nastier.

Drayden took short, rapid breaths. He stepped back again.

The wolf released an awful, guttural noise. It sprung at him.

He raised his arms to protect his head.

A gunshot.

The bullet pierced the wolf right between the eyes. It collapsed to the ground, shaking and twitching.

Eugene was still holding his rifle up, peering through the sight.

Drayden's focus drifted past Eugene and his jaw dropped. He couldn't speak. He jabbed his finger in the air, pointing behind the other privates.

They spun around and recoiled in horror.

Six or seven other wolves bolted toward them.

"Oh my God!" Sidney screamed.

"Run! To the store!" Eugene yelled.

Despite fear crippling Drayden for a moment, he forced his feet to move. The thick grass hindered him as he tried to sprint, like in a dream. Eugene ran up front, heading for the doors.

"Try the gray door on the left!" Drayden shouted.

"Move!" Charlie yelled from behind.

Sidney flew past Drayden.

The wolves would reach them in seconds.

Even with guns, they might not be fast or accurate enough to shoot them all before being mauled to death. Drayden worried about Catrice, who was not a speedy runner. He deliberately slowed to stay near her.

Charlie passed them.

The ground rumbled, thunderous footsteps right on their heels.

"Dray!" Eugene shrieked, his head turned back. He spun around, backpedaling, and fired his rifle in the air with a resounding boom.

Drayden checked behind him.

The gunshot bought them a second or two. The wolves had slowed momentarily before charging again.

Eugene flung the metal door open. He waited outside, holding it. "Let's go!"

Sidney raced inside, followed by Charlie, Catrice, and Drayden. Eugene entered and slammed the door shut.

Everyone doubled over, panting, dripping with sweat.

The store was cool and dark, and smelled musty. The wolves growled and howled outside the door. One of them hustled along the front perimeter of the store.

Drayden coughed in fits, watching it.

Oh no. The main doors.

"Eugene! The other doors. Make sure they can't get in!"

Eugene drew his Glock. "Charlie, get your gun out, dammit. You go that way," he said, motioning right, "I'll go this way. Check for holes or open doors!" Eugene jogged down the length of the store's dusty front.

Charlie went the other way. Drayden, Catrice, and Sidney lingered by the door with their weapons out, just in case.

The wolves paced in front of the store, crying a high-pitched whine. They were emaciated, clearly starving.

Drayden kicked himself for not considering the possibility of wolves in advance. Sam had warned them. Deer were prey. Where there was prey, there were predators.

Eugene and Charlie returned at the same time. Breathing heavily, both lowered their guns. "Don't see any way in," Eugene said. "Those automatic glass doors are stuck shut and the glass is broken but still up. I think we're safe."

"Good," Drayden said. "You and Charlie guard the doors; keep an eye on the wolves. Me, Catrice, and Sidney will scour the store."

Eugene saluted. "Roger that."

"C'mon, you guys," Drayden said to Catrice and Sidney.

They walked past a row of antique cash registers, and up and down the aisles in order. The store had been looted many times over. Not much remained other than dust, garbage, and empty plastic bottles. The shelves were mostly empty, but a few items popped up here and there. Unfortunately, nothing that would be of use. Toys for cats. Wrapping paper.

"Anything we need a shower-curtain liner for?" Sidney asked.

Drayden waved a hand through the air. "No idea."

She stuffed it into one of her pockets.

They found a kids' toy section, with a plastic bat and ball, as well as training wheels for a child's bike.

An idea popped into Drayden's head. If they could find bikes, they could beat the Guardians to Boston easily. He made another mental note.

Catrice was wringing her hands. "No pots."

Drayden stood on his tippy toes to ascertain the layout of the store. "I bet they have some storerooms in the back, like at the Food Distribution Centers back home. The Bureau built those in former grocery stores."

They navigated into the Seafood and Deli section. A door behind the counter led to a room resembling a warehouse, with empty crates and boxes scattered around. On one side of the room was a kitchen of sorts, featuring stainless steel counters and a wide sink. Beside the sink sat a colander, a nutcracker, and balled up aluminum foil. And a metal bowl.

Drayden picked up the bowl and examined it.

It was a little rusty, and had no handle, but it might work.

"I think that's the best we're gonna do," Sidney said.

Catrice hooked her thumb back toward the doors. "There were some empty water bottles laying around the store. We should grab those. Otherwise, we have nowhere to store the water we boil."

"Yeah, good idea," Drayden said.

They reentered to the main section of the store and collected ten empty bottles, stuffing a few in their pants' pockets. When they returned to the entrance, Eugene and Charlie were leaning against a cash register, chatting.

"How about we fire some warning shots?" Charlie suggested.

"Or just shoot 'em all," Eugene countered. "No warning."

Charlie nudged Eugene, drawing his attention to the bowl in Drayden's hands. "You hungry? Dray's gonna toss a salad."

"It's the best we could do," Drayden said. "Shoot what?"

"The wolves," Eugene said, biting down on his lower lip. "We're kinda trapped at the moment."

A few of the wolves had lain down, panting. Others frantically paced and howled.

Even though the wolves might be plotting to eat them, they were only doing what they were supposed to do. They weren't *evil* wolves.

"I don't want to kill them," Drayden said. "The world is rebuilding, repopulating. We can't be killing stuff."

"Dray's right," Catrice said. "Life is evolving again, in a new way. We shouldn't be destroying it. What if these are the last wolves left in the world?"

Sidney rolled her eyes. "I'm trying to save my sister and you're worried about the wolves?"

"So, should we let them eat us?" Charlie asked.

Drayden cocked his head. "No, of course not—that's not what we're saying. If it's us or them, obviously we choose us. How about that warning shot first, to scare them off?"

Eugene twirled his pistol. "Fine. I'm going to fire a few shots out that door we came through. You guys watch through the glass doors, see what they do." He cracked the steel door and peeked through. After he stuck the muzzle of the Glock out, he aimed high and fired two crisp shots, the loud pops echoing throughout the store.

The wolves scrambled away into the tall grass.

Sidney cheered. "It worked!"

"Ah, wait a minute." Charlie raised his finger in the air. "They're still there, roaming in the parking lot now. Sweet."

Eugene returned to see for himself. "I think we gotta kill 'em, bro," he said to Drayden.

Drayden sulked. They did need to leave the store. They had to survive and make it to Boston before the Guardians. "How? If we go out there and we miss, we'll get swarmed."

Eugene surveyed the parking lot. "I think me, Sid, and Charlie can pick them off from in here. There were seven, total. At a minimum we can off a few of them before we venture outside."

The three of them handled their rifles. They checked the ammo, loaded fresh magazines.

"Hold on a sec," Drayden said. "They're—something's up."

The others gathered behind him to watch through the glass doors. A wolf howled in the distance. The pack sprinted away down Route 3a, in the opposite direction, chasing a deer.

The lead wolf snagged it, tackling it to the ground. When the rest caught up, they ravished the unlucky animal.

Drayden's eyes widened. "Let's go, right now!" He led the way to the door, cracking it enough to see outside.

The sunlight blinded him for a second.

"We hug the front of the store and continue north, off the street," he whispered.

"Weapons live," Eugene whispered.

Drayden drew his pistol, even though it might as well have been a toy gun.

"Go!"

He bolted out.

CHAPTER 23

The late afternoon sun cast broad shadows in the heart of Plymouth, Massachusetts.

Sidewalks lined the streets and buildings nestled close together, like in New America. It fell somewhere between small city and large town.

Since Drayden had started a habit of making mental notes to himself, he noted to beware of wolves, especially if deer were around. They'd escaped the pack outside Stop & Shop by pure luck, at the expense of an unfortunate deer. Now they walked with their weapons live all the time.

"Plymouth was where the Pilgrims settled," Eugene said to nobody in particular. "The birthplace of America. Like New America, PostCon."

Charlie carried the metal bowl, a fact impossible to forget due to his constant drumming on it. Occasionally he supplemented the drumming with singing.

"For the love of God, will you pleeease stop!" Sidney said.

"I'm keeping the wolves at bay." To some tune nobody recognized, in a wretched singing voice, he belted, "I'm keeping the wooo-lves at baa-aay."

Drayden coughed. "The wolves might attack just to shut you up."

Catrice chuckled when she looked back at Charlie, who'd stopped drumming and now wore the bowl on his head like a hat.

"It's a little ironic, don't you think?" Charlie asked. "We found a bowl, and now we can't find water. The first half of this stupid expedition, we couldn't get away from water. The ocean, then the first river we crossed when I slipped, then the stream, then the raging river. It was like water every two minutes on Route 6. Route 3a is basically a desert. With wolves. Route 3a sucks."

Nobody discussed the food situation, perhaps because the lack of water was far more serious, or since mentioning food might have revived their insane hunger. They hadn't eaten in twenty-four hours. Drayden was so hungry that he actually *wasn't* hungry anymore. He was weak, and tired. His feet were numb. The cough, which began as a nuisance, had grown debilitating. He was wheezing, and every breath was labored. Other than leave a vile taste in his mouth, the gummy sap he chewed had done nothing. He couldn't even rinse it out.

Sidney, scary good at reading his mind and sensing his needs, rolled up beside him. "Hey, how are you feeling? That cough sounds terrible."

"Thanks for asking." Drayden coughed into his arm. "It's nasty. Don't get too close; I don't want you to catch it."

She rubbed his shoulder. "I don't care. We need you."

"Thanks, Sid."

Eugene, who was walking alone up front, hollered back, "I think if we do find water, we should wait a while to boil it. I know everyone's thirsty. But we risk giving away our location to the Guardians, who will surely try to kill us for real next time. We should focus on getting ahead of them."

"I think we should boil it as soon as we find it," Catrice retorted. "We're on a different road than the Guardians right now, we believe, so we're far enough away. If we get ahead of them, on Route 3 when the roads join, they might see it."

Drayden thought she made a valid point, and it was a chance to team up with her against Eugene. "I agree with Catrice."

She finally noticed Drayden and Sidney walking close together.

"I'm with Euge on this one," Charlie said. "I think the Guardians' guns are a bigger risk."

"What if we check out the next car dealership we see?" Drayden said. "We've passed a few. All the cars outside are rusty piles of junk, but the dealerships have an inside section with a few cars inside. They're protected from rain and stuff."

"Let's try the next one," Eugene said.

Charlie glowed like a kid on the last day of school. "Can I drive?"

"Sure, Charlie," Drayden said.

"Yes!" He resumed drumming.

Drayden processed the random businesses in Plymouth they passed. Plymouth Antiques Trading Company; Cash for Gold Pawn Shop; Martini's Bar and Grill; Dominic's Fine Clothing. Except for the encampments of survivors, nothing he'd discovered on this expedition would be helpful in overthrowing the Bureau. Not only were they failing on their stated goal, he was falling short on his secret one.

He gritted his teeth, pondering what else he should be doing—what Kim would suggest. She would probably say to reach Boston alive and go from there. Hopefully something useful would reveal itself. He debated telling the others about the plot to overthrow the Bureau. Sure, Kim had made him swear he wouldn't tell a soul, yet circumstances had changed. The mission had gone off the rails, plus it was increasingly doubtful they would even make it home. He couldn't though, not without being sure he could trust Eugene. Despite Charlie's convincing defense of the guy, he wasn't ready to fully accept Eugene's confidence.

"Boom," Eugene said, hurrying ahead to the left. "There you go, chief. Time to work some magic."

They approached a spacious lot crammed with ancient cars. Behind it was an enclosed glass room with additional cars inside. In white writing over a blue background, the billboard sign read "Chevrolet."

Using his silencer, Eugene fired two shots into the lock. The bullets obliterated it and shattered the glass door.

"I'd say it's pretty open now," Charlie said.

Eugene entered and the privates followed him inside.

Five cars occupied this glass enclosure. A fine dust coated everything, papers littered the floor, and it smelled wet. One of the hanging lights had crashed to the floor.

"Chev-row-lett," Charlie sounded it out. "Chev...Chev-ro... Shay-vro—"

"Charlie," Drayden said. He inspected the cars, figuring they should focus on the biggest one, which was a roomy black vehicle that resembled the vans in the Palace.

The tires were flat, but otherwise, the structure looked intact. Writing on the back, in the lower left corner, read "Tahoe."

"Guys," Drayden called out, "I think this is the one we should work on."

"Nope." Charlie peeked inside the window of what appeared to be a race car. "If I'm driving, I want this one." He walked behind the red vehicle and read the name out loud. "Camaro. ZL1."

Sidney snorted. "Charlie, we wouldn't all fit. And that car probably isn't the best for roads that have no *road* left."

Charlie released an exaggerated exhale. "Fine."

Drayden opened the door to the Tahoe, thrilled to find the truck unlocked. He sat in the driver's seat and touched some of the buttons and dials around the steering wheel. "Where would the key go in?"

Catrice entered through the passenger side door and joined him inside. "Look, there's a button that says 'Engine Start/Stop.' Try pushing that."

Maybe it didn't need a key. He pushed the button.

Nothing happened.

She sighed. "I guess you still need a key."

"Let's think," Drayden said. "What do we need for the car to work? We need a key. We need new tires. What else?"

"Gas," she said. "I don't think it would last twenty-five years. Does gas evaporate? I don't know."

His hopelessness grew. This car thing was a Hail Mary. They might be wasting time. Whatever, it was worth a shot. "Charlie, you look around for keys. Sid, you search for fresh tires. Eugene, you try to find spare gas. Plan?"

"Roger," Eugene said.

Charlie went to walk away before stopping. "I can drive, right?"

"If we get it running, yes," Drayden said.

He giggled and bounded away.

Drayden and Catrice sat alone in the car—the first time since they'd left New America that it was just the two of them. Although he'd never felt uncomfortable around Catrice, he did now. They gazed into each other's eyes. Drayden yearned to ask what happened to her, to them.

"How's it going?" That was what came out instead, after the prolonged silence.

Idiot.

She grimaced. "I'm scared, Drayden. I'm afraid we're going to die out here. I don't want to die. And I'm so thirsty."

Was it possible she didn't think anything was wrong with them? It could have been what Eugene had said, that she didn't even realize she was pulling away. Or, as Sidney insinuated, she was playing games. "I know. I'm scared and thirsty too. But...how are *we* doing?"

"We're fine."

Drayden coughed a few times. "Listen, Eugene's a great guy; I like him a lot too. I'm just saying, you know...I get it."

She wrinkled her nose. "What are you talking about?"

Charlie returned with a handful of keys. "Are these them? I found them in one of the offices. They don't look like keys, but they have some buttons, like this closed lock and this open lock." He dumped them in Drayden's lap.

Holding one, Drayden searched for some place to insert it. "Where does it go?"

Catrice reached over and hit the Engine Start/Stop button. Nothing happened.

Eugene and Sidney strolled back together, chatting. Sidney walked up to the driver's side door. "We struck out. No extra tires, no extra gas."

It's over.

"This was a terrible idea, guys," Drayden said. "I'm sorry. My bad. Let's go." He hopped out of the driver's seat.

"Hey, it was worth a shot, Dray," Eugene said.

Charlie jumped inside the Camaro. "I'm coming...I had to try this for a sec. My driving career was over before it started."

The group left the dealership and returned to Route 3a, moving a little slower now.

Their dehydration was growing increasingly serious. Besides having a sticky dry mouth, Drayden was dead tired and headachy. Everyone's eyes were more sunken, their skin sallow. Thankfully he'd long passed the point of hunger. His stomach felt hollow and acidic instead.

"It'll be dark soon." Eugene fanned his arm out. "We should sleep in one of these buildings."

Charlie stepped off the road. "I don't know about you guys, but I haven't peed since yesterday. I wanna try to drain the main vein. Hose down the deck, you know? See a man about a dog. Turn the bike 'round. Release the—"

"Charlie!" Sidney yelled. "Enough."

Bikes, Drayden remembered. They needed to find bikes.

Charlie plodded behind a white house that had been a chiropractor's office, according to the sign, while the rest of the team waited in the street.

"Guys! Dray! Come back here!" Charlie shouted from behind the dwelling.

The privates and Eugene exchanged wary glances.

"Nobody wants to watch you hose down the deck, Charlie!" Drayden yelled.

Eugene cracked up.

"No, it's not my anaconda! It's better!"

Even though no one believed him, they marched through the yard and behind the house.

Charlie was waiting at the far side of the short yard. "Look! A creek!"

Drayden whipped out his two bottles. "Nice job, Charlie! Everyone fill up your bottles from the store, but don't drink it yet."

"Any fish in there?" Sidney bent down and swished her hand around the water.

"Don't think so," Eugene said. He walked over to Charlie and patted him on the back. "Should we thank you, or your anaconda?"

Charlie made a silly face. "There you go, Euge, workin' a little humor. I dig it."

A titanic wave of relief washed over Drayden. Major crisis averted. Despite the disagreement over their most urgent problem, he was still convinced it was water. As soon as they boiled it, they could focus on the food crisis and the Guardians.

Although he hadn't even drunk yet, he felt re-energized. Based on the giddiness of the crew, they felt the same. If they could find bikes, they could beat the Guardians to Boston. A tinge of excitement grew inside him. "Now we need to pick a place to camp, start a fire, boil this water, and we're back in business."

Drayden turned to leave and stutter-stepped back. "Don't move," he said to the others.

A few of them audibly inhaled.

"Holy shkat," Charlie said quietly.

They stood face to face with a bear. Apparently, it had crept up on them amidst their jubilance.

Drayden racked his brain for the information Sam had taught them about bears. This was a black bear. They couldn't outrun it, or climb a tree to escape it, and they shouldn't look it in the eye. With black bears, you couldn't play dead. You *could* scare them away if you were lucky. He kicked himself once again for not anticipating it, like the wolves around the deer. Clearly they weren't the only ones who needed water.

A gun cocked. "Dray, step aside," Eugene said in a monotone voice.

The bear roared, a mere ten feet from Drayden—close enough to maul them in less than a second. After staring them down, it paced back and forth. Its sound fell somewhere between growl and roar, but closer to roar.

It was terrifying. Drayden glanced behind, and Eugene was aiming his Glock at the bear.

Three cubs hopped over from the thick brush, frolicking beside their mother. The bear, now stopped in front of them, roared and stomped her foot.

"We can't shoot her," Drayden said. "She has babies. Don't look her in the eye." He stared at the ground to his left. "Everyone get closer to me, in a tight bunch. Make yourself big, raise your arms in the air. We're going to make noise. Get ready. If she charges, stand your ground. Do not turn and run." This was a mother protecting her cubs, not a predatory assault.

The teens encircled him and lifted their arms.

The bear roared again. She charged a few feet and stopped.

Catrice shrieked.

Sweat trickled down Drayden's cheek. He closed his eyes.

"Now!" he yelled.

Charlie drummed on the metal bowl, and the others yelled, and sang, and lalalalala'd.

The bear spun and hauled out of there, like a scared bully, her cubs in tow.

Everyone deflated at the same time.

"And this hopefully concludes the wildlife portion of your expedition," Charlie said.

The group huddled around the fire.

Night had fallen. Charlie and Sidney had gathered loads of wood to make the fire powerful enough to boil water. They'd built it in the parking lot of the Best Western Cold Spring Hotel, still in Plymouth, Massachusetts. While a short distance from the bear encounter, it was roughly forty miles to Boston.

"Can I just say how bad I need a shower?" Sidney asked.

"I can smell my own butt," Charlie said.

Everyone groaned immediately, the chorus of disgust in unison.

Drayden grimaced. "Oh dude, Charlie, c'mon man."

Sidney pretended to vomit. "That is vile, Charlie."

Eugene couldn't stop laughing, and Catrice bit back the chuckles.

"Sorry. But I can," Charlie said, matter-of-factly. "But. Can. Unintended puns all over the place."

Drayden turned his head and coughed. "Moving on. How about that bear?"

Eugene cleaned his weapons with a handkerchief he'd pulled from his pocket. "Dray, I was so close to shooting it. You don't even know."

"The cubs would have been orphaned," Catrice said.

Drayden stared at the fire. "I don't think we should kill things unless we have no choice." He sneezed.

"Bless you," Eugene said. "You guys must have been raised different than me. My old man was tough, mean. It was kind of a take-no-prisoners upbringing."

Drayden gave Eugene a quizzical smile. "Isn't your dad a teacher?"

"Yeah, he is. He's just brutal. High expectations of his son." Eugene tossed a stick into the fire.

For a moment Drayden thought about his own father, and how he didn't seem to care enough to be tough on Drayden. Brutal was bad, sure, but you needed to care to be like that. He shoved the thought away and examined the fire.

It was transitioning from the high flames stage to the hot coals stage. They needed to boil the water over the hot coals; otherwise, the fire wouldn't be hot enough. They'd placed some rocks in the fire on which to place the bowl, suspending it right above the coals.

"I'm soooo thirsty." Sidney shook the full, plastic water bottles in each hand.

They caught Drayden's attention and held it, as if he were in a trance. *Something about the bottles.* It hit him like a hot stone. How could he have been so stupid? He untied one boot, took it off, and removed the laces. After unscrewing the cap from one of his bottles, he tied a loop around the neck, like a miniature noose. Then he tied the other end of the lace to a narrow branch leftover from the fire setup. His contraption approximated a fishing rod with a water bottle at the end. He lowered it over the flames, careful not to touch them.

Charlie poked his bottle with a long stick. "Um, whatcha doing there, Dray? Pretty sure you're gonna melt your bottle and put our fire out."

"I don't think so," Drayden said. "I don't know why it didn't occur to me earlier. The melting point of the plastic has gotta be higher than the boiling temperature of water. And the water in the bottle should prevent the plastic from melting."

Tiny bubbles inside the bottle floated up and disappeared in bunches.

"The flames will be hot coals in a few more minutes," Drayden said. "It may be too hot for this after that. Can you guys do what I did with the bottle and the laces, in case this works?"

They each took off a boot, removed the laces, and built the same water-bottle fishing rod. Everyone studied Drayden's bottle.

The bubbles rose faster and faster. A few minutes later, it boiled.

"Yes!" Drayden removed it from the fire. It only needed to reach boiling to be safe to drink.

The others boiled one bottle each, and Drayden boiled his second one. After that, the fire was too hot. Everyone else had another bottle to boil, and the contents of all four fit in the bowl. After a few minutes, it was done.

Eugene leaned over the bubbling bowl of water. "How do we pull the scalding bowl off the rocks without spilling it or getting burned?"

"How about we pick it up with a shirt or something?" Charlie asked.

Drayden patted him on the shoulder. "That's smart, Charlie. Great idea. I don't want to embarrass you, but you've had a bunch of smart ideas on this trip."

"Really? Thanks, Dray." He fist-bumped Drayden.

Without hesitation, Eugene pulled off his gray camouflage shirt. A sleeveless white undershirt clung to his torso, showing off his impressive physique.

His whole upper body was even more shredded with muscle than anyone could have guessed. And to think, Drayden was attempting to show Catrice he could be as strong as Eugene. What a joke. He would never be as physically powerful as Eugene. Drayden had always been self-conscious about his skinny body. It had come up a few times in the Initiation, when he wound up shirtless beside Charlie. Why fight a losing battle?

"Remind me never to take my shirt off next to Eugene," he said instead, giggling.

Everyone else laughed too, including Catrice. Eugene scooped up the bowl and set it down on the grass where the other bottles cooled.

Catrice touched one of the full bottles. "This first round of bottles is warm but drinkable now."

Everyone gathered around and picked one.

Charlie held his out. "Cheers."

The warm water touched Drayden's lips and splashed around his dry, cracked mouth. It was heaven. He paused mid-bottle to swish some water around his mouth, before chugging the rest of it.

The five parched teens stood in silence, a state of speechless relief. Charlie burped.

Although Drayden's second bottle was also ready to drink, the others needed to wait for the bowl to cool. He decided to save his for later. "I think we should each drink our second bottle tonight.

We're severely dehydrated. But wait a bit first. Before we leave in the morning, we'll go back and hit up that creek and restock."

Catrice tested the temperature of the bowl by resting her finger on the edge. "Eugene, can you hold the bottles while I pour the water in?"

After she filled the bottles with Eugene's help, she passed them out.

Drayden checked out the hotel.

It contained a few separate buildings, most of them two stories tall. The closest resembled a stretched out gray house, with doors to the rooms spaced out across the front. A white railing ran along the second floor. It was dilapidated like all other buildings out in the real world. Still, it was better than sleeping on leaves in the woods.

"Shall we?" Eugene strolled over to one of the doors on the first floor. He tried the knob, but finding it locked, stepped back and kicked it open with a thud. The smell practically knocked them over. Mold.

Drayden flipped on his flashlight and peered inside.

"Gross," Charlie said.

The room must have flooded in the past, as evidenced by the severe water damage and stench.

"Let's try upstairs," Catrice said. "Looks like the pipes burst down here."

Drayden shined his flashlight up the stairs as they climbed, and Eugene busted down the first door. Despite a coating of dust and a mildewy smell, the room had remained undisturbed for a generation. The bed was even made.

"Who wants this one?" Eugene asked.

Sidney peeked inside. "I'll take it."

"You want to borrow my flashlight?" Drayden asked.

"No, it's okay. Thanks Dray." She touched his arm. "Goodnight, you guys."

Eugene kicked open the following four rooms which were identical to the first.

Where will Catrice be sleeping tonight?

She answered Drayden's question pretty clearly when she entered the room next to Sidney and closed the door. After that, everyone took their own rooms.

Drayden beamed his flashlight around the dark creepy space and kicked off his boots. Since the dusty and moldy sheets weren't the best for his cough, he stripped the bed and laid down on the bare mattress.

The water had awakened his body. His ankle throbbed, the cut on his face was sore, and his feet ached. His lungs were heavy, his sinuses stuffy, and most significantly, his hunger had come raging back. It was as if the water had reminded his stomach that stuff was supposed to be in there. He craved that second bottle of water, but if he drank too hastily he would just pee it all out. He needed to wait.

Sleep was coming quickly. As he drifted off, thoughts swirled around his mind. The bear and her cubs; Dad and Wes; and Mom. He wondered if he was so desperate to keep Eugene from killing the bear because they were witnessing a mother doing her job, protecting her kids. He was that cub. Why hadn't his mother protected him like that? He bet that mama bear wasn't off cavorting with some fat old male bear, leaving her cubs to fend for themselves.

In self-pitying mode, he moved on to Catrice, sleeping separate from him for the first time. She probably needed a good night's sleep in her own bed. Or, she didn't want to catch Drayden's cold. Or, since they smelled gamey, she didn't want to embarrass either of them.

His insecurity said those weren't the real reasons. Things were most certainly not "fine" with them. That spark was just about gone.

Although Catrice wasn't weak, she might have latched onto him in the Initiation because he could save her. More accurately, they could help save each other. On the expedition, he couldn't. Eugene could. Eugene was the Drayden of the expedition.

He couldn't help but speculate whether Catrice went to Eugene's room tonight, or vice-versa. If Drayden's body had enough water to form tears, he might have cried.

CHAPTER 24

Drayden had chugged his second bottle of water as soon as he awoke.

Now he, Catrice, and Charlie waited in the parking lot for Sidney and Eugene to return from the creek, where they'd gone to replenish everyone's bottles. They would boil the water later, but who knew when they would find another stream?

"Catrice, I had an idea yesterday," Drayden said. "When Charlie went to take a leak, he said, 'turn the bike around,' which reminded me I wanted to search for bikes. What do you think?"

She chewed on a nail. "It would be a lot easier fixing up bikes than cars. Plus, we know our way around bikes. Where should we look?"

"I'm thinking in people's garages. Isn't that where they would store bikes?"

She shrugged. "Yeah, I guess."

Eugene and Sidney appeared in the distance, approaching with bulging pockets and handfuls of water bottles.

"Success," Eugene said as they arrived. He and Sidney passed out the bottles. "No bears."

Sidney walked right up to Drayden. She touched his forehead and then his cheek with the back of her hand. "How you feeling?"

Drayden noticed Catrice watching.

Good.

He inched toward Sidney, standing closer than he should. "I'm okay, the same. Nasty cough, headache, though that could be dehydration."

"Yeah, I have a terrible headache too."

"Let's move out," Eugene said, his rifle in hand.

"Eugene, we're going to hunt for bikes," Drayden said. "Probably try peoples' garages, once the area gets residential. You know how to ride a bike?"

"Absolutely. I can also drive a van, bus, you name it. All part of training."

Sidney held her stomach. "We need to find food. I'm starving."

Catrice wouldn't look at Sidney. "We either need a place to fish again or an encampment of survivors to ask for food."

Charlie took the lead and they resumed their hike. "Let's do it."

Catrice walked beside Eugene, behind Charlie, and Drayden walked beside Sidney in the rear.

"You see that cluster of oak trees?" Catrice asked Eugene, pointing skyward. "That would be beautiful to draw."

"Oh yeah," he said. "The crowns of the trees blend together, like one enormous tree."

Drayden sarcastically gawked at the trees and held his mouth open in imaginary amazement. All she could muster when they'd been alone was, "We're fine." He could feel Sidney's eyes.

She raised her brows and chuckled, then hooked her arm inside his, shaking her head.

They were still in a business area, real small-town America stuff. Modest buildings resembling houses operated as storefronts. They passed Balboni's Drug Store with its torn navy awning, and The Rock Pub, a diminutive brick bar with even tinier windows.

They'd only walked a few blocks when Charlie stopped abruptly. He spun around scratching his head. "Should we wait to look through garages, or just go in here?"

He stood in front of Martha's Bicycles. It was like a quaint home, with a glass front and a low-hanging brown-shingled roof.

Drayden beheld their first break in all its glory. Finally, some much-needed luck.

The two glass doors were shattered and partially ajar. Eugene pulled one open and walked inside, the privates trailing him. The cash register was unlocked and bare. People had clearly ransacked the shop, but many bikes remained.

Drayden took charge. "Let's pick the five best bikes and see if we can get them working."

"Um," Charlie said, looking sheepish, "I can't ride a bike with gears."

Drayden smirked. He'd forgotten about that. "Well, you find one you can ride."

The others sorted through the bikes and picked four, which were all ten-speeds. Besides having flat tires, the chains and gears were covered in rust. Drayden and Catrice would ride mountain bikes, one red and one black. Sidney and Eugene would ride racing bikes, with curved handlebars, one silver and the other gray. Though not ideal for the terrain, they were in much better shape than the other available mountain bikes.

Drayden examined the black mountain bike. "Let's flip them upside down. Sid, can you search for a pump? Eugene, see if you can find anything to scrape off the rust, like sandpaper or a screwdriver. Catrice, can you get some oil for the chains?"

As they walked off, Charlie returned with a bike of his own. "This is the only one." It was a miniature pink little girl's bike.

Drayden bit his lip, trying not to crack up, but it was no use. He burst into laughter.

"It's not funny." Charlie turned red. "How am I supposed to ride this?"

"In a nice little dress with flowers on it?" Drayden held his sides he was laughing so hard.

"Yeah, ha ha, laugh it up, bro. This is a serious situation."

The others came back and froze when they saw Charlie's bike. They glanced at each other and exploded in laughter.

Charlie stomped his foot. "It's not funny!"

Drayden wiped his tears away. "Charlie, flip it over. And go look for a wrench so we can at least raise the seat."

He turned it upside down and stormed off to the back of the store.

Everyone else made eye contact again and flew off into a new round of cackling.

"It's not funny, dammit!" Charlie yelled from somewhere out of sight.

Sidney was still grinning, a manual pump in her hand. "We got everything. Where do we start?"

Drayden took a few breaths, trying to think of anything else besides the pink bike. "Sid, you pump up all the tires. We'll work on the gears and chains." He took some sandpaper from Eugene and began scraping the rust off the black mountain bike.

Eugene and Catrice worked on two of the other bikes, while Sidney moved bike to bike, inflating the tires. Charlie returned and got started on the children's bike.

"I think it worked." Sidney tossed the pump aside, having filled the last tire. "Let's see if they hold." She snatched sandpaper to tackle the last bike's rust.

After Drayden scraped most of the rust off his, he tried turning the pedals, but they wouldn't budge. Catrice was failing as well.

Eugene grunted and flexed his muscles, employing sheer power to get his going. They made a snapping sound, then spun nicely.

Drayden watched him, again realizing the futility and absurdity of trying to physically match the guy. Not to mention how stupid it was to hope Catrice wouldn't compare them.

"Eugene, can you help me and Catrice start these up? Once they're moving, let's put on the oil."

"Yeah, no problem." He walked over to Drayden's bike and jerked the pedals a few times until they rotated, then repeated the process on Catrice's bike.

With painstaking patience, she squeezed oil on each link on every chain. They let the bikes sit for a few minutes.

"Now run your pedals as fast as you can," Drayden said. They rotated like brand new.

His excitement built, realizing this might actually work. "Moment of truth. Let's try 'em out." He turned over the black mountain bike and wheeled it out of Martha's Bicycles.

Charlie scowled, rolling out the pint-sized pink bike. "This is bull, man."

Drayden hopped on his bicycle and rode around in a wide circle. He wobbled a bit getting comfortable on it, but it worked splendidly.

Eugene, Catrice, and Sidney successfully followed suit. Charlie looked like a giant, needing to stick his knees way out to the side to prevent them from smacking the handlebars. Because of the tiny turn radius of the pedals and the mini wheels, he pedaled furiously just to achieve a reasonable speed.

The others stood over their bikes watching him, trying desperately not to erupt into another round of laughter. Charlie, noticing the peanut gallery, glowed red in the face, fuming.

"What? Yeah, okay, real funny, huge guy on a tiny bike—can we get over it now? Flunks."

Drayden bit his lip and averted his gaze, struggling to swallow the giggles. "Here's the plan. I checked the map. Route 3a goes for another few miles and crosses Route 3, where we believe the Guardians are. We can even stay on Route 3a a little longer, because it crosses Route 3 again a few miles later. Everybody good? Charlie?"

Charlie shook his head and murmured something inaudible.

Drayden rode up front, with everyone else in a group behind him. Charlie struggled to keep up in the rear, pedaling his heart out. Riding on these overgrown roads was nothing like biking in New America with its cracked but clear roads. This ride was bumpy, and required focused attention to dodge bushes, trees, and vast crevices in the remaining pavement. Still, they made rapid progress and reached the junction with Route 3 in fifteen minutes.

Route 3a crossed Route 3 via an overpass. Dripping sweat, they stopped before it and hopped off their bikes. Charlie was gasping for air.

Drayden couldn't stop coughing. After the exertion of riding, he was short of breath and his head pounded. He ducked down, crawled onto the overpass, and rose to his knees to peer down onto Route 3, half expecting the Guardians to be waiting there with ready weapons.

It was deserted, save for a few broken-down cars. Route 3 was a much larger road, a highway, with two-lanes in each direction. The roadway was in far superior condition to Route 3a.

Drayden lumbered to his feet and the others joined him.

"Look!" Sidney pointed south. "A windmill."

An inactive wind turbine, similar to New America's, towered in the distance.

"Maybe we should collect the battery," Catrice said.

"Wow, great idea," Eugene said.

It *was* a great idea. An ingenious idea. If Boston didn't pan out, they could seek out a windmill farm and harvest the batteries. Batteries wore out from constant charging and discharging, like those in New America. Wind turbines also needed maintenance from dirt or rust; otherwise, the blades would stop spinning, as this one had. Although these batteries would have no charge, they would still be viable. The privates lacked a way to transport heavy deep-cycle batteries, but they could come up with something.

"That's brilliant, Catrice," Drayden said. "Let's remember this intersection, in case Boston turns out to be empty. Worst case we won't show up to New America empty handed." He may have found their bargaining chip for the return home.

Charlie doubled over. "We have to find food. I don't think I can go on much longer."

"Dray, how far is it to Boston?" Eugene asked.

"Around thirty-five miles. Thirty to the outskirts."

Eugene rested his hand on Charlie's shoulder. "We can make it today, bud, in a few hours if we're lucky. Hopefully they'll feed us there. We can do it without stopping."

"You're forgetting something," Sidney said. "The Guardians. We'll have to deal with them sooner or later. It's not exactly a straight shot to Boston."

A chill ran down Drayden's spine. He didn't want to face them.

"Let's make a stand here." Eugene fanned his arm out across the overpass.

"We don't know if they've passed here already," Drayden said.

Through his rifle's scope, Eugene scanned Route 3 below. "One of them was shot in the foot; they're moving slower than us. If they are ahead, it can't be by much. We could wait here for a while. With the bikes, we'll catch up to them easily." Eugene stepped further out on the overpass. "This is the perfect place to ambush them. Elevated positioning. Plenty of time to set up, we'll see them coming from a half mile away. Me, Charlie, and Sid can take them out with three bullets."

Drayden didn't want to kill the Guardians. Even though they would kill him, that didn't make it right. Killing was wrong, whether someone would do it to you or not. He didn't need to stoop down to their level of brutality and depravity.

Plus, the Guardians were battle-trained and tested. Eugene might have been as well, but the rest of the privates weren't. Something would go wrong and they'd wind up in a dogfight with superior fighters. Drayden was not scared of them. It simply wasn't logical to go head-to-head with meaner, more experienced dudes. With the bikes, they could beat the Guardians to Boston and never have to face them.

"I'm not trying to pull rank here," said Drayden. "I just think we're best served by riding like crazy and beating the Guardians to Boston. We don't have to kill them."

Eugene twirled his pistol. "Kill or be killed."

"Life is too precious to kill indiscriminately," Drayden countered.

"Even if it's in our best interest," Catrice added softly.

Eugene appeared on the verge of calling them pansies. "Fine. You guys are in charge. We'll follow your lead."

Drayden raised a finger. "Don't forget, we have a secret weapon against the Guardians." He faced Charlie. "If they see that, they won't be able to shoot, they'll be laughing too hard."

Everyone snickered.

"It's not funny," Charlie harrumphed.

"I think we're in Norwell, Massachusetts, so this must be Wildcat Creek." Drayden stood over his bike, consulting the map in the middle of Route 3. "We've gone about fifteen miles. Twenty miles and we'll be in Boston."

Charlie huffed and puffed. "Please...tell me we're resting."

Drayden hacked up a glob of mucus and spat it out. "Yeah, let's take a break, boil this water, and refill the bottles in the creek."

Eugene quickly looked both ways. "Let's get off the road."

What began as a warm, sunny day had transitioned by early afternoon to overcast and cool. While everyone else wheeled their bikes to the metal railing along the side of the highway, Charlie picked his up with one hand and carried it. After depositing their bikes a few feet into the brush, they walked through the thick forest to the edge of Wildcat Creek.

"Please let there be fish," Sidney said.

It was narrow and shallow. "Doesn't look like there are," Drayden said.

Eugene set his rifle on the leafy forest floor. "Dray, I'm going to shoot the next deer I see."

Drayden rubbed his temples. They were starving, in food-desperation mode. Eugene wasn't being unreasonable, and it was clear he wasn't asking for permission. "I hear you."

Besides the food situation, everything else was shaping up. They'd drunk two bottles of water each and were about to drink two more. They'd restock before leaving. Most importantly they were, without a doubt, ahead of the Guardians. The fact that they hadn't passed them meant they must be ahead of them. Not only that, they had gained a nearly insurmountable lead. If they were already ahead of the Guardians at the intersection of Routes 3 and 3a, they were way ahead now. With the short distance between Norwell and Boston, there was virtually no way they could lose, even if they had to walk the rest of the way.

Sidney touched Drayden's shoulder. "Hey, I put some leaves and sticks together for the fire."

"Thanks, Sid. Can you guys find sticks for our water boiling rods?"

"Sure."

Drayden pulled out the paperclip and battery, anxiously awaiting the moment it would stop working.

Thankfully it lit. The yellow flames engulfed the pile of wood. After Sidney returned with a pile of long sticks, everyone pulled off both boots to construct the rods.

Catrice raised her hands above the fire. "I think it needs to get a little hotter. We should wait a few minutes."

Everybody had removed their socks too and stood barefoot on the cool soil.

Eugene unbuttoned and took off his gray camo shirt. "We should wash up in the river."

Drayden found it impossible not to stare at Eugene, and the others apparently agreed.

He also removed his T-shirt, revealing a cut chest and chiseled abs. After rolling up his pant legs he strolled to the creek. Charlie happily lost his shirt to show off and joined Eugene. The girls rolled up their sleeves and pant legs before bounding over to the water.

Drayden held the top button of his shirt, as if he'd frozen in the middle of getting undressed. Back in the Initiation, Tim and Alex were around. They were two normal, average boys, as opposed to Eugene and Charlie, who were both built like Hercules. Drayden was so skinny he could have been a different species. Maybe he'd take his shirt off later. He wandered off, away from the creek, to relieve himself. Having to pee again was a fantastic sign after not going for a full day. He was finally rehydrating. After he finished, he walked gingerly through the brush back toward the creek, as sharp pebbles and sticks in the soil dug into his soles. When the crew came into view, he stopped in his tracks.

Charlie and Sidney washed and splashed in the creek, joking around. Catrice and Eugene stood side-by-side at the top of the shallow bank, facing away from him. Eugene was still shirtless, showing off his hulking back. They were huddled close together. Too close.

The heat rose in Drayden's face. He wasn't imagining anything.

Then Catrice rested her head on Eugene's shoulder.

Drayden clenched his jaw. Such a simple gesture, yet so huge. So meaningful. How could she? And *why*, dammit? He spun around before anyone saw him and stormed back into the woods, whacking branches out of the way.

His chest expanded and contracted erratically. Sniffling, the tears came. But he stopped himself.

No.

If he wasn't good enough for Catrice anymore, so be it. That was her problem, not his. He needed to accept who he was. He was not a strong, tough guy and never would be. He was smart and caring. He needed to stop trying to be something he was not. *You are who you are and you can never be anyone else.* If Catrice preferred to be with the fish-head-smashing Adonis, that was her prerogative. He wasn't going to change to be more like someone else. Smart was better than strong anyway. "Smart > Strong" he pictured in his dorky math head. One day someone else would love him exactly the way he was. That someone might even be on the expedition with him.

He wiped his cheeks with his shirt and forced a smile, trying to expunge the evidence of his crying. He marched back to the group and headed straight for the creek to splash water on his face.

Catrice dangled her hands over the fire, watching him the whole way with a concerned expression.

Drayden refused her eye contact.

The others knelt by the creek, building the water-boiling rods.

"Hey, Dray," Sidney said, giggling, "guess wha—" She frowned when she saw him. She tiptoed over, crouching next to him while he washed up. "What's wrong?" she whispered.

A lump formed in Drayden's throat, so he repeated Charlie's words in his head: *You do you.* He shook his head. "It's…it's nothing. I'll tell you later."

She made a face. "Catrice?"

Drayden raised his eyes to hers.

"Why do you let her hurt you like this? I don't get it, Dray. Sorry. She has a brain, yes, but she has no heart."

To the naked eye, Catrice appeared cold. She did have a heart, though, a warm one. It was terribly wounded, surrounded by stone walls. She'd been sensitive and caring in private. Unfortunately, her heart seemed to belong to someone else now.

Drayden touched Sidney's knee. "Thanks, Sid."

Charlie lugged a bunch of sticks with cap-less bottles dangling from them. "Let's do this," he said as he passed by.

He had uttered Tim's line. It was what he had said at the start of most of the challenges in the Initiation. *Let's do this.* That Charlie phrased it that way didn't go unnoticed by Drayden.

Charlie winked at him.

It was a little "I got your back," from Charlie. Apparently, everyone could tell something was wrong.

Charlie and Eugene passed out two rods to each of them. The group suspended the bottles inches above the low flames, the crackling of the fire the only sound in the world.

The awkwardness between Drayden and Catrice had officially affected everybody, now eyeing one another in uncomfortable silence.

Although Catrice was staring at him, he still wouldn't look at her, or Eugene.

When the water boiled, they cooled the bottles in the creek and drank two each, except for Catrice, who couldn't consume that much. They repeated the whole process once more so they'd have drinkable water for the road.

"All right, good break, team," Charlie cracked. "Creating lasting memories in Norwood, Massachusetts."

"Norwell," Drayden said.

Sidney rested her hand on her forehead. "You guys, I don't know if I can ride any further without eating."

"I'll second that," Charlie said.

"I hear you, but we don't have any food," Drayden said. "Everyone keep their eyes peeled for a lake, a river, or an encampment. Watch for smoke."

Eugene hooked his thumb toward the highway. "Let's move out."

They returned to their bikes hidden in the brush.

"Where the hell did I put mine?" Charlie asked.

"Have you tried your pocket?" Drayden joked.

"Ha ha, very funny. Here it is."

Catrice gripped Drayden's arm before they headed up to the road. "Drayden."

He shook her hand off, ignoring her.

Eugene stopped as soon as he exited the forest and held up his hand. "Get down!" He hustled back into the woods and ducked down with the privates.

A buzzing sound. A humming, growing louder and higher in pitch.

Cars. Approaching them.

"Don't move," Eugene whispered.

Drayden struggled to control his breathing.

Three vehicles appeared in the distance, traveling north like the privates. A motorcycle, a truck with no roof in the back, and a car. They looked rebuilt from spare parts of many cars, colored like dull rainbows.

The loud vehicles thundered past, with two men on the motorcycle, a few in the car, and several in the uncovered back of the truck. Everyone looked dirty, unkempt, and seemingly dangerous. Most were brandishing guns or knives.

One guy in particular, riding in the bed of the truck, caught Drayden's attention. Unlike the rest of the gang, he had short hair, and wore his beard trimmed into a goatee. His face was angular, his eyes light and cold. Something about the way he carried himself indicated he was the leader. But what he held stopped Drayden's heart.

He was waving the Bureau flag in the air.

CHAPTER 25

Despite the light rain, a plume of smoke rose a short distance into the woods off Route 3.

They'd only ridden a mile or two, having waited a while to ensure the scary dudes in cars were long gone. Seeing them answered some questions. For one, working cars did, in fact, exist out here.

Yet it raised many questions as well, like, who was this mean-looking gang? And why were they carrying the Bureau flag?

Nobody could agree on the flag issue. The privates' backpacks, which belonged to the Guardians now, carried Bureau flags for their return to New America. Most likely the flag came from the Guardians. Did that imply they'd killed the Guardians and the flag was a trophy? Had the Guardians given it to them? Neither of those seemed plausible. Hell, was the Bureau outsourcing work to gangs outside New America?

Drayden kept revisiting what Kim had said, that the Bureau controlled the information. He latched onto that nugget and extrapolated it from there. The citizens could only know what the Bureau told them. Presumably, they weren't told everything. Possibly, the Bureau told horrible lies.

A narrow path, worn from frequent use, led into the woods toward the smoke.

Sidney pressed her hands together as if she were praying. "Please, can we go see if they have any food?"

Drayden was starving too. It impacted his physical ability, rendering him weak and tired. His cold had also worsened, and he could tell he was running a slight fever now.

"Guys, c'mon," Eugene said, apparently disappointed in an average person's weakness. "Twenty miles and we're done. Even with the rocky terrain, and well, Charlie's bike, we can be there in two hours. Let's go for it."

Eugene probably didn't need food to operate, running on batteries instead.

"I think Sid's right," Drayden said. "We should try and get food. We're way ahead of the Guardians, so we can spare the time. Besides, Boston is an unknown. It could be deserted. It could be hostile. They could quarantine us for a stretch. There's no reason to expect food awaits us in Boston."

Eugene sighed. "Okay, boss."

They lugged their bikes over the metal highway barrier and left them at the beginning of the dirt path. Under the cover of forest, they walked down the path, stopping once the fire was visible.

The woods gave way to a clearing packed with dozens of shacks. The primitive structures were constructed of mismatched wood, cardboard, and aluminum. Like the path, the ground was muddy, without grass, indicating heavy foot traffic. It was like a little shanty village.

At first blush, no people were in sight. Then a woman holding a young boy's hand emerged from the other side of the fire.

"Listen up," Eugene said, speaking directly to Drayden. "We need mission discipline here. Our goal is to score food and get out. We still need to make it to Boston before the Guardians. Agreed?"

Drayden tilted his head. "What are you suggesting, Eugene? We go in, what did you guys call it, heavy?"

Eugene nodded. "Not just heavy, though. No chit chat. We go in, take what we need, and leave."

"You mean steal it," Catrice said.

"Call it what you want," Eugene said, clearly annoyed. "We have a lot at stake here. It's one meal; they won't miss it, and we'll never see these people again. I know you guys are humanitarians and all, but this isn't the time for a touchy-feely mission."

Drayden pictured Catrice's head on Eugene's shoulder. Here was a chance to show her that he too could be strong and protect her the way Eugene could. If he could win her back, they could be happy again like they were after the Initiation. On top of it, if they could secure that food and escape, this mission was over. They would beat the Guardians. Done deal.

There was one small problem, however. Steamrolling in and stealing these people's food at gunpoint was wrong. Drayden was someone who treated people with empathy and respect, no matter their station in life. He would not sacrifice his own character in the name of achieving a personal goal, whether it be reaching Boston or holding on to the girl he loved.

These poor souls out here were starving, struggling. The privates' lives weren't more meaningful than the survivors'. Everyone's lives mattered. *Life* mattered.

The same inequality poisoned New America, a society that decided his mother's life wasn't as important as a scientist's, so it exiled her. Or a seamstress was expendable, while a Guardian wasn't. It was revolting. Drayden refused to subject these people to the same abuse of power the Bureau wielded. Whoever remained in this PostCon world was bound together in the same battle to keep humanity afloat. They all needed to work hand in hand to achieve their common goal.

"No," Drayden said. "Not only do we go in not-heavy, we go in unarmed."

Charlie made a face. "Dray."

"I'm serious. Otherwise, it's stealing, and it's wrong."

Sidney held her palm up. "Shouldn't we at least carry our weapons? We got ambushed once."

"No. If we have weapons we're a threat, and they may give us food but it will be out of fear, like that first time with Marty. We stole that chicken and moldy bread. We humiliated them, asserted our dominance, forced them to bow before us. I believe in the decency of people. If we treat them with respect, they'll respect us back."

Catrice remained silent. The others' discomfort was apparent on their faces.

Eugene shook his head. "Fine, Dray, you're our leader. You've never let us down. We'll do it your way. I'll stay unarmed, but I'm going to follow behind a bit, just in case. I'm hiding the weapons too."

"Thanks, Eugene."

Everyone disarmed and carried the weapons back to the beginning of the path near the bikes. Hidden off to the side, Eugene covered the pile of guns and knives with leaves and sticks.

"Follow my lead," Drayden said as he marched back down the path toward the village.

The woman and her son lingered around the fire. Both were skin and bones, dirty, and sickly. Still, the boy was cute. He must've been around three.

They were fifty feet away when the boy smiled.

Drayden smiled back, and waved. He checked behind him, and Sidney trailed, followed by Catrice, and Charlie. Eugene hung way back.

The woman looked terrified as Drayden approached. She picked up the grinning boy.

Did she just shake her head slightly at me, or did I imagine it?

Drayden's smile faded. The village was too quiet. The sense of being watched overcame him. The hints of peripheral movement, and the woman's expression, caused his adrenaline to surge. He'd made a huge mistake.

Guns cocked all around them.

Drayden froze.

A gun muzzle pressed against the side of his head.

He began hyperventilating.

The hammer retracted with a click, cocking the gun.

He closed his eyes, trembling. *Catrice. Sidney. I'm so sorry.*

A gun fired.

Drayden shuddered and cried out. Then he opened his eyes. He was alive.

More gunshots in a flurry. Yelling.

"Get 'em! Shoot that boy!"

The shots weren't at Drayden. They were at Eugene, who was racing back up the path.

A few scruffy, bearded guys in dirty clothes chased after Eugene, firing revolvers at him. One man tore down the path with a shotgun.

Is he abandoning us?

Charlie, Sidney, and Catrice had their hands up, so Drayden raised his own.

They stood in a line, side by side now. When he glanced back, he found himself facing the man from the truck with the angular face and cold, vacant eyes. He wore a beige shirt with the sleeves ripped off, and was chewing something. His breath reeked of death.

Drayden swallowed hard.

The man sized him up before moving on to Sidney and repeating the examination. Many other men and women encircled them now. While some held weapons, they remained silent, watching their leader inspect the privates.

Finally, he spoke. "Well, well, today is our lucky day. We was told about you by your friends, the ones you tried to kill. But I thought they was lyin'. They warned us about you. We was ready. They gave us a deer they done killed too. Said they was headin' to Boston so we showed 'em the way." He stopped in front of the girls and rubbed his dirty hands along Sidney's chin. "Gabriel is gonna like you two," he said with a creepy grin. "He's gonna like you a lot. Uh-huh."

Sidney snapped her head back and turned away.

The leader man stepped in front of Charlie and squeezed his arm, shaking it. "Check out this big boy. He'll feed us for a month." He inched closer and stared directly into Charlie's eyes. "And I ain't talkin' about workin' in the fields, boy."

Charlie was unwavering, full of pride.

The leader man cackled, and the crowd assembled around him joined in.

A chill ran down Drayden's spine. He'd never been so scared in his life. This was his fault, and unlike other times he'd screwed up, this time there was no fixing it.

The band of bearded men hurried back down the path into the clearing, their guns hanging by their sides. They doubled over out of breath when they reached the leader.

"Well? Where is he?" he asked.

"He...got away," one of them said. "But there was blood on the bushes. We hit that sucker. He's as good as dead."

Drayden fought to free his hands, struggling against the rope binding them behind his back. It was no use. In the movies, people always managed to magically untie themselves and escape. After a few hours of trying to work them free, all he had to show for it were gashes on his wrists.

He sat in a chair with his feet bound to it, beside Charlie, Sidney, and Catrice, each restrained the same way. They were being held captive inside one of the many huts in the village. A piddling fire in a makeshift fireplace in the corner provided light now that it was nighttime. The light rain had escalated into a major thunderstorm. Rain and wind pounded the hut, and thunder cracked periodically.

Billy, their guard, walked in carrying an antique-looking silver revolver. He wore his brown hair in a mullet—short in front, long in the back—which was matted to his head from the rain.

After a few hours with Billy, Drayden had determined he was a total idiot.

He was a scrawny guy, with a face a little too small for his head, all scrunched up, with a pig nose. Like most of the men in this camp, Billy had a scruffy beard. He alternately guarded the door outside in the rain and ventured inside to taunt the privates.

As with some of the Guardians in New America, if you granted someone an inch of power they took a mile, abusing it. It was especially true for someone who didn't deserve it to begin with.

This time Billy came inside just to make sure everything was in order. He flashed a grin that revealed few teeth, and sauntered back out the door, which remained open at all times. A streak of white flashed outside, and the crack of thunder rattled the ramshackle hut.

Drayden had already effusively apologized to his friends, begging for forgiveness. He couldn't say he was sorry enough for entangling them in this mess. It was one-hundred percent his fault.

He couldn't reconcile it in his mind. He'd done the right thing, stayed true to himself, and approached these people with respect. It wasn't right to steal, bully, and dominate. What had he earned in return? They'd almost certainly lost the race to Boston, but that was the least of their problems. They might never reach Boston at all. Their families would suffer the consequences. And God only knew what these savages were going to do to them.

Throughout the Initiation and expedition, he'd encountered problem after problem and solved every one. With plenty of support, no doubt. This time was different. There was no way out.

Drayden sighed. "Guys, I'm sorry, again." He considered the possibility he was repeating it so he could hear Sidney tell him it was okay—that it wasn't his fault. She was dogged in her defense of him. Resolute.

"Dray, stop," Sidney said. "We don't blame you. We would have died by now if it wasn't for you. We're with you, all the way."

"Yeah, bro," Charlie said. "There were so many dudes with guns, it wouldn't have mattered if we had ours. Heck, if it turned into a gunfight, we'd be dead right now. Probably best we ditched our weapons."

Even so, they should have heeded Eugene's advice about heading straight to Boston. They had an insurmountable lead. How could Drayden have been stupid enough to inject the one variable that relinquished it?

Only Catrice hadn't absolved him of his guilt. One glimpse of her suggested it was due to shock, not because she faulted him. She was quivering, her eyes swollen from crying. She was clearly petrified, and with valid reason.

Drayden yearned to hate her for everything that had happened between them on the expedition. But he couldn't do it. It wasn't his shame for their current predicament either. He still cared about Catrice and felt the need to protect her, like in the Initiation. He desired her affection too.

His expectations might have been misplaced regarding their relationship. They'd only been a couple for a few weeks and weren't close before the Initiation. There was much about her he didn't know. He'd filled in those blanks with his idealistic vision of what the perfect girlfriend would be like, setting expectations she could never live up to. Nobody could. It was a recipe for failure. Catrice was her own person, not a robot built specifically to cater to his needs. Perhaps she didn't want a boyfriend, or wasn't ready for one. Or she desired a different one.

"I'm concerned about Eugene," Drayden said.

"Huh, Eugene," Sidney scoffed. "He abandoned us. I guess he's not so great after all."

"No way," Charlie said. "He might be plotting our rescue right now. He said he was going to hang back just in case. Well, 'in case' happened."

"He got shot, Charlie," Drayden said. "If there was enough blood to splatter on bushes, it was serious. He's probably dead."

Add Eugene's death to list of things that were his fault.

Catrice stayed quiet, save for the occasional sniffle.

Billy the idiot entered the hut and shook his head, spraying water everywhere. His boots dragged mud over the floor as he strolled over to the privates, where he squatted in front of Catrice. He touched her on the cheek, running his filthy fingers down to her lips. "You sure are *purty*. I hope y'all are excited to meet Gabriel tomorrow. I think you're gonna like Gabriel. All the ladies do." He smiled wide and snortled.

Drayden's anger and frustration boiled over. He flailed and tugged to loosen the ropes binding his wrists, to no avail. "Leave her alone, Billy."

He shot up and marched over. "Oh yeah? You don't tell me what to do. I'm in charge. You got that?" He cracked Drayden in the shin with the toe of his boot.

The sharp pain radiated through Drayden's whole leg. Although he fought to conceal his anguish because he didn't want to give Billy the satisfaction, his face contorted in pain.

"Yeah," Billy grunted, "that's nuthin'. Wait till Gabriel gets here." He spun around and walked outside again.

They needed to get out of here, immediately if not sooner. These people were barbarians. No better than what he was trying *not* to be, refusing to steal from them. No better than the Guardians, the Bureau, Nathan Locke, or anyone else who abused their power.

Drayden had always believed people were inherently good, but he wasn't convinced anymore. When pushed by desperation or greed, people succumbed to their basest desires, their animal instincts, and downright savagery. The privates needed to hatch a plan to escape before this Gabriel guy arrived tomorrow. Apparently, he was the real leader, not the sharp-faced guy with the vile breath.

Drayden sneezed a few times in a row. His nose was running, and it needed blowing. Man, he was miserable. Life couldn't get any worse than this. "Guys," he said, quiet enough that Billy the idiot wouldn't overhear, "we have to get out of here. Any ideas?"

"I just want to be back at home." Sidney's eyes welled with tears. "I want to go home," she sobbed.

"It's all right, Sid," Charlie said, "we're gonna figure something out, right, Dray? We'll be home before you know it. Back in our apartments, living next door to each other."

Drayden coughed up phlegm and spat it out. "I wish I had Shahnee here. I need some medicine."

Charlie snickered. "I'd throw my arms around my nurse Jeff if he was here. I'd even let him give me that blue–green shot that scared the crap out of me."

"Yeah," Drayden said. *Wait, what?* "What did you say?"

"I'd throw my arms ar—"

"No, after that. What about a blue-green shot?"

"You know, the Aeru vaccine, or booster, or whatever it's called," Charlie said.

Drayden wrinkled his nose. "Yeah, but yours was blue-green?"

"Yeah. What color was yours?"

"Like, white, opaque," Drayden said. "How about yours, Sid? Catrice?"

"Blue-green," Sid said.

"Blue-green," Catrice squeaked.

Drayden hyperventilated. "Wait, but that...oh my God." A tear rolled down his cheek. Maybe Nathan Locke had arranged it, or someone else who'd wished to dispose of him in the Bureau. He wasn't administered the real Aeru vaccine like the others.

It wasn't a cold.

I have Aeru.

CHAPTER 26

Seated in his chair, Billy tore into a loaf of bread in front of them, the crumbs falling into his lap. Chewing extra slow, he opened his mouth with food inside, making a show of it.

It had the intended effect. Drayden and the others were mesmerized, dreaming of the bread in his hands. Drayden actually felt drool forming. Although he'd stopped crying an hour ago, his cheeks were damp and his eyes felt puffy. He imagined his friends would forgive him for the meltdown. He had Aeru, and he was going to die. They were likely all going to die tomorrow, or sometime soon. But even if they somehow escaped, *he* would still die.

"Awww, what's the matter, tough guy?" Billy asked Drayden, mocking him with an exaggerated sad face. "Cryin' like a baby over there. Save them tears. You gonna need some for tomorrow."

Drayden had never hated anyone as much as Billy the idiot. The fact that this puny, moronic, immoral loser had power over them was sickening.

Billy set his loaf of bread on the chair and walked back outside.

"Okay, this is it," Drayden whispered. "Next time captain moron comes back in, we execute our plan. You ready, Sid?"

She pursed her lips and appeared on the verge of tears. "I'm so nervous. What if it doesn't work?"

"You can do it," Charlie said. "This guy's a weakling."

It wasn't the best idea. She had legitimate reason to be worried. Unfortunately, it was all they could come up with. They also needed to attempt it, given whatever nightmare awaited when this guy Gabriel returned.

When they'd tried to execute the ploy earlier with Charlie, Billy shot it down. Charlie had asked to use the bathroom, and Billy told him to go in his pants. Sidney was going to make the same request, acting flirty in the process. They hoped he would assume she was weak. Little did Billy know that she was a tremendous athlete.

Still, the plan was fraught with shortcomings. Sidney needed to both incapacitate Billy and silence him so he couldn't yell for help. The exact time was unclear, since the clan had snatched their watches. But it was sometime in the middle of the night, and the rest of the camp was quiet, the occupants likely asleep. If the attempt failed, the other privates couldn't even come to her rescue. They would be tied up. If Billy got the upper hand, they would be forced to watch whatever he did to her.

Sidney, while strong, didn't have any fight training other than the rudimentary amount they'd received in Guardian school before the expedition. So Drayden told her exactly what to do. Billy would most likely be behind her with the gun. He wouldn't be expecting an attack and wouldn't be mentally prepared to fire his weapon. If her ambush happened fast, it could work. She would throw a vicious elbow back into his gut and spin around. When he leaned forward from the stomach blow, she would wrap her hands around the back of his head and slam it down into her rising knee. After that, she would tackle him to the ground and choke him.

Drayden could understand her nerves. "Sid, it's either this or we wait to see what Gabriel's gonna do. You can do this. Don't hold back. Hit *hard*. As hard as you can."

She nodded, taking shallow, hurried breaths.

Billy returned and plopped down, dripping water. He grabbed his loaf of bread and bit off a chunk.

Drayden winked at Sidney.

She breathed deeply. "Excuse me, Billy? Would you be so kind as to let me use the bathroom? I promise I'll be good." She pouted her lips. "You can escort me, and we'll come right back."

Billy hesitated, apparently thinking. "You try anything and I'm gonna shoot ya," he said through a mouthful of bread.

"Thank you, Billy, you're the best. I promise I won't try anything." She flashed a sly smile.

Drayden's heart thumped so loud he feared Billy could hear. He was terrified for Sidney, sure something would go wrong.

Billy wiped his mouth with the back of his hand. He got up and set his bread on the chair, blissfully ignorant about the impending assault.

Sweat dripped down Drayden's cheeks. This was the moment of truth.

Billy took a step toward Sidney and stopped. He furrowed his brow, and turned his head back slightly in the direction of the doorway.

Lightning flared and thunder boomed outside.

Seemingly out of nowhere, Eugene appeared behind Billy, drenched. In one motion, he wrapped an arm around Billy's head, covering his mouth, and with the other he slit his throat with a knife. Deep.

Blood sprayed.

Catrice bit back a scream.

Drayden averted his eyes and dry heaved a few times. He vomited bile.

Mother of God.

When he dared to peek, Eugene was kneeling over Billy, smothering his mouth with one hand. He pressed until the body stopped moving. A puddle of dark blood grew wider and wider on the floor. Both of Eugene's hands were covered in it.

It was so quick, so violent, and so brutal. Drayden's mouth hung open.

Eugene scanned the privates' faces and held a bloody index finger up to his lips. After checking once behind him, he dashed to Catrice, wiped his bloody hands on his soaked camo pants and cut her ropes.

She leapt up and embraced him, burying her face in his chest, sobbing. Eugene held her for a second and kissed her forehead. He knelt beside Sidney and tackled her ropes. Eugene's left sleeve was no longer gray but a dark crimson, stained with old blood. After Sidney was free, he cut Charlie and Drayden loose. He pulled out four pistols, handed them out, and cocked his own, quietly.

Catrice was shaking, tears streaming down her cheeks.

Drayden's horror transformed to elation. They were free! Eugene truly was something special. And he looked like hell.

He was pale, gaunt, and twitchy. Judging by his bloody sleeve, he'd indeed been shot earlier.

"Follow me," he whispered. "In silence. We're walking, ducked down, along the outside of the camp to the path, and then we sprint. It's crazy slippery. Got it? I'll go in front. Charlie, you in the rear."

There wasn't time to thank him for his heroics; that would come later. They were forever indebted to this kid.

Eugene stepped over Billy's body and stopped at the door, surveying the camp. He waved his hand forward.

Drayden took one final glimpse of Billy's brutalized body, feeling not an ounce of sympathy for him. He got what he deserved.

Charlie spat on the corpse. "Piece of shkat."

Sidney snagged the loaf of bread and trailed Eugene to the door. He darted out and everyone followed.

In utter darkness, rain pummeled them, the ground thick with mud. Drayden slid all over the place. He could barely find anyone else in the blackness.

Lightning flashed, which allowed him to orient himself. Not much further to the path. They reached it in seconds and ran.

Tearing blindly through the woods in mud was frightening. Each second carried the threat of running head-on into a tree. After a minute, Drayden saw Sidney's back, right before he crashed into her. Charlie barreled into him. The three of them fell, getting caked in cold, slimy mud.

"Dammit," Charlie said.

Eugene hauled them up.

"Sorry," Drayden said.

"No, my bad," Charlie answered.

A lightning burst revealed Eugene on his knees rustling around the bushes. "They didn't find the weapons. They're here somewhere."

The privates squatted with him, searching until they found them. They slung the rifles over their backs and deposited their knives back in their sleeves.

"What about our bikes?" Drayden asked.

"Gone," Eugene said. "They took them. Everybody good? Let's move out."

"Wait," Drayden said. "We should stay off the road a bit. In case they come searching for us or we bump into the Guardians. And I think we need to run now."

"Roger that," Eugene said.

"Let's do this," Charlie said.

Drayden wolfed down his chunk of bread like a wild animal. He even grunted with pleasure eating it, something he'd never done before.

Despite the relative blandness of bread, this piece tasted sweet and extravagant. He didn't let a single crumb go unconsumed. In addition to making him feel immediately revitalized, it lifted his spirits. A tad. There was still quite a bit to be down about. It also left him starving for more.

They'd run as long as possible, until their energy was spent, which wasn't long at all. Not eating for forty-eight hours and being awake all night had left them drained.

It was dawn on Route 3 and the skies had cleared. Rain had a way of refreshing everything, a thorough cleansing of the world, and the air smelled fresh and floral. Rain meant something else too—water.

"Hey, guys," Drayden said with downcast eyes, feeling sheepish, "we should head into the woods and take advantage of this rainwater. We shouldn't drink it off the ground, but some of the leaves might have little drops."

"That's good thinking, Dray." Eugene veered into the woods.

Odd plants which didn't exist in New America covered the forest floor. Enormous leaves fanned out from the center of each, forming a circle. The base acted as a miniature bowl, with a tiny pool of water in it.

Drayden knelt and sucked out the water. "Hey, check it out. Everybody find a plant."

Charlie slurped it up. "This is great. A few hundred of these and we'll be set."

Drayden sighed. "Just get some water in your system. This will all be dried out in a few hours."

They lapped up the microscopic beads of water until they grew tired of it and returned to hiking in silence up Route 3, off the road. Despite running after their escape from Camp Psycho, they'd only made it a few miles.

Drayden couldn't come to grips with the fact that he had Aeru, the same bacteria that had killed billions on Earth, either through infection or by destroying the food supply. It was ironic that in a world where he never felt he fit in, he now had something in common with billions of former people. Because of Eugene's courageous rescue, the future became brighter for the others. For Drayden, it remained grim. He was going to die.

The Bureau never intended for him to return from the expedition. That was why they had given him a fake version of the Aeru vaccine. They probably didn't expect any of the privates to make it home, but with him, they wanted to guarantee it. It might have been Nathan Locke who'd ordered it, or Eli Holst himself. Just because Drayden started receiving the phony vaccine before he'd confronted Locke didn't mean Locke wasn't responsible. Maybe he was being proactive, knowing he'd eventually have to eliminate Drayden. The Bureau, and Locke, were one step ahead. They'd won. He wouldn't get to exact revenge after all. Now it made perfect sense that nobody had discussed their employment or living arrangements upon their return.

How would his mother feel about her affair with Nathan Locke now? It led to her exile, which led to Drayden entering the Initiation, which led to the expedition, which led to him catching Aeru and ultimately dying. His mother's selfish escapade actually precipitated her own child's death. His mother had killed him and here he was, worried about failing to avenge her. Drayden yanked off his green Yankees cap and shoved it into his pants' pocket.

He wondered what would happen when they reached Boston, if they indeed found people there. They could quarantine him, refuse to admit him, or possibly even execute him. At the very least, they'd surely separate him from his friends, which would also clear the way for Catrice and Eugene.

She walked with her arm interlocked with Eugene's, clinging to him like an orphaned baby animal to its surrogate mother. In any other circumstance it would enrage him, induce tears, and generally drive him mad with jealousy. However, considering what had occurred, she deserved a pass. She had not spoken since the rescue, appearing almost catatonic. The unknown horror they were forced to contemplate upon Gabriel's arrival was absolutely grounds for shock. They could have been tortured, enslaved, killed, or eaten. Or even worse, all of the above.

Catrice's public display of affection for Eugene might have been more than that too. Drayden needed to finally accept that she had moved on from him. She'd made her choice, and hell, who could blame her?

Drayden *thought* what he needed to do was accept who he was, with Catrice and in life—his choices, his values. He needed to generally stop trying to be someone else, and specifically stop trying to be like Eugene. As long as everyone was true to who they were and accepted it, things should work out the way they were supposed to.

Yet that exact philosophy resulted in the disaster at the crazy village. It didn't make sense. Maybe he was wrong, and he *did* need to be more like Eugene—tough, brutal, savage—or they couldn't succeed out here. Was Eugene's way superior to Drayden's way on an absolute level?

Eugene's way > Drayden's way.

"Hey, Euge?" Charlie said.

Walking up front with Catrice, Eugene turned his head back questioningly.

Charlie cleared his throat. "On behalf of everyone, I want to say thank you. I don't know what else to say. You're a total stud."

Drayden and Sidney chimed in, thanking him too.

Eugene checked the ammo in his rifle. "Thanks. You're welcome. I wasn't going to leave you guys behind. I would have died first."

They'd been walking for over an hour, and until then nobody had uttered a word to Eugene about his dramatic rescue. It wasn't that they weren't grateful. On the contrary, they could never repay him enough. It was that they were traumatized, because they'd watched their friend savagely murder a man. They were in clinical shock. The awkwardness of the past hour was akin to what occurred when you accidentally saw someone naked, like your mother. Nobody discussed it afterward and both parties pretended it never happened.

Sidney was walking beside Charlie, chewing her nails. "How did you escape, Eugene? Are you hurt? They said you got shot."

"I'm all right." He glanced at his arm. "A bullet grazed my shoulder. I rubbed my bloody hands on the bushes so they would think I was mortally wounded and stop searching for me. It worked. I was nearby after that, in the woods the whole time waiting for a chance to get in. Even after the whole camp was asleep, that pesky guard of yours kept going in and out. Every time I would decide to go for it, I'd have to abort. Then I said, 'screw it.' That's when I came in."

Sidney snickered. "Right in the nick of time. I was about to attack Billy. That was the guy's name."

Drayden studied Eugene, curious if hearing the guard's name, giving him an identity, elicited any remorse or grief. He didn't seem upset about it.

Eugene had become decidedly darker the past two days. Gone was the childlike wunderkind, replaced by a much harder, brooding, intense man. It was as if his Guardian identity had overtaken his persona now that it was desperately needed. The expedition was clearly wearing on him as well.

Sidney looked at Catrice, then at Drayden, before shaking her head.

"What is it?" he asked her.

"Can I get any love here? I was about to risk my life in a fight to the death and all everyone can do is fawn over poor Catrice. It's unbelievable."

She was right. Drayden had been guilty of the same thing during the Initiation, taking Sidney for granted. She was such a badass it was sometimes hard to remember that she wasn't superhuman.

He walked up beside her. "You're totally right, Sid. I'm sorry. What you were about to do was crazy brave. Just because Eugene came in doesn't change that. You've stepped up time after time."

"Thank you," she said, with little emotion.

"You're a legend, Sid," Charlie said.

Eugene nodded and said, "You would've won that fight."

"You guys, I'm sorry, stop," Sidney said. "I'm not fishing for compliments. I just...I don't know what I want." She threw her hands in the air. "To be appreciated or something, I guess. Forget I said anything. I simply refuse to let my sister be taken from me. *Refuse.* We have to make it to Boston."

Since people seemed to be airing their grievances, Drayden had something to get off his chest. He hurried to catch up to Eugene and strode beside him, opposite Catrice. "Eugene, thank you, again. Thank you, thank you. I can't say it enough times. But I also need to apologize. I'm sorry."

Eugene chuckled, as if he thought it was a joke. "For what?"

"For not trusting you. I wasn't sure you were really one of us. I thought you might still be working with the Guardians. Until now, that is." Eugene had put Drayden's jealous suspicion to bed for good, with authority. He was on their side.

"Are you serious, Dray?" Eugene appeared hurt. "How could you think that? After everything I've done?"

"I know; that's why I'm apologizing. You've saved us time and time again, and none bigger than that last one. God, it sounds so stupid now, but I thought you didn't actually try to move the tree over the river. And I was surprised you didn't kill any of the Guardians, given how perfect a shot you are."

Eugene threw his head back. "C'mon, kid. Ten of me couldn't have moved that tree. I was a little worried about my back after what happened to Charlie too. During the gunfight...I mean, I never had a single clean shot. Those guys are pros. They were skillfully covered. If I had an opening, I would have connected. But I'm the outsider here. I get it. You guys did the Initiation together. Nothing to be sorry about." He punched Drayden in the shoulder.

It ached. "Oh yeah, you shouldn't touch me. I have Aeru."

Eugene frowned. "Wait, what? How do you know?"

"In our hours of captivity, we determined the Bureau gave me a fake vaccine, different from the others. Mysteriously, I'm sick and everyone else is fine. I'm running a fever now on top of the nasty cough, both signature symptoms." Drayden thought about Shahnee. She'd told him they'd know the vaccine didn't work if he developed a cough and fever. He desperately hoped she didn't know his vaccine was fake.

Eugene looked stunned. "I'm...I'm sorry, Dray. I'm so sorry." Ignoring Drayden's advice, he wrapped his arm around Drayden's shoulders.

While nobody had explicitly stated it, everyone knew what having Aeru foretold. Drayden lowered his head.

"You guys?" Sidney asked. "Do you think the Guardians are ahead of us now?"

It was difficult to tell. Drayden attempted the math. They'd ridden their bikes approximately seventeen miles from where Route 3a intersected Route 3. It took them between two and three hours. Most people walked three miles per hour, but one of the Guardians was injured. If they walked two miles per hour, it would have taken them over eight hours to reach camp Gabriel and the crazies. Call it a six-hour lead when Gabriel's clan captured them, which was sometime in the afternoon. The Guardians had several hours of daylight to catch up, cutting that to a slim lead. Other variables complicated it as well. Had the Guardians camped for the night? The privates and Eugene had restarted hiking before sunrise.

"I think it's probably pretty close," Drayden said. "They might be ahead. It depends on whether they stopped to sleep or did any walking in the dark. We should be on alert. They could be close by."

"I don't know if I can go on," Charlie said. "I'm so weak. We didn't sleep last night. We haven't eaten in two days, and that bread woke up the monster in my belly. I'm a few minutes from eating bark off a tree."

Drayden felt the same way: completely exhausted and mentally fried from stress. A raw hunger stirred up some primitive, ancient instinct to find food. Fifteen or twenty miles on bikes was one thing, but walking that distance was not trivial.

A plume of smoke billowed above the tree line in the distance once again.

Eugene stopped when they reached it, raising his eyebrows.

Drayden shook his head. "I don't think it's worth the risk. Not after...you know."

A woman's bloodcurdling scream suddenly pierced the morning silence.

CHAPTER 27

"Whoever that was, we need to see if she's okay," Drayden said. "But we'll be real cautious and abort if we sense trouble."

Charlie cringed. "I didn't like the sound of that scream. That wasn't a stub-your-toe scream."

They maneuvered through the thick bramble, now only a hundred yards or so from the smoke.

"Guys, let me up front." Eugene stormed past them. "If we go in, we're doing it my way."

Drayden didn't have grounds to object anymore, for obvious reasons. Nonetheless, the "Eugene way"—ready to fire, take no prisoners—didn't feel right, despite the disaster at Camp Gabriel.

"Eugene, you mean heavy, right?"

"Yeah. Guns live. Ready to act. Nobody's getting captured this time, I don't care how many of them there are. If we're in trouble, we fight."

Unable to forget the last encampment, Drayden thought they should abort right now. But they did need food, and he couldn't shake the sound of that scream. Charlie was right; as far as screams went, that was an ominous one.

Eugene waved his arm downward and crouched. The others followed his lead and squatted. Everyone held live weapons except

Catrice, who still wore a glazed-over expression and continued to shadow Eugene.

Drayden opted for the Glock since it was easier to carry and was less intimidating. If this was a friendly camp, he didn't want to scare the crap out of them with an assault rifle.

Several ramshackle wooden huts came into view, surrounding a fire. This village didn't sit in an expansive clearing like camp crazy. It existed amongst tall trees, on the other side of a hill. From where they were huddled, no people were visible.

Sidney whispered, "The last time we saw no people, it was a trap."

"We should get out of here," Drayden said.

Eugene stood up halfway, inspecting the camp. "Wait. Is that... what is that? Is it a body?"

A person appeared to be lying atop the hill, sprawled out. Their angle made it difficult to tell for sure.

Someone wailed in the village, her sobs reverberating through the woods.

Eugene raised his rifle. "Let's go. Stay tight together. Weapons ready." He advanced, looking through his rifle's sight, his finger on the trigger.

Catrice followed him closely, remaining unarmed. Sidney glared at her before following, trailed by Drayden and Charlie.

Drayden's breathing became labored and shallow. Vivid memories from the last camp flashed through his mind, the terror fresh. A chill ran down his spine when they reached the top of the hill.

The man on the ground was dead, with a bullet wound to the chest. A fresh one, oozing bright red blood.

"Sweet mercy," Charlie said, digesting the scene down the hill.

Bodies were scattered everywhere, probably fifteen or twenty.

Drayden's heart broke. It was a massacre.

"My God," Sidney said.

Eugene eased down the hill, his rifle raised, scanning the area. The dead were all men, and they'd been shot.

"I think we know who did this," he said.

Sidney scoffed. "The Guardians."

"Freaking animals," Drayden said. How could they? And why? These men were unarmed. The Guardians didn't care about the villager's lives; they were simply an obstacle to acquiring food, so the Guardians had slaughtered them. It was such a despicable and unnecessary waste of life. Supremely selfish, unbearably arrogant.

The amount of barbarity displayed on this journey was enough to last a lifetime. A battle raged in the real world between brutality and humaneness. Brutality seemed to be winning.

But it wasn't exclusive to the real world, because it was happening in New America too. The Bureau didn't respect life. More specifically, they didn't respect certain lives. Some were more important to them. The Bureau was wrong. Life's value couldn't be measured solely by one's contribution to society. Life, to be alive, was a magical thing, and the idea you could rank it by skill was ludicrous. The Bureau was playing God, as the Guardians had in this camp.

Movement inside one of the shanties grabbed their attention.

"Three o'clock." Eugene whipped his rifle to the right.

Everyone trained guns on the hut. Inside, scared teary faces of women and children peeked out through a window with no glass. The whole village seemed crammed into one shack.

Drayden holstered his pistol and raised his hands in the air as he approached the window. "We mean no harm; we're friendly. Please, don't be frightened."

People inside the hut shrieked and cried. They scooped up their children and cowered on the far side of the room.

"Please, it's okay. We're here to help," Drayden pleaded.

A little girl dashed outside the shanty, coming right up to him with a big smile.

He knelt, smiling back. He extended his hand, and she shook it. "Hi, my name's Drayden. What's yours?"

She swayed back and forth. "Susie."

"How old are you, Susie?"

"I'm six."

"Susie, can you tel—"

"How old are you?"

"Oh. I'm sixteen."

A haggard woman with frizzy hair and dark circles under her eyes barreled out of the hut. "Susie! Susie, no! Get away from them!" She scooped the little girl up and squeezed her tight.

"Mommy, this is Brayden, he's sixteen."

Drayden raised both hands in the air, noting that a mother was thinking of her child's safety before her own, as she was supposed to. "Please, wait! We're friendly. We're not like the men who did this."

The woman blew a strand of hair away from her face, but she stayed. "They was dressed like y'all."

Susie pointed at Catrice and Sidney. "They didn't have pretty girls with them."

Catrice was blank, vacant. Sidney made an "aww" face. "Bless your heart, sweetie. You're a very pretty girl. You remind me of my little sister."

"We know who they are," Drayden said. "We're chasing them. We're trying to stop them. Can you help us?"

She wept. "We're peaceful people. Why would they do this?"

"They're bad men. I'm sorry," he said. "We want to make them pay. Unfortunately, we need food. We haven't eaten in days."

"They wanted food too. When we said we didn't have none to spare, they started killin'. Then they went house to house and took whatever we had."

Drayden's heart sank. He felt awful thinking and asking about food when they'd suffered such a horrific loss. It was selfish and insensitive.

Susie's mother wiped her tears. "Our men was brave. None of them told where most of the food was."

Although Drayden hated to ask, they were starving. "I'm so sorry for what happened here, ma'am. But do you have some you could spare? We don't need much."

She grew indignant. "My husband just died protecting that food. And you want me to give it to you?"

"Ma'am, again, I'm sorry. If we don't catch them, they'll get away with this. Your husband's death will never be avenged. We haven't eaten in days. We cannot catch these guys without eating something. Anything, no matter how little, we'd take it."

Susie jumped out of her mother's arms. "Can I show them, Mommy?"

The woman scanned the privates' faces. "As long as y'all promise to get revenge for what they done."

"We will, ma'am," Sidney promised.

"Go, Susie."

Susie practically tumbled down the hill and everyone chased after her, including her mother. Susie stopped in front of a pile of leaves.

Charlie scratched his head. "Um, thanks, but no thanks? I ate leaves yesterday, so..."

"Charlie," Drayden said.

"Push them leaves off to the side," Susie's mother said.

Eugene scattered the leaves with his rifle, revealing two wooden doors built into the ground.

The group collectively gasped when he hoisted them open. The underground bunker held dozens of loaves of bread, some moldy; many heads of lettuce; and what appeared to be meats covered in salt.

Susie's mother knelt, pulling out two loaves of bread, two heads of lettuce, and five tubes of meat shaped like miniature baseball bats. She stuffed the lettuce and bread in a plastic bag from the bunker and handed it to Sidney, and gave the tubed meat to Charlie.

He sniffed them. "What are these?"

Susie's mother looked confused, pausing before answering. "Sausages. It's pork. We keep pigs, goats, and chickens down the woods a bit."

"Do we have to cook it?" Charlie asked.

She scratched her neck. "Where are y'all from? It's cured and dried. You can eat it straight away."

"Thank you," Drayden said. "Thank you so much. I wish we had something to give you in return. All I can offer is that we're going to catch the guys who did this to your village."

Eugene stepped forward. "Ma'am, how recently did those men come through here?"

"Bout twenty minutes."

"*Twenty minutes*?" Drayden echoed. "Jeez, they were so close to us."

"They could be close to us right now," Sidney said.

The privates rotated around, surveying the woods.

"Wait." Drayden rubbed his chin. "We didn't hear any gunshots."

"Their guns didn't make any sound," Susie's mother said.

"Silencers," Eugene said. "They all have them. They probably didn't want us to hear the shots. It's possible they knew how close we were."

"Do you know if there are people in Boston?" Sidney asked Susie's mother.

"Don't know. Those evil men wanted to know too." She eyed the top of the hill. "They grabbed ol' Hal, asked him to make sure they were going the right way. He showed them. Then they shot him dead."

Drayden checked his map as they hiked off the side of Route 3. They were roughly half an hour behind the Guardians, which at a pace of three miles-per-hour, translated to a mere mile and a half. They needed to find a way to leapfrog ahead of the Guardians that didn't involve walking right past them. It would be impossible on the same road.

Where in the world were they? Few landmarks existed. Drayden guessed they were around Weymouth, Massachusetts, barely fifteen miles from Boston's outskirts. It was most likely early afternoon, based on the position of the sun. Route 53 ran parallel to Route 3, a short distance away.

"Ohhhh," Charlie grunted. "This is sooooo good." He chomped at the sausage.

The group had shared one loaf of bread and one head of lettuce. Now they savored their sausages as they walked. Everyone agreed they should eat half and save the rest.

Drayden bit into the salty, chewy, spicy meat. It was unlike anything he'd ever eaten, and tasted vastly different than the chicken he'd first experienced a few days prior. It was delicious. Although his Aeru symptoms had continued to worsen, he had energy and a clear mind after eating. He'd put his hat back on as well. Despite his growing anger at his mother, he needed her strength.

"Guys," Drayden said, "I think we should switch over to this Route 53. It runs parallel to Route 3. It's the only way we can pass the Guardians without accidentally running into them."

Charlie spoke with his mouth full of sausage. "Is it faster?"

"No. Technically it's a little longer."

"So, we'll fall further behind," Sidney pointed out.

"Yes," Drayden said.

"We won't catch the Guardians at the rate we're going," Catrice said, speaking for the first time since their rescue.

Drayden couldn't help but notice she seemed like herself again after eating, as if she'd emerged from a coma. She no longer clung to Eugene, and didn't even walk beside him. If Drayden were Eugene, he would slow down a bit to walk next to her. Eugene continued to prove himself different from Drayden in every way, though. He didn't seem to care that she wasn't walking with him anymore.

"What do you suggest?" Drayden asked her.

She picked at her fingernails. "I don't know. I'm just saying, what we're doing right now...we'll lose. We need to run, or find bikes, or if lucky, a working car."

"Can I drive?" Charlie asked.

"I think Eugene should drive since he already knows how," Sidney said. "You'd probably drive us off a cliff."

"I'm pretty sure we're not finding a car," Drayden said.

After discovering the massacre, Drayden was convinced they needed to beat the Guardians to Boston, as Eugene had been saying all along. The Guardians had shown how far they were willing to go to win.

If the Guardians beat them to Boston, one of two things would happen. They could ambush and kill the privates and Eugene as they arrived. An infinite number of places existed for them to hide. The privates wouldn't see it coming even if they knew it *was* coming. Or they could enter Boston and tell any number of lies about why the privates should be turned away. Either way, the privates would be screwed. If the privates and Eugene arrived first, those options would be theirs, among others.

The group approached a ramp off the highway, and the faded green sign beside it was still standing.

"Let's take this exit." Drayden refolded the map as he walked. "Derby Street. We go about a mile, then head north up Fifty-Three."

The condition of Derby Street was much worse than Route 3. It too was wide, like a highway, but seriously overgrown. After fifteen minutes, they reached the intersection with Route 53. It featured buildings on each corner, three of which had been reduced to piles of rubble. The one standing was a brown house with a flat roof and smashed glass walls. The sign read "Dunkin' Donuts."

They turned left, heading north. A narrower road, Route 53 was clearer, mostly covered in grasses and shrubs.

"Those friends of yours are some pretty evil dudes, Euge," Charlie said.

Eugene tilted his head from side to side. "Yes and no."

"Um, yes and yes." Charlie held up his index finger. "One more thing. Yes."

"I agree what they did was brutal, but it wasn't illogical. They asked for food first. When the villagers declined, the Guardians had two choices. Leave, or do what they did. They needed food, so they couldn't leave."

Those were hardly their only two choices. Killing every man in the village? Killing the man who gave them directions *after* they'd secured the food they needed? Just a tad extreme. Since Eugene had been a Guardian from the age of eight, the Guardian mindset had been drilled into him. He didn't perceive the fault with that argument. It was so black and white, so devoid of nuance. Life wasn't black and white, but shades of gray.

Drayden's way wasn't the wrong way after all. Eugene's and the Guardians' was. They weren't tough; they were monsters. Drayden wasn't soft; he was kind. They weren't strong and he wasn't weak. His strengths weren't physical; they were of the mind and heart. And he was going to show all of them how strong he was. He was going to unleash the strongest Drayden ever to win this battle. He wouldn't accept defeat at the hands of the Guardians, the Bureau, Eli Holst, or Nathan Locke. He would find a way to beat his enemies using his greatest weapon—his mind.

The second he completed that thought, he nearly coughed up a lung. His deteriorating health was the main risk to his grand plan. He couldn't die before they reached Boston, or become so weak he couldn't follow through.

Sidney sidled up to him, rubbing his shoulder. "I'm worried about you. What can I do to help?"

"Thanks, Sid. If you want to help, you should probably keep your distance. I don't want to make you sick. We need you."

She wrapped her arm around his waist as they walked. "I don't care. I don't care if I get sick. If I do, we'll be sick together. We need you. *I* need you. I'll take the risk to make sure you're okay."

Drayden gazed into her kind brown eyes. He loved Sidney in that moment. Everything with her was so painless. No drama, no games. She was the one person who always defended him, whose belief in him never wavered. Sidney tended to him. The only one who'd ever cared for him that much in such a way was his mother. Before she got herself exiled anyway.

He touched his hat and felt warm inside. He wrapped his arm around Sidney's shoulders and kissed her on the cheek. "Thank you, Sid."

Catrice gawked at them, her face twisted in disgust.

Drayden frowned. *What's she getting miffed about?*

She'd made her choice, and silently announced it to the world. He did feel the need to check on her, as he often did, to ensure she was all right. She was devastated by the capture and rescue at the camp. Something about the experience had hurt her more deeply than the others. But he didn't feel like he could or should be the one to approach her and inquire. Her rejection of him had been so public, so humiliating, so awkward. He couldn't embarrass himself further by chasing after her once again. If she wished, she could come up to *him*. Did she? No. Drayden squeezed Sidney even tighter.

Her satisfaction was evident.

Eugene stopped to examine a house on the right.

The dwelling was in top-notch shape—PreCon condition—and smoke rose from the chimney. An expansive field of crops stretched out behind the house, along with a barn, a windmill, and several other sheds. Farm equipment dotted the field.

"Whoever lives here has their act together," Eugene said. "We haven't seen anything like this yet."

Charlie pretended to knock on a door. "Pardon me, sir, would you happen to have five working bikes we could have forever? Yeah, and one of them needs to be an eight-year-old girl's bike, please. In return, we can give you nothing."

Eugene chewed on his lower lip. "They probably don't have bikes, but if they did, where would they keep them?"

Sidney looked at Drayden. In unison, they answered. "The barn."

CHAPTER 28

Whoever lived at the house must have been home, based on the chimney smoke, so Eugene led the privates through the woods past the property, emerging near the back side of the barn. He peered through his rifle's sight to assess the scene.

"We're clear. It's only about forty feet to the back of the barn. We sneak in, check for anything useful, and get the hell out of Dodge."

They were in a life or death situation here. If they didn't slip ahead of the Guardians, they were dead, one way or another. Charlie had highlighted the absurdity of asking the residents for assistance. Still, if the barn contained anything helpful, they were going to steal it. It felt wrong.

"Go." Eugene bolted, leading the way.

They reached the oversized barn door in seconds. Eugene slid it to the side, leaving it open.

Although Drayden had never seen a barn, it was pretty much what he expected: ancient wood beams, hay in a loft, rusty farm equipment, even a pitchfork. A beat-up tan car missing wheels rested atop cinderblocks in the barn's center.

They scoured the space, and failing to find bikes, regrouped at the car. According to the writing on the back, it was a Jaguar. Besides missing tires, it was rusty, dusty, and clearly hadn't run in ages. Wires jutted out from the dashboard.

Charlie kicked the bumper. "Damn. Hey, at least it doesn't have flat tires."

"So much for a lucky break." Sidney lowered her eyes.

Catrice chewed on her nails.

Drayden felt a rush of anxiety. They were going to lose. He sensed the others coming to the same realization. There just wasn't enough time to find some other solution, to continue searching for bikes or a working car. Unlike in the Initiation, they didn't have the vitality to run, surely not fifteen miles. The food had recharged the batteries enough to prevent a spontaneous coma, not to complete a half marathon. With Drayden's lungs full of mucus from the infection, he couldn't run much at all.

"Let's go, guys," he said, wearing the defeat on his face.

He turned to lead the way out, only to find two barrels of a shotgun in his grill.

"Hold it right there, son."

Drayden froze and raised his hands in the air.

The old man's short gray hair and leathery skin were reminiscent of Premier Eli Holst, and they appeared around the same age. Despite his elderliness, the man's eyes were clear and alert. "Let me see everyone's hands," he said, speaking with proper grammar and no peculiar accent.

Drayden's pulse quickened. They unequivocally didn't have time for another hostage situation. He was in front, so he couldn't see the other privates or Eugene.

The old guy rotated the barrels of the shotgun to his left, away from Drayden's head. "I said, put your hands up," he said to someone behind Drayden.

Drayden took a quick peek.

Sidney, Catrice, and Charlie held their hands high.

Eugene did not. He stood defiantly. "No."

The old man seemed perplexed. "This is your last chance, son. Put 'em up or I'm going to shoot."

"No, you won't," Eugene said emphatically.

Has he lost his mind?

"Um, Euge?" Charlie mumbled.

The old man raised his eyebrows, now apparently intrigued. "Is that right? Why not?"

"Because you're a dead man if you shoot, and I don't think you want to die," Eugene stated. "There're five of us. We're all armed. That's a simple double-barrel shotgun you have there. You could shoot one or two of us before you'd have to reload. Your head would be full of bullets by then."

The old man's mouth curled up a tad into a faint smile. "You might be right. But you're the one I'm going to shoot. You'll die too."

"Then do it." Eugene's piercing blue eyes bored holes in the man.

Drayden shook his head in awe. Eugene truly *was* like Rambo, once again demonstrating why a young corporal was selected for this mission ahead of more senior volunteers. He was so brave, so tough, so skilled, and insanely bright. While he'd won the gun chess-match with the old man, the whole interaction was unnecessary. It didn't have to be a battle.

Drayden dropped his arms. "Sir, we're peaceful. We're sorry we're in your barn." He extended his hand. "I'm Drayden."

Eugene groaned.

The man regarded him for a few seconds and lowered his shotgun. He shook Drayden's hand. "Professor Alan Worth. May I ask what you *are* doing here, on my property?"

Drayden took a deep breath. "You got a few minutes?"

He gave Professor Worth the three-minute summary: New America's situation, the expedition, the Guardians, Camp Gabriel, the slaughtered village, and their urgent need for speedier transportation.

"Sounds like you have a real problem." The professor leaned against a wooden post.

The other privates and Eugene huddled around Drayden now.

"Yeah, you could say that," Drayden said.

"Dray, we gotta move," Eugene said.

Professor Worth rubbed his chin. "One quick question. Do you have any food you can spare?"

"No," Eugene blurted.

Drayden scowled at him. "Yes. Well, here's what we have. One loaf of bread, one head of lettuce, and we each have half a sausage. That's the first food we've had in two days, and we're rationing it. We're happy to share, though."

"May I have the loaf of bread?"

Eugene snickered.

Drayden snatched the plastic bag from behind Charlie's back, and handed him the loaf.

The man took it, smiled, and handed it back to him. "Thank you, Drayden. I don't want it, but I wanted to know if you would give it to me. If you wait here for a minute, I'll bring something that may assist you." He strolled to the front of the barn, opened the door, and headed for the main house.

Drayden locked eyes with Eugene. Although Eugene may have been tough as nails and the bravest guy in the world, all they needed to do was be friendly to the man.

Eugene was antsy, chewing on his lower lip. "This is taking way too long. We can still beat the Guardians. We gotta hustle."

Sidney squinted, attempting to view the farmhouse. "Maybe he's fetching us bicycles. He said he'd bring something that would help us."

Professor Worth returned, carrying a white plastic bag. He handed it to Drayden. It was full of vegetables—carrots, peppers, celery, and string beans.

"Thanks a lot, Professor, that's very generous of you." Drayden shook his hand once more.

A little kindness goes a long way, Drayden thought as he turned to leave. He couldn't hide his disappointment though. The expedition was over. A bag of vegetables was a nice consolation, and sure would taste delicious. But they simply couldn't catch the Guardians. He walked toward the barn's back door, deflated.

"Drayden?" the professor asked.

He spun around.

"The veggies aren't what I was talking about when I said I would bring something that might help."

"Sir?"

He held a set of keys in his hand, dangling them in the air.

Drayden eyed the beat-up Jaguar on cinderblocks. Was this some sort of sick joke?

Professor Worth tilted his head. "Don't you want a ride?"

"Whoa, this guy's not playing with a full deck," Charlie whispered. "I think he's going to take us for a pretend ride in the Jaguar. We'll sit inside and he'll go 'vroom, vroom.'"

Professor Worth went to say something but pressed his lips together. "Follow me. Very carefully, single file. Do not deviate from my path." He led them out the front of the barn and through an empty field, stopping at an unpainted wood shed on the verge of collapse. Before opening it, he paused before the privates and Eugene, like he was about to begin a one-man show.

He parted the doors and stepped off to the side, gesturing inside the shed, a sly smile on his face.

Drayden's heart skipped a beat.

Massive tires. Mounted spotlights. A hulking, mean-looking green truck stood inside.

Drayden held his Yankees cap in his hand so it wouldn't blow off in the wind. The afternoon sun shone in his eyes, making him squint. The truck was a "Jeep," and instead of windows or a roof, it sported a "roll bar," according to Professor Worth.

The wind blasted Drayden's face in bursts, blowing his hair back. Zooming in the Jeep was a thrill.

In reality, they weren't going that fast. Vegetation, including trees, covered Route 53 in many places. They bumped and flew through the air, and skidded, and swerved. It was a blast. Professor Worth had clearly done a lot of driving. Charlie rode up front, with everyone else squeezed in the back. Drayden sat on one end next to Sidney, then Eugene and Catrice on the other side. Charlie had asked if he could drive, as expected, but the professor shot him down. Laughed at him, in fact.

Drayden had checked the map before they left. "Professor Worth, after Route 53, can you take Route 3a, then I-93?"

"Yes. I know the way."

"Drop us off right at the intersection of 3a and 93."

Professor Worth turned his head back and raised his eyebrows. "Not into Boston?"

"No."

Sidney squeezed Drayden's leg. "Why not straight into Boston?"

"Because we're making a stand against the Guardians."

Nobody knew what Boston was like. It could be a police state, where the Guardians would command a lot more respect than five teenagers. If both groups arrived in Boston, it could devolve into a he-said she-said situation. That could be true even if the privates arrived first. What if Boston enforced a quarantine period? Arriving a few hours before the Guardians would prove meaningless. If the Guardians beat them, they might be shut out of Boston entirely, with their families paying the price.

Yet it was beyond logistics. The Guardians were evil, and barbaric. They needed to be stopped. Someone had to shut down their crusade of cruelty. There was no limit to how far the Guardians would go to destroy him. He would destroy them first. Except he wasn't sure he could or would actually kill them.

Something struck Drayden. The Guardians weren't on this mission to escort the privates. *It was the other way around.* The privates' presence was to ensure the Guardians reached Boston. But why?

"We'll be on the outskirts of Boston, near Dorchester," Drayden said. "Far enough away that nobody from the city will interfere."

Eugene grinned. "Now you're talkin."

Catrice leaned forward. "Professor Worth, are there people in Boston?"

"Yes. I don't know much about it. I've never been there."

"Why don't you live there?" Drayden asked. "And how are you alive?"

"Natural immunity to Aeru," Professor Worth answered. "I don't know why, though. Most of the people who survived had some sort of immunity. I used to be a math professor at MIT. Originally, I avoided the quarantine because I didn't want my fate to be decided by a bunch of incompetent politicians. Not to mention a closed-off society is ripe for government brainwashing, corruption, propaganda. I didn't realize how serious the Confluence was until it was too late. I was shut out of the city. After that, I assumed I would die, as my wife did, but I never got sick. If I had known my wife would die, I would have stayed in Boston. I did try entering ages ago and was turned away. I never went back."

Drayden recalled Kim's claims about the Bureau. They controlled information. It was becoming clear that nobody outside the Bureau likely knew the truth about New America.

Professor Worth slammed the brakes, and everyone flew forward. He drove around a fallen tree on the road.

"Sorry about that."

Eugene took in the scenery outside the Jeep. He appeared disinterested in learning more about the world outside the walls, or Professor Worth. He and the professor hadn't quite recovered from their standoff earlier, and had yet to speak to each other.

Professor Worth continued. "You see, I've come to understand the Confluence. It had to happen. Humanity was on a crash course with self-destruction. If it wasn't super bacteria, or inequality, or cyberterrorism, it would have been nuclear weapons, climate change, or something else. The Earth and humans needed a fresh start."

Charlie tapped the professor on the arm. "How do you avoid getting robbed by bad guys like the ones we ran into at Camp Gabriel and the cannibals?"

Professor Worth bellowed a deep old-man laugh. "That would be a long conversation. The short version? Weapons, safe rooms. My whole property is booby-trapped. It's a miracle you kids didn't get injured running to my barn. Many people have died over the years trying to steal from me. Over time you learn how to coexist. People learned the hard way not to mess with my property, and then learned to work with me. I'm familiar with Gabriel's camp. I even have some deals with them. They're a violent group. You were lucky to escape."

Charlie leaned his head back. "Saved by Eugene."

Professor Worth regarded Eugene through a small mirror that hung up front. "Ah yes, Eugene. I like him. Very brave, very clever. Watch out for that one."

Eugene revealed nothing. He chewed on his bottom lip so hard it trickled blood.

Professor Worth seemed excited to have people with whom to speak, to teach, and to help. "The Confluence brought out the worst in everyone. Gabriel was probably a nice guy, like a pharmacist, Pre-Confluence. Given how tenuous daily survival is out here, now he's a savage leader."

The road became clearer, and Professor Worth sped up. "You kids are too young to know, but the Confluence didn't happen on one day. It's not as if God snapped his fingers and humans disappeared. People died slowly, one region at a time. The world spent much time in chaos, disarray, lawlessness. People robbed homes of neighbors who died; they murdered people who had things they desired. Of course, what was valuable Pre-Confluence and what was worthless reversed. People stole the wrong things. Money, cars, electronics like smartphones, and jewelry all became worthless. Pots, matches, medicine, and water became the new gold. Guns became diamonds."

Their surroundings became increasingly commercial and residential.

"We're on Route 3a, now," Professor Worth said.

"Ah, one of my favorite roads," Charlie said. "Wolves."

Professor Worth looked puzzled. "What was that?"

"Watch out for wolves. They love Route 3a."

"How do you have a working car?" Drayden asked.

"It's my hobby, fixing up cars."

Drayden snickered. "We tried to fix up a car from a dealership, but it didn't work."

"If you had a year, you wouldn't have gotten it working. Fuel is the major problem. My cars run on ethanol. I make it myself from my corn. Modifying the engine to run on ethanol is fairly simple."

Drayden wished he could spend more time with Professor Worth. In addition to being knowledgeable, he was a survivor. He'd figured out how to thrive in the wild all on his own. Drayden could learn a lot from him. He'd also make quite an asset against the Bureau.

Sidney placed her hand on Drayden's thigh and gently interlocked her fingers with his.

He squeezed back.

Professor Worth drove onto an extended overpass above the streets below. It became a narrow bridge that crossed over a river.

"This is the Neponset River," Professor Worth said. "Almost there."

The road curved down to the right and ran alongside an elevated roadway. They drove up a ramp and onto the highway.

The skyscrapers of Boston emerged in the distance.

This was it. I-93.

Professor Worth stopped the car.

Drayden touched him on the shoulder from behind. "Professor... thank you, from the bottom of my heart. We may still fail, but now we have a chance." He started to ask if he could come visit in the future, after Boston, before remembering he had no future.

The professor nodded. "You're welcome. This was the most interesting day I've had in years. Good luck to you all."

"You got a plan?" Charlie asked Drayden.

"Nope."

Eugene cocked his pistol. "Here's my plan."

CHAPTER 29

The late afternoon sun glistened off the skyscrapers in the distance, making them glow.

Boston's skyline was much smaller than New America's, as if all but a few tall buildings had fallen.

Drayden examined I-93 in both directions.

It wasn't as damaged as other roads, resembling an actual highway, probably because it was elevated. A few industrial buildings lined the streets below. Roughly a half mile to the south, the vegetation exploded, as if Mother Nature had vomited.

If a brilliant plot lay dormant somewhere inside Drayden's brain, now would be an opportune time to pop it out. Unfortunately, nothing came to him. He hadn't the faintest idea how they would defeat the Guardians. Suddenly a two-hour head start seemed piddling.

Sidney coughed. "I know we have stuff to do, but I'm dying of thirst."

"Me too," Charlie said. "My mouth's so dry I'm spitting cotton."

Drayden glimpsed south down the highway, away from the city, toward the vegetation. "Let's walk down there." Hopefully something they saw would trigger an idea for the upcoming battle.

They hopped the cement divider between the northbound and southbound lanes. Drayden and Sidney led the way down the gentle slope of the southbound lanes.

"Let's be on alert in case I'm wrong about our lead over the Guardians," Drayden said. "I believe we're around two hours ahead, but it'd be pathetic if we got surprised by them."

"Are we sure fighting them is the right move?" Catrice asked, avoiding eye contact with Drayden.

"Absolutely," Eugene said. "This must be done."

"I think there's too much uncertainty about what would happen if both groups arrived in Boston," said Drayden. "What if they believed the Guardians over us?"

In the heart of the vegetation eruption, they crossed over the Neponset River. To the right of the highway, a five-story office building sat alone on the river's bank, surrounded by marshland. The wide structure consisted of brown stone with black windows.

A green sign over the highway indicated an exit lay ahead for Granite Avenue, Ashmont. Exit 11b.

Drayden pulled out his map of Boston. "This is the Neponset River Reservation. I guess that's why it's so…nature-y here. Let's take this exit ramp on the right up ahead."

The exit ramp ran downhill and curved to the right, turning 180 degrees until they were facing north again at the bottom. It deposited them right in front of that office building on Granite Avenue, which ran parallel to the elevated I-93. A sign read "2 Granite Avenue." Although the parking lot was heavily overgrown, the building appeared in decent shape. Even the windows were intact. Marshland and trees surrounded the building and the parking lot, with I-93 rising above it in the back.

A much larger marsh, a swamp overflowing with tall reeds and wild plants, occupied the other side of Granite Avenue. Water, presumably the Neponset River, meandered deep in the marsh.

Drayden digested the landscape. "Anyone ever been in a swamp before?"

"First Avenue smells like a swamp," Charlie said.

"There's water out there. Let's check it out."

For the first few steps they trudged through wet grass, which quickly became thicker and muddier. The marsh smelled rotten, and the reeds were nearly as tall as Drayden in some places. While the sun's reflection off the river was visible in the distance, the tall reeds obstructed much of the view.

"It's not much further to the river." Drayden checked behind him. "Everybody good?"

Charlie pinched his nose shut. "Smells like a rectum."

Drayden faced forward and slipped. "Oh shkat!" It all happened so fast, he didn't know what hit him. He found himself on his back and felt as if he were falling, sliding. His legs flailing, he desperately grasped at the reeds.

Someone snagged his collar, choking him for a second. Hands braced him beneath his arms, and Charlie scooped him up. Cold, wet mud coated Drayden's gray camo pants.

He lumbered to his feet and straightened his clothes. "What the heck happened?"

The others huddled around him. A deep pit, essentially a spacious muddy crevice in the ground, stood before them. It was invisible until you were on its precipice because of the tall wetland weeds. It stretched wide on both sides.

"Jeez. I did not see that coming. Man, if I fell in there..." Drayden didn't care to complete the thought. His brain started performing the mental gymnastics to solve his hypothetical rescue. Tie a rope out of the reeds and drop it down to him? It had to be fifteen feet deep, and slick with mud everywhere. "Thanks, as usual, you guys."

They navigated around the hole and slogged their way to the river. Unlike the crystal-clear streams they'd encountered, the Neponset River was mucky and green, full of organic matter.

Charlie dipped his hand in the water. "Um, I know I'm not one of you smart guys, but we don't have any bottles. Or that bowl."

Drayden smacked himself in the forehead with his palm. "I'm such an idiot. You're right, Charlie. My bad. That water looks gross anyway; we shouldn't drink it."

The water, boiling it, a fire...

An idea was crystallizing in his mind about the battle with the Guardians. Though he couldn't grasp it yet, something was there.

Sidney rubbed her hands together. "I'm getting kind of nervous about this confrontation. How exactly are we going to kill the Guardians?"

Eugene peered back at Granite Avenue. "Perched on top of that office building would be ideal. Good angle, right over the highway. We'll see them coming half a mile away. Me, you, and Charlie are accurate enough shots."

"What if they don't come up this highway?" Catrice asked.

"They were headed up Route 3," Drayden said. "Anything's possible, but this is pretty much the only way they can go."

Eugene licked his lips. "We'll be ready for them."

The privates, visibly uneasy about the idea, looked to Drayden.

He put his hands in his pockets. "I don't think we should kill them."

Eugene snapped his face away for a second, obscuring it. When he turned back, his piercing eyes dug into Drayden. "You can't be serious."

"I am."

Eugene was incredulous, speechless for a moment. "And you want to do what, negotiate with them? Reason with them? Talk about their feelings?" He sneered.

Eugene had never spoken to him like that before. He was condescending, obnoxious. "No." Drayden's face grew hot. "I think we shou—"

"Do you realize they'll kill you?" Eugene stepped closer to him. "Not only would they not hesitate, they'd enjoy it. Even if they didn't need to kill you to beat us, they'd *still* do it."

Charlie draped a hand on Drayden's shoulder. "I kinda agree with Euge. Dray, it's not like we're killing nice guys. These are wicked dudes."

Sidney shrugged. "I'll follow your lead, Dray, but I wouldn't have any problem killing them. They deserve it."

"I'm with you, Drayden," Catrice said.

Drayden twirled the paperclip and battery in his pocket with his right hand. His left hand touched something else. What was that?

The gummy sap.

The plan was forming in his head all on its own.

It was hard to argue they didn't deserve it. Killing them would guarantee the privates and Eugene could enter Boston alone. The Guardians would definitely slaughter him if given the chance.

Trying to kill each other suggested going head-to-head with them at their greatest skill. The privates did have the advantage of surprise, and the time to set up for the clash. But a gunfight played to the Guardians' strengths, not Drayden's. Fighting was what they did. It was all they did. They'd call on their vast experience and physical skill. He would lose that battle.

Yet it was more than that. Faced with the same choice as on the Route 3a overpass, his decision remained the same. Killing wasn't what he was about, or who he was. He wasn't a murderer. Just because the Guardians would kill him didn't require him to kill them. He was better than that. He refused to accept a lowest-common-denominator world, in which the most evil among them made the rules and dictated the values. He could win this fight without betraying his identity.

"I'm not saying they don't deserve it," Drayden said. "But what would that make us? No better than them. Killers. Barbarians like they are. There's too much brutality in this world already. I think—"

"It's a brutal world, Dray." Eugene cocked his head. "The only way to combat brutality is to match it."

Drayden's eyes narrowed. "It's *not* the only—"

"What are you so afraid of?" Eugene stepped closer.

"Let me finish, goddammit!" Drayden got right in Eugene's face.

"Don't be a coward!" Eugene screamed, the tendons bulging in his neck.

"I'm not a coward! I'm not afraid of them! I'm afraid of turning into them, like you." His nose was inches from Eugene's.

Then it clicked. Drayden's eyes widened. He looked past Eugene.

I've got it. The plan.

Everything fell into place. He knew how to defeat the Guardians without resorting to senseless murder, unless left with no other option.

Eugene stepped back. The others observed them in silence.

"I have a plan," Drayden said. "We win. Our way. And if something goes wrong, we always have the option of killing them. Hopefully it doesn't come to that."

His mind raced. They had things to set up. Suddenly, time was of the essence. What to do first?

"What's the plan?" Sidney asked.

Drayden tugged on his left ear. "We need to start a fire."

"I think it's too wet." Catrice walked in place, her feet slopping the mud with each step.

Drayden pulled the gummy sap out of his pocket. Thank God for Sam and everything she'd taught him. One of the uses of gummy sap was to start a fire in wet conditions. It was highly flammable. "This will light," he said. "It's sap. Once it's burning, we can pile on some of these reeds and grasses."

Charlie scratched his head. "But the Guardians will see it. Gives away our advantage."

"I want them to see it," Drayden said.

He looked confused. "Oh. Okay, then."

"Uh," Drayden said, struggling to put the pieces together in his mind, "Sid, Catrice...do you still have the Guardian baseball hats in your pockets?"

They pulled them out.

He held his hands in the air. "Can you...can you guys stand next to each other, and turn around?"

Charlie smirked and crossed his arms. "Dray, if you wanna check out their butts, I really don't think this is the time."

"Knock it off, Charlie. I'm not...never mind."

The girls stood side by side with their backs to Drayden.

Hmmm, could work.

"Good. You can turn around. Sid, do you have that shower curtain liner from the Stop & Shop?"

She dug through the myriad pockets on the Guardian uniform pants and pulled it out. "Yup."

Eugene shook his head. "I wish I knew where you were going with this, but I have no clue."

Drayden viewed the roof of the building. "You're going to like this plan."

CHAPTER 30

The beauty of the setting sun over the marsh caught Drayden by surprise. Despite the situation, he took a moment to catch his breath.

From the roof of Two Granite Avenue, the sun was a giant, deep orange disk, the sky on fire around it. The bottoms of the purple clouds glowed red.

The calm before the storm.

Drayden faced the others. "Is everyone ready? Everybody know what they need to do?"

"Booyah, Dray-man." Charlie fist-bumped him.

"It's a smart idea, Dray." Eugene sounded almost apologetic. He'd chewed his lip bloody again.

"Let's do this," Sidney said.

Catrice nodded, still refusing to directly acknowledge him.

The expansive roof provided an unobstructed view of both I-93 and the marsh. They would need both views, both lines of sight, both firing lines if necessary. A security station, like a miniature house or shack, sat near the marsh side of the roof. It provided access to the roof from the inside stairwell. Otherwise, the roof was a vast, open space.

Sidney and Catrice both donned their military caps, with the flat tops, as instructed. They tucked their hair up, hiding it under the caps. That detail was critical, since Sidney was a brunette and Catrice a blonde. It didn't make them look *exactly* alike, because they had different body types. Sidney was taller and thicker, much more athletically built. Catrice, on the other hand, was stick skinny, and the opposite of athletic. But it was the best they could do. Hopefully from a distance, they would appear similar enough.

Deep into the marsh, right by the Neponset River, their small fire raged, thanks to the gummy sap. It unleashed a steady stream of smoke into the sky, likely visible from quite a distance away. The Guardians couldn't miss it.

The other setups had been arranged in the marsh as well. Now it was time to wait for the Guardians, whose arrival could be imminent if Drayden's calculations were correct. The privates and Eugene needed to take their positions ASAP.

"We need to get going," Drayden said with authority. "Don't misinterpret my attempt to spare the Guardians' lives for a softness toward them. They're despicable human beings. They murdered twenty people in cold blood. They're savages. Sparing their lives is about preserving *our* identity," he said, jabbing his finger into his chest, "and has nothing to do with them. If it comes down to it, if it's a question of us or them, we take them out. Shoot to kill." He paused, scanning their faces, to ensure his message was clear. "Let's do this. Everyone get into place."

Drayden felt the urge to comfort Catrice, but decided against it. He reminded himself that she'd dumped him without a word.

Eugene likewise offered her nothing, either unaware of, or indifferent to, her fear.

As per the plan, Eugene and Charlie remained on the roof. They headed over to the highway side to watch for the Guardians. Catrice,

Sidney, and Drayden climbed downstairs and exited through the front door. Catrice strode silently out into the marsh.

Drayden touched Sidney's arm. "Sid, I'll meet you at the bottom of the highway exit ramp. I want to check something."

She drew her head back. "What?"

"It's nothing; I'll be right back. I'll meet you out there." Without giving her a chance to pry further, he jogged around the building, hugging the walls, heading to its rear. He located the back door and tried the knob.

Locked.

He picked up a rock and smashed a hole in the glass, hoping Charlie and Eugene didn't hear, then stepped back a few feet and waited.

Neither boy peered down to investigate.

Phew. He reached through, unlocked the door, and entered. A short walk down a corridor revealed the staircase that led up to the roof. *Check.* Now he knew how to access the roof through the back door without being noticed. He left through the rear door and jogged up Granite Avenue.

Sidney was waiting for him at the bottom of the curved ramp that led up to the highway. "What was that all about?"

Drayden doubled over, out of breath. "I...I wanted to make sure the back door was open, in case everything goes wrong and we're running from the Guardians, searching for a place to hide." That wasn't totally a lie. It was one of the reasons, just not the primary one.

She eyed him suspiciously.

"You got the head of lettuce?" he asked, changing the subject.

She pulled it out of the plastic bag and handed it to him.

Professor Worth's vegetables were vastly superior to the lettuce from the slaughtered village, so they hadn't eaten it. Drayden set it atop the metal guardrail and waved at the roof of the office building.

The bottom of the ramp offered a clear view to the building. Further up, heavy tree cover blocked the view between the ramp and the building.

Eugene waved back from the roof, followed by a thumbs-up.

Drayden plunked down on the guardrail, a stone's throw up the ramp from the lettuce. He and Sid carried their pistols, having left their rifles on the roof. Charlie and Eugene held their rifles, ready to act. Everything was in place.

"Soooo, now we wait." He tried to relax and enjoy these few moments of peace.

Sidney offered a sly smile. "Whatcha want to do?" She draped her arms over his shoulders and connected them behind his neck.

Drayden's heart fluttered. He'd never been close to Sidney like this. He stood, resting his hands on her hips, their faces so close. Sidney was beautiful.

He thought about Catrice, his guilt sneaking up on him. He couldn't help it, wondering if she could see them from where she was hiding in the marsh. He didn't check. Even though it was over with Catrice, he still worried about her, cared about her.

Catrice's default state was frightened. Often her fear wasn't warranted, or at least not the magnitude of it. But this time, it was, and then some. Drayden had gone out of his way during the Initiation to keep her out of harm's way. In this operation, not only was she in harm's way, she had a greater risk of death than anyone else. As the architect of the strategy, Drayden himself was responsible for endangering her life. It had to be that way. The plan couldn't work otherwise. He felt terrible for not saying anything to her when they left the roof. She must be shaking with fear. And quite possibly, she was watching him cozy up to her nemesis.

Screw it.

He'd bent over backward trying to make her happy, and she embarrassed him over and over. She picked the Guardian barbarian—the Guarbarian—over him. He bet she didn't feel the same way about Eugene now. He was a far cry from the innocent charmer they'd met before the expedition. Which version was the real Eugene anyway? Hell, Catrice might have accepted her dangerous role to prove to herself and everyone else that she, too, could contribute to their victory on the expedition.

Drayden sat back down and wrapped his arms around Sidney's waist, pulling her close.

She sat on his lap, facing him.

He brushed his hand on her cheek, her skin so soft against his hand. She had a lot riding on the outcome of this fight, as did he. She had Nora, her little sister, who needed her. Besides their lives, they each had personal reasons they needed to vanquish the Guardians. All of them hinged on Drayden's plan.

His mind played out so many different scenarios. The various ways it could go wrong flooded his brain. The Guardians taking a different route didn't even make the list, since it was unlikely, though it was still a risk. What if they didn't fall for the trap? They might not. This wasn't their first rodeo. It was dusk now, light fading by the minute. What if the Guardians showed up after it was dark? The scheme wouldn't work at night. What if someone from Boston saw the fire and interfered, screwing everything up? His head was a mess.

The team had endorsed the plan because they blindly believed it would work. They didn't perceive the shortcomings he did. If Catrice did, she hadn't said anything. Drayden had a gut feeling something would go wrong. Although the privates and Eugene had discussed specific contingencies if things didn't work out properly, they couldn't prepare for every scenario.

Of course, Drayden had one wrinkle to the strategy he couldn't divulge to anyone. He did, however, need to provide Sidney some explanation about why he would deviate from the plan right at the start.

He cleared his throat. "Sid, I'm not feeling too well. That short jog I did practically killed me. I'm thinking I won't run alongside you. I'll cover you from a distance. I just...I think I might be too slow, and the whole plan will be blown if we're slow."

"Um, okay," she said, struggling to hide her disappointment. "I'd rather have you there with me, but if you don't think you can do it...where are you going to go?"

"I'm gonna hop the guardrail and head toward the back corner of the building through the parking lot. There's another whole swampy area there and thick tree cover. I should be able to move undetected." Drayden hadn't lied yet, he'd only omitted some information. The short jog had, in fact, almost killed him. And he *was* going to hop the guardrail rather than run down the ramp beside her. But he was going to do other things too.

She rubbed his chest. "Don't worry, I can handle this part by myself. Should we let the others know we're changing the plan?"

"No," he blurted. "It shouldn't affect them. It'll just be you down there, instead of me and you."

Thank God he could always count on Sidney to handle whatever was required of her.

She looked out over the marsh, her jaw clenched. "Do you think this is going to work? Really. After we reach Boston, will we get to go home?" Her eyes moistened.

Drayden held her hands. "I do. I believe it'll work. Even if it doesn't, we'll still find a way to win. After that I think it may take us a while to handle business in Boston, whatever that is, and then we'll get home. You'll see your sister again, safe in the Palace."

Drayden didn't mention his own improbable return, since this story was all fantasy anyway. He hadn't a clue whether they'd win this battle or not, and no idea what would happen after. He thought it highly unlikely anyone else would make it home either. They would all have to pray the Bureau showed mercy on their families and allowed them to remain in the Palace. They'd left New America with one-way tickets, as people used to say back when airplanes flew. Deep down, Sidney probably knew it too, which was why she asked. But it was much easier not to face the harsh reality.

She cupped her hands over her mouth, sobbing in short bursts. Tears streamed down her cheeks.

Drayden hugged her, rubbing her back. Given how strong a person she was, it was easy to forget that she was human too. Her love for her sister had pushed her to do what needed to be done, but it didn't mean she wasn't scared. Everyone expected her to step up, to deliver. It struck him how much she needed support as well.

Sidney rested her head against his chest. She pulled back, wiped her eyes, and smiled. "Sorry. I try not to think about her, because I always start to cry." She shook out her hands. "I'm better now. Thank you, Drayden."

He gazed into her eyes, their faces now an inch or two apart.

Her warm breath kissed his lips. She tilted her head a tad more and closed her eyes.

The head of lettuce exploded.

Sidney tumbled off his lap.

"Jesus!" Drayden yelled, flopping off the guardrail himself. He checked the roof.

Eugene was kneeling with his elbow rested atop the roof's wall. His Glock remained in place, aimed directly at them, or where the lettuce innocently sat before it was assassinated. He'd shot it with his silencer on to alert them.

It meant the Guardians were in sight.

Charlie jumped up and down on the roof, frantically gesturing toward the highway.

Drayden's stomach twisted in knots. Holy freaking shkat, it was finally time to do this. He took short, rapid breaths and drew his Glock. But his feet wouldn't move.

Sidney grasped him by the arm and yanked him up the highway exit ramp. She flew ahead of him, pumping her arms, her pistol in her right hand.

Drayden wheezed, struggling up the ramp, which ran uphill, curving to the left. Thick trees lined it on both sides, making it tunnel-like, providing superb cover.

Out of breath, he reached the top of the ramp.

Sidney was crouching behind the guardrail, viewing the highway. Her chest heaving, she motioned toward the south.

Drayden knelt beside her.

The sky's brilliant canvas of pink, purple, and blue was fading. I-93 ran downhill away from them, curving to the left. They hid on the southbound side, with the northbound lanes on the other side of the concrete barrier.

In the distance, three silhouettes carrying rifles marched up the northbound lanes. One of them was limping.

CHAPTER 31

"Guess it was Captain Lindrick's foot you shot," Drayden whispered to Sidney. They remained behind the metal guardrail where the highway and the exit ramp met. "Well done."

"I was hoping for Duarte, but Lindrick'll do."

Captain Lindrick hobbled, putting little weight on his right foot. The limp made him seem much older and weaker. If the Guardians had noticed the smoke, they revealed no sign of it.

Sweat dripped down Drayden's cheeks and dampened his back. With shaking hands, he cocked his pistol.

"When do we go?" Sidney asked.

"Not yet. When they're about two hundred feet away." Drayden noted the Guardians weren't wearing the privates' backpacks. They must have taken what they wanted and left them.

They were still about a quarter mile down the highway.

The timing was critical to the plan. The Guardians first needed to see them, and then give chase. The distance between them would be significant later.

As the Guardians neared, their heads turned toward the smoke.

They looked awful. Dirty, gaunt, ashen. Drayden didn't care to imagine the nightmares they had experienced the past three days.

Considering the trauma the privates had endured to reach Boston, they must have survived their own horrors as well.

He wiped his sweaty palms on his pants. Allowing the Guardians to inch closer was nerve-racking, but the strategy had to be executed with discipline. Two hundred feet was close enough to yell. When the Guardians eventually began shooting, Drayden had to ensure he and Sidney weren't hit.

"Sid, get ready," he whispered.

The Guardians carried their rifles in the low-ready position— ready to act but facing the ground.

Drayden was trembling. He took a deep breath and exhaled. *You can do this.* He touched Sidney's shoulder. "Let's go."

The two of them strolled side by side onto the highway, heading toward the city up the southbound lanes. They walked a few steps; enough for the Guardians to notice them. It needed to appear as if he and Sidney were simply jaunting north, unaware of the Guardians' presence.

"Now, Sid!"

Drayden spun around and dropped to his knee, taking aim at the Guardians, who were preparing to fire themselves. He squeezed off five high-speed rounds.

Sidney also knelt and fired.

The Guardians scattered. Duarte jumped behind the guardrail bordering the northbound lanes, and Greaney dove down onto the asphalt. Lindrick took a knee and fired a flurry of bullets at Drayden and Sidney.

"Get down!" Sidney screamed.

She and Drayden scampered back to the guardrail and ducked behind it.

The Guardians methodically approached, using the cement barrier between the north and southbound lanes for cover.

Drayden fired two more shots from behind the guardrail.

Almost time.

The Guardians took cover.

"It's time, Sid!" Drayden said.

She grabbed him by both cheeks and pecked him on the lips. "You ready?"

He nodded. They jumped to their feet, fired once more at the Guardians, and dashed out of sight down the ramp.

Sidney blew by him.

Drayden hopped over the guardrail on the side closest to the office building. Before escaping into the trees, he glanced back.

The Guardians were charging the ramp. Lieutenant Duarte and Sergeant Greaney led the way, with Captain Lindrick struggling to keep up.

It was a relief that they bit and were following. All according to plan, though Lindrick's lagging could become a problem.

Drayden ducked into the heavy foliage beside the highway ramp. Dodging tree trunks along the way, he stumbled down a steep embankment to the swampy area below. At the bottom, he surveyed the marshland surrounding the building. He bolted, splashing through a trifling stream in two giant strides. The water soaked his boots and socks, chilling his feet, but he continued running as hard as he could.

This part of the plan would be the most difficult for him. He needed to reach the roof of the building before Sidney arrived in the marsh. It was going to be close.

Drayden whacked tall reeds out of the way, powering through his burning legs and heavy lungs. He leapt through the mud with increasing urgency.

Right now, Sidney would be sprinting down the exit ramp, the Guardians in tow. Since she moved like lightning, she would have to ensure she didn't get too far ahead. They needed to observe where she went so they could follow. If she let them get too close, however, they could shoot her. Hopefully she was managing her speed accordingly.

Drayden reached the parking lot, sprinting his heart out. His wet feet sloshed around in his soaked boots, and he was totally out of breath.

Charlie and Eugene would be watching Granite Avenue with their rifles drawn. If the Guardians neared Sidney enough to shoot, they needed to protect her. Catrice would have heard the gunshots on the highway, and she would be in position in the marsh, ready to go.

Drayden flung the building's back door open. He darted inside, sliding all over the linoleum floor with his wet boots. His lungs were on fire, his wheezing audible. How in the world could he climb five flights? He could barely breathe. Maybe he messed up his own role and wouldn't make it in time. He could miss the whole damn thing.

He jumped up three and four stairs at a time, grunting, wiping the sweat out of his eyes. Two stories, three, four, five.

Drayden entered the makeshift house on the roof and stopped for a second to gather himself. Sweat poured down his cheeks. He had to be quiet now. He couldn't be breathing heavy and sure as hell couldn't cough.

He nudged the door to the roof open, on the side opposite where Eugene and Charlie stood, and tiptoed down to the edge of the house, near the roof wall that overlooked the marsh. He stopped there, staying out of sight in case they turned around.

A little to his left, both boys were leaning over the waist-high roof wall with their backs to him. Propped up on their elbows, rifles aimed, they watched the action through their scopes.

Drayden struggled to catch his breath. He scrunched his face up to choke back a cough desperately trying to escape.

He'd made it in time. Sidney was racing down Granite Avenue, just shy of the marsh. Duarte was a few hundred feet behind her, with Greaney right behind him. They were a little far, but within sight of her, which was all that mattered. Captain Lindrick trailed way behind Sergeant Greaney.

Running for her life, carrying her pistol in her right hand, Sidney's face glowed bright red. She veered left into the marsh. Once inside, she took broad, hopping strides, fighting to move swiftly through the mud.

From the Guardians' angle, she would have gone out of view. They would have witnessed her enter the marsh and disappear among the tall reeds. A line of trees along the marsh's edge blocked the view into its depths. They would see the smoke from the fire deep in the marsh, and hopefully assume she was headed there. Once the Guardians reached the marsh and entered, they would be able to see her again through the reeds.

Drayden bit down on his lip.

Now that she was trudging through the swamp, dealing with the mud and the weeds, she had slowed. The Guardians were gaining on her, fast.

C'mon, Sid. Move, dammit.

She arrived at the mud pit and dropped down out of view.

From the roof of the office building, she was visible lying down on the mucky marsh floor. From inside the marsh, though, she'd be hidden.

Immediately after she laid down, Catrice jumped up, just *past* the mud pit. Sporting her Guardians cap, she bounced toward the fire, carrying her pistol in her right hand.

The Guardians cleared the line of trees and charged into the marsh, chasing after Catrice. Except they believed it was Sidney, still running for their "camp" at the fire by the river.

The Guardians followed Catrice in a straight line with her path to the fire. They were headed right for the mud pit.

The privates and Eugene had tinkered with the mud pit, turning it deadlier. They covered the first few feet of it with the shower curtain liner, which they concealed with mud, weeds, and reeds. It was totally invisible. By the time you stepped on it, finding only air beneath, you were done. Even if the Guardians veered left or right of the shower curtain, the pit was wide and malicious enough.

"Euge," Charlie said. "Euge, we got a problem. Lindrick is way too far back. He's gonna see the other guys drop in the pit. He's not gonna fall for it."

It was a serious problem. With the limp, Lindrick couldn't keep up with Greaney and Duarte. Little did he know the limp would save him from nose diving into the mud dungeon.

Catrice was not the athlete Sidney was. The Guardians were rapidly closing the distance—much closer, and they could shoot her. But they were headed straight for the pit. Almost there.

Drayden contemplated how Lieutenant Duarte and Captain Lindrick believed he was weak. They were wrong. While he wasn't ruthless or skilled with weapons, he had his own skills. He was about to prove that he was stronger than they were.

Duarte and Greaney were ten feet from the pit. Duarte raised his rifle at Catrice.

Five feet from the pit.

They disappeared, as if they vanished into thin air.

Yes! Drayden pumped his fist in the air. *It worked!*

Catrice continued moving toward the fire, as instructed.

The other Guardians screamed like crazy from inside the pit, trying to keep Captain Lindrick from falling in. He stopped just short of it.

"Oh shkat," Charlie said.

Drayden's smile faded.

Sidney.

She lay in the weeds, mere feet from Captain Lindrick, who was raising his rifle at Catrice.

No!

He lowered the weapon, and looked around, confused.

Catrice slowed to a jog. From Lindrick's position, she was a sitting duck. Target practice, if he decided to shoot.

"Euge!" Charlie said. "We gotta take him out. He's gonna kill Sid or Catrice. We have to do it, Eugene!"

"Yeah." Eugene stood upright, holding his rifle in the air.

Charlie glanced up at him for a second, before looking back through his rifle's sight. "You want the shot? Or you want me to do it?"

Eugene didn't answer.

"Eugene! We have to shoot him, dammit!"

Eugene set his rifle down, drew his Glock, and held it to Charlie's head.

"I don't think so, Charlie. Drop it. Now."

Charlie gawked at him. "Euge, what are you doing? It's me."

"Drop it. Now!" Eugene barked.

Charlie dropped his rifle on the roof.

Drayden snuck up behind Eugene and shoved his Glock into the back of Eugene's head. "You drop yours, you two-faced snake."

Eugene turned his head back a tad. "What the—you gotta be kidding me. Drayden?"

"I said drop it, you shkat flunk."

Eugene sneered. "What, you gonna shoot me? You refuse to kill people, remember? Hell, you couldn't even hit me from there."

Drayden drove the muzzle into the side of Eugene's head. Hard. "How about from here?"

Eugene dropped his weapon.

Drayden peered into the marsh.

Captain Lindrick raised his rifle once more, aiming it at Catrice.

Catrice. No.

"Charlie, grab your gun! Shoot Lindrick! Now, Charlie!"

Charlie fumbled for it and aimed.

"Take the shot, goddammit!" Drayden screamed.

Eugene kicked Charlie in the head, knocking him over. He cried out. The rifle tumbled to the ground.

Oh my God.

Drayden couldn't hit Lindrick from here. Nor could he pull his gun away from Eugene.

Catrice!

Wait...what if...

Drayden held his Glock right by Eugene's ear, aiming it up to the sky. He pulled the trigger. The gun fired with a loud pop.

Eugene let out a horrible scream and collapsed to the rooftop, his hand over his ear. He writhed around in pain, moaning.

Captain Lindrick spun around, spotting them on the roof, and prepared to fire.

Sidney jumped up from the weeds and shoved him in the chest toward the mud pit.

Lindrick started falling backward. He flailed his arms, his feet sliding out from beneath him.

Drayden held his breath. It happened as if in slow motion.

As Lindrick fell back, he pointed his rifle at Sidney.

No.

Sidney backpedaled as fast as she could.

Lindrick fell into the pit, but not before firing one shot as he went down.

Sidney!

She fell onto her back.

Dear God, no.

She didn't get up.

Drayden's heart stopped. "Sid!"

CHAPTER 32

Drayden hopped down five or six stairs at a time, hyperventilating and crying.

No, Sid. No no no. Not you. Please, Sid, please be all right.

Third floor.

He practically fell down the stairs, sliding like they were covered in ice.

Second floor.

He'd instructed Charlie to restrain Eugene somehow and ensure he wasn't overpowered. Shoot him in the leg if need be.

First floor.

Please, please, please.

Drayden barreled out the front door.

Sidney and Catrice strode side by side through the marsh, heading back toward Granite Avenue.

He released a huge breath, his tears turning to joy.

Thank God.

He wiped his eyes.

The girls broke into a jog when they spotted him. Sidney, all smiles, leapt into his arms, wrapping her legs around his waist.

Drayden held her tight, weeping once more.

"You did it, Drayden!" Sidney sobbed. "You did it. Thank you."

He set her down, his hands on her hips. "I thought we lost you. I thought you got shot."

She beamed, wiped the tears from Drayden's eyes, and kissed him on the lips. Not a deep kiss, just a kiss.

Drayden held her briefly before letting go.

Catrice had tears in her eyes as well.

"Are you okay?" he asked her.

Crouching down, she covered her face, sobbing into her hands.

"Catrice...?"

He didn't know if it was the moment, everything that had happened, or if it had something to do with him and Sidney.

"Dray," Sidney said. "What was the gunshot? Did someone try and shoot Captain Lindrick?"

Wait until they heard this. Especially Catrice. Her boyfriend had double-crossed them.

"It was Eugene. He stabbed us in the back."

Catrice looked up, her eyes puffy and red, the shock apparent on her face.

"What?" Sidney asked, her hands on her cheeks.

Drayden recounted the tale of Eugene's betrayal on the roof.

"Sid, if you hadn't pushed Lindrick into the pit, we were screwed. He would have shot Catrice, or you."

Glaring at Catrice, Sidney pushed closer to Drayden and locked her arm inside his. "How do you feel about picking Eugene over Drayden now?"

Catrice wrinkled her forehead and wiped her tears. "What are you talking about?" she asked. "I didn't pick Eugene over Drayden. I don't know what you mean."

She seemed genuinely confused, Drayden noted.

Catrice's expression morphed to anger and her face flushed red. She looked at Drayden, then to Sidney, and back to him. "How could you?" she hissed.

He cocked his head. "How could I? How could *I*?"

She stared at the ground, shaking her head, fresh tears streaming down her cheeks.

"Hey!" Charlie shouted, having emerged from the office building with four rifles hung over his shoulder. He was guiding Eugene, whose arms were bound behind his back, forcefully shoving him along.

Eugene's face was a mess. His nose and lip dripped blood, as did his right ear.

Charlie must have given him a beating.

The Guardians periodically fired their guns from the pit and yelled for help.

When the two boys reached the others on Granite Avenue by the edge of the marsh, Eugene refused eye contact with everyone. Charlie had used a T-shirt to bind Eugene's hands.

"You like that?" Charlie eyed the shirt. "Hey, Euge, thanks for teaching me the handcuff knot! Came in real handy, bud."

Drayden got right in Eugene's face.

Eugene stared through him.

Drayden jutted his jaw. "Why?"

Eugene finally looked into his eyes. "Seriously, Dray? You still don't get it?"

"No. Enlighten us."

He tilted his head. "What's my name?"

Drayden paused. "Eugene?"

"My full name, dummy."

"Corporal Eugene Austin."

Eugene snickered. "Eugene Austin. That sound like a real name? Sounds like a movie star name. Plus, who has two first names anyway?"

"I have two first names. Charlie Arnold." Charlie shook his head. "Jerkoff," he mumbled.

"Austin is my middle name. Eugene Austin *Lindrick*."

"No way," Charlie said.

Drayden scratched the back of his neck. "So, wait. Did you change your mind when Charlie was going to shoot Capt...your father? Or were you against us the whole time?"

"C'mon, Dray," Eugene said. "Mister smart guy. Oooh, you and Catrice are so amazing; I'm in awe of you guys, blah blah blah." He laughed. "You can't figure this out?"

Drayden stood tall. "It was all an act."

"You have no idea what this mission was really about. We lied about my name from the time we met, didn't we? After we split from the Guardians, my job was to get you to Boston. Alive. No matter what."

"What about...you kept trying to convince us to kill the Guardians."

Eugene groaned. "Dude, try to keep up. I knew you were too weak to ever kill them, no matter how much I prodded you. But I needed you to trust me. I also needed to reconnect with them. Their assignment was to follow us, and protect themselves. If we attacked them, it wasn't my responsibility. That was their duty, to fight us off. They failed. I did not. I did my job."

Catrice approached Eugene, her face pale and swollen. "Do you even like drawing?" she asked, barely a whisper.

"I couldn't draw a straight line. And I don't know the first thing about stochastic calculus."

Sidney bit down on her lip and chuckled.

Catrice shot eye daggers at her.

Drayden felt terrible for Catrice in that moment. An emptiness swelled in his heart for her, because Eugene had made her a fool. She didn't deserve that. The poor thing had opened herself up to two people, probably for the first time ever. Eugene had played her like a violin. Meanwhile, Drayden ditched her at the first sign of trouble, for her nemesis of all people. She'd trusted them both, in an innocent way.

What have I done?

Drayden gripped Eugene by the shirt with both hands. "I may never have muscles like yours, but I'm stronger than you'll ever be. What a waste of talent you are. You and your buddies can talk about how weak I am in the mud pit together, while *we* enter Boston. You should have plenty of time to discuss it, you worthless piece of shkat."

Eugene spat in his face.

Drayden's face flushed hot. He wiped off the spit, pulled his Glock, and shoved it against Eugene's forehead.

Eugene didn't even blink. "Do it. Do it, you coward!"

"Drayden, no!" Catrice shrieked.

He held the gun firm.

Eugene pressed his head into the muzzle.

He stared into Eugene's piercing blue eyes, which revealed an evil Drayden didn't know could exist. A masterful, cunning evil.

Drayden lowered his weapon. "Nope. I'm not a killer. And you're not worth the bullet." He stepped back. "Charlie, drag him to the pit."

Charlie pushed him, steps at a time. "Hey, Euge. With your hands tied behind your back, you're gonna eat a nice mud pie when you face plant in the pit. Enjoy, bud. Well deserved."

Eugene remained silent until they neared the pit.

"Guardians, do not fire! It's Corporal Eugene! Hold your fire!"

"Get control of the situation, Corporal!" Captain Lindrick yelled.

"I've lost, sir. Catch me when I fall, my hands are bound!"

Charlie paused a few feet from the pit. "Any last words, Euge?"

Before he could answer, Charlie shoved him with all his strength. Eugene tumbled into the mud pit, fighting to get his legs underneath him as he went down.

Charlie grimaced. "That had to hurt."

The Guardians fired bullets out of the pit with reckless abandon.

When they stopped, Drayden spoke. "Captain Lindrick, I'm a little confused. I was wondering if you and Lieutenant Duarte could help me figure out who's in charge of the mission now." Drayden couldn't fight back a smile, wishing he could see their faces.

Sidney patted him on the back.

"Savor your moment, Private," Lindrick said. "It won't last. This isn't the end."

"It could be, if we were soulless barbarians like you guys. We could have killed you. We could kill you now."

"Private, this mission didn't go as planned."

"You think so, Captain Obvious?" Drayden was knowingly crossing the line. Lindrick must be fuming.

"Listen up, son. If you let us out of here, we call a truce. We all enter Boston, together. You can't enter alone, because you don't understand the true purpose of this mission. If you go into Boston alone, you'll embarrass yourself. This has nothing to do with what you believe it does. Most likely, the leaders of Boston will kick you out the second you arrive. Unless you have us with you."

Intriguing.

Drayden tugged on his left ear. "If you tell me the true purpose, I'll consider letting you out."

"No deal," Lindrick said. "Only if you let us out first."

"Fine, have it your way," Drayden said.

Charlie and Sidney shook their heads at him.

He winked. "Have a good time in the mud pit!"

"When I get my hands on you," Lieutenant Duarte snarled, "you're going to wish I would shoot you."

Drayden nodded. "Luckily you have plenty of time to polish that knife of yours now." Even though he understood you should be gracious in both victory and defeat, he simply could not help himself. "Once we're in Boston, we'll send someone. To arrest you."

Drayden exited the marsh alongside his friends. It was mostly dark now, with a hint of violet light left in the sky. They marched up the exit ramp, back onto I-93, and headed north toward the city.

The heart of the city lay about five miles away. Perhaps they had walls that started further out.

Drayden walked alone, now unsure of the Sidney and Catrice situation. The Guardians' comments about the true purpose of the mission still ate away at him. He'd suspected they were up to something, but he never did uncover their goal. It gave him an uneasiness as they approached Boston.

I-93 was elevated above the streets below, which had become city-residential. Crowded houses, apartment buildings, and businesses lined the highway. After an hour of walking, a towering wall came into view.

"We need a white flag to wave," Drayden said, choking on his words from extreme thirst. "To show them we're friendly. Charlie, you have your T-shirt?"

"No, I used it to tie up Eugene."

Drayden felt a tinge of anxiety about removing his shirt in front of the girls, as if regarding his skinny torso would compel them both to lose interest in him. He shrugged it off. He was who he was. A skinny kid. He removed his Guardian camo shirt, and then his T-shirt, and put the camo shirt back on.

"Everyone sling your rifles over your backs and raise your arms in the air."

When they did so, Drayden waved the T-shirt above his head.

Although no guards were visible as they approached, a gate did exist in the wall where I-93 intersected it. Cameras, instead, cast a watchful eye at the highway.

The privates stopped in front of the gate.

"We made it to Boston," Sidney said. "I can't believe it. We actually made it."

Charlie searched around for a button or a handle. "Soooo, how do we get in?"

The gate began to open.

CHAPTER 33

Drayden led the way.

Maybe for the last time, he thought, coughing.

The government in Boston would never admit him into the city with Aeru symptoms.

In New America, no gates ever welcomed anyone from outside the city. This one, however, appeared designed to do just that. Rather than open to the highway on the other side as it did back home, it revealed a building similar to a garage. Inside, the ceiling rose two stories, and the cement floor was worn. A shiny white sign dangled from the ceiling. On the left it read, "Protective Suits," with an arrow leading straight ahead, presumably through the green door. On the right, it read, "No Protective Suits" with an arrow pointing right, at a red door. The room featured cameras in each corner, focused on the center of the room.

"I think the Guardians would have been stumped right here," Charlie said.

"Red it is." Drayden walked through the red door.

They entered a windowless, low-ceilinged room made entirely of metal. The same cameras existed in each corner. Cavernous boxes lined the walls.

"Attention," a man's voice said over a speaker system. *"Deposit all weapons in the boxes. Any weapons found beyond this point will lead to immediate expulsion."*

The privates tossed their pistols, rifles, and knives into one of the empty boxes.

Drayden noticed the adjacent box, which was open. It contained flashlights, some fishing rods, a shovel, and a few other guns.

"Proceed through the red door," the voice said.

The privates entered yet another garage-like room, this one with high ceilings and a metal bench in the middle of the space. People milled around behind a glass-covered second story. They resembled the Guardians, albeit with navy blue uniforms.

A voice boomed over the loudspeaker, *"Have a seat on the bench."*

The privates sat, with Drayden on one side, Sidney next to him, Charlie, and then Catrice.

"Do you realize what's going on?" Drayden asked with wide eyes. "They have a procedure for people to leave and reenter the city. They let people out here."

From a door beneath the glass, two men emerged and approached the privates. They wore full-body white protective suits, helmets with glass shields, and carried pistols. The taller one with a mustache spoke.

"You kids lost? What can we do for you today?"

"We've come from New America," Drayden answered, "which you probably know as New York, to speak to your leader. The leader of New America sent us to seek help. Our city is in grave danger."

The two men exchanged a perplexed glance. The mustached man said, "Uh, is that right? That's a little above my pay grade, but Immigration can sort all that grave danger stuff out for you. Either way, you gotta clear medical. Head through that red door and follow the signs. I'll let Immigration know you're coming."

How many times would they have to recite their story? The short version sounded preposterous coming out of Drayden's mouth. The Guardians may have been right about getting laughed out of Boston.

They entered a white corridor, reminiscent of a hospital. Staff paraded around in full-body protective gear. Others in plain clothes reinforced the notion that Boston allowed people to come and go. While some were clearly fishermen, the rest looked like miners. Covered in black dust, they wore hard yellow hats with miniature headlamps on them. Signs overhead separated the entrants by health status—whether they had symptoms of illness or not.

Drayden's anxiety grew. He'd be segregated from his friends here. "You guys, I guess this is it. I have to go right; you go left. I don't know what's next, but it's possible, even likely, that I won't see you again." He sighed. "You guys have to bring this journey home. Tell our story. Don't leave out the part about the Guardians and how they may have been on a different mission. The city should send someone to find them, although I don't mind making them sit in the pit for a while. Make sure to talk to the most senior person you can, and then find a way to get back to New America. Ask the government of Boston for help." Drayden paused to gather himself. "I'd appreciate if one of you guys could find my father and brother. Tell them I love them."

Sidney stepped up and embraced him. "Dray, this isn't the end. We're going to see you after this. If they put you by yourself, we'll come back for you. We're not leaving Boston without you, okay?"

"Yeah, Dray," Charlie said. "C'mon, bro. Even if we die too, we're sticking together. We'll break you out if we have to."

Catrice covered her mouth with both hands.

"Enough of this nonsense." Charlie corralled Sidney and Catrice. "We'll see you in a little bit, Dray. Don't worry." He dragged both girls up a corridor to the left.

Drayden's heart beat in his ears. He took the corridor to the right, which led to a room containing many beds, three of which were occupied.

A man in a white protective suit met him. "Hi, I'm James. I'm the nurse. Have a seat on that bed in the corner."

Drayden plopped down, shivering.

"Before I take a blood sample, why don't you tell me what your symptoms are."

He took a deep breath. "About three days ago, I developed a terrible cough, like thick, mucous-y. I had a sore throat and stuffy nose the first day or so, though they've gone away. I started running a fever on and off too."

"Follow me," James said. He led Drayden out the door, down a corridor, and into a smaller room with one bed. "Lie down here."

He collapsed onto the bed, which was heavenly.

James whipped out an alcohol swab, an elastic band, and a syringe. He drew two vials of blood from Drayden's left arm. "The doctor will see you in a few minutes. Try to relax."

When Drayden started to doze off, the doctor entered, also wearing full protective gear. He thought he was hallucinating for a moment. She looked like his mother.

The doctor was a short Korean woman. "Hi, what's your name?"

He sat up a bit. "Drayden Coulson."

"I'm Doctor Park. Let me explain what's happening. You do have symptoms that are consistent with Aeru infection, which is why we put you in an isolated room. We're running the blood test now. If it's not Aeru, we can still likely identify what type of infection you have."

"How does that work?" Drayden could never escape his love of science. "How long does it take?"

"Around an hour. Essentially, we read your immune system to determine what it's reacting to. It's a genetic test. Your genes tell us if you have an infection and whether it's bacterial or viral. If bacterial, which one it is. If this test had existed before the Confluence, we never would have had the Aeru superbug issue. Doctors prescribed antibiotics for every illness in the old days, most of which were viral. Antibiotics are useless against viruses. Prescription abuse allowed bacteria to grow drug-resistant."

Drayden nodded. "Yeah, we learned all about that in school. What happens if I have Aeru?"

Her eyes softened. "There's no cure. We're working on that. We have some treatments. Basically, we'll make you comfortable, and then...well, we wait. We have a unit solely for handling Aeru patients. The same goes for pretty much any bacterial infection. Aeru isn't necessarily deadlier than the others; it's just so much easier to catch."

"Are people still catching it out there?"

She checked her watch. "Yes, but much less frequently than, say, a decade ago. Sit tight, Drayden. I'll be back soon." Doctor Park patted him on the leg and left.

He sank further into the bed, his eyelids growing heavy. His thoughts turned to his mother, and the remarkable chain reaction her exile had triggered. A month ago, he was like any other kid, leading a mediocre life in the Dorms. He'd been in such a hurry to figure out what happened to his mother that he'd never stopped to think about *why* it happened. He'd always thought she was perfect, but in the end discovered she was flawed like everyone else. Hopefully she'd never caught Aeru and was alive, because he really needed to talk to her. That was his final thought before closing his eyes.

Doctor Park shook him awake. She rested on the edge of the bed, a big smile on her face. "You have a cold."

Drayden sat bolt upright. "A cold? I have a cold?" He was so happy he hugged Doctor Park, banging his face against her helmet.

"Yup. Common cold virus. You should be better in a few days. You can go left out that door and follow the signs to Immigration. Good luck, Drayden."

He leapt out of bed and ran down the hallway, a zip in his step. Although his spunkiness was probably psychological, he even felt a little livelier. He'd still need to figure out why he received a different Aeru vaccine than the others, and whether it was fake, but he was too excited to worry about that now.

The signs led him to a steel door with no handle. He stood outside, unsure of what to do, when the thick door rose with a wheeze.

Drayden found himself in a tight chamber, like an elevator, with a similar door on the other side.

The door behind lowered and clicked a few times. A burst of air whizzed through the chamber, sucked into vents in the ceiling. A minute later, the airflow stopped, and the door in front rose.

The following room resembled an office, and several people slouched on folding chairs. Many numbered doors lined the walls of the beige room.

Drayden approached a woman in a navy Guardian-like uniform, without protective gear, who sat at a desk. When he gave her his name, she directed him to room number four.

He entered the room, an office with a desk, a few chairs, and a dark green couch along the wall. Sidney, Catrice, and Charlie sat there, regarding him like they expected the worst.

Drayden pretended he was about to cry. "Guess who doesn't have Aeru?"

Sidney screeched and hugged him. Catrice sniffled, wiping her eyes with both palms. Charlie wrapped his thick arms around Drayden and hoisted him in the air. "Attaboy! Think a measly superbug could stop you?"

Drayden noted that Catrice hadn't spoken to him yet. "So, what is this?" he asked. "Have you guys talked to anyone yet?"

"No." Sidney pulled Drayden to the couch and nestled close to him. "We all had clear blood tests and they sent us here." Charlie and Catrice joined them on the couch.

A few moments later a stocky African-American man with glasses entered and sat at the desk. He shuffled some papers around on his desk and held a pen in his hand. "How can I help you?"

The others looked at Drayden.

He delivered the three-minute summary of New America's current state, the expedition, and the Guardians, concluding with, "Please, sir, it's urgent that we speak to your leader. The Premier of New America himself sent us."

The man scratched his chin, set his pen down, and leaned back in his chair. "Are you messing with me?"

"No, sir."

The man hunched back over his desk, mumbling. "Always...the *last* one of the day...never get a fisherman..."

"Sir, we don't intend on staying here," Drayden said. "We're not hoping to move to Boston. We just need to speak with the leadership. And, well, we could use some assistance getting home."

The man threw his hands in the air. "Hell, it's a crazy story. It'll certainly be the most entertaining thing they hear down at the mayor's office all week." He seemed amused. "You kids sit tight; let me see what I can do."

"Sir?" Drayden asked. "We haven't drunk anything in over twenty-four hours and have barely eaten in four days. Do you have anything you could spare?"

"Absolutely. I'll have some snacks delivered. If you want to freshen up there's a bathroom down the hall, the way you came in." He headed for the door and stopped, pinching his nose. "I'd *highly* recommend freshening up." He hurried out of the room.

Charlie smelled his own armpit and looked like he might faint. He peered over his shoulder at his butt.

"Don't say it," Drayden said.

"My butt speaks for itself."

"Jesus, Charlie," Sidney said.

A few minutes later another man carried in a pitcher of water, four glasses, and four chicken sandwiches.

The privates scarfed everything down.

Drayden would never complain about food being boring or gross ever again after the expedition.

CHAPTER 34

The following morning, the privates waited inside an office at the Boston Capitol building. Formerly the Massachusetts State House, it resided in the Beacon Hill neighborhood of Boston. The Immigration department allowed, or rather encouraged, them to shower at their offices. They'd also provided cots on which to sleep, and fresh clothes. The privates wore blue jeans, white T-shirts, and green flip flops. Drayden wore his green Yankees hat, and they each carried their Bureau pins in their pockets. Everyone had acknowledged the generosity of the Boston government, which had taken first-rate care of them.

Drayden got the giggles when Charlie stood to adjust his jeans in the crotch area. The clothes were used—donated—and didn't fit well. His and Charlie's jeans were the same size, leaving them baggy on him and exceptionally tight on Charlie.

Charlie grunted. "Between all the frigid water on the expedition and now these jeans, I'd like to reiterate that I'm never having kids."

Sidney smirked. "I'll reiterate that those aren't the only reasons."

They sat in four chairs at an expansive oval conference table that could seat twenty-five.

While they awaited someone from the government, Drayden took note of the office. It was nothing like the ornate ones in the

Bureau headquarters. This one was minimalist, austere even. Thinking about Kim Craig, as well as Harris von Brooks's words before they departed, he made a mental list of all the bases he needed to cover with the Boston authorities.

A smartly dressed, middle-aged woman entered, closed the door behind her, and approached the privates.

"Hello, my name is Taylor Vasquez. I'm the Head of Foreign Relations." Smiling, she shook each of their hands and walked all the way around the table so she could sit across from them. "I'm sorry. We're swamped today. Why don't you briefly tell me who you are and why you're here."

Drayden sat up straighter and cleared his throat. "My name is Drayden Coulson. This is Charlie Arnold, Catrice Zevery, and Sidney Fowler. We've come here from New America, which you probably know as New York. We were sent here by the leadership of New America to seek help. Our city is in grave danger. I guess I'll start by—"

"Whoa, hold on a sec." She held her hand up, her consternation apparent. "Did you say *New America*? I'm sorry. I don't mean to sound difficult, but do you have any proof?"

Drayden pulled out his Bureau pin and tossed it across the table.

Taylor Vasquez examined it and blanched. Regarding the privates in seeming amazement, she ran her fingers through her black curls before standing. "I'm...I'm sorry. Would you excuse me for a moment? I'll...I'll be back in a few minutes." She hurried out the door.

The privates were dumbfounded.

"Looked like she saw a ghost," Charlie remarked.

After about forty-five minutes, Ms. Vasquez returned. Four others—three women and one man—followed her. They sat in the chairs across the table from the privates.

"I'm sorry for the delay," Ms. Vasquez said. "Other people, important people, need to hear this. Joining us on the end here is Mayor Michelle Sullivan, who's the highest-ranking official in Boston. She's been mayor for two years. Beside her is Jason McCarthy, who was our mayor ten years ago, and advises Mayor Sullivan now. Additionally, I've brought the mayor's Chief of Staff, Christiana Silva, and her Secretary of Defense, Susan Murphy. The most powerful people in Boston are in the room right now. Please continue, Drayden."

He took in the furrowed brows and curious eyes of the Boston leadership, immediately noticing they were mostly women, unlike the male-dominated Bureau. The mayor, Michelle Sullivan, looked to be in her thirties.

Drayden launched into their tale once more, delivering the more thorough fifteen-minute version. He started with the supposedly equal zone system in New America, concluding with the Guardians, and their claims about the unknown "real" purpose of their sojourn.

As he described the nature of the expedition, an image popped into his mind. On the boat, beside the tanks of extra water, were several boxes, wrapped in chains, sealed with locks. What was in those boxes? Perhaps the expedition was all about delivering their contents. The privates were sent to help the Guardians transport them to Boston. That had to be it.

Drayden scrutinized the faces of their hosts, expecting shock.

Their expressions suggested something else. Confusion? Pity? They looked like he had just explained the world was flat, and they let him finish even though they knew it to be false.

A nervous heat enveloped Drayden's face. He shifted in his chair.

The group of leaders appealed to the mayor.

She folded her hands on the dark wood table, tilted her head, and wrinkled her forehead. "Drayden, we know all about New America."

"Excuse me?"

She sounded like she was breaking bad news to someone. "New America has been known to us for ages, but it's notorious as a hostile colony."

Drayden exchanged a befuddled glance with the other privates, who appeared equally stunned.

"Mayor Sullivan, someone needs to go capture the Guardians right away. We need to find out what they know. They're in a mud pit in the Neponset River Reservation about five miles south of here. It's in a marsh across from Two Granite Avenue."

Susan Murphy, the secretary of defense, stood. "I'll handle this. I'm sure the border police are familiar with that mud pit." She hustled out of the room.

Drayden set his elbows on the table. "I don't understand what's going on."

Mayor Sullivan turned to the former mayor. "Jason, you want to take this?"

Jason McCarthy was an older man, with bushy white hair and even bushier white eyebrows. He got up and paced. "I'm certain you kids don't know much about the world today. Your government, the Bureau, hasn't told you the truth. We estimate the Confluence wiped out approximately ninety-six percent of the world's population."

Drayden did the quick math in his head. That implied around three-hundred million people remained on Earth. Not much compared to the many billions Pre-Confluence, yet it wasn't exactly like humanity was hanging on by a thread as they were told. Three-hundred million was a lot of people.

"Many cities around the world enforced quarantines, as they did in New York. While lots are known to us, there are probably hundreds more. Over time, the world collectively rebuilt some technology, reestablished radio communications. It also developed vaccines against bacterial infections like Aeru. Many of these cities began trading goods, as everyone did Pre-Confluence. Boston produces a lot of fish and beer. Rio de Janeiro produces sugar, beef, and oil. London exports chemicals and medicine. We trade with other cities along the eastern seaboard in America, such as Jacksonville, Florida. They export much of our fruit. Today's trading is done by ship."

Drayden couldn't believe his ears. How was this possible? All this commerce and communication, and nobody in New America knew? "Hostile" was ringing in his ears. How and why was New America considered hostile?

"We used to trade with New America," Jason McCarthy said. "Years ago. Your city lacked the technical knowledge to develop its own vaccines, not to mention boats. So, we would send our ships to a port downtown."

Drayden remembered the dock at Pier Fifteen, where they'd launched the expedition. The gate had carved deep grooves in the wood, as if it was often used. Now he understood why.

McCarthy stopped pacing and looked over the privates' faces. "New America was famous for exporting one thing: drugs. And I'm not talking about medicine. I'm talking illicit drugs. Marijuana, opium, cocaine. New America is the drug-producing capital of the new world."

Drayden's jaw dropped. He recalled the narcotic painkillers from the Initiation.

"What the hell?" Charlie asked.

"I believe New America stopped producing and began importing most of its food years ago," McCarthy went on. "Most of your food production facilities produce drugs now. You also produce most of the world's tobacco and alcohol, which allows your government to trade with a veil of legitimacy to mask their principal export—drugs."

Kim Craig had told Drayden about the surveillance cameras and said none existed in the Meadow. He wasn't sure why then, but now that made sense.

"Unfortunately, New America began having trade disputes with other colonies, like ours. They cut us, and others, off. It became more and more isolationist, confrontational, attacking boats that approached. We really have no idea what's gone on there the past few years. The fact that you still have food means New America does maintain trade relationships with other colonies, but we're not one of them. Based on the looks on your faces, they've also done an exceptional job hiding the truth."

McCarthy sat back down and spoke directly to Drayden. "It is possible this power-storage problem is real, that deep-cycle batteries have worn out. Because of the structure of New America with its zones, there's no incentive to invent, to innovate. Everyone is paid the same wage and nobody can advance. So why bother? As such, your colony has dramatically lagged the rest of the world in technology. Plus, since it cut others off, it hasn't experienced the shared progress the rest of us have achieved. We've made advances against Aeru, and can travel. But I would caution that the power story may be false propaganda. The Bureau may be expelling people so they don't have to feed them, and can hoard more spoils for themselves. Or they cannot import enough food anymore because of New America's isolation."

"Holy shkat," Sidney said.

"The Bureau needs to be stopped." Catrice grimaced. "Can Boston...invade New America?"

Mayor Sullivan picked up Drayden's Bureau pin from the table and played with it. "Jason forgot to mention the other thing your city is known for. Its military. Let me ask you, how many people live in New America? And how many are Guardians?"

"Around one hundred thousand people live there," Drayden answered. "Roughly fifteen thousand Guardians. At least that's what we're told."

"Exactly," the mayor said. "Fifteen percent of the population are military. That's much, much larger than anyone else. Nobody would dare try. There's also no incentive to invade anyone else these days. Land is plentiful and travel is difficult."

Drayden's head was spinning. "We were taught that our abundant Guardian population was due to the huge National Guard presence during the Inequality Riots. The quarantine trapped them."

"That may be true," McCarthy responded, "but once the Bureau found itself with this gargantuan police force, it decided what type of state it wanted to be. Drugs and other illicit products are some of the most expensive and hard-to-obtain items today. Very profitable."

Catrice leaned forward, tucking her hair behind her ears. "Do you think the whole Bureau is in on this?"

"I doubt it," Mayor Sullivan said. "Probably the senior leadership, including some of your senior Guardians."

All the pieces were falling into place now. The growing sense that *they* were escorting the Guardians. The heavily secured boxes on the boat, followed by the revelation that New America's main business was drugs. Drayden felt confident now that the boxes contained drugs, but what else had they held? And why deliver them to Boston?

"Mayor Sullivan, can you tell us a little about Boston?" he asked.

"We still consider ourselves a city of America," Mayor Sullivan said. "We're led by a mayor and retained the name Boston. We're much like we were Pre-Confluence, only a little fairer. We hold elections every four years, and no mayor can serve more than one term. We don't believe there's one right system of governing. Capitalist, socialist, democracy, communism—you need a balance. We believe in the competition and creativity that capitalism breeds, with the strong social safety net that socialism espouses. The problem with all forms of government is corruption. We root it out. Corruption is up there with murder in Boston." She observed the faces of her deputies.

Drayden wondered whether a more corrupt government than New America had ever existed.

"We have no zones; we are one city. People here work and own businesses. In the early days, we offered massive pay for people to go outside the walls to do our work, where Aeru might infect them. Now we have vaccines and protective suits, although there's still risk. Jobs outside the walls continue to pay well. We mine, fish, and farm outside the city. People who are entrepreneurial and successful can grow wealthy and enjoy the fruits of their achievements. But we set a limit on how much money wealthy families can leave to their children, which benefits everyone, even the children. It's a high limit—people need that incentive to create wealth. Their heirs are allowed enough to ensure they are always comfortable, though not so much that they fail to become productive members of society. Money is then put back in the pot to support those who are not as successful."

Drayden held his head in his hands. Beyond technological development, he couldn't fathom how much it would transform life overall if people in New America were rewarded for their achievements. If they could move up.

Mayor Sullivan continued. "We imprison people who commit crimes and try to rehabilitate them. We don't exile. We care for our sick, less fortunate, and elderly. Boston is a wonderful place."

Drayden shook his head. "We need to get back to New America immediately. Mayor Sullivan, can you help us? What's going on in New America is a humanitarian crisis. They're exiling innocent people—murdering them. I appeal to your sense of compassion. Any help is welcome. Weapons to use against the Bureau, manpower, deep-cycle batteries in case the Bureau is telling the truth about the power problem. We could use a ride home too."

"I feel for you, Drayden, I really do. Unfortunately, there's not much we can do. I understand you came in with some weapons; we'll resupply you with ammunition. Obtaining batteries these days is a major problem, so your best bet is to visit an old windmill farm near New America. We can help you research that before you go. As for getting you home, we haven't sent a boat to New America in many years. It would probably be attacked. The next boat making a trip down the East Coast, however, could drop you off a few miles away. It would be our pleasure to put you up as our guests and let you enjoy life in our city until then."

"That's very generous, Mayor Sullivan. Thank you," Drayden said. "We just have a few details to work out. We need proof we made it to Boston, because the Bureau threatened our families if we didn't make it. Can you give us something?"

"I'll personally draft a letter on official Boston letterhead for you to deliver to your Premier," the mayor said. "I'll also give you several blank sheets of letterhead so you can each carry one, in case you become separated." She stood, walked to a table on the side of the room, and returned with a gold coin in her hand. "Take this. It's an old commemorative coin with Boston's seal on it."

Drayden read the inscription. *Bostonia Condita AD. 1630.*

The privates each thanked her for her consideration.

He recalled his final conversation with Kim Craig, and though they no longer needed help finding someone trustworthy, he figured if Kim's aunt were alive, she'd want to know that Kim was alive too.

"One more thing," he said. "I know this will sound crazy, but do you know a Ruth Diamond?"

Charlie, Catrice, and Sidney looked at him like he'd lost his mind.

The mayor checked with the other senior officials, and they all shook their heads. "I'm sorry, no," she said. "We haven't rebuilt electronic records yet."

The door flung open and Susan Murphy entered. "I sent a team down to the mud pit you described." She hesitated. "The Guardians were gone."

The privates returned from an evening walk through Boston Common. They stopped in front of the former XV Beacon Hotel, their temporary home. A stone's throw from the Boston Capitol, it still functioned as a quasi-hotel. Now it accommodated visitors from other colonies who'd come to Boston to trade goods.

"I miss Eugene," Charlie said. "But the nice Euge, not the evil one."

"I still can't believe it," Sidney said. "He must be like an evil genius."

Charlie wrapped his arms around Catrice's shoulders. "Don't feel bad. He had us all fooled, not just you."

Drayden cringed at that comment. Catrice had been quiet the entire day and remained so.

Sidney waved a finger. "He didn't fool Drayden."

"Yeah, he did," Drayden said, trying to make Catrice feel better. "I thought I'd look like a paranoid jerk for making sure he didn't double-cross us in the marsh."

"Fine, but it's not like you fell in love with the guy," Sidney said. "You even told him you didn't trust him."

Catrice blushed and balled her fists. "Why does everybody think I had something going on with Eugene? All I did was talk to him. Jeez."

After an awkward silence, Charlie fanned his arm across the skyline. "I think I'd rather stay here than return to New America. Boston rocks."

"Aren't you forgetting our families?" Sidney asked.

Drayden thought about Dad and Wesley, hoping they were safe. "I can't believe that stuff about New America. Who knew, right? It's crazy to think about. We suspected the Bureau was corrupt, but not like that."

Before the expedition, Drayden had committed to help overthrow the Bureau. Back then, all he thought they were doing wrong was exiling people unfairly. Little did he know he was only scratching the surface of their duplicity.

"I can't believe we're a hostile colony." Charlie rubbed his chin. "We don't seem hostile."

"What about the drugs?" Sidney asked. "Who would have thought? Alex was onto something, dealing drugs."

Charlie put both fists on his head and pulled them away in a brisk motion, extending his fingers out. He did it again. "You know what this is?"

Sidney looked flummoxed. "What are you *doing*?"

"You see this?" Charlie repeated the fist thing. "This right here."

"What, Charlie?" Drayden asked, annoyed.

"Mind. Blown."

Drayden whacked him on the arm. "You guys, I need to tell you something. I wasn't honest with you about why I entered the Initiation." He told them about the forced exiles in the Dorms, and that he'd found out when he overheard the conversation between Lily Haddad and Thomas Cox.

"Holy shkat," Charlie said. "Thank God we passed."

"That's not the craziest part though," Drayden said, finally realizing his friends' need to know about the overthrow plot outweighed the risks of telling them. He gave them a rough outline, which was all he knew anyway. "This time I didn't tell you guys what I was up to because I didn't want to endanger your lives. Look what happened to Thomas Cox. He was executed. So, there's already a plot in the works, and Kim Craig said it involves some Bureau members and some Guardians." Drayden recalled Kim's note, the one he wasn't supposed to open unless she was dead. Against her advice, he was going to open it when he returned to his room. Circumstances had clearly changed.

"That's great." Sidney held a hand up. "We can try to get involved, right?"

Drayden shrugged. "I'm not sure. Knowing Holst, he's already onto it. We might need our own plan."

"I have a plan." Charlie lumbered up the steps to the hotel, yawning. "It involves sleeping for about three days."

Everyone headed inside.

Catrice gripped Drayden's arm. "Can I talk to you?"

He glanced at Sidney, who gave Catrice some serious stink-eye before entering the hotel.

Catrice dragged him a few feet down the sidewalk so the two of them were alone.

Before Drayden had a chance to say anything, she hugged him, weeping a little into his shirt. Although he wasn't sure what to do, he hugged her back. He was kind of with Sidney now.

"I'm sorry." Catrice pulled back. "About everything on the expedition. I was so scared, and everything reminded me of my parents. I guess physical separation doesn't mean I've escaped them. Between your mother possibly being alive, the suffering we saw, and being held captive...my mind was back in my parents' apartment. It was traumatizing. After our capture and rescue, I don't even remember the entire next day, like I blacked out."

She wiped her tears. "The expedition was really difficult for me. But one thing that never wavered was how I felt about you. I don't understand why everyone keeps saying I had something going on with Eugene. I didn't at all; I was never interested in Eugene like that. I just enjoyed making a new friend."

It was remarkable how effortlessly Catrice could make Drayden like her again. Had he imagined everything? Or was she playing mind games? Her recollection of the expedition was quite different from his.

"Catrice...I...I'm sorry for how difficult the expedition was for you. That's just not what I saw. It was pretty clear to me and the others that you ditched me for Eugene. You barely spoke to me. If you were having such a hard time, why wouldn't you talk to me about it? With Eugene, it was like you were conducting a four-day interview. I've never seen you talk so much."

Though Drayden didn't want to fight, he grew bitter recounting the details. "From the time we met Eugene, you never gave a single indication that we were a couple in front of him. But you did rest your head on his shoulder when we stopped to boil water the last time, and you did lock your arm inside his for around five hours. I don't think I misread the signs."

Catrice's eyes narrowed. "You know, I've never had many friends, something Sidney loves to point out. Because of you mostly, I've learned I don't need to be afraid of people. Eugene was one of the first friends I've ever made. Maybe I don't understand how to do it right yet, what you're supposed to do, and how you should act. You and I were already together. I didn't think you were so insecure that talking to Eugene would make you leave me."

Her cheeks glowed red, which happened when she got upset. "What did you actually see, Drayden? Me talking to Eugene. That's it. I didn't know I wasn't allowed to talk to other people. I don't recall resting my head on his shoulder, and it didn't mean anything if I did it. If Charlie were standing next to me, I would have done the same thing. I have no recollection of locking my arm inside his either, but if it was after the camp, I was literally blacked out. Being tied up like that wasn't too different from what happened to me at home, okay? Holding his arm sure as heck didn't mean we were a couple."

Catrice had tears in her eyes again. "Did I not cuddle up to you every night? I'm shy, and it's embarrassing, like, hanging on your boyfriend, being all public with everyone watching. I guess I don't know what I'm doing yet. I think you imagined a lot of things that weren't there, Drayden, and I bet Sidney was real helpful getting you to see them, wasn't she? So just like that, I talked to Eugene, and you leave me in four days? What kind of person are you? What kind of man do you want to be, Drayden?"

He had no answer. He was so confused.

Catrice shook her head, crying. She stomped past him and entered the hotel.

If the expedition had taught Drayden anything, it was that he needed to accept who he was. He was a skinny, smart, compassionate, yet insecure and inexperienced boy. He probably needed to tack on neurotic to that list.

He stepped into the hotel, walked through the black and white lobby, and rode the elevator to the fourth floor. As he approached his room, he tried not to dwell on everything that went wrong on the expedition, but what went right. He'd defeated the Guardians, led his friends safely to Boston, and uncovered the truth about New America.

All he'd needed to do was embrace who he was.

The privates' rooms were grouped together on the fourth floor. His was 406, Charlie was in 405, Sidney was in 404, and Catrice was in 403. Catrice's room and Sidney's were directly across the hall from each other. He stopped in the hallway between both rooms and looked at Catrice's door, full of sorrow and regret. He raised his fist to knock, then hesitated.

The door behind him opened.

He spun around.

Sidney stood there, a weak smile on her face. She leaned against the doorframe in a white T-shirt and sweatpants. "Hi."

Butterflies flitted inside Drayden's stomach. He smiled back. "Hi."

"My turn. Can you talk?"

Drayden peered back at Catrice's door and let out a deep breath. He hated how much he craved being appreciated and needed, but that was who he was. Sidney needed him too.

He stepped inside her room, wrapped his arm around her waist, and closed the door behind him.

ACKNOWLEDGMENTS

I assumed writing my second novel would be easier than the first, but I stand corrected. I needed a great deal of help and encouragement along the way. From those who edited my work to those who offered passing words of praise: thank you.

I'd also like to thank Anthony Ziccardi and everyone at Permuted Press, especially Michael Wilson, Devon Brown, and Madeline Sturgeon. I would be lost without you guys. *The Expedition* would be a word salad of disparate plot elements without the keen eyes of editors Deborah Halverson, Maya Rock, and Felicia Sullivan. As with *The Initiation*, the first person to untangle the writing was Christiana Sciaudone. Credit for the gorgeous cover goes to designer Cody Corcoran. Many thanks as well to Simon and Schuster, and to all the booksellers and librarians I've met along this journey.

To my young beta readers—Jack Babu, Taylor Manett, Samantha Miller, and my daughter Lily—thank you for keeping me grounded in a young adult's world.

I so appreciate the help of Jason McCarthy, photographer Greg Berg, and Captain Ryan Bryla of The United States Navy.

There were many difficult writing days I couldn't have survived without the guidance and wisdom of author Renita D'Silva.

A special thank you is needed for my wife Michelle, daughter Lily, and parents for their unwavering support.

Lastly, for the lovely poem "Memory" by Violet Wiggins Newton used in this book:

Newton, Wiggins. "Memory." *Poetry Explorer.* Accessed August 28, 2018. www.poetryexplorer.net/poem.php?id=10112480.